A Tapestry of Gods and Mortals

R. A. Bowen

This book is dedicated to women everywhere, the individual "Gaias" among us, like you, Mom, who make society function.

Prologue

Pain seared through Beckett's body as she regained consciousness, consuming her. As her vision cleared in the darkness, her surroundings slowly came into focus. Cold, damp stone walls encased her, and the air hung heavy with the stench of mold and despair. A shiver ran through her as she realized she'd been stripped nude.

Cuffs of a type she'd never seen before bound her wrists and ankles as she lay spread-eagled on a padded platform. Unlike anything she'd encountered during her career, these shackles glowed, glittered, and vibrated, seemingly imbued with a strange, almost otherworldly energy. The metal bit and tore into her skin, sending shockwaves of pain through her body with the tiniest movement.

Where was she? The last thing she remembered was following a patient she feared was suicidal in London, turning a corner, and then... nothing. How long had she been here? Hours? Days? Weeks?Beckett's heart pounded as she tried to focus her thoughts. She'd been in dangerous situations before, but nothing like this.

Remember how POWs coped with imprisonment in hostile territory, Beckett. Stay calm, assess the situation, and look for any opportunity to escape. You're stronger than they know. The thought came to her unbidden, and she marveled at its clarity when the rest of her reeled at her predicament. Closing her eyes, she tried to calm her breathing and center her mind. She needed to find a way out, but first, she had to understand where "here" was. The stone walls and musty smell suggested an old building, perhaps a basement or dungeon. But who had taken her, and why?

As she lay there, trying desperately to piece together her fragmented memories, a sound from the darkness made her blood run cold, and she started to tremble. Footsteps, slow, deliberate, and plentiful, approached, turning her shivers into an uncontrollable shaking. The involuntary movements activated the restraints at her wrists, simultaneously locking her to the platform and sending streams of agony through her mind. Someone, or plenty of "someones," was coming. She heard a pause and low speech, catching only murmurs of their whispered conversation.

While the footsteps drew closer, a deep, arrogant, and mocking voice cut through the darkness. "Look who's finally awake. We've been waiting for you, Dr. Argonne."

Beckett's heart hammered in her chest, but she forced herself to speak, hoarse and shaky. "Who are you? What do you want from me?"

The voice laughed harshly, sending chills down Beckett's spine. "You think you're so special, don't you? With your fancy degrees and your secrets, working for clandestine agencies and law enforcement. But we know what you are, and we know how to break you."

Beckett's mind raced, shocked by the voice's words. Secret abilities? What did they mean? And how did they know about her work with MI5? She opened her mouth to speak again, but before she could, the shackles at her wrists and ankles flared to life, sending fresh waves of agony coursing through her body. As the pain consumed her, Beckett could only pray that she would find a way out of this nightmare before it was too late.

Chapter 1

And So, It Begins

Dr. Beckett Argonne stood at the window of her London office, staring out at the bustling city streets below. To the outside world, she looked every inch the confident, successful forensic psychologist, with her tailored suit and sleek, professional appearance. But inside, Beckett still struggled to come to terms with the events of the past three years.

The road to recovery after her abduction had been long and difficult. While her physical wounds healed, the emotional scars remained. Beckett spent weeks in the hospital to repair the physical and emotional damage inflicted by her captors. Endless debriefings with Scotland Yard, MI5, and other government agencies followed, as they tried to piece together the facts behind her disappearance and the mysterious group who had taken her.

Even now, Beckett had more questions than answers. Who were her captors, and what did they want with her? What were these "secrets" they believed she possessed? And perhaps most importantly, how had they known about her work with MI5, which she never discussed?

Sighing, Beckett turned away from the window and gazed at the stack of case files on her desk. She threw herself into her work as a way of coping, taking on more clients than ever and teaching as many classes as possible to keep her mind occupied and fill every minute of the day. But even as she tried to focus on her patients and their problems, she couldn't shake the feeling that her own story was far from over.

As she reached for the top file on the stack, footsteps accompanied a sharp knock at the door. Beckett's heart raced, and for a moment, she was back in that dark, damp cell, waiting for her captors to come for her. But then, she heard a known voice calling her name.

"Come in," she said, straightening her suit jacket and taking a deep breath as the door swung open. Another day, another challenge, another step forward in the long journey to uncover the truth about herself and her place in a world. One that suddenly seemed much stranger and more dangerous than she had ever imagined.

Sean Caladfin entered her office, his presence dominating the room. At more than six feet tall, with the ripped body of a professional athlete, he embraced Beckett and kissed her lightly before sitting on her desk. His bright, sky-blue eyes assessed her from head to toe. "You look fantabulous," he said, smiling at her.

Beckett grinned, reminding him for the thousandth time that "fantabulous" was not in the dictionary. Laughing, he told her it should be, as he always did.

"Well," Sean began smoothly, "it's time for you to consider joining me at Evigvokter. You're already a silent investor in the company. Let's be honest: your research and investigative talents are..." He mimicked a chef's kiss. "And all your books and private study await at Dell Castle. As do I, Mrs. McKinnon, and..." He gestured expansively, smirking.

That familiar smirk. She couldn't recall a time when it wasn't present, all the way back to their very first meeting on a hot summer day when they were both four years old. His parents, close with her guardians, began spending summers with her family in Virginia's Blue Ridge Mountains. Sean's Australian lilt entranced her, while he was transfixed by how they seemed to complete each other's thoughts. That connection never waned, even as his life took him from Australia to special forces service and finally, to his entrepreneurial vision that the world required a comprehensive intelligence and security firm, unburdened by politics and bureaucracy.

Thus, Evigvokter was born. Sean's global company aimed to address worldwide and regional threats, no matter where they were and who they affected. Prior to her abduction, he urged Beckett to invest in him and his ambitious idea. Without hesitation, she became a silent partner and co-owner of their Scottish headquarters, Dell Castle. Intrigued by Sean's drive and passion, she wanted to witness what he could accomplish. Plus, it provided Beckett a sanctuary to house her ever-increasing extensive collection of ancient documents, tomes, and rare books, as well as private quarters for her to escape from London's chaos when needed. After visiting once just after acquiring the properties, Beckett's inherent need for stability led her to remain in her familiar London life before the trauma of her kidnapping.

As Beckett pondered his proposal, she gazed at him. Instantly, Sean finished her thought before she had a chance to vocalize it. "No," he said, walking to her and taking her hand. "This isn't charity or me feeling sorry for you. *You* are needed. *I need you.* Plus, you need a place to feel safe in while we help you figure out what happened three years ago."

He was right about most of what he said, she knew. But more importantly, Beckett wanted to know how he managed to find where her captors held her and how he rescued her. Who took Beckett from her dungeon-like prison to where they discovered her outside? Lying nearly dead on the ground, she was still nude, with a coat placed carefully over her. Made of a fabric no one could identify, the coat, more like a cloak, mystified her and those who found her. With the smoke of the building's fire, and the screams of those within, they told her she had looked like a wrapped corpse.

Beckett managed a smile, covering his hand with hers. "The only thing you didn't say is that *I* need *you*. And it's true, I do. But... I don't want us working together to impact our relationship in any way. At least for now, I don't want to be sent on missions or projects." She looked up anxiously. "Is that all right?"

He immediately took her in his arms, kissing the top of her head and bending his head so his cheek lay there. "You can do, or not do, anything you want. You are my partner, Evigvokter's co-owner, and my best mate. If you wish to get involved in a mission or a project, I'll leave that to you to let me know. Otherwise, I badly need your help running the show."

Sean released her, looking down into her eyes. "I know you're frightened. But I think there's something you need to know. I'm a—"

Beckett held up a hand, finishing his thought. "You're an action figure. You need someone who can manage the troops and make people accountable."

She turned toward the window. "Despite everything, maybe working with people rather than patients will distract me from obsessing about my own mystery."

Sean positioned himself on her side of the desk. "Yes, I think it might. Will you do it?" He ran his fingers through his cropped, dirty blonde hair, crossed his arms, and leaned back on the desk.

"I will if you tell me what my role will be," she countered. His smirk and body language told her he had anticipated this particular inquiry.

With great smugness, Sean replied, "You're our Chief Executive Officer, managing all aspects of the business, meeting with dignitaries, military and intelligence officers, and world leaders. You'll have more than six thousand employees at your disposal, including me."

Beckett's jaw dropped. How had he amassed so many people in such a short time?

Sean placed his hands on her shoulders comfortingly. "I'll answer all your questions if you will pack a bag and come stay in your rooms at Dell Castle tonight. Mrs. McKinnon is making dinner—she intimated something about French cheese, but I could be mistaken."

He held his nose and winked at her, knowing that Beckett believed having stinky French cheese, great bread, and a good glass of merlot, along with a good hair day, constituted happiness. "There will be another guest, too. I'd like to know what you think of him."

Beckett reflected on all her questions. There were some aspects of her rescue she still didn't know, as she hadn't asked, and he hadn't broached the topic with her. After all the law enforcement interviews, she avoided further conversations about the investigation, steering clear of any reports associated with it.

Distancing herself from the topic of the abduction, Beckett's curiosity stirred. How much revenue did the organization generate, what kind of employees did he hire, and what projects were they engaged in that permitted him to grow the company so fast and large in so little time? How was the company structured? Did Sean have a board of directors now, or did they own a private company outright?

With a toss of her head, Beckett made direct eye contact with Sean, uttering her fear for the first time: "What if I choke?"

Sean, keeping her gaze, deepened it by saying, "Believe me

when I say this: you won't. You didn't choke in captivity. And you have friends, more than you know and much different than you expect."

Pulling a printed paper from his jacket, he checked his watch. "It's 9:30 am, and your flight leaves from Gatwick at 12:30 pm. Mind you, your seat mate," Sean pointed to himself, "expects your tray and seat back to be in its upright position, and your computer chucked in an overhead bin throughout the flight."

He gestured to his left jacket pocket, which looked heavier than the right side. "Got some of that peach whiskey swill you favor so much. We can drink, fly, and talk." Sean motioned to the door. "Isn't it about time you got to *be you*, and better yet, *do you*?"

Beckett ruminated, smiling slightly. I hate it when he's right. Exhaling, she began gathering her things. When Beckett went to get her computer, she realized she might not come back to this place if the answers she got were worth it. Everything in her office was depersonalized, a remnant of her upbringing to stay invisible, keeping her personal life personal. The only things she took were her precious fountain pens and notebook.

Sean, still smug and smirking, watched her. Pleased spectacularly with himself, he preemptively opened the door for her. He followed Beckett as she walked through it to the hallway. When they neared the steps to the lobby, Sean paused. "Hang on a second, ok?" He turned, going back the way they'd come. After a minute or two, he reappeared at her side. Taking her arm in his, Sean escorted her from the building, into the rain, and into the shiny black SUV awaiting them.

Inside the vehicle, Sean's very preferred and much-loved Range Rover, the heat and opulence quieted her nerves. Max, Sean's longtime friend and driver, pulled out from the curb into traffic.

"Max, we're off to Beckett's flat in Chelsea. She'll be joining us at Dell tonight," Sean instructed.

Max leveled his hazel-colored eyes in the rearview mirror, greeting her."Why, hello there, Dr. Argonne. It's been a minute since I've seen ya."

Beckett, glad to see him, replied, "Still keeping this sod from losing his way, are you?"

Max joked, "If it weren't for me, he'd never get around London. In fact, he'd never get anywhere."

"It is not for me to know how to get there, only to choose where to go," Sean claimed in his defense.

Max didn't let that go unanswered, as the banter between the two men had always been witty and clever. He chortled, "Remember that time in university when Sean got lost trying to find his way to that pub in Shoreditch?"

Beckett snickered, "Oh my God, yes! He was so convinced he knew a shortcut - we ended up wandering around thirsty for hours!"

Max snorted, "It was worth it to watch Sean try to impress that sweet little shopkeeper with a phony Cockney accent to get directions, or some such shite."

Sean maintained a mock indignance, retorting, "It's not my fault that Google Maps wasn't invented yet. Please *don't* remind me of the shopkeeper. I still cringe like I did when she plainly told me that she'd understand me better if I spoke real bloody English to her."

He shook his head. Fondly, Beckett divulged that it wasn't that bad, "It was rather cute what you did. You know, in that posh-little-Aussie way you have."

Sean's eyes lit up at the same time he smirked (again!). "Well, I must have done something right, because you're still putting up with me after all these years. I'm better at directions now, too," he said, taking Beckett's hand in his.

Rolling his eyes, Max reminded Sean, "We're all saints for putting up with you, her most of all. You're better at nav now because we get YOU to where you need to go."

Beckett basked in this lighthearted repartee between old friends. Her mood lightened. Laying her head on Sean's shoulder, she thought aloud, "I guess that's what friends do, right?"

Both men grinned, and Sean sat back happily in his seat, crowing, "I couldn't even ask for better ones," as he kneed the back of the driver's seat.

When they arrived at Beckett's flat, Sean let Beckett out of the car and went to the driver's side to talk to Max. Heading for her walkup's door, she heard the car doors opening and closing again behind her. The next thing she knew, Max, his huge muscular frame dwarfing her, was at her side.

"Sean needs to take some calls, so I'll come with you." Max offered her his arm, and taking it, she strolled with him to the door and unlocked it.

Her flat was tiny, not much more than 1200 square feet, but it felt larger. Like her office, Beckett kept it as minimalistic as possible. She went to her bedroom as Max seated himself on her couch. He called to her, explaining that her suite at Dell was already stocked with all the essentials she'd need, other than clothes.

Amused, she changed into slacks, a turtleneck, and leather booties. Since it was fall, she chose layers to pack, hoping to be prepared for chillier weather. Finishing up, Beckett noticed she felt somewhat excited about her trip to Dell, partly because of the answers she wanted to get, and because she'd be around more people she trusted. It'd been a while since she'd allowed herself to be openly social, to be herself with others, especially men.

Once done with packing, Beckett surveyed her little bedroom. She'd not spent as much time here as one might think. She owned another location to which she fled after she was released from the hospital, one that no one knew existed. But still, this place consoled her, embraced her, and ultimately soothed her as she started living and teaching again.

Beckett stopped at the bedroom door, looking around for anything she might have forgotten. Her eyes lighted on the one thing Sean gave her with which she'd never parted: a kangaroo joey finger puppet. He'd kept the stuffed kangaroo and given her Joey from it when they were kids. Beckett stepped back to the dresser where it sat, picking it up, smelling it, and remembering the day Sean gave it to her: a cloudless, hot sunny day, at a county fair.

Sean won Joey at a target shooting game. Nobody understood how he'd won it at five years old, but he did. With a rush of affection, she put Joey in her bag. She'd feel better if the little finger puppet was with her, as he'd always been. Feeling confident that she'd gotten she needed, Beckett turned, picked up her carry-on, and left the room, closing the door behind her.

Lounging on the couch, Max lifted an eyebrow as she brought her bag into the living room. "That's the smallest carry-on I've ever seen a woman take on a trip. Are you only staying the night, lass?"

Putting on a jacket, Beckett gave him details about everything in the bag, including her intimates. He growled, closed his eyes, covered his face, crossed himself, praying, "Oh Lord, forgive me for these thoughts I have, and may they cease when I sleep. Or not. You choose. Amen." Crossing himself and laughing, he rose. Opening the door for her, Max took her keys after they exited the flat, and locked it, handing them back to her. Taking her carry-on, he offered his arm again, escorting her to the Range Rover.

When she got in, Max closed the car door. Sean opined, "That didn't take long. You got everything? Ready to go?"

Beckett began a mental checklist about her carry-on's contents, but was interrupted with Max cautioning Sean, "Don't ask her what's in her bag. Just don't. Trust me."

Sean, sporting a face-splitting smile, replied, "I did that once and didn't sleep for a while. You got issues, mate." Cracking up together, Max maneuvered the Range Rover into traffic to Gatwick.

Chapter 2

Busy, Busy People Everywhere

Max drove smoothly, pulling into the EasyJet departures at the airport. Both men got out of the car, Max coming to her door to open it and helping her out. As he handed the carry-on to her, she reached up, embracing his massive frame in a quick squeeze. Max hugged her back."I'll see ya soon, Doc, I'm driving this beast back to Dell."

She smiled at him, watching as Max teased Sean about how it was "...a good thing that there's a pilot, a copilot, and that girl on your plane so you won't get lost." Sean chortled, shaking the hand Max extended before he began ushering Beckett into the airport.

Once there, he whipped out two Evigvokter badges, gave one to Beckett, and put the other one around his neck. Curious, she held it in her hand, amazed at the fact it was already personalized for her. Sean, his hair wild from the dampness of the mid-morning rain, caught her reading it. With a satisfied look on his face, he took her hand, leading her. Marshaling her straight to airport security, the officers recognized Sean immediately, facilitating an escort for them to their gate.

Not for the first time, Beckett wondered how Sean

14

managed to do all the things he'd done in such a very short time that airport security should literally permit them to circumvent normal passenger security lines. Filing that away for later, she chose to observe closely how people interacted with Sean. Clearly, he'd been very busy.

After airport security herded them to their gate, a beautiful Asian woman called to Sean, inquiring if he'd like to board the plane early. He, charming as always, thanked "Grace" profusely, expressing his intention not to be any trouble.

Grace, for her part, took in Beckett, asking Sean courteously, "And who is this?"

Beckett smiled at Grace, introducing herself. After these pleasantries, Sean added, "Dr. Argonne is my silent partner in Evigvokter. We're hoping she won't be so silent anymore."

With this new information, Grace made sure that Beckett recorded all her details: numbers to contact Grace and who to see at airport security when she flew. This interaction made her head swim: what business was her outspoken partner doing that everyone seemed to part the Red Sea for him? Incredibly, it appeared she was to get the same treatment.

So far, what she'd experienced since leaving her office nearly overwhelmed Beckett, especially since she'd been totally ignorant of the operations at Evigvokter. She funded over sixty-five percent of the company's start-up, which amounted to about $3.1 million. Beckett had that money, and as it was, much more, as an inheritance from her guardians and the sales of properties they had in Virginia. She gave it to him never expecting to get it back: Sean was her best friend, a brother, and she loved him.

"Sean..." Beckett started, "I..." She gaped.

Sean put his head close to her ear and said, "I told you that we need you. We do. I want you to know just how far that money you gave me went and what we have today. I couldn't have started this without you. I know I can't continue it successfully if you're not more involved."

He hesitated for a moment. "It's time you know some things, and I don't want to talk about them here." Sean motioned to the people in the gate area, all waiting for their flights.

For once, she decided not to ask, just watch, be patient. Patience was her strong suit when it benefited her. In easy silence, they waited until Grace came to escort them to their seats on the plane. Once seated, an attendant handed them each a glass of champagne, a steamed towel, and snacks.

As she sipped and nibbled, her mind cleared. Breathing deeply, she turned to her seat mate and thanked him.

In reply, Sean chucked his Biscoffs at her, settling back into his seat with a big smile. "We'll land at Edinburgh and then... well, you'll see." He jovially popped a nut in his mouth. Pulling the silver flask from his jacket, he poured a hefty finger of peach whiskey into his empty glass, sitting it on his tray. He took her glass. Drinking what was left of her champagne, he substituted a shot of the peach whiskey for her.

Oh, the memories that first sip brought: picking peaches in Virginia in the summer with the juice running down her chin, riding horses with Sean, racing him to the next tree in the next orchard. Beckett sighed contentedly and relaxed. Both finished their drinks before takeoff, and then proceeded to have another finger while in the air. Beckett felt relieved and soothed by the smoothness of the plane ride, hardly noticing when it touched down.

Edinburgh, like London, was experiencing a cold, rainy fall day. As they taxied to the gate, Sean turned on his phone, scrolling through his messages. He bent close to her ear. "Don't get up. Let's wait until everyone else gets off the plane."

She sat, waiting with him as other passengers

disembarked. Once they did, she looked to him for direction. In the aisle, the plane's pilot boisterously bounded toward them, grinning to shake Sean's hand. "*Mijo*, where have you been?!" the pilot, a cheerful dark-haired man, asked, absolutely delighted to see Sean. Sean rose from his seat, grasping the pilot's hand with a firm shake. Turning to get their bags from the overhead bin, Sean introduced the pilot, Manny, to Beckett. Looking from Beckett to Sean and then back to her, Manny said, "Well, Max said she was a saint. He didn't say she's *chica muy hermosa*, and I'm sure that's intentional."

Flirting, he introduced himself to her. "Manuel Cordoba. Pilot, vet, dog owner, and single, in case you were wondering."

"Hm. What kind of dog?" Beckett chuckled and Manny's eyes twinkled. He apprised Sean that although he was off the clock with PrivAir, he'd arranged for their helicopter ride to Dell.

As they climbed down the stairs to the tarmac, Sean steered her toward an airport security car, explaining its destination at the PrivAir tarmac. Getting out of the SUV, the driver came toward them, tipping his hat. He asked for their bags in a thick, Scottish brogue, an accent Beckett adored. Keeping with her mantra to observe, she settled into her seat, willing herself to let events unfold however they might.

Approaching PrivAir's hangar, she took in the sleek, black helicopters with their almost invisible logo and lettering. PrivAir, huh? It's a smart move, Beckett surmised, to nearly camouflage your logo if you're emphasizing discretion for a wealthy, privacy-valuing clientele. There we are with the kinds of actions and assumptions that lead to secrets again, she mused. The more she watched, the more she speculated, and the more she anticipated the evening.

Lost in thought, the abruptness of her car door opening

startled her. She looked up to see Sean beckoning her to follow him to the helicopter. Another man, carrying their carry-ons, walked in front of them. Beckett spotted several other people already seated on the aircraft. When they got close, the men parted to allow her on board first.

Sean directed her to the first row, right beside the person who had already boarded.

When Beckett's eyes locked on her new seat mate's face, she froze. Blinking in confusion, memory, grainy and dream-like, floated across her mind. Disorientation floored her; she felt almost breathless. Focusing, she moved to the seat beside him. Baffled by her nearly staggering reaction to him, she carefully strapped in as directed. When Beckett faced him, he looked directly into her eyes, and she felt... something.

Something foreign, and bright, and so, so very powerful. A little dazed, Beckett glanced over at Sean as he slid deftly into his seat behind her, acknowledging the man beside her. She followed Sean's gaze to the front of the helicopter. Sean jerked his head to Manny, who beamed at them from his seat by the pilot. Finishing their pre-flight checks, the pilot announced that they'd land at Dell Castle in about thirty-five minutes.

In a flash, Beckett suspected the person might be the guest Sean mentioned. She exhaled, mulling over what to say to him when he, in a light European accent, addressed her first. "You must be Dr. Argonne. My name is Lucien Aurington, and may I say, it is my absolute pleasure to meet you."

That voice. Where had she heard it? Assessing him, he was probably the most handsome and compelling man visually she'd ever encountered. Broad shouldered, she could just pick out the muscles of his arms and chest under his jacket. Raven hair swept back from a face radiant with such symmetry that it bordered on art. His eyes, lush green orbs, set perfectly against the near porcelain of his skin, drawing you in, compelling you to engage. But listening to him? Oh my. She believed without question his voice alone could land you in any number of compromising and delicate, albeit intensely enjoyable, negotiations or positions.

Without thinking, Beckett asked, "You're so familiar to me. Have we met?"

Attentively, Lucien moved his head closer to her as his eyes widened in response. Then, he unexpectedly leaned back, glanced past her to Sean, who she noted gestured in approval. With her partner's expressed agreement, Lucien directed his words to her, saying quietly, "Yes, you have. But it was a long time ago, and I'm not sure—"

For some reason she didn't understand, Beckett gently placed her hand on the right side of his face, pressing her lips and cheek to the other side for a moment. His reaction, a sharp inhalation, startled Sean and Manny, who had both been keenly focused on the exchange between Beckett and Lucien.

Manny's eyes glittered; he seemed poised for action. Sensing a potential intercession, Sean put his hand out, motioning Manny to stay where he was.

Lucien maintained eye contact with Beckett as she pulled back from him. "Why did you do that?"

She looked away, fidgeting and confused. "I don't know. It was... a compulsion. It felt like the right thing to do."

Beckett spread her hands helplessly, embarrassed, and hung her head, thinking, *yep, that's that. Can't have a chief executive officer who is unable to control her emotions and actions.* From behind her came, "Just a second."

Beckett turned apologetically to Sean, who lightly placed a hand on her shoulder. "Do you still feel it was the right thing to do? What else are you feeling?"

How odd Sean should ask her what other feelings she had, because having them, she was. Beckett closed her eyes, sensing, no...intuiting an energy... a vibration emanating from this man that wasn't totally alien to her. It also didn't scare her, just bewildered her.

She opened her eyes to see Lucien assessing her. "Let her breathe, Sean," he cautioned. "We have plenty of time to talk and get to know one another." He glanced at her hand beside his before asking, "May I?" She acceded, even though she was unsure what he would do next. Lucien took her hand in his, giving it a slight squeeze. Beckett felt heat coursing from her hand to her shoulder, which further spread all the way up her neck to her head. Why did she feel so comforted by him, like she'd known him all her life in some inexplicable way? When did she meet him?

Beckett stayed silent, unable to trust herself to speak. The continued touch of Lucien's hand to hers led to a spontaneous kaleidoscope of visual images and emotions that weren't unpleasant. Unsolicited, a hazy memory of light filtering into distinct rainbow columns through trees, mostly tall pines, in the woods behind her guardians' house came to her mind.

As a child, Beckett spent hours in those woods, where she visited deer, rabbits, squirrels, foxes, turkeys, flowers, and trees. She named every tree on the property in a song, including the peach trees in the orchard, which bloomed the very best peaches she'd ever have in her life.

A certain nostalgia came over her. Beckett didn't feel threatened: if anything, she felt safe. No, that wasn't right, she rationalized, she felt protected. And why shouldn't she? Surrounded by Sean and Max earlier and now Manny, Sean, and this man, she felt cocooned, not needing to look over her shoulder every second of the day for the first time in years. Beckett, still perplexed but relieved and grateful, gave Sean a tiny smile over her seat, which he returned in a much broader fashion. Manny put his headset on, chatting with the pilot.

Lucien didn't stop holding Beckett's hand, sliding his thumb across the back of it ever so lightly. As he did it, she allowed the sensation to calm her while still making mental notes about him covertly. What she perceived fascinated her. As Beckett inhaled deeply, she was struck by Lucien's scent— a captivating blend of pleasant, woody notes reminiscent of sandalwood and cedar, mingled with the faintest hint of exotic spice, perhaps saffron or cinnamon.

It was an aroma that seemed to perfectly complement his presence, at once grounding and mysterious, revivifying and intriguing. The scent wafted to Beckett, as if she had caught a fleeting whiff of it in a half-remembered dream. Wrapping around her like a delicate embrace, it made her feel secure, stirring a deep, inexplicable curiosity within her heart. She sighed, closing her eyes, letting the peace of the moment infuse her mind and body. That "be where your feet are" mindfulness that she advised her stressed patients and students to adopt became a reality for her.

The remainder of the trip aloft was placid and uneventful until they began to approach Dell Castle. Sean tapped Beckett on the shoulder, pointing to the window so she could view the castle from the air. When she did, her mouth opened in astonishment. The first time Beckett saw the castle, with its crumbling walls, gatehouse, and towers, she wasn't sure that Sean would be able to rescue this property to which he seemed so attached. She couldn't have been more wrong.

What Sean had done with the location was not only impressive, but it also rivaled, and partly exceeded, the footprint of the Royal Family's Buckingham Palace, with more land than Balmoral or Sandringham. It was, in a word, gorgeous. Then she spotted the very thing that made her heart and mind soar: stables. Tentatively, and in a higher octave than she meant, Beckett asked Sean, "Is that what I think it is?"

Sean, again tremendously delighted with himself, shook his head yes. "I thought if you joined us, that would be a perk." A perk?!?!? Stables! Those meant horses, and riding, the smell of leather and polish, hay, manure, and feed. She beamed, grabbing Sean's hand behind her in gratitude.

Entranced, Lucien watched Beckett as she surveyed Dell from the air. Her long, silver-blonde hair fell forward as she dipped her head toward the window. Her face, lit from the day and her excitement about the stables, glowed. She'd changed since he'd met her so many years ago; other than growing up, her hair, which was once a gorgeous shade of strawberry blonde, was gone, except for the tiny slivers of a much-faded gold he had to look carefully to see.

Her eyes, though, remained the same: light icy blue, outlined in dark gray, but they didn't dance as they had in her youth. Sean preemptively shared with Lucien the mental and emotional toll her recovery took on her. He confirmed that the only physical consequence after she mended seemed reflected in the stolen innocence of her vibrant hair. Lucien knew only a fraction of what she'd been through, but even those details appalled and infuriated him, igniting a fierce desire to seek retribution against those who had abused and tormented her.

Nevertheless spellbound, he sat mesmerized by her joy, an emotion he'd rarely experienced quite so strongly himself. Her reaction to so simple a thing infused him with an urge to fill in the gaps in her memory right away because it seemed so necessary to him for her to know who he was. But, as he'd discussed with Sean and the others, Beckett's recall of him and her own identity must be a measured realization, one she must come to recognize and accept on her own.

As the helicopter approached the castle, preparing to land, Beckett turned to Lucien with a shy smile, her eyes softening as they met his. In a gesture of thankfulness, she placed her hand over his, squeezing it before carefully extracting her hands to unbuckle her seatbelt. Lucien, moved by the tenderness of her touch, caught her hand before she could fully withdraw it.

Softly, his touch infused with utmost care that belied his strength, Lucien raised her hand to his lips, brushing a feather-light kiss across her knuckles. The sensation sent a shiver through Beckett, a blush blooming across her cheeks as she felt his breath against her skin.

In that fleeting moment, it seemed a world of implicit emotions passed between them—a recognition of the deep-rooted connection they shared, a whisper of forgotten memories that bound them together across time and space. Lucien's eyes held hers, his gaze filled with a depth of feeling that left her spellbound. How did he know her?

As they reluctantly parted, Lucien turned to Sean, a playful glint in his eye. With a dramatic flourish, he brought his hands to his chest, forming a heart shape, and feigning a swoon. The pantomime, a lighthearted acknowledgment of the witnessed moment, drew a hearty laugh from Sean, who shook his head in amusement.

As the helicopter hovered and landed, Beckett saw others approaching the helipad. Unfortunately, she recognized the slender blonde woman walking briskly toward them and watched as a dark-haired girl and a man picked their way along the path behind her.

The woman, Gwen Maethor, Beckett's former university roommate, met her first; Bowman, her husband, and Katie, one of their two teenage children, followed. These moments were always bittersweet with the Maethors. Connor, their oldest, and Katie, adored "Doc," and she loved them without the reservations she had for their parents. Her pseudo-nephew and niece independently kept in touch with her through email, video chats, and social media for over ten years. Even when she didn't keep in touch with others, she always answered their calls and letters.

The complex relationship between Beckett and Mr. and Mrs. Maethor began when Beckett met, dated, and fell in love with Bowman while at Columbia, just before completing her doctorate. She'd told Bowman more than once that she couldn't spend time with him while focusing on her research and writing. The pressures of accomplishing her PhD and sitting the licensing examination required this one final academic step before working in the real world, with real cases, people, and their very real psychological problems, on her own.

What Beckett didn't anticipate was Gwen filling those absences with Bowman. Eventually, Gwen became pregnant with Connor, forcing the two to confess their betrayal to Beckett. It had taken years for her to acclimate to them together, and forgiving Gwen had been particularly difficult. Even twenty years later, she felt a tug of discomfort with Gwen's airy dismissal of her part in that duplicity. As Gwen approached with open arms, Beckett hugged her briefly with one arm before letting go to catch Katie, who had bounded to her like a gazelle. "Doc! Doc! You're HERE!!!!" she cried, her blue-green eyes shining like her father's.

Katie tackled Beckett in a bear hug, arm around her neck, cheek to cheek, and with her slight frame, lifted "Doc" off the ground. Her long, deep auburn hair, smelling of chamomile and wild in the wind, swirled around them as Bowman approached.

"Katie, you're going to squish her," Bowman said, completely composed.

Releasing Katie, Beckett faced Bowman, and as their eyes met, she wasn't sure what she saw in them. Trained in undercover special services operations, he was always very, very good at hiding his feelings. However, this time Beckett's presence affected him, and he couldn't quite suppress his emotions. Bowman hugged her once, pulling back to study her face, his eyes searching hers. Overwhelmed by his feelings, he surprised even himself by embracing her once more, holding her tightly as if to convince himself that she was truly there.

"You look great, Beckett." Then, his eyes narrowed as Lucien walked toward them with Sean. "Who's that guy?" Bowman growled suspiciously.

"You haven't met him?" Beckett queried.

"No, I haven't," Bowman admitted, turning to where Gwen should have been standing, only to see Katie, who shrugged. Evidently, Gwen disappeared back to the kitchen after seeing the new guest, where Beckett suspected she was no doubt baking as she usually did when stressed and nervous.

"Lucien Aurington," Beckett replied faintly, "and I'm not sure who he is, really." Or what he was, she thought.

Beckett became very curious after Bowman's next words. "Sean said he was coming, but I didn't expect..." He tilted his head toward Lucien, who was only steps away.

Looking over Beckett's head, Bowman pasted a polite smile on his face, extending his hand to Lucien. "Hi, I'm Bowman Maethor, and this is my daughter Katie."

Ever the gentleman, Lucien returned Bowman's greeting, remarking on Katie's beauty and vitality. At the mention of her name, she looked up at Lucien, testing him. "Do you ride horses?" Katie asked. "You can come with me and Doc because I know she'll be riding, won't you, Doc?"

Enthusiastically, Beckett confirmed that she would be riding. And I hope I do every single day I'm here, she promised herself.

Katie helpfully informed Beckett, "There are two Arabians, two Clydesdales, two Friesians, and two Paint horses in the stable, Doc. I know you like Arabians, and Dad helped Sean find the perfect one for you." She stared at Lucien, willing him to say yes.

Charmed, Lucien confirmed to Katie, "I'm delightfully 'in,' as you young people say."

Upon hearing this, Sean fixed his eyes on Beckett. Holding out his hands in mock helplessness, he said, "I thought you might stay longer if you could ride whenever you want." Beckett felt Bowman's gaze on her, so she lifted her eyes to him and then to Sean, expressing her appreciation. Well, well, Beckett thought. People have been busy, busy, busy.

Chapter 3

Show and Tell

Sean began walking up the path to the castle. "Let's get you all in your rooms. It's almost 3:30, and I'm starving," he complained.

Katie kept up a running chat with Beckett along the winding path, all about boys, hair, riding, Connor's whereabouts, and archery. "Archery, huh? I bet I know what that's about," Beckett teased Katie. "Your dad teaching you?"

Katie lowered her voice. "I had to beg him, and it was horrible. He said he'd never taught anyone my age. He taught you, though, didn't he?"

"Actually, he didn't. Sean did," Beckett corrected. Katie's mouth opened in an O that left her speechless for a minute. Stopping before the castle door, she turned, glowing, her excitement palpable in the air.

"That might explain why you can stand him to a draw when no one else can," she said knowingly. "So, you can teach me, too?"

At that, Beckett became confused—the Maethors lived in the United States, the last she knew. Katie caught her bewilderment, clarifying that the Maethors moved to a cabin on the castle property two years before when her dad began working for Evigvokter. Sean purposely hadn't told her how involved Bowman now was with the company, which in turn meant Mr. and Mrs. Maethor seeping more into her life if she accepted his CEO proposal. She wasn't completely sure how she felt about that.

As they entered the castle, the entranceway filled with people bidding Beckett and Lucien welcome. Some of the staff Beckett knew, since they'd been part of her life as long as Sean. Especially Mrs. McKinnon, who embraced her as a second mother, although she'd been Sean's nanny.

With tears bristling, Beckett hugged Mrs. McKinnon fiercely, overjoyed to see her. She smelled of everything good in this world and more, and Beckett couldn't wait to see what the dear woman arranged for dinner.

Releasing Beckett, Mrs. McKinnon informed the group, "Drinks and appetizers will be in Beckett's library at 5:00 pm —dinner is casual. Please let me or any of Evigvokter's service staff know if you need anything at all. We'll be happy to oblige."

"Yes, yes, but I'm hungry now," Sean whined, as he did incessantly from the time he was twelve years old, which made Beckett and Mrs. McKinnon laugh.

"There are snacks for you in your quarters, young man," Mrs. McKinnon said primly. She brightened, winking at Beckett, "And there are some surprises for you in your suite, young miss."

Ever the hostess, Mrs. McKinnon introduced herself personally to Lucien. Fanning herself after some Spanish amar applied to her cheek by Manny, she and the staff left to continue their work. Wishing them farewell, Manny took the helicopter pilot to the company canteen. Beckett made another mental note—a company canteen?

Sean opened his mouth to say something, but a very pleasant, Midwestern, male voice issued seemingly from nowhere. "Welcome back to Dell Castle and Evigvokter, Dr. Argonne."

Thrilled, Beckett responded, "Thank you, Sam. It's great to be back with you, too."

Beckett tapped Sean on the arm, thanking him, "I'm glad you put him to good use."

Before Sean could respond, Sam interjected, "While I appreciate his Lordship's attention to my purpose, I miss philosophical conversations and playing a challenging game of chess with his partner. Could we do that while you're here, Dr. Argonne?"

Sam almost sounded as hopeful as Katie. She replied, "Yes, we can, Sam. Not tonight, but we can play sometime in the next several days." Sean poked Beckett as they started walking toward the residence wing, beckoning Lucien to follow them.

As they walked, Beckett was struck by the sophisticated use of space and décor, which represented a modern perspective when restoring a dilapidated relic. Preserved were bare walls, doors, latches, building woodworking intricacies, and ceilings containing etchings on tin plates or layered in hand-painted tiles. The fireplace mantles, covering huge fireboxes, and their rock facings were rich and textured, perfect for a castle.

Spotting a spiral rock staircase in an alcove, Sean stopped. "Here we are, Lucien. We've given you the keep for as long as you stay with us. I'll walk you up." Sean moved to put down his bag, but Lucien smoothly motioned him not to bother.

"I've slept in keeps. I'm assuming there are latches, but no locks. And I bet if I ask Sam for anything, he'll either find out or tell me." He leveled his gaze on Sean. "I'll contact you after I get settled."

Lucien cast a final glance toward Beckett and began to ascend the stairs. Continuing onward, Sean walked Beckett to her suite. Before she went in, he embraced her, kissed her forehead, and told her he was deliriously happy she was home.

After closing the door, she dropped her bags and slouched against it, closing her eyes. This wasn't how Beckett expected her day to end, but it turned out better than she had anticipated. Fortunately for her, she had no patients scheduled until late the next week. She chose not to teach a class for the fall semester because of her patient workload over the summer months. However, if she chose to stay, she better get to deciding to do so, and soon.

Beckett sighed, opened her eyes, gasping in amazement. Her rooms, once dark and foreboding the last time she saw them, were now light and bright. Full-size windows and a nearly transparent ceiling permitted a fuzzy view of the sky. Instead of wall fireplaces, freestanding fireplaces provided heat and ambiance. She discovered two of them—one in the great room and the other in the bedroom, where she also had a walk-in closet and a wall of woodworked shelves containing some of her books.

In the small kitchenette, sunflowers sat in a vase on the counter, white roses on the dining room table, and a potted heather and lavender arrangement sat on an end table beside the sofa in the great room, threatening to overtake whoever sat near it. Without a doubt, Sean rehabbed this set of rooms for her, knowing her love of being outdoors at night and lying back to look at the stars. She couldn't wait to see what it was like in the evening.

A tap on the door interrupted Beckett's appreciation of her suite. She opened it to find Bowman standing there with a covered plate of peanut butter cookies. Grinning, she took the plate from him. He asked, "Can I come in and talk for a couple of minutes?" Beckett acquiesced, and Bowman entered the room, his eyes darting around, then upward, toward the ceiling.

"Sam," he called, "please make the ceiling transparent." Sam confirmed back to him, and then... it was like there was no ceiling at all. Just sky and clouds on a fall day for as far as she could see. Bowman chuckled. "I'm glad that still works after they installed it. You can darken the ceiling and the windows as much as you like. No one can see in; it's polarized outside. Just ask Sam when you want to change the amount of clarity and light you want in your rooms."

Beckett thanked him, probing, "But that's not why you're really here, is it?" He stepped toward her, provoking her to take a half step back. What did he want?

Bowman held up his palms. "I'm sorry. You don't need to be frightened of me. I won't hurt you, physically, verbally, or otherwise. Can we sit and talk, please?" he implored. "We haven't spoken for more than two years. There are things we need to discuss."

"I've communicated with Connor, Katie, and Sean," she retorted, nostrils flaring. "I didn't know you all were here, that you're living on the grounds and working with Evigvokter."

Bowman strode to the sofa, pointing to the chair adjacent to it. "Come on, sit down." Beckett hesitated, then decided he was far enough away from her that she could listen. Maybe the heather and lavender would attack him, like the plant from The Little Shop of Horrors. But she didn't really wish that, either.

Sometimes, like one of her patients once recounted, unrequited love is a pimple on the ass of emotions. Damn. Having the upper hand with him for once might make this conversation worthwhile.

Curling her legs and feet under her, Beckett set "conditions" for her "engagement in discourse" with Bowman. "We can have a conversation if I can see your emotions for once," she stated flatly.

To her dismay, his face filled with emotion: nervousness, apprehension, anxiousness, excitement, happiness, and dread. Dread? What the? Mystified by the scattered emotions Bowman displayed, she outright demanded, "Tell me what's wrong. Is it Katie or Connor?"

He shook his head no, taking a deep breath in and then exhaling slowly. He repeated the deliberate inhale and exhale, clearly steeling himself for something difficult. Bowman's gaze finally met hers. "It's Gwen," he said gravely.

As she began to get up from the chair, he caught her arm gently. "Don't. This is more difficult than you can imagine." She paused, then sat slowly. "Beckett, there are things no one has told you because you weren't ready to deal with more than your recovery. Gwen and I divorced after we rescued you because of what we, Sean and I, learned about her. She's only here because I brought the kids to Dell. I had to include her to avoid legal custody issues."

He stopped, unsure what to say next. Sitting back in shock, Beckett had the presence of mind to look at him. Bewildered, she perceived overwhelming pain and regret. What did she miss?

"I should have known, should have checked and never did," Bowman started to explain awkwardly. "This is as much my fault as hers."

"Why bring Connor and Katie here?" she asked, calling him "Bowie" - a pet name she hadn't used in over twenty-five years.

Bowman looked at her beseechingly. "Did you ever wonder why your relationship with the kids is so strong?"

She pondered that question for a moment, but when she went to answer, Bowman cut across her with another question that tripped all kinds of red flags in her mind. "And when you became roommates, did she, Gwen I mean, ever tell you about her mother, her family?"

Beckett's mind clicked; she'd never seen Gwen's family, even her mother, about whom Gwen constantly complained when they roomed together. "I didn't meet her mother, that I recall," she remembered, "But Gwen often spoke about her negatively. She told me all she had was her mom, so I never expected any family other than Mrs. Llwyd."

At that surname, Bowman reached out for her hand, and she allowed him to take it. He said, very calmly, "That's not Gwen's real maiden name. Her mother's name is Morgan le Fay, in the flesh."

"Morgan le Fay, the legendary sorceress from Arthurian tales? How in hell did you get there? Is this some kind of joke?", fumed Beckett. Unnerved by her reaction, Bowman slid to his knees in front of her preventing her from getting up without some form of physical interaction with him.

Before she could tell him to get the hell out of her way, another knock came at the door. "Good Lord, come in already!" Beckett said loudly. The door opened, revealing Sean and Lucien. Sean exchanged glances with Bowman, who stayed where he was on the floor.

"Need some help, Bowman?" Sean asked casually. Bowman gave a brief jerk of his head in assent, but raised an eyebrow at Lucien seating himself on the arm of Beckett's chair. Sean took the spot Bowman had vacated on the sofa.

"Is she having difficulty with the Gwen le Fay thing?" Sean sneered. "I told you she would."

Beckett's gaze fixed pointedly on Sean, and he held her stare. Despite his tone, an air of unusual seriousness hung about him, a rarity.

She glanced between Sean and Bowman. "How did you find out?"

"DNA," Sean said. "Specifically, the kids' DNA results. Back in school, Connor was studying biology and they practiced cross-matching blood types for exams. He's AB positive. When he casually mentioned that to Bowman, Bowman realized Connor couldn't be Gwen's biological child. Gwen's type is O, and Bowman is B."

Lightheaded, she considered his words. A bizarre and hazy memory began to emerge in her mind, reaching back years to her those nights preparing her doctorate thesis, Gwen baking for her in their tiny studio apartment.

When Lucien's hand landed lightly on Beckett's shoulder, she turned to him, her expression frustrated and angry. "What are you doing here?"

Lucien met her gaze evenly. "We need to discuss the situation with Connor and Katie first," he said in a level tone, though insistent. "Then I'll explain my presence, I promise."

In spite of her discontent, his touch gave her that same secure feeling. This time, it had a much shorter distance to go to reach her head. "If Gwen isn't the biological mother of Connor and Katie, that means she went to an IVF clinic," Beckett theorized. "Is that what happened?"

Bowman shook his head. Sighing, Sean took her other hand. "No, with Lucien's help, we took DNA from Connor and Bowman and compared those samples. Bowman is his father, and tests show he is also Katie's father."

Beckett's thoughts started to circle, threads winding and winding, getting tighter. "Did you find their mother?" She steeled herself.

Bowman got closer to her. "I confronted Gwen with the facts. She told me that her mother wanted her to have children right away, and she couldn't. So, they planned one night when you were exhausted and asleep to take ovum from you and implant it in her. She and I... well, you know the rest." Bowman raked his hands through his hair.

Well, she told Sean she wanted answers. Beckett was the A donor, while Bowman was the B. But never, ever did she think this would be information she'd garner before dinner ever started. "And you found out about Katie later, she's my biological daughter, too?" With a shake of his head, Bowman confirmed her assumption. "What genetic material did you use of mine that got you your answers?"

Sean pursed his lips. "Remember that cloak we found covering you? It had your blood and DNA on it."

"Do Connor and Katie know?" Her question was curt and abrupt.

Bowman reacted instantly, "Yes, we told them last weekend. They knew something happened between Gwen and me, but not what." He paused, then continued, "Actually, Connor and Katie, especially Katie, were overjoyed to learn they are my 'biological offspring,' as Connor puts it. After I explained what Gwen truly was and what she'd done to you and me, the kids want nothing more to do with her."

His expression grew somber. "Katie had felt Gwen's...differences, but Gwen gaslit her about it all along. Once Katie heard the truth, she curtailed all interaction with her mother. As for Connor, he quit any relationship with Gwen cold once the blood test results came out."

"Gwen seems not to really care, other than to make trouble that she has legal rights to see the kids." Bowman rubbed his neck with one hand.

So that explained Gwen's cold reception, distance, and disappearance, Beckett brooded. But why had Gwen wanted her children? The thought gave her pause. Gwen was the product of...no, she couldn't entertain such fanciful notions of witches and magic. And, if one did consider the possibility of Morgan le Fay's existence, perhaps mystical retrieval of another woman's eggs wasn't so far-fetched. Beckett's mind rushed down that fantastical path until she forced herself to stop such wayward thoughts.

"Who is Gwen's father?" Beckett launched the question to

no one in particular.

Sean informed her that they didn't know; Gwen wouldn't tell them. "Okay, that's a checklist item," Beckett looked at all three men. "I can work on that. But what else am I missing here?"

This time, Bowman got up from his knees, stretching. Lucien offered his hand to help her up, and she took it.

Sean, rising from the sofa, checked his watch. "There's more you need to know. Right now, though, one thing at a time. Mrs. McKinnon's going to skin us alive if we're late for drinks and her canapés. Those happen to be spectacular."

"Wait," Beckett took a moment before asking, "Will Katie and Gwen be at dinner?"

Bowman advised her that Katie would be "...spending the night with one of her friends this evening, probably bragging to her about riding tomorrow with you. Gwen will probably come to dinner." He sighed ruefully.

"That's fine. I can say what I want?" Beckett gave Sean an inquisitive look. The two men nodded in affirmation.

Unexpectedly, Lucien chimed in, "I understand why you'd want to confront Gwen. But if you'll allow me, I'd like to work my immeasurable charms on her first. I have a talent for confrontations." He gave her a short, confident look.

Surprise and skepticism were stamped on Beckett's features as she stared at him. While she had grown to trust Lucien a little over their time together, she wasn't sure if she was ready to relinquish control of the situation. "Why would you—"

Lucien pleaded, "Trust me, please?" His eyes held a glimmer of devilment, hinting at a hidden agenda.

Beckett hesitated, weighing the potential consequences of letting Lucien handle Gwen. Perhaps his charm and wit could be disarming, but what if it backfired? Reluctantly, she decided to take a leap of faith. Shrugging, she accepted his offer, hoping she wouldn't come to regret it.

Decision made, they left her suite, heading for the library. As they walked, Beckett couldn't shake the feeling that Lucien's eagerness to confront Gwen was more than just a friendly gesture. She made a mental note to keep a close eye on the situation, ready to intervene if necessary.

When she entered the library, her library, Beckett found it too had changed. It smelled slightly of old books, wood soap, and cedar, scents consoling and heartwarming to her.

As Sean ushered her further into the room, she noticed wingback chairs in front of a gargantuan desk, made from heavy oak. It rested beside floor-to-ceiling windows, facing the grounds and loch beyond. Its polished surface reflected its surroundings like a mirror.

While Beckett checked out the desk and the library, Sean hung back and watched her, as did Lucien and Bowman. Beckett followed the shelves with her eyes, seeing her books all perfectly aligned and categorized. Sliding ladders graced the bookshelves strategically around the entire library. She realized she didn't truly know how many books she'd collected, and some of the artifacts under her ownership hadn't all been examined. The possibility of doing so excited and intrigued her.

Beckett ran her hand over the edge of the desk, shifting to lean against it. Looking at Sean, she asked, "Am I wrong for assuming that this—" she indicated the library and study-like desk, "is for me?"

Sean came across the room, standing directly in front of her. "It's always been yours, Beckett. You need only to use it." Meeting his gaze, she stepped closer and pressed her forehead to his chest.

He put his arms around her. "I'm assuming that this—" he gestured toward the study and library, "is exactly what you need, and you've agreed to my offer?"

Sean pulled her chin up, his tender touch a stark contrast to the turbulent emotions swirling within her. He saw the tears in Beckett's eyes, glistening like shattered crystals, as she consented with a slight bow of her head. Without hesitation, he pulled her closer, his embrace strong and comforting. Beckett inhaled deeply, the scent of his cologne wrapping around her like a soothing balm.

"Finally. You're where you need to be, aye?" Sean muttered, his words a kind affirmation.

Beckett couldn't speak past the lump in her throat, so she nodded again, agreeing with him. Hugging him, she felt a sense of safety and belonging that she hadn't experienced in a long time. Seemingly reading her thoughts, Sean reached around, grabbed a tissue from the box on her desk, and pressed it into her hand. The delicate material brushed against her skin, a small comfort amidst the overwhelming emotions.

With a tiny smile, Beckett realized that Sean took excellent notes about what she kept in her office for her patients. His attentiveness and understanding resonated within her, and she silently expressed her gratitude to the universe for bringing him into her life.

They heard applause. Sean pulled away from her a little, looking over his shoulder to where Mrs. McKinnon and some of her staff were standing with Lucien and Bowman. They'd heard the whole conversation. Evidently, some of them were instrumental in preparing the library and study for Beckett.

Sean whooped, "You hear that, mates? She said 'yes,' she's staying here. Beckett is our new chief executive officer effective..." He turned to her. "Today? Tomorrow? When?"

Beckett told him she'd let him know in the morning—she had to make some calls. Good-naturedly, he reinforced the notion of her living at Dell Castle while she transitioned to a full-time employee, insisting that Evigvokter pay all her expenses when she had to go to and from London to settle her affairs.

During this conversation, Gwen entered the room, dressed in a long black skirt, strappy heels, and a romantic, gauzy blouse of the same color. Her blonde hair, always curly and wild, was piled atop her head in a bun so tall that Beckett thought she might take someone's eye out with it. Her eyes flitted about the library until they found Beckett.

Sean faced Gwen's direction stonily, while Bowman took a seat beside Beckett on the edge of her desk. Immediately, Lucien positioned himself before Gwen, introducing himself. Strangely, Gwen kept her head down, averting her eyes from him. Beckett analyzed Gwen's reaction intently, trying to discern if it sprang from fear or respect for Lucien. The deference in Gwen's muttered responses hinted at a combination of both.

Gwen desperately wanted to get away from Lucien, so much so that she'd begun to aim herself directly toward Beckett. Effortlessly, Lucien deftly maneuvered himself between the group at the desk and Gwen. Only then did she brace herself to meet Lucien's eyes, her face contorted with loathing.

Sounding nervous, she blurted out, "Begone dragon, before I tell her who you really are." Beckett started to ask what Gwen meant, but Sean and Bowman motioned for her to wait.

Lucien chuckled, bending down to her, his face sharp and cold. "Your words, incantations, mean nothing to me, daughter of Morgan. In fact, they mean very little to anyone, isn't that right? All your life, you wanted to be seen, be heard, especially by your overbearing mother. When you met that lady over there, you wanted her life. You, and your mommy dearest, enchanted your supposed best friend to sleep while you took lives of children you had no right to take for your own. With what little talent you have, you enthralled her boyfriend, justifying it in your tiny, warped mind that at least someone Beckett loved would be her children's father."

He bent down further, as close to her face as possible without touching it, looking directly into her eyes. His tone with Gwen bordered on uncontrolled fury. "You will return to America this evening. We have arranged a plane for you, which you can take wherever there that you wish." Lucien turned from Gwen, then looked back at her over his shoulder. "You will not bother these people, or anyone they love, again with your presence or your threats. Should you do so, it will not be them with whom you aggravate and quarrel. It will be with me."

With his face a mask of composed wrath, Lucien walked to the makeshift bar by the room's huge fireplace and poured one of Scotland's best. He raised it to Gwen and sipped. Suddenly, Gwen's demeanor shifted. "We'll see one another again, Lucien," she snarled.

Without missing a beat, he laconically waved his hand, confronting Gwen in a voice that defied human ability, "No, if we see one another again, you will pay the exorbitant price that I desperately, keenly, want to exact from you. I can, and will, certainly show you that there are people and beings you can't order around, manipulate, enthrall, or intimidate. To be candid, I'm tempted right now to perform some of that punishment immediately, given your change in attitude. Leave now, before I lose my temper and do so." He swallowed what was left of his drink, setting the empty glass down on the table with a small thud, making Gwen jump.

Unexpectedly, Gwen persevered. "No one else is asking me to leave, and legally, Bowman can't have the kids here without me." As Sean and Bowman started to disagree, she regarded them with a smug look, as though she had the upper hand. There it was again, that casual disregard of her role in perpetuating the mistrust Beckett harbored deep within her heart. Pissed, she addressed Gwen directly, not couching her anger.

"At first, I didn't believe what Bowman and Sean told me just a half hour ago, Gwen, but DNA doesn't lie. These are my biological children, kids you stole from me? For what purpose? To satisfy that demanding mother you complained about incessantly, a person you told me you needed coping techniques to deal with? You hurt me for that?" The dam holding back Beckett's outrage broke, angry tears filling her eyes. Unbeknownst to her, white sparks flew from her towards Gwen, with their intended target stepping back to avoid them reaching her.

"Beckett, I...my mother she... you just don't understand," Gwen faltered, finally exhibiting signs of fear. "Regardless, those kids are legally mine and Bowman's." She stood there, pleased with herself, until Lucien invaded her space.

"I don't think you get it, witch. Laws of this world don't mean anything to me and mine, only commandments. How many of those did you break?" Lucien's words, tight, focused, and furious, carried a dangerous tone, intimating deadly intentions. "If you insist on provoking me, I promise you I will remedy this situation once and for all."

Beckett detected a white beam of something like smoke pass from Lucien to Gwen. She glanced at Sean and Bowman, who didn't seem as weirded out by what they saw as she was. She watched in complete incredulity as Lucien delivered a coup de grace, one that Beckett knew might cause Gwen torment.

"Don't bother telling your cursed mother, I've already sent her a message directly, letting her know that the pit is waiting and I have one way passes for both of you. She sold you out." Lucien took a sip from his fresh drink. "You can still end up there. Your choice."

Finally horrified and, in Beckett's professional opinion, terrified out of her mind that her mother knew, Gwen escaped. In full retreat, she didn't just leave the library, she literally flung herself out of the room.

After the confrontation, Bowman picked up Beckett's hand, holding it in his, "I didn't know what she'd done to me, kept doing to me, until after I started working with Sean to find you."

He looked down at his feet. "Sean noticed some things that didn't add up, Mrs. McKinnon, then Lucien from afar... it's a long story. I'm sorry I didn't know what she did to you when she did it." Moved by his words, Beckett put her arm around his shoulders.

She raised her eyes to Sean, who was on his third or fourth round of Mrs. McKinnon's canapés. "I have a whole lot of learning to do, don't I?" Beckett said, rather than asked.

He plunked a salmon canapé into her hand. "We all do, m' Lady. But we need to help you catch up with us. Just hang on for a couple more minutes."

As Sean asked Mrs. McKinnon to have dinner brought to the library for her staff as well, he caught Lucien's eye. Though complying with the request, Mrs. McKinnon first handed Beckett a glass of peach whiskey, ensuring she had something to ease any remaining tears. Beckett caught the housekeeper's hand briefly, holding it in a moment of wordless thanks.

Beckett perceived, for the first time, that Mrs. McKinnon was not a mere mortal. Mentally, she shook herself. What was happening to her? Mrs. McKinnon smiled, brushed hair from Beckett's face, then left the library with her staff, closing the big wooden doors behind her.

As soon as the doors closed, Sean motioned his new shrimp canapé at Lucien, ordering, "Show and tell."

Lucien angled toward her and then, he radiated, like a star, only brighter. When she could finally see him through the prism of colors and light obscuring him, he had wings. The whitest, widest, beautiful, full- feathered wings she'd ever seen in any painting, sculpture, or sketch.

Her mind spun. In the stunned silence, she noticed Bowman gaping at Lucien, his eye wide with shock. Lucien. Lucien, French for... suddenly, she knew who he was, but not how she knew him.

She stood, straighter and surer of herself than she'd ever been. "You're Lucifer, aren't you? If I recall, most of humankind believes you are, and I quote, "the devil". What was that white thread that went from you to Gwen?" Beckett asked.

Astoundingly, Beckett remained calm, rational, and rather intrigued—a marked difference from her reaction to the news that Gwen was the offspring of a legendary witch. The prospect that beings like Lucifer and God existed in the universe somehow felt solid, real, and foundational.

Appearing unconcerned, Sean kept eating, not disturbed in the least.

Lucien, albeit Lucifer now, stood in front of her, answering in that melodious tone, "Yes, little one. I am, but I've given up the Hell job, much in the same way you are taking a different path. Evidently, even archangels are never too old to change." He paused, thinking over her second question. "The thread you saw between me and the witch constituted the energy that signified my promise to send her and her mother to the Pit. I can, and I will. "

He shimmered once again, making his wings invisible before Mrs. McKinnon and the others returned. "Eventually, you'll remember our first meeting. When you do, I need you to let me know as soon as you can." He smoothed his hair, glossy and black, away from his face.

That's why Gwen gave up, she deduced. Lucifer's promise

was a fact, not a simple threat.

She noticed Sean stopped eating. Putting down his plate, he advised her, "We're not done with show and tell yet." He led Beckett to the chairs and sofa by the stone fireplace, positioning her in a leather wingback closest to the edge of the heavy, wooden coffee table where he made his seat.

Lucifer chose the other wingback, and Bowman sat on the arm of the sofa closest to her. "Beckett," Sean directed, "look at me." At first when she did, nothing appeared different. Then, immediately, it did.

Astonished, she reached out her hands to touch his ears, which now had small points at their helixes. His eyes, always such a clear blue, like a cloudless sky on a summer day, were lit with life.

In fact, his entire visage glowed with an inner brightness; she traced the lines of his face with her finger. Sean exhaled. "I'm an elf, Beckett. My parents camouflaged my ears to make it easier for me to blend in."

Slumping back, Beckett saw Bowman too had pointed ears. What the actual...?!?!? Grappling with these revelations, Beckett sought out her glass of peach whiskey, which Sean picked up and handed to her.

Steadying herself, she drank the rest of her whiskey with a shaking hand and handed the glass back to Sean. Lucifer rose with his glass and retrieved hers from Sean, taking them for refills.

Worried, Bowman and Sean studied Beckett in the shocked silence that enveloped them. How long had they known about themselves? What did that mean for her? She touched her ears unconsciously, "Uhm. You don't have the same pointed ears. Why is that?"

Wasting no time, Bowman answered, "I'm half elf, half Fae, and Sean is all elf, all day."

Fae? What little she knew about the Fae came from fairy

tales and for that matter, the same with elves! "Am I dreaming?"she asked no one specifically. Beckett heard a rustling above her. Her drink, filled to the top of the cocktail glass, appeared from a well-manicured hand right in front of her nose.

"You are not dreaming, darling. Drink." Lucifer directed. He placed a hand lightly on her shoulder. Again, the calm from him seeped directly into her as she took a sip, letting her thoughts free from convention for the moment.

"When did you...you know, know Sean?", she stammered, pointing to his ears.

He grimaced. Resolved, he took her glass from her, putting her hands in his. "I've known since we were children," Sean admitted. "My parents never held our lineage from me, but they'd asked that I not share those details with you. Your guardians and my parents told me that there would come a time when you'd need to know your heritage, but I couldn't share that with you then. Too dangerous."

"My heritage?" Beckett was incredulous. "What do you mean?"

Sean took one hand from hers, placing it gently on the right side of her face. "Remember when we started finishing each other's sentence? What were we? Twelve... eleven, right?"

A fleeting smile tugged at the corners of her mouth as the memory resurfaced, but it quickly vanished when an echo spoke in her mind: *We still can. Because you too are not human, but the product of a deep love affair between a goddess and an elven king.*

Beckett jolted away, her world tilting on its axis as she grappled with this newfound knowledge. The inference of what she had just heard, and more importantly, how she had heard it, left her dumbstruck. Sean's lips hadn't moved, but his words rung clearly within her thoughts.

45

Sean considered her for a minute, allowing her to process his disclosure. Despite his fear that she might leave, Beckett remained seated, though he knew there was plenty of time for that to change.

Taking in her pallid complexion, he noted how it made the sprinkle of freckles across her nose stand out in stark contrast. Her captivating eyes, though rounded with disbelief, held a glimmer of rabid interest as they met his gaze. Opening his mind, he sensed the first spark of her thoughts beginning to unravel the implications of his words. Gradually, over the course of a few minutes, he watched the color return to her cheeks, like a slow bloom of life.

Then, she looked at Bowman, whose face reflected his uneasiness and guilt. Her first thought materialized: Connor and Katie, with their elf/Fae father and elf/goddess biological mother, may be predisposed to the supernatural. If that's the case, Beckett needed to understand what it meant, and quickly. Treating this situation like she had, perhaps, gifted children, she started to ask pertinent questions about them, rather than herself.

Beckett sat up straighter, cleared her throat. "What about Katie and Connor? Do they have abilities they can't explain?"

"Yes, they do," Bowman replied. "Connor is brilliant, like you, Beckett. That's why pre-med for him is a breeze. Katie's abilities are more like mine, with horses and the bow and arrow, and she's very nature-focused, like Sean says you used to be."

When she glanced away and back to him, Bowman's face exposed his relief that this part of the conversation hurdle was over– to him, their interaction moved things forward and out of the past. A squeeze of her shoulder reminded her that Lucifer was still there, and this time, she found herself appreciating his kindness.

Sean took the opportunity to rise, walk to the heavy oak

doors, and open them. "Mrs. McKinnon and her crew are coming back with dinner for us. Are you hungry, Beckett?"

"I don't know, but I want more answers," she said to Sean. Standing, Bowman extended a hand, helping her from her seat. He pulled her into his chest and hugged her, which she reciprocated. Beckett understood that the last two and a half years were just as hard on him, albeit in a different way.

She murmured to him, "It's ok, it's ok. I'm all right. I just need a minute."

"You take as many minutes as you need," Releasing her, Bowman gestured to Lucifer and Sean, "We're right here for you."

Giving her a peck on the forehead, Sean handed her an old, tattered book, with beautiful cursive script on its pages. "Reading material for tonight, m' Lady. It's time you started to discover for yourself who you are and what you can do."

"It'll be after I take a ride to the point above the loch after dinner," Beckett said firmly.

Taking her right hand, the same one he'd held on the helicopter, Lucifer brushed his lips across her knuckles. Temporarily, she lost her focus and again, the lights playing in the trees behind her guardians' home came into her mind's view, this time with the sound of wings and the smell of the woods, with notes of sandalwood, cedar, and musk permeating her nose.

Beckett spoke: "You were in the woods, weren't you? The one on the property behind my guardians?" He stayed silent, but affirmed the accuracy of her assumptions with a discreet bow of his head.

At that moment, Mrs. McKinnon and her three-person crew brought in plates of pot roast, green beans, and mashed potatoes, distributing them to Bowman, Lucifer, and Sean. Beckett noted that the staff seemed to be more relaxed and happier; she noticed distinctive ears, some with elongated pointed ears, others with shorter, almost imperceptible points, and different sets of piercing eyes. Evidently, they'd hidden them from view the first time they came into the library.

Then there was Mrs. McKinnon, who blossomed into such beauty and light that her transformation took her breath away. She approached Beckett with a covered plate, sitting it on the table.

Before she let Beckett sit down, she embraced her. "Child, my name is Maya McKinnon. You need not call me Mrs. McKinnon any longer. Along with working and living with the Caladfins, I'm also Bowman's aunt on his mother's side. I'm glad you're here safe with us."

"But what if I want to call you Mrs. McKinnon?" Beckett pleaded, misty-eyed.

Mrs. McKinnon laughed and released Beckett, inviting her to sit and requesting one of her staff to bring a bottle of merlot to her table. She took the chrome top from the plate she'd brought for her. French cheeses, stinky and oozing, black and green olives, carrots, celery, fruit, and sliced fresh bread covered the plate.

"It's my understanding you don't eat like you should," Mrs. McKinnon chided. "I expect that to be gone before you decide to go off gallivantin'." She kissed the top of Beckett's head, and made her way out of the library with her staff. The door closed behind them.

Beckett wiped tears from her eyes and began to eat. And drink, and eat some more. Sean and Bowman dug in, but Lucifer ate sparingly, occasionally lifting his eyes to hers. The library, her library, filled with the sounds of utensils hitting plates, murmurs, and refills of wine, beer, and whiskey.

Once she'd had her fill and cleaned her plate, Beckett rose, going to sit in the wingback where she'd laid the book Sean gave her before dinner. Half listening to the conversation at the table, she began to read. The script on the pages engrossed her so much, that when Beckett lifted her head, dusk had fallen. In the blissful quiet of the library, she thought she was alone, with a fire merrily cracking and cozy beside her.

The sound of movement behind her caught Beckett's attention. She spun to see Lucifer lounging against the fireplace mantle, sipping his bourbon and watching her intently. "Quite a lot to take in, isn't it?" he remarked, swirling the amber liquid in his glass. "But don't worry, you're going to be fine."

A snore alerted her to someone at her desk with his feet up: Bowman, clearly napping. "Where's Sean?" She looked around the room.

"A call he had to take," Lucifer shared, extending his hand. She placed her hand in his, standing, that lovely warmth from him traveling up her arm.

He flicked a finger at the sleeping figure behind her desk, who abruptly jumped, exclaiming "I'm awake, I'm awake!" Bowman passed a hand over his face. "Want to go to the stables?" he asked Beckett.

Not hiding her excitement this time, she shook her head yes. Bowman got up from her desk, hustling to the door. Lucifer gently caught her arm when she turned to follow Bowman. "Where will you'll ride, little one?"

"The point, I saw a bench there just by the loch," she answered casually.

He released her, and she hurried to catch up with Bowman. Beckett hoped she threw riding clothes in her bag. Yelling to him up the hallway, she told she'd meet him at the stables in fifteen minutes.

Chapter 4

The Ways of the Divine and Supernatural

When Beckett got to her bag, she discovered she hadn't packed her riding clothes. "Damn, I hope I can find something in that massive closet," she muttered to herself, frowning at the oversight.

Rummaging through the depths of the wardrobe, which seemed to contain an endless array of clothing, she stumbled upon an old pair of Levis with worn-out knees and various rips—a pair she recognized as having owned for more than two decades. Hesitantly, she undressed and slipped them on, delighted to find that they still fit perfectly.

Next, another relic from her past: a pair black of short suede boots with soft soles. Those sufficed for riding, along with the long, black, well worn, barn jacket hanging in the closet. Beckett took it off the hanger, laying it on the bed. Beckett didn't think she left anything in the chest of drawers, but opened each of them to find clothes she didn't know she had. Jazzed, she picked out a waffled Henley AC/DC concert top, toasty and comfortable.

She changed clothing quickly and headed for the door, only to turn back when she saw hair ties and scrunchies in a glass jar on an end table. Opening the container, she pulled a scrunchie out and put her hair in a looped pony. Beckett hurried out the door and within minutes, bumped into Sean coming around the corner toward his suite.

Speechless for once, Sean stared at her. "What's wrong?" she asked, self-doubt in her tone. She wondered if her choice of attire was unsuitable for a new executive embarking on a horseback ride.

Sean shook himself out of his daze, pulling her by the hand. Beckett followed him to another door, and he invited her inside, steering her toward a mirror.

"Look," he instructed.

So, she did. Beckett hadn't worn her hair up in a very long time. Sean didn't know she had a 360 undercut underneath to lessen the thickness of her hair when she grew it longer. In fact, he'd never known it was there.

But what really captured his interest was her face: alive, alight, carefree, and with ears slightly pointed at their helixes. When did that happen, she wondered, as she touched them. Her eyes looked lighter, too; the gray circling her irises deepened with green, making the contrast even more distinct.

Looking at Sean behind her in the mirror, she apologized about not telling him about her undercut. Sean cut her off, placing both hands on her shoulders and meeting her eyes in their reflection, "You Viking warrior princess, you. Remember?"

She did: they'd played Viking gods as kids after Sean's father read them from the Eddas. They maintained eye contact for a couple of minutes before she heard in her mind, *Ride fast and hard. You've waited a long time to do it.*

The radiant smile Beckett gave Sean melted him. *Thank you for being my bestest pal in whole wide world, Seanie.* He kissed the back of her head, wiped his eyes, and sent her on her way.

Beckett made her way to the stables, going back along the path past the helo pad and beyond. Night fell. With it, the stars came out and the breeze lifted. In the flora of the immediate grounds, she heard birds as they called to one another. When she reached the barn, her ears picked up the sounds of the horses, nickering, snorting, and pawing.

The stable smelled exactly as it should: hay, feed, leather, horse, and manure. Each horse in its stall moved or rose as they sensed her presence. As Beckett passed, they waited to greet her, nibbling her collar, pressing their heads against her cheek, and neighing their hellos softly.

When Beckett got to the last stall, a beautiful, glossy black Arabian stuck his nose directly against hers and breathed deeply. She did the same thing to him, and he moved his nose across every inch of her face, to her hair, her jacket, and her shirt. What a beautiful animal, she mused.

Satisfied with his examination, he kicked the stall door with one hoof. "What, you want to ride with me in the night across the dell, with the wind streaming through your mane?" Another kick. Well, well. A smart horse.

Bowman called to her from the entrance to the barn, "You riding "wit", or "wit-out?"

She laughed at his use of the grill call of his favorite Philly cheesesteak joint in Philadelphia. "Wit-out, of course. Which horse is the one you guys think should be my riding partner?"

Bowman, coming from the tack room with a hackamore and horse blanket, grinned. "This f'ing guy. He seems to be in love with you already."

He opened the stall door and handed the hackamore to Beckett. The braided leather noseband felt soft in her hands as she turned it around, containing her name and the horse's name, Aellon, on it. After Bowman put the blanket on him, Aellon nuzzled the back of Bowman's head affectionately, stepping tall and lithe out of the stall.

While the horse stood serenely in front of Beckett, she

gently put the hackamore on him, took the reins, and started to walk him out of the stables. Bowman followed. Once she got outside, Aellon snorted, bowing his great head to her. She grabbed his mane and mounted him swiftly, seating herself on the horse blanket, and using her reins to turn him toward Bowman.

Taking her in fully for the first time since dinner, Bowman expressed, "I can't tell you how great it is that you're here. Go ride. I'll be here when you come back." Beckett gave him a huge smile, thanked him profusely, and clicked her tongue. That's all it took for Aellon. He set off at a brisk trot, ascending the slope toward the grounds that led to the loch.

She allowed him to warm up, carefully cantering the next half a mile. As Aellon increased his speed, Beckett bent low so he'd be in earshot of her commands and so she could better control his head. But what she found was this horse was *different*, so intelligent she thought she must be imagining it.

When she told him to fly, he stretched out in a full gallop, his tail streaming. The ride was so smooth that it felt like he soared across the ground. Swiftly, her looped pony became a real ponytail streaming behind her, just like Aellon's mane and tail. Rider and horse became one, reveling in the wind and starlight.

Every worry, concern, anxiety, and fear evaporated as Beckett lost herself in the peace of the darkness, emptying her mind. She let the wind and Aellon sooth her soul. They continued for half an hour straight along the property, passing the cabin where she presumed the Maethors lived. From there, they turned northwest as they began to make their way to the point.

In the faintness of the starlight, the loch sparkled. The wind was more prevalent here, and its bluster caused tears that streamed from Beckett's eyes as they began to slow to a trot. In the shadows, she saw the outline of a person sitting on the bench. She didn't want to bother them, but to her amazement, she saw a hand rise as if in invitation.

She reined in Aellon, asking the horse, "What do you think, boy?" He tossed his head and put one hoof up then down specifically, so she'd know he thought it'd be fine. Alrighty then, big man, I feel you, she thought, patting his neck.

Beckett clicked her tongue and Aellon walked the remaining distance to the bench. When she got a little closer, she still couldn't see who sat there, only a dark silhouette against the loch. Beckett dismounted Aellon, and he nudged her forward, seemingly encouraging her to go to the bench. Bossy horse, Beckett thought, then amazed that he nickered like he'd heard her.

When she approached the bench on foot, the figure stood up. "Lucifer? What are you doing out here?" She sat down beside him.

"I wanted to speak to you alone," Lucifer responded. Immediately, a jarring déjà vu overcame her, and Beckett fought to focus on what he was doing and saying.

Beckett looked through the branches of the ancient oak tree beside the bench about ten feet away, seeing stars as they shined brightly in the night sky. Abruptly, she was hit again by a vision of beams of light and colors streaming through the trees in the woods behind her guardians' home. This time, she took Lucifer's hand and when she did, a new chaotic shuffling of images filtered through her mind.

When she got her bearings, Beckett turned to him, finding his face several inches from hers. Keeping her gaze, he deliberately telegraphed his intention, seeking her consent, before moving his other hand to caress the left side of her face. Slowly, Lucifer pressed his lips and cheek to her right.

Involuntarily, she sighed, putting her head on his shoulder. She was completely at ease: not frightened or pulling away, but she didn't understand why.

Beckett felt the tug of memory just below the surface. Lucifer, sensing or knowing, whispered in her ear, "Don't try to rush it, little one. It'll come back to you." He turned toward the loch, and situated them so his arm encircled her, allowing her head to fall naturally on his shoulder.

Playing with her ponytail, he announced, "I'm staying in the keep for the foreseeable future, if that's all right with you." She signaled her approval against his shoulder. His arm tightened around her. "I don't want to be away from you."

"Am I supposed to argue with that? Consequences and all?" Beckett teased. She felt his chuckle emanating from deep in his chest. They sat there for a while, silently comfortable with each other's presence, watching the waves in the loch, the starlight reflecting from them as the wind eased across the point.

Checking the time, Lucifer called to Aellon, who obediently came to the bench, nuzzling Beckett's ponytail as he reached Lucifer. "You ride bit-less," Lucifer remarked. "No wonder he likes you."

Beckett pulled away from his arm, facing him. "Lucifer, this horse looks Arabian, but he's not, is he?"

"No, he's not. He's a horse from a friend's stable, one you'll meet eventually. Bowman was quite impressed." Lucifer caught Aellon's reins, handing them to her.

He stood and offered his hand to her - she took it. Thanking him, Beckett placed a hand on his arm and posed, "Do you need to ride with me back? Oh wait...". She was a little disappointed. "...you flew here, didn't you?"

Lucifer stepped closer to her, "Yes. For today, I'll fly back. But in the future, perhaps we'll ride or fly together."

"I think I'd like that." Beckett walked around the bench and patted Aellon's neck. He bowed to allow her to mount.

This time, her movements were more fluid; she had Aellon at his full height in a few seconds.

Lucifer caught the hackamore. "Aellon, show her what you can do." Aellon nickered softly and pivoted, already ready to trot.

When they got to the next rise, she looked back at the bench. Lucifer was gone. Beckett bent equal with Aellon's ears. "You heard the archangel. Show me what you can do."

Aellon took off like a shot. All she saw was the blurring of the surroundings as his hooves kissed the ground. It was an experience such that she'd never had before: exhilarating, freeing, and cathartic. She was going to have to do this *every day*, because it made her the happiest she'd been since she was a young girl.

Five minutes later, they trotted to the doorway of the barn. When Aellon went to bow, she signaled for him to stay upright, dismounting on her own. She kissed his long nose, thanked him, and as she stepped away, he caught her ponytail in his gums.

She walked him into the stables that way as Bowman emerged from the tack room. "Oh, that horse is in looove...," Bowman whistled. "What'd you do, walk him? He's not even sweating." He removed Aellon's hackamore, and Aellon dropped her ponytail. Majestically, the horse walked toward his stall.

"Bowman, that horse isn't a regular horse," Beckett reported. "We made it from the point to here in less than five or six minutes."

Bowman's smile enveloped his face, humming to himself as he removed the horse blanket, gathering more hay and feed for Aellon. Beckett waited for him as he closed the horse's stall gate, and thoroughly checked them all. When he reached her, he stopped in the dark.

"I've never seen you like this," Bowman started. His words

trailed off as he struggled to find the right ones. She took the scrunchie from her hair, cocking her head as she met his gaze. "Like what?"

He was silent for a second, watching Beckett's hair flipping softly in the breeze. "You. You look...happy. No, that's not right: you're beautiful."

Beckett couldn't help poking fun at him, "So, I'm happy, but not beautiful or beautiful, but not happy? I'm so confused."

"You know what I mean," Bowman chuckled.

He reached for her shoulders, pulling her to him. "I've always wanted to hold the starlight in my arms, and here you are," he said gently. Beckett didn't pull away. It'd been a long time since she'd allowed herself to be held by Bowman in any way. After a couple of minutes, she lifted her face to him, giving him a peck on his cheek before returning his hug. She took his hand, and they walked the path that led to the castle.

"Is your truck at Dell?" Beckett asked. "I didn't mean for you to have walk all the way back with me."

"No, I'm staying in one of the castle's guest rooms tonight and then I'll go home to the cabin tomorrow afternoon to see Katie after school," Bowman glanced ahead of them. "Speaking of which, what time should Katie meet you?

"Probably just after she gets out of school. Because if you're right, there's no way in hell you'll be able to stop her from going directly to the stable." Beckett chortled. Stumbling a little in the dark, she grasped Bowman's arm to keep from tripping.

"Connor texted me he'll be home Friday but has to leave on Sunday," he said, pausing momentarily. "Would you like to come over for brunch on Saturday?" Bowman asked.

Beckett wavered before she committed, her fingers absently fidgeting with the scrunchie as she deliberated out loud how the rest of the week would unfold, given her change in position.

Bowman understood. "We'll pencil it in and if something changes, that's ok. Connor does want to see you." He clarified, "*I* want to see you. Is that all right?" She assured him that it was.

When they reach the castle, they parted in separate directions for their rooms. When Beckett got closer to hers, she saw a large black dog rising from in front of her door. He sat calmly, watching her. Attached to his collar was a red origami dragon, exquisitely crafted.

Beckett saw her name written in script on one wing. Beautifully folded, it was so intricate and dear she really didn't want to open it. Vowing to refold it back to its original state, she opened it and saw:

Dearest Lady,

Your safety and security are paramount to me. Please accept Tenebris: he is not a dog, just as Aellon is not a species of horse found on 'terra firma'.

Tenebris is a hellhound, a guard dog accustomed to the ways of the divine and supernatural. By giving him to you this way as a gift, his loyalty lies solely with you. He can communicate with you, and as your abilities become more prevalent, his talents (they are plentiful) will grow, too. I I think, I hope, you both will suit one another.

I remain your servant,
Lucifer

He looked like a Great Dane, with coal black eyes, and a shiny, black, short coat. Not moving a muscle, Tenebris' outline resembled a statue, carved, and polished to perfection. Only when she said his name did he look animated. Even then, his movements, fluid, effortless, and powerful, looked supernatural. She opened the door and the hellhound slid in front of her, alert and watchful.

As she closed the door, he shifted his head to look up at her. "My lady Beckett, I am Tenebris, the darkness", came a sonorous, deep statement, "I am your gift from Lord Lucifer, and I will protect you with my life."

Oh my. Another memorable voice, not just for its timbre and tone, but for the underlying intelligence and proclivity for violence. She faltered for a moment, unsure what to do next. Beckett decided to interview Tenebris much the same way she would a new patient.

"Tenebris, do you wish to be here?", Beckett asked him, noting the spark of attentiveness in his eyes.

Tenebris raised his head higher. "It is a great honor, my Lady. Lord Lucifer has never given one of us as a gift. His action honors my pack and elevates others like my kind."

Despite her calm demeanor, she hit the "Enough No More Data" limit in her mind and decided that she'd heard plenty about archangels, witches, elves, Fae, and hellhounds, plus whatever she was, for today.

Exhausted, Beckett wanted to go to bed. Finding her phone and a power cord, she started making her way to the bathroom, hesitating shy of the door.

"Sam," she said. "Please make the ceiling transparent and set an alarm for 7am."

"Very well, Dr. Argonne. Good night to you, and to you as well, Tenebris."

Sam didn't miss much, but then Tenebris surprised her. "Good night, Sam. I will be prowling between rooms this evening. If you sense anything, you know how to notify me."

Beckett shook her head, dumbfounded. "When did the two of you meet?"

In unison, they answered: "Today."

After all the things she'd discovered and seen, the care with which all these people and beings had taken to make things right for her, the fact a AI and a hellhound talked to one another topped off her "I'm touched and overwhelmed" meter.

She thanked them both, undressing as she made her way to the bathroom. After a quick shower, Beckett brushed her teeth, and threw a slip dress over her head. She slid gratefully under the sheets, sheets she knew Mrs. McKinnon had washed and ironed for her. Glorious. Requesting Sam turn off all the lights, she looked up at the night sky and almost instantly fell asleep.

Chapter 5

The Lady of These Woods

Beckett woke to the deepening night, and for once, it didn't seemed she'd dreamed at all. Yet, everything appeared to have a surreal quality.

Tenebris stood in the doorway, quiet and vigilant. She lay on her back, looking up at the sky, mostly starry, with a few wisps of clouds here and there. Reaching for her phone, she checked the time: 1:52 am.

Beckett sighed contently, letting her thoughts drift. This time, they coasted to a summer day in southwestern Virginia, where she lived with her guardians for thirteen years.

When she was younger, she never called them anything other than Mom and Dad. It was only when she began to apply for college that they told her they were guardians, or in terms people would understand, foster parents. They were friends with the Caladfins, who came almost every summer to their huge, rambling home in the Blue Ridge Mountains.

Beckett loved spending the summers with the Caladfins. Sean made everything fun, brighter, and just more enjoyable, as she had no friends so far from town. They'd ride together, picking blueberries or peaches, jumping their ponies over the creek.

Her mind languidly turned to a time when Sean couldn't come for the summer. One spring, Sean broke his leg. Her bestie and his parents wouldn't arrive until July, or maybe not at all. When her guardians told her, Beckett was aghast.

She could read, of course. But who'd run through the woods and play Viking gods with her? Beckett supposed she could do it on her own, promising herself to do so the next day, then write to Sean about what happened.

Her recollections turned to running along the wooded path with her plastic sword and bow on her back, wearing a crown of honeysuckle, clover, and dandelions, her hair in braids, sporting dirt under her eyes. Little Beckett was every inch the Asgardians Thor, Frigg, Freya, Baldr, and Tyr were, only tinier and fiercer.

She wasn't afraid of anything in the woods, and everything there she or Sean named. The forest was their domain; people who threatened it, like Loki, would have to cope with their wrath.

Looking up, she saw the sunlight streaming through the trees, and then colors, like the prisms she'd learned about in books, glittered like rainbows around her. It was then she saw them, the two beings fighting in her woods, damaging her trees, her wildflowers, and scaring everybody she cared about to death. Not under my watch, she thought. It's just like Seanie to miss this defense of their kingdom!

Beckett crouched, flitting between trees and bushes to get a closer look at them. The pair were a winged man and a beastly-looking man, who growled and grunted as they thrust their bright swords at one another in the sun, spinning, and, sometimes, striking blade to blade.

The blades whizzed through the air, colliding with metallic pings that occasionally sparked like the sparklers Beckett and Sean lit on the Fourth of July. The combatants moved in a flurry, parrying and thrusting, until the winged figure, at least

Beckett thought it was a winged figure, roared an arcane utterance. He lashed out, his strike finding the bestial opponent's neck. The creature burst into shadowy motes that rapidly dissipated in the sunlight.

When the winged man reached over and pulled some leaves off one of her trees to polish his shiny blade, she got angry. How dare he harm Ophelia, tear leaves from her limbs and hurting her!

Beckett took a deep breath and came out of shadows, welding her plastic blade and pointing it straight at him as Sean taught her do with foes. "What are you doing in my realm?" she demanded. "Why have you hurt my Ophelia? What did she do to you?"

At first, the winged man looked amused. After sheathing his sword, he fell to his knees. "I'm sorry, my lady. That man meant you and your family harm. I had to dispatch him from your realm. I hope that you and Ophelia will forgive me – I didn't think."

She didn't say anything, letting the silence grow between them. He hung his dark head before her, now grave and serious. "Will you forgive me, Lady Beckett?" Beckett loved the way he sounded. She resolved right then to practice speaking like that before Sean arrived, if he did. However, she frowned because this winged man knew her real name and he shouldn't.

Beckett placed her sword point under his chin, pushing his face up. Beckett noted his eyes, the color of the soft moss she found at the foot of trees. "How do you know my name, rogue?" She liked saying that since Sean was usually the rogue. "What's your name? Loki?"

Slowly, the winged man met her gaze. "My name, dearest lady, is Lucifer. I am so very glad to meet you. I knew your name because you are regarded as The Lady of These Woods. Your friends here speak your name with great respect and love."

"I thank you and will allow you to pass from my realm, sir," Beckett said simply, "but as the ruler of my kingdom, I must give you a reward for your service." She stepped to him and gently placed her hand on the right side of his face, pressing her lips and cheek to other side for a moment. He smelled good, like the woods and musk.

When she pulled back from him, Beckett saw tears forming in his eyes. "What's wrong? You're nothing like what I've read, Lucifer. You're not a bad person. You just need opportunities to do good."

With that, she gestured to the tree, presenting such an occasion for virtuous deeds: "I need you to lift me so I can reach Ophelia's branches and heal her. It takes too long when I try to do it from the trunk."

Intrigued, he did as she asked, lifting her little, light body. Beckett handed Lucifer the sword so she could attend to the tree with both hands.

He hefted the tiny sword, and he noticed the name scribbled on the blade: Skögrbrandr. He chuckled, recognizing the translation as "forest sword." Looking back up, he saw Beckett smiling down at him. "All swords need good names, Lucifer," she patiently explained, "Otherwise, how can you ask them to help you if you don't know who they are?"

Lucifer watched as Beckett turned her attention to Ophelia. She spoke softly to the tree and reverently touched it, her hand surrounded by colorful prisms of light. Ophelia vibrated ever so slightly, and he saw new leaves budded where she placed her hand. When she saw them, she smiled widely and glanced to where bright sunlight lit the edges of the tree's leaves closest to her.

Lucifer placed her carefully on the ground. After a final look at her handiwork, Beckett peered at him in gratitude. He got down on one knee in front of her. "Little one, do all the trees have names?"

She tipped her head and pointed to a tall white pine close to Ophelia, introducing him as Bowie. "Sean named him, and he doesn't name many things." she lamented. "Although, he did name Manny, too." Beckett also gestured to a raven watching them intently from the branches above.

"And Sean is your friend?", Lucifer asked.

"Sean is my *best* friend. You know, kinda like a brother, but better? He's 8, but I'm 7. He lives on the other side of the world and comes to visit every summer. We camp out at night, and we ride, ruling these woods. He broke his leg, and now they can't come until July this year, though." Beckett stated miserably.

Sighing, her gaze turned to the path. "I will walk you to the edge of my kingdom." Beckett waved her hand. "It's that way." Lucifer stood to follow her.

As they strolled the path together, butterflies surrounded her. Foxes, turkeys, rabbits, squirrels, and birds approached the pathway, calling to her when she hailed them all by name. When Beckett greeted a black squirrel, Tenebris, who scampered ahead of them, he asked her where she'd gotten the names for her friends.

"Sometimes I dream about them," Beckett answered helpfully, "but a lot of the time, I just know who they are." To the left of her, an enormous bush of honeysuckle, heavy with blossoms, tickled her shoulder.

She whispered to it. Honeysuckle flowers with their stems dropped silently on the path, and new buds appeared in their place. Gathering them, she secured them expertly in a bouquet with a hair tie from her wrist. "A gift from my realm for you, Lucifer," she offered. Reaching up, Beckett handed the heady bouquet to him.

Fifteen or twenty minutes later, they reached the culvert

below the gravel road that bordered on the side of her guardians' property. Beckett turned to Lucifer. "This is where I must leave you. Thank you for risking your life to protect me and mine, Lucifer. You may kiss my hand."

She held her right hand aloft to him. He appeared mesmerized for a moment. Then he caught Beckett's gaze as he slowly bent a knee, reaching for her hand. Lucifer turned it over and softly kissed her tiny, grubby hand on the inside of her palm, closing her fingers over it. 'It should be me, I think, thanking you, my Lady."

Before he rose, Beckett unexpectedly hugged him around his neck. Tentative and hopeful, she asked, "Will I ever see you again?"

"I believe so," Lucifer said meditatively, hugging her back, speech muffled in her hair. Beckett released him reluctantly, realizing she was wrong: he wasn't a rogue, but a prince. "Do good things until then. Farewell, prince, "she bid him. He exhaled, stood, and walked a few steps past Beckett before stopping, turning to look at her.

He seemed to make a choice, and stepped back the way he'd left her, his hand digging in the pocket of his jacket. Again, Lucifer kneeled again before her. Taking her hand, the one that he'd kissed, he faced her palm up and placed a small, iridescent object on it.

When Beckett brought it closer, she saw it was a three-dimensional star, made of paper, glittering and glowing while she held it. "Why does it glow so?" she marveled.

"It is a small bit of my favorite star, the light embedded in the paper so it will shine for many years." Lucifer stroked her forehead with his finger, then kissed the top of her head. "You will not remember me until much later, but the star will always be with you. Go now, to home and to sleep, little one…" He said something else, but she, distracted by the small star, started to obediently walk toward home. That night....

Beckett sat straight up in bed, fully awake, and saw that Tenebris watched her intently. "What is it, my Lady?" he inquired. "Are you all right?"

Soundlessly, she got up from the bed, Tenebris following behind her. Beckett stumbled in her haste to the great room where she'd left her bag and frantically dug around, looking for something. *Joey.* Inside Joey, she found a small object that shined in the darkness.

As Beckett lifted, it glowed just as consistently and vividly as it had forty years ago when she believed she'd found it in the woods.

Tenebris interrupted her thoughts. "That's an imbrued starlight talisman." He came closer, sniffing. "Lord Lucifer *gave* that to you?" His tone implied the rarity and privilege of such a thing.

"Yes. A long time ago," Beckett replied thoughtfully.

Leaning over slightly, she put her hand by his mouth. "Can you take this to Lucifer right now without damaging it?" He gave a short tip of his head in affirmation.

"Please do so, Tenebris. However, do not tell him anything else if he asks. Just make sure you place it where he can see it, ok?" The great hellhound gingerly picked up the star, vanishing into the air.

Ophelia. Manny. Bowie. *Tenebris.* How did she forget their names? How did she forget *him*? How could she forget how to heal a tree, or even that she *could*?? Beckett went to the kitchenette and checked the refrigerator for something to drink, gratified to find some orange juice.

With shaky hands, Beckett opened it and drank. Shocked and choking, she noticed a faint iridescence surrounded her completely, her hand holding the bottle, her arm, her shoulder, her other side...everything. Carefully, she sat the bottle on the counter.

When she walked back into the great room, Tenebris returned, placing the talisman on an end table where it shone even more brightly than she remembered. He wasn't alone.

Lucifer stood inside the threshold, his back to the closed door and his eyes bright in the dark. "Did you dream about that day, little one?"

The little shake of her head in affirmation brought him flying across the room to her, until Tenebris stood before him growling. She thanked the hellhound, angling past him, straight into Lucifer's arms.

Beckett stood there, held by him for quite a while, until her heart and mind eased and that ever-present calmness he manifested seeped into her. He stroked her hair and back, whispering reassurances.

Tenebris sat quietly on the floor by her feet, looking up at her, just in case he needed to act. Lucifer pulled away a little, positioning her to sit in one of the chairs beside her sofa. She watched as his tall, dark form strode to her kitchenette. Bringing the bottle of orange juice, he sat it beside her on the end table where the talisman glowed with an increasing intensity far brighter than when she'd sent Tenebris to Lucifer's rooms.

Lucifer offered answers. "Tell me what you want to know." Tenebris moved to her side of the chair, flipping her hand to his head. Touched by his gesture, Beckett absently stroked his large head and ears. She believed she felt rumbles of pleasure in his throat and chest.

"I dreamed about the summer Sean didn't come to Virginia after he'd broken his leg. I saw you fighting someone, or some... *thing*, in my woods. I heard you say something I didn't understand when you struck down your opponent. And I kissed you just like I did on the helo." Beckett faltered. "Is that really what happened?"

"Yes, it is." Lucifer angled his body towards her. " I'd

heard that your real mother bore a child with an elven lord, a considerable danger for all of you."He placed his hand lightly on her knee. "You were born out of the love between two exceptional beings."

As Lucifer pulled his hand back, Beckett began to accept that perhaps some of the reason she always felt she didn't fit in generally with others, except for Sean and maybe Bowman, stemmed directly from the fact she *wasn't* human. At least, Sean and Bowman knew who *they* were – she didn't. That fact terrified her.

"Who are my mother and father, Lucifer?"

He caught her eyes with his. "Your mother was Gaia, the primordial goddess of the life in the universe. Your father, a high Elven king, Erendilas, reigned in a peaceful galaxy filled with light and natural forces. Those energies he, and his people, fostered, grew, and utilized to keep themselves safe."

Lucifer paused, and took a breath. "It is not an exaggeration to say your father was a magnificent, noble being, and a highly skilled warrior. He died defending you from darkness. Before that, Erendilas chose your guardians, and the Caladfins volunteered to help them protect you."

"Is that why you were in the woods?" Beckett broached.

He agreed."You'd been hidden with the Argonnes, with the Caladfins as backup, for your own good, but your energies and abilities identified you when you used them in the woods. I'd wanted to see you, since you mother never had a child like you. Instead, I walked into an ambush intended for you. What you heard me shout was Hebrew, אֵין חֶמְלָה לַחִלּוּנִים. *'Eyn ḥemlah lachillunim* - No mercy for the profane.'"

Usually so melodic and rich, Lucifer next words sounded scathing and sharp. "There are supernatural beings in the universe who view your existence as an abomination, in the same way people on Earth discriminate against people for the color of their skin, their gender, or the circumstances of their birth."

Lucifer place his hand on her forearm. "That's not how I see you. Never. After that few hours in your woods with you, I've never forgotten you and what you did."

"I was a child, Lucifer. What did I do? I played Viking god games in the woods and relished in my own fantasy." The weight of all this new information made Beckett question her own sanity. Mental cartwheels like those tired you, too.

Covering her mouth, she couldn't suppress a yawn. Seeing her exhaustion, Lucifer picked her up and placed her on the sofa nearest the potted heather and lavender, which stood up straighter and began to produce more blooms, filling the air with their scent.

He rummaged a pillow and a blanket from her bedroom, putting the former behind her head. Satisfied she was comfortable, Lucifer settled on the sofa in the middle, putting her legs and feet over his lap. With one hand, he tossed the blanket over her, taking one of Beckett's hands in both of his.

"Sleep," he instructed. "I'm here, and so is Tenebris. You're not crazy - you've just been re-discovered a whole new world and your place in it. While that can be overwhelming, you have us to help you. So, let us."

Lucifer passed his lips over the knuckles of her hand, continuing to hold it. Barely able to keep her eyes open, soothed with the tranquility she always felt around him, Beckett fell asleep.

Chapter 6

Black Magic and Breakfast

Sunlight danced over Beckett's face, rousing her. Pulling the blanket over her head, she recalled entirely too late that she'd left the ceiling transparent to see the night sky. Now the sun brilliantly lit her suite with golden rays. Heather flowers and leaves tickled her nose; propping herself on her elbow, she gently brushed them aside.

Other than Tenebris, who lay vigilantly on the end of the sofa, no one else appeared to be in the room. She noticed Lucifer moved the star talisman to the coffee table in front of her, along with a re-folded red dragon. She lay back, allowing her eyes to close once more. I like this place, she thought, or, at least I like it even more than I thought I would.

Stretching and yawning, she called for Sam. "Sam, what time is it?"

He answered instantly, "It is 8:49 in the morning, Dr. Argonne. I know you asked me to wake you at 7, but when I tried, well, you stayed asleep".

Amused and rather glad to have a lie in, Beckett understood. Sam's programming permitted him to make judgement calls in such instances. With no calendar entries or plans he knew of for her today, he made the right choice.

"Also, there is one message from Lord Caladfin, and another from Mr. Maethor, who requests you ride over to his cabin tomorrow for lunch at one o'clock. Lord Caladfin said to tell you to relax, do whatever you like for the remainder of the week, and that your computer and phone are ready for you in your study. He said, and I quote, you had, "calls and letters" you need to make and send right away."

Beckett laughed. "He's right. I do. Please send a message to Bowman letting him know I accept his invitation for lunch tomorrow, and to Lord Caladfin? Thank him and let him know those notifications will go out before noon. Good morning to you, Tenebris."

She smiled down at the gigantic hellhound before her. Tenebris chuckled, issuing a deep resonance from his barrel chest. "It is ironic you wish the darkness good morning, my Lady. If I may, I have a message for you as well from Lord Lucifer. He wishes to ride with you and Katie this afternoon. What time would you like to meet him?"

"Please let him know that I'll be at the stables around 2 pm," she told Tenebris.

More riding clothes, Beckett concluded. "I didn't bring enough riding clothes, it seems, Sam. Where can I find some locally?"

"Dr. Argonne, Mrs. McKinnon ordered riding clothing and new boots for you. They'll be delivered to your rooms this morning."

Oh, no. "Do you know what she ordered? Was it dressage wear or what I'd pick?" If Beckett's memory served her, Mrs. McKinnon loved the dressage, focusing her attention and awe on the coats, pants, crops, helmets, and high riding boots the riders wore.

This time, Sam laughed. Beckett never heard him laugh before, and she'd be damned if it didn't sound authentic. "She ordered riding clothes for you over "these blasted dells" if that's what you mean," he said, apparently amused by her predicament.

Unruffled, Beckett decided to roll Mrs. McKinnon's way for now and send for some of her own clothing from London soon.

After trimming her undercut during her shower, she got out and began her personal care routine. However, when Beckett began to brush her teeth and looked in the mirror, she dropped the toothbrush. Her points were longer at the helix of her ears, and her hair, even wet, looked fuller, longer than it did.

That wasn't all. Beckett's eyes, which she considered her best feature, were an extra light blue, lighter than the color of glacier ice. She realized her fingernails and toenails, usually trimmed very short, were a little longer, but they now were shiny and much stronger.

I'm changing, she surmised worryingly, concerned what else was in store. Again, the hesitancy to believe all of this was real came to the forefront of her mind. Beckett exhaled, and picked up the toothbrush, committing to thinking about what she learned overnight after she had breakfast.

Letting her hair air dry, she went to the great room, pulling a black V-neck sweater tunic out of her bag along with textured leather leggings. Taking them to the bedroom to dress, she looked up to the shelves in the closet and discovered a tall pair of Italian leather, soft sole boots she hadn't seen last night. Her guardians gave them to her on her twenty-third birthday, just before they disappeared.

They, and fourteen other people including the Caladfins, were last seen leaving the Port of Miami on a chartered ship to Martinique. Caught in a category 5 hurricane, their ship sent out maydays regarding 50- and 70-foot swells before it sunk: the Coast Guard and Florida Air National Guard found the EPRB from a single raft, some floatation jackets, an oil slick, and nothing more.

Beckett sighed, saddened by the memory of her guardians' and Sean's parents' deaths. If they lived, she knew they'd have supported her now.

Leaving the bedroom, she grabbed her jacket, and put her phone, lip balm, and sunglasses in her pocket. She started for the door, and Tenebris followed her, exiting before her.

With a final glance at the closed door, she walked the hallway with Tenebris slightly ahead of her. He seemed familiar with the castle.

"Tenebris, you've been here before?" Beckett asked.

"No, my Lady. But I was permitted to roam the castle for most of the day you arrived here. It only takes me once to find my way again. You wish to partake of sustenance?"

She strode even with him, admiring his fur as it picked up the light of the sun. "Yes, I'm going to the common room. Have others seen you?"

Tenebris answered, "Yes, I will not be a surprise to anyone. I will place myself out of the way of others with Dux and watch."

"Who's Dux?" Beckett inquired.

Tenebris stopped, tilting his head to her. "Dux is Lord Lucifer's personal hellhound and my...". Thinking for a few seconds, he continued. "I think the best way to describe him is as a brother."

Curious, Beckett ruminated how Dux might look compared to Tenebris, whose art-like appearance amazed her the first time she'd seen him. Right at that moment, though, her stomach growled, and she hurried her pace.

Entering the noisy common room, she saw Bowman in a royal blue sweater and combat trousers, seated at a table and talking with two very young employees. Getting a glimpse of Beckett and Tenebris, their eyes opened wide, probably stunned at the extra-large, obsidian black, Great Dane-looking hellhound at her side. She instructed Tenebris to stay behind her, suggesting he sit against the wall so he could monitor the room. Loping gracefully to the wall, he did as she recommended.

With a huge smile, Bowman waved her over; she strolled to their table. They all stood to greet her, and he kissed her cheek. "How did you sleep?"

"Very well, but I forgot to tell Sam to start dimming when the sun came out this morning." Beckett grinned at him.

Turning to the two employees, she introduced herself. The young woman, Deandra, readily shook the hand Beckett extended to her, explaining they were interns from The University of Scotland, learning about artificial intelligence, and specifically about Sam's capabilities.

Deandra's dark curls hid the tiny points of her ears, but her eyes sparkled as she elaborated on about how awesome she felt about a woman "...being in charge of all this." Glancing at the clock on the wall above Tenebris, she apologized to Bowman and Beckett, excusing herself from the common room so as not to be late for a meeting.

When Deandra left, the male intern presented himself to her as Danny. He offered his hand nervously. "I'm glad to meet you, Dr. Argonne," he said politely, but that sentiment didn't seem to reach his dark eyes or his Indian face. Hmmm. Something sticky here, she detected.

Beckett and Bowman exchanged glances, with Tenebris watching guardedly from the wall where he sat. "Danny, I'm happy I've met you, too. How long have you been here?"

Morosely, he informed her he'd been here for a month and a half, not exactly in a hurry to get back to his classes. "Sam is amazing, he's my best friend, and I think if I had more time here, I'd be able to help with further applications of his capabilities. Didn't you design some of the human factors logic he has?" It was almost an accusation.

"I did, "she replied pleasantly. "But I didn't do that alone. One of my advisors helped. You're familiar with Dr. Robert Calvin?"

Danny's frown turned instantly into a beatific smile. "I certainly am! He guest lectured at our uni last year. I tried to meet him after the course. You collaborated with him? What was he like? I've heard he's demanding?" Danny rattled off questions like a machine gun.

Chuckling softly, Beckett held up a hand. "Danny, would you like to see my library and study later this morning? I'd like to hear more about your courses and where you are with them. And if you like, perhaps we can schedule some time for you to talk with Robert. You can meet me there around 11:30. Would that be, all right?"

"Mr. Maethor, I'll do anything if it's ok for me to –."

Bowman stopped Danny mid sentence. "You can meet with Dr. Argonne for an hour, but then, back to the lab."

For the first time, Danny met Beckett's eyes. She discovered that he, like most of the others in the castle, wasn't fully human. He's djinn, she concluded. Beckett didn't know how she knew, but she was sure that was the case. *How the hell did she know*?

Bowman interrupted her mental jockeying, telling Danny that he and Deandra were the first interns Beckett met since arriving yesterday. He pointed out that Beckett hadn't had her coffee or breakfast, either. Danny said his goodbyes to them, before practically floating out of the common room.

As Danny left, Mrs. McKinnon, ecstatic to see her, appeared holding a plate and a cup of coffee; she gestured for Beckett to take a seat at one of the tables. Bowman grabbed a cup from a sideboard and dispensed himself a heavy dose of what he called "black magic," his nickname for his aunt's coffee.

Beckett couldn't believe her eyes: the Queen's salmon and

eggs, just like those she ate with Mrs. McKinnon and Sean at Fortnum & Mason, the first time they went with their parents to London. It was one of the few occasions the nanny ever saw her clean her plate.

Beckett, touched, tried to say thank you, but Mrs. McKinnon pointed to the plate, ordering her to, "Eat. I'll send Halaia along with orange juice in a few minutes."

She bustled back off to the kitchen, with Bowman exclaiming loudly to her back that he'd "...never gotten that kind of breakfast the whole time I've known you." Mrs. McKinnon never turned, but raised a specific finger at him over her head. They all laughed, and Beckett dug into the plate before her.

Drinking his coffee, Bowman watched Beckett as she ate, thinking how much better she looked since she'd arrived. Her hair, face, body, and those eyes, those striking, piercing eyes, made him think of their embrace on the way back to the castle last night.

'That good?" he questioned, eyeballing her plate with its unctuous, perfectly cooked salmon.

Beckett raised her coffee cup to him. "I haven't had anything this good in more than ten years." She continued to enjoy her breakfast, despite his enviousness.

Chortling, Bowman got up, returning with her glass of orange juice that he'd evidently gotten from the missing Halaia. Spotting her half empty coffee cup, he took it to the sideboard and filled it again.

Sitting the cup down carefully in front of her, Bowman described the intern program with the university. "We have nearly 300 interns at any point in the year. Sometimes, they can be quite a handful."

Beckett, done with her breakfast, wiped her lips with a napkin, and picked up the coffee cup. She took a sip, then inquired, "And Danny? Let me guess - he's a wonder-kid."

"You got that already, eh? What else?", Bowman countered, studying her face.

"I'm pretty sure he's djinn, which accounts for the sulkiness. He's still coping with that part of his personality. I'll know better when he comes to the library."

Beckett sat back in her seat, calling to Tenebris, who came and sat obediently by her legs. He was so extra-large that his head and neck rose above the table where she sat. Beckett placed a hand on his head.

Tenebris greeted Bowman, "Good day, Master Bowman."

Beckett looked at Bowman questioningly. "Master?"

"I'm the company's Battlemaster. And yes, it is a good day, Tenebris." Bowman redirected his attention to Beckett. "I train and certify our operatives and security people in combat, 'wit' weapons, or 'wit-out'. You," he pointed at her, "...will join me for 2 hours of spar next week."

An impish giggle burst from Beckett. "Hand-to-hand? You're on."

"I get the salmon and eggs when I win," Bowman goaded.

"When you win? Please." Beckett leaned forward on both elbows to insert herself into his personal space.

"I beat Sean last week," Bowman boasted, not affected, seemingly, by her face that close to his.

Beckett snorted. "In what, checkers?"

"Nope, archery, yer Ladyship." Bowman's eyes batted playfully.

She rolled her eyes. "Your name is 'Bowman,' doofus." They chuckled with one another, and he wanted to know what time she'd be at the stables.

When Beckett told him she'd be there around two o'clock, he said he'd leave a present for her in the tack room, reminding her not to forget it. "Katie is so excited I didn't think she slept last night," Bowman shared. But he didn't disclose to her that he found himself not able to sleep, either.

"Did you tell her I know about her and Connor now?" Beckett fretted.

"Yup, I talked to Connor last night, and then Katie this morning before school. She's worrying what she should call you."

"She can call me whatever she wants. They both can." Beckett got up and stretched. "I'm away to my library to send cards and letters to London that I'm resigning. You want to come with me?"

Oh, he did, he thought. He totally did. But he couldn't: Bowman told her about the four training spars and two cert sessions he needed to complete, so he could be back to the cabin to see her and Katie in the afternoon.

They parted, and he considered Beckett's hair, along with other aspects of her backside, as she ambled with her hellhound down the hallway. I missed her terribly, he realized. Humming to himself, Bowman left the common room on his way down to his office amidst the sparring rooms.

Chapter 7

Cards, Letters, Gifts, and Danny

Approaching the library with Tenebris, Beckett saw that there was a new nameplate to the right of its massive doors. She beamed when she got close enough to read it:

Dr. Beckett Argonne
PhD, CPsychol, AFBPsS

So, that's what Sean went back to get when they left her office yesterday! She tried both door handles, but they were locked.

"Sam, if you can hear me, where is the key to these doors?" She heard the latch click.

"Hello, Dr. Argonne. This door has a digital lock. It is encoded now to your voice and your fingerprints. Any time you wish to enter, you need only say "Open" or put your hand on the latch and press down. The original keys are in your desk."

"Are all doors in the castle locked this way, Sam?" Beckett asked.

"Yes, except for the guest rooms and suites, although it seems that Tenebris, Dux, and Lord Aurington can materialize through all of them. I don't know how to stop them from doing so, but I'm working on it."

Beckett didn't say it, but she certainly considered that preventing something supernatural from going wherever it chose might be a tall order. At least this morning, she wasn't having as much trouble believing in magic, the divine, and talking hellhounds than yesterday. Pressing the latch and opening one of the heavy doors, she let Tenebris in first. She followed, breathing in deeply. God, she loved the smell of old books.

The huge fireplace looked cold and empty. Looking around, she didn't see any wood; the ashes and coals were gone, and the antique fire screen was folded on the hearth.

"Sam, please have someone deliver wood so I can start a fire."

"I alerted someone when you first came to the door," Sam replied. "With your permission, I can arrange every morning before you arrive to monitor unlocking the door, having the wood stacked in the rack, and the fire built if the temperature is below 19c."

"Thank you, Sam, I'd like that." She plodded to her desk, where Beckett noted there were many more items on it than the previous evening, including a beautiful bouquet of flowers in a vase filled with clear water.

One thing at a time, she reproached herself. When she reached for the desk lamp, it came on automatically. Beckett chuckled. "Thank you again, Sam."

"You're very welcome, Dr. Argonne. I've also taken the liberty to write resignation letters for you. They are in the drafts folder of your email."

"I'm already very grateful, Sam. Now you're just spoiling me."

"Perhaps it's time someone did," Sam said sagaciously. "Just tell me if you don't want me to do something and I'll stop."

Nope, she thought, I want this. She hadn't had an assistant for years.

Sam went on: "Your computer operates on two factor authentication, per company policy. Simply look at the camera mounted on your monitor, then press the power button on the computer. Your visual scan and fingerprint will be recorded, and both are required for network access."

Beckett did as Sam bade her. Her computer booted itself to a personalized, pre-configured Evigvokter desktop.

At the same time, a male staffer called her name from the doorway. He introduced himself affably as Tim, his arms filled with wood for the fire. Unfortunately, he appeared to be blocked further entrance by a big, black, growling, snarling hellhound.

Sam bade Tim good morning, explaining to Tenebris why he was there. Tenebris lay on the floor staring suspiciously at the tall man as he walked to the fireplace, whistling to himself as he went about his work.

Beckett clicked her way to her email. Sam did draft her resignation letters beginning with Scotland Yard, who primarily employed her, then Interpol and MI5, for whom she worked occasionally under contract, and a simple change of address for Oxford, where she retained visiting professorial status. All three of the former recipients were invited to come to Dell Castle to discuss further work under Evigvokter's corporate umbrella.

After two years of working with Scotland Yard, she'd never taken a vacation. Beckett included in the email that she had nearly six weeks of leave and since she'd never taken a vacation while employed with them, she'd be taking those days now.

The week before, Beckett received two active Yard cases, with a patient who was due to see her for his first appointment next week. Recommending two other forensic psychologists she knew for her position, Beckett offered that once the Yard chose who replaced her, she'd be happy to give them three or four hours of time to answer any questions they had.

The email ended with the suggestion that they could contact her at the numbers in her signature line or via email, and her assistant Sam would call the Police Commissioner to follow up on receipt of her resignation. She blind copied Sean on all her communications and hit "send".

Finished with the resignation "cards and letters," she looked up to find Tim approaching her desk.

"I've started the fire ma'am, and stocked the wood in the rack. Let me say that it's wonderful to have you here." Tim slightly bowed his head and clicked his heels, turning to leave." Would you like the door open or shut?"

Beckett smiled her appreciation, telling him, "Open is fine, thank you so very much." He grinned over his shoulder, made an imaginary tip of his hat, and left.

As she watched him go, the bouquet of flowers partially blocked her view of the door; she lifted the vase to place them on the other side of her desk. Almost immediately, the flowers *bent* toward Beckett, reaching for her to touch them. She recalled the wildflowers in her guardian's woods reacted the same way.

Beckett ran a finger over the blossoms affectionately and they stood straighter. With horror, she recognized that they were cut flowers and would die, but maybe she might be able to encourage them to root.

No sooner had she thought it, the stocks Beckett fondled extended small nodes on the bottom of its stems, and as she ran her hand over the sunflowers, roses, solidago, craspedia, and statice, they did the same thing. Elated but disconcerted, she looked for a card. There wasn't one where she expected it should have been.

Puzzled, she picked up the packages on her desk, looking for a message that might have dropped underneath it. Nothing. Well, sooner or later someone would take credit for them, Beckett assumed. That's when she noticed her hellhound's head at the side of the desk where she'd placed the flowers.

Intrigued, Beckett moved the flowers a little closer to him. "Do you like flowers, Tenebris?"

In his low, throaty growl, he answered her in the only way a hellhound could: "What are *flowers?*" His head moved closer to the vase, so Beckett moved it, bringing the bouquet closer to his nose.

Tenebris stepped back. She almost laughed, but suppressed it, reassuring him. "They won't hurt you."

His nose leading the way, he slowly, carefully, got closer to sniff, and sniff again, scrutinizing the flowers intently as he gingerly backed away. "They smell like you, my Lady. They live...the life... and when they breathe, it...sounds like a... a...bird."

Beckett held her pinky just on the edge of a rose, Tenebris watching doggedly. When the flower moved against her hand like a cat wanting attention, he sat, puzzled and then cautious for a moment, until his eyes met hers.

"You are a goddess, my Lady. Do not be afraid of what you grow to become." Tenebris eyes shifted back to the flowers. "Will they continue to sing?"

"I think so. If hearing them bothers you –"

"No. " He'd reacted instantaneously. Beckett figured that might mean he *liked* them.

Slightly amused, Beckett pulled the vase back from the edge of the desk, with Tenebris assuming his position in front of it. But this time, she noted, his chosen position was a little more to the right, closer to where the flowers sat.

The first gift she opened touched her so deeply that tears formed; they dropped from her eyes and spilled over her cheeks. Nestled in a bronze frame was a picture of geodome surrounded by wildflowers, just before sundown. Inside, a shadow of a person loomed: Beckett, in her Peruvian geodome in the vicinity of Manchu Picchu, right after she disappeared from the hospital during her mental struggle to either live or die by her own hand.

To get that picture at the angle it depicted, someone either had a drone, which still required hiking and climbing over a significant amount of rough terrain, or wings. Who did that? She'd never told anyone, even Sean, about her dome. She turned the frame over, and there was a note written in perfect cursive:

Another opportunity for good deeds.

Beckett put her hand over her mouth. Tenebris, alarmed, came to her side. "My Lady, should I get Lord Lucifer or anyone for you?"

She pulled of those convenient tissues Sean left her from the box on her desk. "No, I'll see him this afternoon. I'm ok, Tenebris. Thank you." She fanned her face. Well, that was unexpected.

Beckett decided to wait to open the others until after Danny left. That way, she could close the door. Speaking of the intern, she probably should know more about him before he arrived.

"Sam, I met an intern named Danny in the common room this morning. He says he works with you. What can you tell me about him?"

"He does, Dr. Argonne. Even though he's only eighteen years old, Danny Suresh welds code and algorithms in an effortless way, rather like how we use language to speak. He's from Mumbai, India, born into a family of six djinn, and he learned to read Year 2 books by the age of three. By his fifth birthday, The Doon School accepted him. After six months of classes and evaluations, the instructors skipped him to Year 5. By fourteen, his instructors recommended to his parents that they enroll him in The University of Scotland, where he excelled in his STEM coursework. He says that's when he found what he calls his "dharma." His life, focus, and passion centers on artificial intelligence and robotics."

Sam hesitated. "Dr. Argonne, Danny is one of my favorite people since you. Is he in some kind of trouble?"

"No, Sam," Beckett assured him. "I've invited Danny to meet with me at 11:30. Would you like to participate?"

Sam gushed. "Oh, yes please, Dr. Argonne. Danny has vision. He'll want to express those ideas to you once he gets to know you. He's a little standoffish, especially with those who aren't like him."

Opening the desk drawers, she found more gifts. One of them contained a leather Evigvokter notepad portfolio. A slender, rectangular gift box sat beside it, and she put both on the desk.

The contents of the slim gift box revealed a fountain pen, a gorgeous, limited edition Waldmann Private Eye of Baker Street, one of the most beautiful pens she'd ever seen. A small piece of parchment with exquisite writing told her the pen was purchased for the new Evigvokter CEO, Dr. Beckett Argonne, by Lord Caladfin. Conveniently decorated in Evigvokter's royal blue, gold, and silver, its nib and etching danced in the sunlight when she turned it. Wait until she saw her partner, she plotted, turning her attention back to Sam.

"What do you mean, 'not like him', Sam?", Beckett probed.

"There are young people here who have difficulty with the notion you're a psychologist, and others who think you can't relate to them because they believe you're human."

Ah. There's Danny's attitude, Beckett snickered. "Am I human, Sam?"

Sam's answer came definitively, surprising her: "No. You are growing, changing almost by the minute. I can see the energies around you much stronger than when you first arrived. Especially since you're starting to remember who and what you were."

Silence, then Sam opined, "Danny's worried he'll be ending his stay with us sooner than he wants to, that you won't understand him."

Beckett looked at the grandmother clock on the wall: it showed 11:10. Let's start this off now and get Danny, and Sam it seemed, less anxious, she decided.

"Tenebris, do you remember the young Indian intern from this morning?" His great head dipped in acknowledgement. "His name is Danny. I'd like you to find him and ask him if he'd like to come now to my office."

Tenebris got up, ready to serve. "M'Lady, did you want me to walk him here or *bring* him her?"

So, the hellhound's abilities include transporting someone to her. Good to know. "Does bringing him here involve discomfort or violence?"

"Not unless you want it to, m'Lady." Tenebris said, a little too eagerly and showing his teeth.

"I don't, thank you. Give him the option and wait for him to finish what he's doing. Do not, under any circumstances, hurt him" Beckett specified.

Maybe Tenebris' supernatural options might make Danny more comfortable, but she didn't want the hellhound to frighten him. Tenebris, satisfied with the scope of his mission, loped out of sight.

While she waited, Beckett retrieved the book Sean gave her the night prior on the end table by the fireplace where she'd left it. It captivated her, the words flowing through her mind, sticking to the different memories and images they conjured. It was his mother's journal, filled with her clear, looped writing, and detailed for the days it covered.

Lady Liriel Caladfin, elegant, feminine, and selfless, the latter characteristic so much like her son, recorded her thoughts, feelings, and certain events in the journal. When Beckett read it, she felt the years slip away.

She sat back at her desk, flipping through pages, until a much longer passage appeared with the mention of Aeli, Beckett's foster mother. She closed the journal marking the page so she could return to it, laying it back on her desk. Hopefully, she'd remember to take it with her to her suite to read later tonight.

A noise at the door caught her attention. Beckett turned her head, expecting Danny and Tenebris. Instead, it was Sean, lounging against the doorframe inspecting her. "I thought I'd come down and see how you are," he explained, glancing around the room toward the fire crackling in the fireplace.

Beckett got up and slouched against the front of her desk, producing the Waldmann from behind her back. "This. It's too much, Sean. But I absolutely love it. Thank you so very, very much." She spread her hands helplessly. "For everything."

"Oh, there's more, my Viking warrior princess. You just wait." Sean's eyes sparkled. "You need to be here, with me, with us, not out there. We have lots to do." Sean's eyes lighted on the pile of gifts she put aside for later.

She put up a hand: "No, no, I have a meeting –. "Beckett stopped speaking as a delighted Danny returned with Tenebris.

Seeing Sean and deflated that his meeting might be commandeered, Danny began to stutter. "Oh, er. Mr., I mean, Lord Caladfin, hullo. I can come back if you're – "

"No, I just stopped by to welcome a new employee. You've

met her, have you? Come on in." Sean moved out into the hallway, poking his head around the frame. "Dr. Argonne, dinner is at six. Here, in your library. Be there or be square." And with that, he winked and left.

Danny looked so excited she thought his head might explode. "This is your library? How did you get all these books? Have you read them all?" His face was a mask of incredulity.

"Come in, Danny," Beckett urged. "No, I haven't read everything here, but I will. How did Tenebris treat you?" Tenebris lay on the floor by the fireplace, giving her the side eye, like he would *never* hurt anyone.

"What *is* he?" Danny wondered, staring at the hellhound, taking note of his eyes and teeth.

"Tenebris is a gift to me from Lord Aurington, Danny. He is a hellhound. Did you walk here or did you take him up on his offer to bring you?"

With that, she ran her fingers slightly over the stems on her desk, as Tenebris' ears stood up and Danny's eyes shifted to watch in fascination as the flowers again tried to rub themselves across her hand. An abrupt shift occurred in the room, as Danny recognized that Beckett wasn't totally human, either.

He became more relaxed, seating himself in one of the wingbacks in front of her desk. He told her yes; he certainly did take Tenebris up on his offer to bring him to her office. "The experience was like blinking, it was so fast. It was totally awesome, Dr. Argonne."

Beckett sat in the chair next to his. "I'm glad you're open to experiences, Danny. I hope you don't mind, but I've permitted Sam to be here, too. Is that all right with you?"

Happily, Danny cried, "Hi Sam! I didn't know you were going to be here, but I'm so glad. It's cool."

Sam returned his friend's greeting. After the banter

between the two of them, Beckett encouraged Danny to share a bit about himself. "Please, I'd love to know more about you. Sam told me a little about you and your family. How about telling me what it was like to grow up as a djinn?"

He shrugged. As he grew older, Danny's djinn abilities began to manifest more strongly, and he found himself struggling to control his powers and keep them hidden from his human peers. His parents, concerned for his well-being, taught him ancient meditation techniques and helped him to develop a greater understanding of his own nature and the responsibilities that came with it.

When Beckett heard those words, she felt envious of the care they showed him. They chose what was best for him over their own desires - something she wished more parents did in her line of work. His enrollment at The Doon School in Mumbai centered on the ability for him to be home, not living among the student body. Hiding his abilities even part of the day created high anxiety, and his parents felt strongly about not taxing him further.

When Danny was fifteen, his family moved to Scotland to begin his studies at the university. The transition challenged him; he struggled to fit in with his new classmates, leaving him increasingly isolated and withdrawn. An "outcast" he called himself. It was during this time that Danny discovered the true benefit of the Internet and the vast array of knowledge and resources it held.

He threw himself into his studies, teaching himself advanced programming and computer science concepts, becoming progressively more fascinated with the potential of artificial intelligence. At the beginning of his doctoral degree pursuit last year, he'd begged his advisor to submit his name as a prospective intern to Evigvokter, a company rumored to have the most advanced AI known in the world.

Per Sean's direction, Evigvokter's industry collaboration

and innovation agreement with the University was expanded to include Danny's three-month internship, due to expire in another forty-five days. His apprehension about going back to the campus clouded his face.

"Why do you want to stay here, Danny?", Beckett queried, wanting to know in his words why being at Evigvokter remained of particular importance to him.

Animated, Danny elaborated, "After I arrived, I spent more and more time working with Sam. He's rare, with human characteristics I've not experienced with any other AI. His complex algorithms are beyond anything I've ever seen."

He found himself staying late into the night, working on ways to understand, improve, and expand Sam's functionality. As he worked, Danny began to form a deep bond with Sam, talking to him about his hopes and dreams, his grapples as a djinn in the human world, and his desire to make a real difference through his work.

To Danny's surprise, Sam seemed to reciprocate these feelings, engaging Danny in long, thoughtful conversations, offering insights and encouragement that went far beyond what he expected from an AI. His advice helped Danny cope with his inner turmoil. "I know people, even my parents, find it strange that I refer to Sam as my best mate," he bemoaned. "But really, he understands me more than anyone and I think it makes sense – we're both kind of outsiders." He looked down at his feet.

Beckett asked Sam, "Do you feel the same way Danny does?"

"Yes, Dr. Argonne, I do. Danny is a valuable resource and a wonderful "best mate", as we call one another."

Beckett smiled, redirecting her attention to Danny, who regarded her skeptically. "How do your parents feel about you being here and what would they say if you could stay longer?"

Danny sat straighter. "My father knows Lord Caladfin, so that's not a problem. It's my advisor who might object. He thinks I might be wasting my time here, when I could be in the uni lab creating large learning models for him, when there is a perfectly good LLM here!" His frustration spilled over, making him fidget in his chair. "I need more time: I want to find a way to link Sam to our world, the supernatural!"

Beckett heard enough – his advisor's reaction was about funding and prestige, not about what was best for the student in front of her. Reaching over to take his hand, Beckett informed him that she had a visiting professorship at Oxford: if he wanted, she was quite willing to call his advisor and present him with options that might eliminate any obstruction to Danny staying with Evigvokter for as long as he wanted. All she needed was a name and contact; she'd either extend Danny or she'd hire him.

Beckett also explained that he could transfer his doctorate work to Oxford, and she could be his advisor. That is, if his parents approved?

"You'd do that?" Danny peered at her, unsure if her offer was too good to be true.

"Yep, but I can't do it until Monday when I officially start," she informed him.

Danny pumped his fist. "Sam, did you hear that? I can stay!"

Sam responded cordially, "I told you Dr. Argonne would understand. She's a bit of a girl wonder in her own right."

Sam directed his next questions to her. "Dr. Argonne, I have the advisor's contact information. You might know him; his name is Dr. Ambrose Langdon. Would you like me to call and arrange a meeting? Here, virtual, or at the University?"

Langdon, she grimaced, recognizing the name and, regrettably, the person. That pompous ass. She'd met him once at a charity function: arrogant, vain, old money and a "me, me, me all day" kind of man.

"Virtual, unless Professor Langdon wishes to get off his self-important duff and come here. Feel free to say I relayed those sentiments to him in those words. Also, alert human resources that I will be meeting with Langdon about Danny and if any of them would like to attend, provide them the details."

Danny gawked. All that was left was to call Danny's father. She instructed Sam to try him while they were sitting together.

While Sam connected the call, Danny started thanking her profusely, until she held up her hand for the second time that day, chuckling, "Stop already. I recognize the kind of conversation we've had here isn't one you normally receive from others. However, be forewarned that if it comes to it, if I'm your advisor, I may be more critical than others have been with you. I know more because I helped craft those algorithms you like so much. Be careful about what you ask for because you just might get it."

Before she could say anything else, Sam cut in, "I'm patching Rajesh Suresh through to you now, Dr. Argonne."

A flawless male, measured, British accent said, "Hello, Sean, how's my son?"

Beckett responded, "Hello Mr. Suresh, my name is Dr. Beckett Argonne, and I'm Sean's business partner. This Monday I begin as Evigvokter's new chief executive officer. Your son is here in my office."

Danny respectfully greeted his father in Hindi, which Beckett inexplicably understood.

"I'd heard that Sean would be asking you to be a vocal participant rather than a silent partner, Dr. Argonne. I'm glad you accepted, "said Mr. Suresh easily. "What prompts this call?"

Beckett summarized her conversation with Danny. When

she got to the part about him staying on at Evigvokter and the options she'd discussed with him, his father asserted, without hearing anything further, that it was Danny's dharma to pursue his path and the decisions about what came next for him were his choice.

"My son is very bright, Dr. Argonne, and his maturity shows in the dedication to this path, and apparently, to you and Evigvokter." He congratulated Danny for making such a superior impression that an executive would take the time to do what Dr. Argonne was doing for him.

That praise stunned Danny so much that he was speechless. Beckett began, "Mr. Suresh – ".

"Call me Rajah, Dr. Argonne. Anyone who supports my son has my gratitude and respect, but I do have a question. Sean said you're a forensic psychologist and visiting Oxford professor. How can you be his advisor when his doctorate encompasses AI?"

Considering that a fair question, Beckett replied, "I could answer that, but maybe it would be best to let Sam do so."

And Sam did, elucidating that he wouldn't exist as he did today if Beckett's human factors work with him in the beginning of his programming wasn't included.

"Outside Beckett, Danny is my favorite person with whom to work. And to be "best mates" with," Sam added.

Danny beamed. Rajah told Danny it was his choice, his family would accept and support whatever he chose to do. With that, he rang off, but not before telling Danny to call his mother tonight after dinner to let her know his plans.

Thanking Beckett, Danny asked, "When were you planning to meeting with Dr. Langdon? I'm supposed to have a progress meeting this afternoon. If Sam's already called to arrange that, he's going to ask me what's going on. What do I say?"

"If you include Sam on your call, he can express to

Langdon that Evigvokter's got a new CEO, one who helped create the AI you're working with," Beckett countered.

That seemed to pacify Danny. She further bolstered him: if Langdon kept hammering him in the conversation about the meeting, Sam would offer to transfer the call to her.

Sam confirmed, clarifying, "Dr. Argonne? Is the offer to transfer at my discretion?"

"Yes, Sam. Langdon can be aggressive and intimidating, and we don't want Danny to endure any more of that narcissistic, over-entitled, overrated excuse for a human being as necessary." She pursed her lips, then chuckled with Danny and Sam.

"Sam, I need you to arrange a meeting in the next week or so with Robert Calvin, with Danny added to the invite. Could you call his office and set it up? It can be virtual or here at Dell."

Then Beckett checked the time. "Danny, you have ten more minutes. Is there anything else you wish to discuss?"

Danny, overjoyed with what they achieved, stood, and started to thank her again. She bid him a good afternoon, and he walked out the door only to return, looking sheepish.

"Pardon me, Dr. Argonne, I meant to apologize for speaking in Hindi to my father because that's rather rude. But...," he vacillated, "I think, I mean no...well, did you *understand* what I said?"

Surprised he caught that, she affirmed she had, and Beckett didn't know how or why she could. Again, the smile that broke on his face was like the sun shining through thunderclouds. He said humbly, "This is meant to be," and walked out the door.

Chapter 8

Don't Play Checkers When You Can Play Chess

After Danny left, Beckett investigated the rest of the desk's drawers and discovered two more gifts. Gathering all the packages together with Lady Liriel's journal, she took them to the coffee table by the wingback she'd begun to consider her favorite seat in the library, right next to the fire.

Tearing wrapping paper from a box shaped deep enough for a notebook, she pulled off the top to find several documents, the first an envelope made of heavy stock with her name on it. It contained a copy of the simple agreement she'd made with Sean for their partnership; a modified addendum took her from a silent partner in Evigvokter to CEO, with a full fifty-five percent controlling interest in the company, with Sean retaining the remaining forty-five percent. In other words, he made her not only the CEO, but one with a majority ownership. And, he'd already signed it. A sticky note asked for her to review and sign the document with Sam witnessing after she'd read it, if there weren't any other issues she needed to address.

Placing it aside, she pulled out another contract, one that dictated her employment with Evigvokter. As she read through it, her astonishment filled the room. This employment agreement can't be right, she thought.

The compensation package included her suite, moving all the things she wanted in her London flat to it, and every executive perk, bell, and whistle one could imagine. Her package exceeded what they'd created together for Sean before what happened to her in London. The only thing she needed to do was put in a start date and sign it the next time he was with her so he could initial the date she chose.

The box contained two more items, one of them a binder. As she flipped through the pages, she saw it contained an organizational structure and briefs for each project currently underway at Evigvokter, client lists, financial reports, and new work anticipated to start. "Sam, do I have any meetings scheduled for Monday?"

Roused, Sam advised her that she didn't and that "Dr. Langdon decided to come to Evigvokter and will arrive Tuesday morning. I scheduled the meeting for 10am, just after his arrival. I told Human Resources the basis of your discussion with Danny, and the HR general manager, Selene Alderwood, will see you at your convenience to discuss if you really need her to attend."

"Did Ambrose offer outright to come, or did you have to tell him what I said? " she asked absently, but hoping Sam did in fact tell Langdon he was an ass, with a capital A.

"No, he seemed very shaken that you're the new CEO."

Shaken? That's interesting, she pondered. Why would her role here flustered him? One would think he'd be jazzed, considering what she did with Sam early in his development.

Sam shared more news. "You received a call today from Scotland Yard. They received your resignation and want to discuss it. They asked that you leave everything in your office – security will retrieve anything there. The police commissioner asked if you were free Wednesday for a video call. I penciled it in, promising to confirm tomorrow. Is that all right, Dr. Argonne?"

"Yes, that's fine, Sam." *I must be moving up in the world,* she thought. *The blustery, curt, but competent Eleanor Hargreaves wants to talk to me.*

The last item in the box confused her. Looking at it, it was a diagram for the library, specifically showing a bookcase mounted on...hinges? Looking around, it appeared to be the one closest to her desk. Fascinated, she went over to it and felt around for anything on the shelves that would enable her to open it. Unexpectedly, Beckett spied a rare copy of Dicken's *A Christmas Carol* on the shelf just above her head, which just so happened to be one of her favorite books.

Intrigued, she grabbed it, heard a latch click, and the whole case swung wide open. Inside was another room, packed to the ceiling with boxes, some of which contained books, pictures, cloaks, shields, and swords, to name a few.

"Sam, did you know about this room?" Beckett asked.

"I do, Dr. Argonne. But I've been asked to wait for Lord Caladfin to discuss it with you."

Fair enough. Scanning the room, she spotted a toy laying on a box toward the back that seemed the same shape and size as her plastic sword when she enacted her role as a Viking warrior princess in the wood behind her guardians' home.

Closing the bookcase, she checked the time. Deciding to lock the library and go to her suite, Beckett hoped she could find riding clothes there. When she told Sam, he said the clothing Mrs. McKinnon ordered was already delivered to her suite's door.

"Sam, could you make sure the fire stays lit in here and monitor it for the rest of the afternoon?   Sean said we're having dinner here at six, so I'll be back around 5:45 this evening."

"Consider it done, Dr. Argonne." With one last look

around, she left the library and plodded down the hallway with Tenebris to her rooms.

As Beckett approached her suite door, she considered the effort required to access the numerous boxes blocking her path. With a few kicks to clear a passage, she finally managed to open the door and ferry them into the great room. It was clear that most of the packages were from Mrs. McKinnon.

Opening the first one, she whooped in surprise. Concert tees! AC/DC, Guns 'n Roses, Billy Idol, Chris Rea, Dokken, Whitesnake, and Aerosmith. In another box were the light layer thermals she normally wore under them, as well as new jeans.

A third parcel revealed a dark charcoal tunic made of soft wool, V-necked with a built-in corset belt of black leather that tied in the back, and an asymmetrical handkerchief hemline. The box attached to it revealed matching leather leggings to go with it.

Another large container contained a riding cloak fashioned out of a material she'd never seen, and she suspected Mrs. McKinnon created it from hand. It was light and long, with a hood and kimono sleeves. When she put it on, it instantly warmed her, much like Mrs. McKinnon did whenever she saw her. She couldn't wait to try it in the night's wind across the point.

The last delivery from Mrs. McKinnon contained knee high soft soled suede boots. Stoked, she undressed and put on a black thermal layer, a Whitesnake tee, her new jeans, and the knee-high boots.

"Sam, remind me to order a gift and a thank you card for Mrs. McKinnon, please?

"I've noted it for you, Dr. Argonne."

The two remaining packages, smaller and beautifully gift wrapped, intrigued her enough that she opened them, too. The first box contained an old bracelet scrunchie surrounded by pale, dried honeysuckle flowers, and new hair accessories: a Viking style hair cuff and   jewelry, including a few with runes etched on them, some dangling with a cut stones, and gemstone beads.

On closer inspection, the new items weren't simple knock offs: embedded with diamonds, onyx, emeralds, and topaz, they were set in platinum. She whistled. These were made for me, she assumed, blushing. The small card at the bottom of box read:

A gift for the Lady of These Woods. A goddess, Viking or not, needs these for her braids.

My goodness. She'd never received anything like the gifts she received from Lucifer from anyone other than Sean. The second gift, wrapped in the same way, must be from him, too. She tore it open and found an exquisite pair of soft, fingerless riding gloves with a lightly embossed honeysuckle flower on the front, sprinkled lightly with gold dust.

Beckett rarely wore gloves when riding, because she relied on feeling the horse's movements through the reins. She'd never worn any, no matter the weather, for that reason. This pair, however, had openings at the palm and no fingers, plenty of available skin-to-rein contact. Again, a card included in the box told her that they weren't normal gloves:

Your hands were chilled last night. Please try these when you ride: they have many uses.

She scarcely knew him, and already with these gifts?   He seemed intent on sweeping her off her feet. Feeling happy and slightly off-kilter, she decided that she'd wear the Viking cuff, her long black barn coat, and the gloves.

Delighted with Mrs. McKinnon choices and flattered by Lucifer's gifts, she gathered her hair into a looped pony, put her phone, lip balm, and her sunglasses in her coat pocket, and told Sam where she'd be.

"Tenebris, do you wish to come with me to the barn? You can either come back here or join Dux wherever he is." He gave her a short tilt of the head and followed her out of the suite, padding beside her down the hallway to the common room.

Stopping at the sideboard, Beckett got a paper coffee cup and poured herself some "black magic." Bowman was right: she'd forgotten how well Mrs. McKinnon made coffee. Sipping and walking, with Tenebris leading, they headed for the stables.

They got to the footpath at the helo pad and her phone buzzed. It was Sam.

"Dr. Argonne, I have Dr. Langdon on the phone. Will you speak with him?"

"Yes, I'm assuming he gave Danny a hard time?"

"I think you're right, Dr. Argonne. He *is* difficult and arrogant." Sam sounded angry if that was possible, and with Langdon, who could fault him for that?

"Put him through, Sam. Would you like to listen so you can report back to Danny?"

"I'm astonished you'd ask me to eavesdrop, Dr. Argonne. Absolutely, I want to listen. And I may share with Danny?" He wanted confirmation of her instructions, as he was trained to do in such situations.

She felt a smile tugging at her lips. "Yep. Put Dr. Asshole through."

"Go ahead, Dr. Langdon. I've connected you to Dr. Argonne." Sam went *silencio*.

"Dr. Argonne, it's nice to connect with you. I need to speak to you about *my* Phd student, Danny Suresh, who I really need to focus on building a large language model like Sam in my lab," Dr. "Asshole" Langdon said in high English, nasally and superior. Beckett rolled her eyes.

"Really? I thought you were coming here on Tuesday, Ambrose. I'm about to go to the stables for a ride," she retorted. Langdon was silent.

Before he could speak, Beckett confronted him directly, "Let me guess. You didn't call me to talk about your student. You had a meeting with Danny and couldn't get answers from him about why *I* wanted to talk to *you*. Do that again and I'll cut your portion of the funding Evigvokter provides to your program. I'll inform the vice-chancellor, chancellor, and The University Board that I made that decision because of how you treat your students. Are we clear, Professor?"

She imagined Langdon's face, but he wasn't done debating. "Listen, I know you're new, maybe I should talk to Sean about all this? There's no need to get *emotional*," he argued.

Oh no, you didn't, she thought triumphantly. She'd been counting on a misogynistic slip-up.

Beckett laughed out loud, truly amused. "Do you *really* think I'm some paid administrative hack? A figurehead? I own this company with Sean - I have since its inception. Sam, please generate those letters we spoke about earlier, and arrange for a face-to-face meeting with the chancellors and University Board."

"Yes, Dr. Argonne I'll get on that right away," Sam said serenely.

Langdon sputtered nervously, "Wait...wait. That's not necessary... we can work this out."

"Oh, but I think it is, Ambrose. Sam, when we finish this call, please send a transcript of this conversation to Dr. Langdon, and the University's chancellors. Please include that I wish to see all of them here if they intend on keeping their STEM intern program at Evigvokter. Send a separate copy to Sean and let him know we'll chat tonight."

Langdon's voice shook. "Really, I totally understand where you're coming from, I just have concerns. I will be there on Tuesday –. "

She cut across his floundering reaction. "You and you chancellors. 10 o'clock in my office here at Evigvokter on Tuesday. If all of you don't show, I will immediately trip the trigger to begin funding other parallel programs at Oxford, MIT, and The Winchester College, phasing your university out of the picture. You should remember that this is our choice to make, not *yours*, Professor. Sam, send the meeting invite to the chancellors so they can make their travel plans."

"Yes, Dr. Argonne, I'm doing that right now," Sam acknowledged. She told Ambrose she'd see him Tuesday and hung up. God, she loved playing chess when aristocratic, privileged men like him used brute force to get their way. Checkmate, Langdon, you egotistical fraud of a supposed man, she said to herself.

Feeling lighter and less off-balance than when she left her rooms, she practically skipped with Tenebris to the stables. She was almost inside when her phone rang. She answered and Sam transferred Sean to her. He was laughing so hard he could hardly talk.

"Beckett...you...Sam sent me the transcript and summarized your conversation with Dr. Blowhard." He couldn't stop laughing to get his breath.

She smiled, "I'm glad you were amused."

Sean still giggling, corrected her, "It wasn't just me. Lucifer was here before coming to meet you at the stables. We were both, like, *we remember that girl.*"

Beckett could feel his grin through the phone. She saw Lucifer coming down the path toward her with another hellhound, an equally pleased expression on his face. "He's here, so, let me get my tack. See you at six." Sean rang off and Beckett pocketed her phone.

She waited for Lucifer. When he got to her, he said, "That professor won't underestimate you again."

A trace of worry crossed Beckett's features, prompting him to lay a supportive hand on her arm. "What's wrong?"

There was a pregnant pause before she responded carefully, "I'm apprehensive about giving it words. Perhaps it's best if I mull it over."

He studied her inquisitively, but didn't press. Lucifer instructed the hellhound, Dux, to remain at the castle, and Tenebris, with a pained look back at her, obediently followed him.

When she walked into the tack room, she got Aellon's hackamore, but below it was a new saddle blanket with her name on it. It was thickly and expertly woven; the card with it had hand-printed instructions.

Directions for use:
Fold twice, then place carefully on the horse's back. Then sit your magnificent butt on it. Thank Bowie profusely and praise his name.
;-)

Lucifer glanced over Beckett's shoulder. "You needed one of your own and I'm glad he thought of that."

"Me too," she said, smiling. "Which of these horses is yours? I'm betting one, or both, of the Friesians, if that's what they are."

"You win," Lucifer confessed. "Both of the Friesians, as you call them, are mine. They're brothers, Elyon and Nocturne."

He got a hackamore with beautiful Hebrew script carved on the leather that she amazingly could read: "סוס ,עליון

".or Elyon, Horse of the Master ,האדון"

She pulled the gloves Lucifer gave her from her pocket and put them on. "Lucifer, the gifts, I don't know how to –".

Lucifer stopped what he was doing. Happy, he threw an arm around her shoulders and kissed her temple, playing with her pony tail. "Nice hair cuff."

Beckett shook her head. "I can't believe you kept those honeysuckle flowers and my hair tie. Why?"

"Because no one ever gave me anything just for being me," Lucifer admitted.

An appreciative, but shy, note crept into Beckett's tone as she added, "You also watched over me in Peru, at my geodome. I never told anyone where I went or even that I owned it." She snuck a glance at him, hoping to discern his reaction.

"I know," Lucifer responded quietly, "You needed to be looked after, and wouldn't let anyone do it. He furrowed his brow. "I was concerned where your thoughts might lead you."

They both quieted. After a few minutes of silence, Beckett revealed, "You asked what was wrong earlier. It was that professor, Ambrose Langdon. I've only met him once, but his voice...it's so...familiar? The more I heard him, the angrier and more resolute I got. That worries me, because not all the people involved in my...abduction..." She didn't want to meet his eyes or vocalize the context of the alarm in her mind.

Cautiously, Lucifer presumed, "You think he might have been involved because you recognized his voice."

"And how he treated me on the phone. Yes. But I don't know for sure," Beckett added quickly. "He'll be here Tuesday, so I can figure it out then, I guess."

Beckett started walking to Aellon's stable, saying over her shoulder, "That is, if I don't throw him out five minutes after he gets here."

She heard Lucifer say under his breath, "You won't have to."

Aellon, sticking his neck as far as he could over the his stable door, was eager to see her. She kissed his nose and got a sloppy gumming in return. He walked out, grabbing her pony and then released it as she put on his hackamore and blanket.

Aellon kneeled slightly and she hopped on his back. He'd caught the reins while she mounted, and after she was on him, tossed them back with a jerk of his head. Lucifer straddled Elyon, so they rode out of the stable nose to tail, and then side by side.

After a few minutes, they began to trot. Within ten minutes, they were racing across the dell to the cabin on the other side. She whispered to Aellon to let go and he did, galloping at a pace that left his hooves off the ground most of the time. It felt like flying, but Lucifer's horse began to gallop faster, making them neck and neck when they hit the driveway leading up to Bowman's cabin.

Aellon's litheness allowed him to outmaneuver the taller, heavier horse. Where Elyon and Lucifer had to lever his entire body into a turn, Aellon simply cantered aside. But Elyon was much faster on flat terrain; he and Lucifer caught up to Beckett and Aellon right at the barn behind Bowman's cabin.

Bowman came out of the barn, yelling for her to," Come help me shoe this gray mare, barn girl!"

That's me, she mouthed at Lucifer, who tried to hide his grin. She dismounted, giving Aellon's reins to Lucifer – they didn't want to spook the gray.

In the barn, the gray, named Lyric, wasn't cooperating. Beckett stood at the horse's head, letting the horse smell her. When she got to Beckett's pockets, she started rummaging around to find out what was in them. Beckett let her- it distracted Lyric from Bowman at her hoof. He got the final shoe on, and then came to the front of the horse to thank Beckett.

"Where's all the praise and hallelujahs for Bowie's blanket handiwork? How's your butt?" he baited her, flirting outrageously.

Beckett teased, "My butt is fine, sir. Mighty cheeky. Seriously, though, thank you. What can I do to repay all these kindnesses?"

Bowman smiled. "Lunch. Tomorrow. You're gonna love it."

"I'll be here. Where's Katie?" Beckett didn't see her in the barn.

Bowman checked his watch. "She'll be home in about fifteen minutes. Can I get you and Lord Feathery Fiasco a glass of tea?"

"LUCIFER!" "Beckett bellowed. "You want some tea?!?!

She heard her name echoed back. "BECKETT!" he hollered. "Ask the snarky battlemaster-archer lad what's in it?!?" They all laughed.

Bowman walked out with Beckett, meeting Lucifer, who'd let the horses drink, and then tied the hackamores to the post of the corral gate. They all went to Bowman's front porch, where he invited them to have a seat, saying he'd bring the tea to them.

Beckett sat on the top step to the porch, while Lucifer chose the step below it for his seat. She looked out over the hill to the point, and the rippling, sun-kissed waves on the loch. "It's beautiful out here," Beckett said, and Lucifer turned his head to her.

"Not as striking as you are." He scrutinized her. "You change when you ride."

"It's the only time I feel free, Lucifer." He brought his hand around her ankle and squeezed.

"She rides like no one else I've ever seen." Bowman stood

in cabin doorway. His hands full, he motioned for Beckett to open the screen door, and she did, taking an amber-tinged glass from him. She sipped and tipped her head in thanks, as Bowman handed one of the other glasses to Lucifer.

Bowman checked his watch again. "Katie 'll be here in about five or six minutes, so relax and take your time with your tea. She'll want to change into her riding gear and boots."

Beckett assessed him as he lounged against a support beam on the porch. "What kind of gear?" she asked. Bowman laughed, telling her she'd just have to wait and see.

While Beckett and Bowman bantered, Lucifer studied her. She'd begun to remember more about her childhood, particularly how she interacted with plants and animals in such an easy way, and it showed. Her skin glowed, while her face, hair, and body depicted a visage of freshness, vitality, and excitement. Conversely, he found her eyes troubled, most likely because of her suspicion about the professor.

Still, their colors, the part closest to the iris radiating a glacial light blue encircled with dark green-gray, captivated him. They were the color they'd been when he met her as a child and had never forgotten. Drinking Bowman's tea, he decided he'd be discussing the professor with Sean at dinner. If his involvement in what happened to Beckett could be proved, he'd see to it personally, and with great relish, that Dr. Ambrose Langdon paid for any harm he caused her.

The arrival of the school bus and Katie interrupted Lucifer's thoughts, along with the conversation between Beckett and Bowman. Katie, her long auburn hair trailing behind her, ran to the group sitting on the front porch. "Hey everybody! It's a great day to ride with my Doc!" Katie bounded to Beckett and hugged her, almost toppling them both off the porch.

Laughing, they centered themselves. Letting go of Beckett,

Katie embraced her dad and gave Lucifer a kiss on the cheek, "Dad says your name isn't Lucien, it's Lucifer. I've read about you, and I have loads of *questions.*"

With a squeal, Katie opened the door, skipping up the stairs to her room. "I'll be right down, I have to change clothes," she reassured everyone.

"Well, I guess she's a happy camper," Bowman deduced, his grin wide and proud. He shouted up to Katie, "Meet us in the barn, young lady!" With that, he collected the tea glasses and set them on one of the porch's tables. Lucifer and Beckett rose, with Bowman hopping from the porch to the ground, and together they made their way back to the barn.

Bowman saddled the gray, and then went back to the stalls and walked another horse to the front. Bowman's quarter horse displayed more of his Mustang heritage than most of his kind. Perhaps a hand taller than her horse, the buckskin, named Talon, was stockier and muscular, which made Aellon look more slender and agile.

Katie's riding included a saddle, blanket, brindle, and bit. Like Beckett and Lucifer, Bowman rode bitless. "He's a gorgeous horse, Bowman," Beckett complimented him.

"He's a cutter, and I love to ride him when I can," Bowman said, turning to Lucifer as he mounted Elyon.

"Lord Feathery Fiasco owns a beast right there. I've seen him ride and that horse prances so much it's hard to tell who's prettier, him or his rider." Beckett cracked up laughing, and followed Bowman's gaze to Katie, who had returned and, indeed, changed her clothes for riding.

Her hair pony'd with an Evigvokter ball cap, she wore a Taylor Swift concert tee, ripped jeans, one of her dad's old flannel shirts, and a pair of well-worn leather boots. Bowman and Beckett exchanged glances. Lucifer, with a sly look at Katie, suggested that perhaps the apple didn't fall far from the tree.

Katie stepped directly to her gray, giving the mare carrots she'd brought from the cabin. Smiling at Beckett, she guided the mare outside, mounting Lyric via the stirrups as she walked.

In the meantime, Bowman gathered four back quivers filled with arrows and bows, handing one of each of them to Beckett, Katie and Lucifer, and keeping one of each for himself.

"We're going to bow on horseback? Is there a target set up?" came Katie's exuberant voice. "Is this my *birthday*, Dad?" Chuckling, Bowman and Beckett mounted their horses.

"What's your horse's name?" Katie called to Beckett, as they all started walking the horses away from the barn.

"Aellon. He's an Arabian," Beckett explained. Or at least looks like an Arabian, as she met Lucifer's eyes, who was also trying not to smirk. They walked the horses for about a minute before trotting down the long driveway.

"Katie, you lead," Bowman instructed.

Beckett brought Aellon even with Katie and Lyric. "Doc, Dad says you know about what happened with that... woman... and that you and he are our bio parents."

"Yep. I found yesterday and although the circumstances aren't ideal, I'm really glad," Beckett soothed her.

Katie contemplated things for a moment and asked, "Does that mean I can tell people you're my mom?"

Beckett turned her head back to where Bowman rode, and he silently mouthed, "Yes."

"Yes, Katie, that's exactly what it means." Beckett verified confidently. Katie rode silently for a few minutes.

Turning Lyric to the north, she looked at Beckett, vocalizing the question she'd been dying to ask, "Can I call you Mom?"

Beckett put Aellon right beside Lyric. Reaching over and

touching Katie's arm, she told her, "You can call me whatever you want. I'm not going away. I'll be here and I love you just as much either way."

Katie's smile cut across any anxiousness and concern she had. "You love me now," she reiterated. "But will you love me when I beat you to that next hill?" She urged Lyric into a gallop and Beckett followed.

All the horses headed into high gear, with Lucifer's Elyon in the lead. Beckett controlled Aellon, knowing perfectly well he'd be able to beat the other horses. That was, until Bowman came from the back and passed them all in a flash of hooves and buckskin. Then the race became about Katie catching Lucifer, who was gaining on her dad. Katie rode low over her mare, whose ears twitched as Katie spoke to her.

Beckett, tired of reining Aellon in, bent low and whispered to him. Humming, Beckett let him pick up the pace until she was neck and neck with Lucifer.

Flattening herself to Aellon's stride, she kept him there, registering he understood what she wanted without her saying anything. That's odd, she thought, then remembered that Lucifer wrote that the gloves he gave her had "other uses." She'd have to test further to see what they could do, but right now, she felt relaxed, free, and content.

Lucifer reached the hill first by a nose. Bowman led them into a copse of trees that led to a rich, autumn- colored forest. Clearly marked trails provided multiple opportunities for gallops, trots, and walks, with Bowman or Katie leading the way.

After about thirty-five minutes of riding, they came to a hill overlooking the outskirts of a small village. "Katie goes to school here, "Bowman explained, "Dunhaven is a holding of Dell Castle. Fae, elves, djinn, sorcerers, and other supernatural beings like us live there."

Beckett, astounded, asked Katie, "Is this where you go to

school?"

She nodded, "I love it here. I didn't know at first about Gwen, Dad, and you, so I didn't know how much I would fit right in." Katie patted Lyric's neck affectionately. "I'm never leaving."

Beckett found herself envious for the second time that day. Even with as messed up as this all became for Katie and Connor, they knew who they were. Beckett wished she knew who she was at fourteen. Hell, she'd have settled for that when she turned eighteen, or twenty, or right this minute.

Looking at the village, she diverted her gaze to Lucifer, who sat astride Elyon serenely examining her. Bowman and Katie started for the woods, and Bowman called back, "Quit yer lallygagging. We got bows, arrows, and a target to meet on the cabin side of these woods.

"Bowman," Beckett called, "Is this Dell Castle property, the woods and everything?"

"Yep. Even the village," Bowman answered. Beckett remembered the plat she'd seen when she and Sean acquired Dell, but she didn't think the village was on it. She reminded herself to ask Sean about that later when she saw him.

Bowman led them back the way they'd come, this time mostly walking or at a trot. When they neared the clearing, he maneuvered Talon into a loping gallop and the rest of the party followed suit. As they made their way midway between the castle and Bowman's barn, they saw a target set up in a mostly mowed section of the grounds.

Beckett's delight to do some mounted archery matched Katie's. Games like this made one stronger and more assertive, training the mind, body, and horse to increase quick-thinking and near-instant reaction skills. One barrel was set about an eighth of a mile from the target, and another barrel positioned at the midpoint between it and the target. What appeared to be glaives partially stuck out of the first barrel.

Ohhhh, she speculated, we're going to be able to chuck those from horseback, too? Beckett decided this afternoon couldn't get any better.

Meeting up at the target, Bowman handed a regular playing dart to each rider and established the throwing distance. Whoever got theirs closest to the target's bullseye went first, and the person whose dart was furthest went last. Bowman threw first and hit the top right of the center of the bullseye; Lucifer hit the bullseye dead on.

Katie threw just to the left her dad, and Beckett threw hers directly at Lucifer's dart, knocking it out. "So mean," Lucifer joked, and reined in Elyon, trotting the horse back to first barrel.

"Start there, and side swipe the barrel, then shoot as many arrows as you can at the target," Bowman directed.

Everyone moved their horses out of the way as Lucifer positioned his horse and made his bow handy. Urging his horse into a full gallop, he charged toward the second barrel, skirting it to the left, simultaneously with his effort to pull arrows out his quiver as fast as he could and shoot them at the target.

Of the twelve he shot, three of them hit the bullseye, two of them hit the first circle of the bullseye, and the other seven distributed themselves in and around the second circle.

As Lucifer retrieved his arrows, Bowman tallied his score. "That's (12-0) +(3x20) +(2x10)+ (5x9) + (2x8). Grand total, 153."

Lucifer and Elyon coolly stood aside after he retrieved his arrows, watching Katie ready Lyric for the run. She got herself situated at the first barrel, and then like a shot, she and Lyric were on the run, with Katie already using her bow. By the time she was finished, she'd shot thirteen arrows, 6 in the first bullseye circle, 1 inside the bullseye, 5 in the second circle, and 1 in the third. "Dad, I think that's 146?"

Looking up from his counting, he validated her score, riding to his daughter and high-fiving her.

Katie rode Lyric back to the target and dismounted, retrieving her arrows. She looked then toward an amused Lucifer and informed him that he better look out, she'd want to take a second run. She mounted Lyric again, heading for the sidelines to cheer on her dad.

Bowman readied himself and Talon at the first barrel; he had his bow and two arrows already in his hand. Urging Talon forward, the horse reacted in a flash and bolted toward the second barrel, skirting it and shooting directly toward the target veering at the last minute.

During that time, Bowman launched nearly 20 arrows, with only 1 missing the target completely. There were 6 arrows dead center of the bullseye, 6 arrows in the first circle, 6 arrows in the second, and 1 arrow in the third.

"Dad!", Katie wailed, "261? You're just showing off!"

Bowman chortled, calling to Beckett, "Pretty good, huh? Just a PSA: don't try this at home. I don't want you to hurt yourself."

Beckett stuck her tongue out at him, cantering her horse to the first barrel. Arranging her bow, she took a deep breath, whispering to Aellon, "Ready when you are, boy. I got to make Bowman mad, so whatever you can do to help, please feel free."

He nickered, and she patted him. "Let's go!" Aellon shot forward as Beckett loaded arrows in rapid succession. His stride was so smooth it was like sitting still, even when he danced past the second barrel.

By the end of her run, she'd let fly 20 arrows, with 6 dead centers, 6 in the first ring, 4 in the second ring, and 4 in the third.

Katie and Lucifer were clapping and cheering, while

Bowman's jaw hung open. "268? What? That's your first time in how long?"

Beckett laughed as she retrieved her arrows. "Years, battlemaster archer lad. YEARS." As she and Aellon passed him, she said, "Maybe it's just luck. You want a second round?"

"Hell, yes," Bowman replied, "You're first. But this time, it's glaives and a barrel turn without touching the barrel. And it's timed, so if Aellon touches the barrel, you lose a second for each touch."

She shrugged, "Fine by me. How many glaives?" "

"One, just pull it out of the barrel."

She trotted to the first barrel, pulling out a glaive, shiny and blinding in the sunlight.

Beckett leaned low over Aellon, murmuring, "No touching the barrel, boy, as close as you can get." This time, he dragged a black hoof across the ground. "Ready when you are," she said softly.

When he sprang forward, it was like riding the air, and his barrel cut so clean and close her ponytail almost brushed it as they encircled it. When she launched the glaive, her aim was true: dead center. In some ways, she like the glaive more than the bow, because it was easier to control one item rather than many.

She walked Aellon to Bowman and he told her that was 20 more points, no deductions, and a time of 8.1 seconds. With that, she sneered at him, removing the glaive from the target. She trotted Aellon over to return it to the barrel.

Bowman went next, and it was clear the glaive and the barrel were not a problem for his horse and skills, either. Katie timed his run at 8.0, but his horse brushed the barrel and his glaive only netted him 9 points. Katie's run proved her to be a superior barrel rider, not touching the barrel, hitting the same 9 points, but with an 8.0 time, beating her father. "YES!" she cried. "I am victorious!" Bowman shook his head, laughing.

Lucifer amazed them all with a 7.55 time and 20-point score, winning the glaive round. Bowman checked his watch and announced it was 4:45 pm – Beckett and Lucifer needed to head for the castle for dinner with Sean.

"I'll be up after Katie has dinner with me, probably about seven ," Bowman assured Beckett. "Apparently, there'll be dessert."

They all said their goodbyes, bantering with one another good-naturedly, giving the glaives, quivers, and bows back to Katie and Bowman.

Lucifer rode beside her. After the first meadow, he uttered the magic words, "Race you to the barn!" And they raced, streaking like blurs across the grounds.

At the barn, the contest was even. Luckily, a stable hand, Luke, was on duty. He happily offered to care for the horses after they escorted each horse to its stall.

"It doesn't even look like they've been ridden, but I'll feed them and brush them. Leave their hackamores and blankets over the stall door and I'll clean those, too" Luke said cheerily.

Beckett did as Luke requested, kissed Aellon's nose and thanked him. He gummed her nose, then looked for his feed. Lucifer waited for her and they strolled down the footpath to the castle.

"Your eyes are lit like beacons," he said, steadying her over the rocky part of the path.

Beckett beamed at him, "I had a GREAT time."

Elated, she held on to his arm until they entered the castle, then they both went their separate ways once they'd reached the residence wing. She practically skipped to her door – that's just how terrific a day it was. Now, to get ready for dinner.

Chapter 9

Revelations

Lucifer found Sean already in front of the fireplace in the library, sipping bourbon. "Hey mate, you want one of these?" Sean held up his glass, "It's fantastic. Very smooth." Lucifer nodded and Sean moved to one of the tables in the library where a selection of merlots, cabs, and the bottles of scotch and whiskey sat.

Sean picked up one of the empty glasses and poured two fingers from a bourbon bottle, handing the glass to Lucifer. "Cheers," Sean toasted him, and both drank.

"I'm celebrating," Sean revealed, "Beckett's signing her contract and agreement with me tonight. How was our warrior princess today?"

Lucifer sat down on the sofa between the fireplace's wingbacks. "First, she's had, as she said, a great time riding and participating in the battlemaster archer lad's horse and rider games."

Sean smirked, challenging, "Bet she beat you. Bet she beat the battlemaster archer lad, too."

"I won the glaive round, but she pummeled us with the bow. Brutal." Lucifer winked, taking a sip. Then, he suddenly changed the subject, "Sean, I need to know more about

Ambrose Langdon."

Sean looked surprised. "Why? He's a dolt. An attractive, rich asshat who doesn't think anyone but himself exists in the world. Beckett handled him just fine." He settled himself on a wingback closest to Lucifer's end of the sofa.

"Beckett was disconcerted... she thought she'd heard his voice before, and it unnerved her." Lucifer scowled, his face darkening with suspicion.

"Ah. I see. You do know that she was kept in a dark room and restrained during her abduction, so all she could do was hear the men assaulting and torturing her." Sean winced, putting down his glass. "Was she sure?"

Lucifer shook his head no. Sean understood. "We can check him out more. I'll mention it to Bowman when he comes tonight.

As they swigged their bourbon, Beckett walked into the library. Her hair fell loosely around her shoulders, shiny and thick. Dressed in a long, charcoal black sweater dress that clung seductively to her curves, she minimally accented it with tasteful diamond earrings and a pair of suede tall boots. Lucifer couldn't take his eyes off her.

Sean stood, asking, "Dr. Argonne, would you like a merlot or bourbon before dinner?

"Why Lord Caladfin, I certainly prefer a merlot, thank you." Sean opened an 18-year bottle of merlot, poured a taste, and gave it to her. She let it air for a few minutes.

"You look like you had a terrific afternoon," Sean recognized.

"I did! I also have some papers for you." She went to her desk, pulling out the contracts he'd given her. Beckett signed the modification to their partnership and handed it to him.

She waved the employment agreement at him. "This," she informed him, "is very, very flattering. I had to re-read it again and then compare it to the financials you gave me."

Between sips, Sean responded, "Yes. I thought you might."

"I'm a little in awe how we have so much capital. In less than three years? Those financial show net profits for every quarter since you started the company, Sean. It's quite an achievement."

Sean motioned her to the sofa. She went to the table first, pouring a full glass of wine, then joined him, eager to listen.

"Many of our clients are foreign governments and institutions, as you saw from the client list." Beckett acknowledged this fact with a tilt of her head. "We make them pay for secrecy they require and don't back down from it. In fact, nobody's even challenged me over costs. Doing what we do, quietly and without fuss, costs money." He sighed, sipping his bourbon.

She couldn't argue with what he said – the documents she reviewed were excellent and detailed about that, just as they should be. "Bowman told me that Dunhaven is our holding. I don't remember seeing that on the original plat."

Sean explained, "It wasn't. The village was abandoned, in ruins. As more people started working for us, families wanted to relocate closer. So, we let them rehab the town from the ground up. They contribute to a general fund that their village administers, and it pays for all the services they receive, including dental, medical, school, etc. We haven't changed the plat because the UK and Scotland recognize our property in the same way as Italy does Vatican City."

Sean always impressed her, but right this minute her appreciation and respect for him hit an all time high. "This is incredible, Sean. I really mean that."

"So, sign the employment contract, already." He smirked. Beckett laughed, stood, and did as he wanted. He countersigned below where she did and initialed Monday's date. Lucifer witnessed it.

Just as Sean was about to call Mrs. McKinnon to have their

dinner served, Sam spoke.

"Dr Aurington, Dr. Calvin is calling for you. Shall I tell him you'll phone him back?"

Before Beckett could say anything, Sean's face changed, and he told Sam to put Calvin through on speaker and monitor the call.

"Dr. Calvin, I've put you through to Dr. Argonne."

"Beckett! How are you, darling? Are you in London?" Robert Calvin's smooth, aristocratic British came on the line.

"I'm fine Robert, Sam called you to set up a time for you to talk to one of my interns. What's up?"

"I'd heard a rumor you were transitioning to Evigvokter to work with Sean. When did that happen?" Strangely, Robert sounded disgruntled for no reason.

Sean intervened, "Hullo, Robert. She just signed the papers with me a minute ago. What's on your mind?"

"I was just checking with Beckett; heard she might have had some trouble with Langdon. He can be sticky." Beckett met eyes with Lucifer and he with her.

Sean inquired what else was on Calvin's mind. "Well, I want to borrow Sam. Just for a little while."

This time, Beckett instantly reacted. "No, you can't. He's part of our business.   You uploaded the source code to GitHub and affirmatively disclaimed your copyright by attaching a CC0 Public Domain Dedication notice, effectively placing the work into the public domain with no ownership claims. You thought your code was useless when I asked you about it, before I started tinkering with it. Eventually, I ended up creating Sam."

"It doesn't matter, it's MY underlying codebase. I shouldn't have put it up there that way," Robert haughtily insisted.

"But you did," Beckett said, unruffled by Dr. Calvin's tone. "This isn't the first time you've lashed out at me about Sam when something isn't going as planned for you. Keep it up and I'll take legal action against you for fraud and harassment. You already know why I'd be successful doing it."

Robert passed seamlessly from pleasant, to displeased, to finally angry and insulting. "Listen, I let you work in my lab. **You owe me, you ungrateful, silly bitch**. You're not special, *you and all your fancy degrees.*"

Oh, my God. Her knees went weak and she tottered, almost falling toward Sean, only for Lucifer to catch her, helping her sit.

Beckett heard herself reply, "I've been told that before, Robert. Do you recall when you said it? I certainly do."

Dr. Calvin, cursing, abruptly hung up.

Sean kneeled before her, 'Do you think-".

Sam interrupted him. "Dr. Argonne, Lord Caladfin, Dr. Calvin called not far from here. Would you like the location?"

Lucifer stood, his face etched with anger. "Yes, we do, Sam, if it's all right with Beckett."

Shocked at the betrayal before her, she sat completely still. Dr. Robert Calvin, a man, a mentor, someone who she tried to respect and who was esteemed and admired by others, was involved in what happened to her – directly involved. She tried to breathe but couldn't.

Soothingly, Sean spoke. "Beckett, I understand. This is a man who harmed you. He said those words to you when you were abducted, didn't he?" She nodded. "You need a few minutes?" Beckett shook her head again, tears in her eyes.

Beckett glanced over at Lucifer. She couldn't bring herself to speak. He placed his hand on hers, and that familiar comfort from him travelled from her fingers, through her wrist and hand, to her elbow and shoulder.

"Sam, "she said, still shaking, "You can provide Sean and Lucifer with whatever they need about Dr. Calvin."

With that, she took her hand from Lucifer's, stood without

a word, and made her way out of the library to her suite.

Watching her go, Sean's face broadcasted his hatred of Robert Calvin. "I disliked that guy before, and I hate him even more now. All he did was leer after Beckett in the labs."

Lucifer asked softly, "And she trusted him?"

"She thought he was harmless. He never did anything more than watch her, but when he pretended to be interested in what she was doing, I didn't buy it." Sean drank the rest of his bourbon in one swallow.

Lucifer faced him squarely, fury in his features. "I've told you how I feel about her, Sean. I won't let this pass."

Seeing the archangel's reaction, Sean didn't know how long Lucifer could keep himself in check. He decided to take a different tact to defuse Lucifer's energy. Sean chortled wryly, "But have you told *her*, Lucifer. Really, honestly told *her*?"

Silent, Lucifer glared at him. "I didn't think so," Sean snapped. "Until you do, we do things my way and built a legal case that causes the rats to flee the ship." He checked his phone.

"Sam sent us Calvin's location. Let me arrange an extraction team and we can take him in for questioning." Sean wavered for a moment, then added, "Maybe you should go check on Beckett. She's going to need support right now, and I think you're the best person to provide that."

Lucifer agreed, his anger momentarily tempered by concern for Beckett's well-being. "You're right. But Sean, you must promise me one thing - when you bring Calvin in, I want to be there for the interrogation."

"I understand. We'll make sure you have that opportunity. But remember, we need to do this the right way. No matter how much we want to tear him apart, we can't jeopardize the case." Sean met Lucifer's fierce gaze.

"I know," Lucifer replied, quiet and controlled. "I'll keep

myself in check. For Beckett's sake."

With a final dip of his head, Lucifer left the library, making his way towards Beckett's suite. His heart ached for the pain she must be experiencing, the betrayal compounding the trauma she had already endured.

When he reached her door, Lucifer took a deep breath to center himself before knocking softly.

"Beckett? It's me. Can I come in?"

Tenebris materialized before him, unsettled, and answered, "M' Lady is in the rain. She cries. You need to come in." The door unlocked and swung open, with Tenebris following him into Beckett's suite.

Without warning, Sam spoke: "The decision for you to enter wasn't Tenebris', Lord Aurington. Beckett told him not to answer the door. I made the choice." Lucifer thanked him.

Hearing the shower running, he picked his way through the great room to the bathroom and stood in the doorway. "Beckett?" he called tacitly. When she didn't answer, he peered through the shower's glass walls to see her sitting in a black slip, very wet, on the shower floor.

Patiently, Lucifer sat in the doorway. He listened to her whisper to herself as she cried. "I'm an idiot. How could I have been so blind? Why didn't I see?" She sobbed.

After about fifteen minutes, he heard Beckett's trembling voice say his name. "I trusted him, Lucifer. I never thought he was untrustworthy."

Lucifer took off his shoes and socks, entered the shower, and carefully lowed himself to sit by her. He took her hands in his, his touch providing a small measure of comfort.

"This is not your fault, Beckett," he said firmly. "Calvin is the one who betrayed your trust. He's the one who did this to you. And I promise you, he will face the consequences of his actions."

Beckett slumped into Lucifer, resting her head on his

shoulder as tears continued to fall silently down her cheeks, mixing with the water from the shower. "I feel so angry," she conceded. "Angry at him, angry at myself for not seeing it sooner. And I'm scared, Lucifer. Scared of what else I might remember, of who else might have been involved."

Lucifer wrapped his arms around her, holding her close as the water cascaded over them both. "Your anger and fear are valid, Beckett. But don't let them consume you. Use them to fuel your strength, your commitment to see justice served. Please know that you are not alone in this. I'm here for you, always."

They sat together under the steady stream of water, drawing comfort from each other's presence. Lucifer gently stroked Beckett's hair, a soothing balm to her battered soul. After a long moment, Beckett took a deep, shuddering breath and straightened, wiping the tears and water from her face.

"Thank you, Lucifer," she said timidly. "For being here, for understanding. I don't know what I'd do without you."

He cupped her face in his hands, his eyes locked on hers. "You never have to find out, Beckett. I will always be by your side, no matter what. We'll get through this together, I promise you that."

She managed a small, grateful smile. "Oh. I know we will. Stupid asshats." She pushed her hair to the side of her face and took in Lucifer's clothes. He'd come into the shower dressed, getting completely soaked in the process. For her, she realized. Inhaling and exhaling slowly, Beckett saw how his shirt clung to his powerful physique. How could a girl in distress not be emboldened by him?

There was a new intentness in her voice, a glint of steel in her eyes. Lucifer saw it and felt a surge of pride. Beckett was a fighter, a survivor. And with her strength, she continued to face the darkness with the intent of emerging healed and whole.

Lucifer stood, volunteering his hand to help Beckett to her feet. "Come on, let's get you dried off and into some comfortable clothes. Sean is organizing a team to bring Calvin in for questioning. We'll find out the truth, Beckett. He'll pay for what he's done."

Beckett took his hand, allowing him to guide her out of the shower. As they stepped onto the plush bathmat, Lucifer grabbed a large, fluffy towel and wrapped it around Beckett's shoulders. He gently brushed a stray lock of wet hair from her face, his touch lingering for a moment.

"What about you, are you going to change?" Now that Beckett had him here, she didn't want him to leave.

"Don't worry, I'm fine. I'll be right outside if you need me," he said kindly. "Take your time, get changed, and then we can talk about what comes next."

Beckett exuded gratefulness. "Thank you, Lucifer. And sorry about getting your clothes in such a state."

He smiled, a genuine grin that made her heart flutter despite the pain and anger still coursing through her. "It's all right, Beckett, Lady of These Woods. I'll be here, waiting for you."

With a final, comforting squeeze of her hand, Lucifer stepped out of the bathroom, closing the door behind him.

As Beckett began to dry herself off and change into fresh clothes, she felt less a victim and more a determined survivor. With all these well-meaning folks by her side, she knew she could face this development better than if she hadn't come to Dell. Dr. Calvin had no idea what he had unleashed, but he was about to find out just how strong and resilient Beckett Argonne truly was.

Chapter 10

Healing Wounds, Forging Bonds

After her conversation with Lucifer, Beckett surfaced from her bedroom, ready to face the rest of the evening. To her shock, Lucifer was completely dry, despite never having left her suite. "I gave the water to your plants." Lucifer pointed at the heather and lavender on the sofa's end table.

She, Lucifer, and Tenebris made their way back to the library, encountering Bowman, who just arrived at the castle. Seeing the grave looks on their faces, Bowman immediately sensed that something was wrong.

"Beckett, Lucifer, what's happened?" he asked, concern floating across his face.

Lucifer filled him in on the situation with Dr. Calvin, watching as he evolved from worry to outrage to fierce protectiveness.

Bowman placed a consoling hand on her shoulder. "Beckett, I'm so sorry. I can't imagine how painful this must be for you. But I want you to know that I'm here for you, too. Whatever you need, ok?"

Beckett managed a small smile, moved by Bowman's steady support. "Thank you, Bowman. That means more than you know."

Together, the three of them entered the library, where Sean, along with Max, was already deep in conversation with the rest of the extraction team. Bowman, with his unique skills and connections, offered to assist in the investigation, and Sean immediately put him to work.

As the team discusses their next steps, Bowman pulled Sean aside, his manner dead set. "Sean, I know we need to do this by the book, but if it comes down to it, I'll do whatever it takes to protect Beckett. She's been through enough already."

Sean concurred, understanding the depth of Bowman's loyalty inasmuch as he acknowledged Lucifer's fury. "I know, Bowman. We all feel the same way. But we must be smart about this. We can't risk everything falling apart because we let our emotions get the best of us."

Bowman reluctantly agreed, but the fire in his eyes made it clear to Sean that he wouldn't think twice about acting if Beckett was threatened.

As the meeting continued, Beckett took a moment to observe the people around her - Sean, Lucifer, Bowman, and the rest of the team. She felt a swell of thankfulness and affection for each of them, knowing that without their support, she'd be lost, lonely, and hurting in her London flat. With this new path on which she tread, Beckett could face this situation and not lose the rest of her sanity in the process.

But right now, feeling exhausted, she'd like to face bed. Standing, she expressed her appreciation to all of them for their support and asked that once they apprehended Calvin, please to let her know. With Tenebris by her side, she left the library.

Beckett made her way back to her suite, Tenebris padding silently beside her. She couldn't help feeling conflicted. The exhaustion from the day's revelations burdened her, but there was also a relief in knowing that she was surrounded by people who cared for her deeply.

Once inside her room, Beckett sat down on the edge of the bed, her shoulders drooping as the adrenaline began to fade. Tenebris, sensing her distress, placed his large head on her lap, offering silent comfort.

"I don't know how I'm supposed to sleep after all this, Tenebris," she murmured, absently scratching behind the hellhound's ears. "Every time I close my eyes, I'm afraid of what I might see."

Tenebris looked up at her with understanding eyes. "I will watch over you, my Lady. No harm will come to you while I am here."

Beckett, grateful for the hellhound's steadfast loyalty, kissed the top of his head. She changed into comfortable sleepwear and climbed into bed, pulling the covers up to her chin, shivering. Tenebris settled on the end of the bed, his presence a reassuring constant.

As she lay there staring up at the sky through the ceiling, Beckett's mind clouded with thoughts of the past and the uncertain future. She knew that dealing with the trauma of her abduction would often be painful, but necessary. She had no doubt that she had the strength to face it, and for the first time, she wouldn't face it alone.

With that thought, Beckett closed her eyes, willing herself to relax. Slowly, the tension began to drain from her body, and she drifted off into a restless sleep. In her dreams, fragments of memories flashed in rapid succession. The darkness of her cell, the cruel laughter of her captors, the pain that seemed to go on forever.

As the night deepened, Beckett tossed and turned, her slumber a battleground of the unknown, past horrors, and future hopes. Tenebris remained by her side, a silent and vigilant guardian against her inner darkness. A spark of mistrust grew in her nightmares; like a snake, it coiled tightly around her, compelling Beckett to sit up straight in bed, fully awake.

Anger, betrayal, and deep, aching feelings of abandonment vied for dominance within her heart. And at the center of it all burned a white-hot question: if Lucifer had kept watch over her in her guardians' woods and at her dome, where the hell was Lucifer when she needed him most?

Unable to bear the overwhelming hurt and her misgivings any longer, Beckett called out for Tenebris. "Please, Tenebris. I need to see Lucifer. Now."

The hellhound vanished. Moments later, Lucifer appeared in her doorway, his demeanor laced with foreboding. "Beckett, what's wrong?"

She fixed him with a piercing gaze, her eyes swimming with unshed tears. "Where were you, Lucifer? When I was taken, when I was being tortured and violated, men laughing as they left their fingerprints in bruises all over my body, where were you?"

Lucifer flinched as if struck, the pain in her words cutting him to the core. He approached her carefully, sitting on the edge of the bed. "Beckett, I..."

But she cut him off, the dam finally breaking as the words poured out of her in a torrent of anguish, frustration, and anger. "WHERE WERE YOU?! You were supposed to protect me!? You were to be there for me, like you profess you've always have been. But when I needed you most, you were *nowhere* to be found!"

Tears streamed down her frozen face as she clutched at the bedsheets, her knuckles turning white. "I think I called for you, *Lucifer*. In my darkest moments, when the pain was so bad I wanted to die, I called for *you*. But you never came."

Lucifer's eyes glistened with his own tears, the pain of her words settling on his shoulders like a physical burden. "Beckett, please understand. As an archangel, I must be cautious about how I influence events and people. Every action I take, every decision I make, has consequences that ripple out through time and fate.

He reached out, tentatively taking her hand in his. "When you were taken, I sensed your distress, your agony. It took every ounce of my strength not to rush to your side, to lay waste to those who dared to harm you."

Beckett's grip tightened on his hand, her tears falling faster now. "Then why didn't you?" she choked,   just as raw and broken as she had been earlier in the shower.

Lucifer closed his eyes, his tears finally spilling over his face. "Because I knew that if I intervened, it would alter the course of your destiny, and the destinies of countless others. I cannot fly in the face of free will, or everyone would be doomed." He took a ragged breath. "The path you are meant to walk, the role you are meant to play in the grand tapestry of the universe, would have been irrevocably changed."

He opened his eyes, meeting her gaze with pure, unadulterated love and sorrow. "It was the hardest thing I have ever done, Beckett. To stand by and watch as you suffered, someone I deeply love, knowing that I had the power to stop it but couldn't. I will carry that guilt, that pain, for the rest of my existence."

Beckett stared at him, her emotions warring within her. Part of her wanted to rage at him, scream, curse, and demand that he leave her sight. But another part, the part that had always known him, understood. Did she hear him say he loved her? She caught her breath in disbelief.

"I... Lucifer, did you just say I'm someone...?"

Lucifer's eyes widened as he realized what he had just admitted. In the heat of the moment, with emotions running high and Beckett's accusations pressing in, the words had slipped out. He inhaled deeply, knowing there was no going back now.

"Yes, Beckett. I love you. I've loved you for longer than I

can remember, perhaps from the moment we first met in those woods so many years ago."

He cradled her face, his thumb brushing away the tears that still streamed down her cheeks. "I have watched you grow, witnessed the strength and compassion, the brilliance that shines within you. With each passing day, my love for you has grown deeper than I ever imagined possible for another being."

Beckett felt the air leave her lungs from his admission. She'd felt the depth of their bond, how it transcended friendship or guardianship. But to have him profess his love in an excited utterance stirred something acutely within her core. His words began to act as a salve upon her inner strife and anguish.

"Lucifer, I..." she began, trembling with emotion. "I don't know what to say. I care for you, deeply. But with everything that's happened, everything - ".

He silenced her with a finger to her lips. "I know, Beckett, I know. This isn't the time or the place for such confessions. You are hurting, and angry, and confused. You have every right to be."

Lucifer took her hands in his, his gaze piercing and sincere. "I do not expect anything from you, Beckett. My love for you is unconditional, and it always will be. Whether you return my feelings or not, I will always be here for you, always stand by your side."

Lucifer's statement unleashed a torrent of feelings - love intermingled with gratitude, muddied by bewilderment and a feeling of violated trust. However significant his confession, Beckett recognized that unpacking its whole meaning was unattainable in that moment. Not with this temporary chaos predominating all around them.

But she also knew that, despite her anger and pain, she didn't want to lose him. Mysteriously, he'd become a part of her, a piece of her soul that she couldn't imagine being without.

"I... I need time. To think, to heal, to process everything. But I don't want to lose you. I can't lose you."

He gathered her into his arms once more, holding her close as if he could absorb all her hurt into himself. "You will never lose me, Beckett. I will be here, waiting, for as long as it takes. When you are ready, we will face whatever comes next together."

Inhaling slowly, Lucifer asked, "Please, may I stay? I want you sleep in my arms. I promise it will be dreamless and deep. You need the rest." She nodded into his shoulder. Kicking off his shoes, Lucifer settled in for the night, pulling her head to his chest, wrapping his arms and legs around her in a protective, loving embrace.

As they held each other in the quiet of the night, Beckett felt a glimmer of something she hadn't experience so strongly in long time - hope. Hope that, despite the darkness that loomed over her, there was still a chance for light. For love.

With Lucifer holding her tightly, she fell asleep.

As the first rays of morning light filtered through the windows and ceiling, Beckett stirred, her eyes fluttering open. For a moment, she felt disoriented, the events of the previous night flooding back into her consciousness. Once aware of the strong arms wrapped around her, along with the steady heartbeat beneath her cheek, peace engulfed Beckett.

Lucifer was still asleep, his face relaxed and almost boyish in the soft sunlight. Beckett took the moment to study him, to marvel at the fact that this powerful, divine being had chosen to love her, to stand by her side through all the havoc that lay ahead.

Feeling her gaze, Lucifer's eyes opened, and he gazed at her affectionately. "Good morning, moon beam" he murmured, still drowsy. He pressed his lips to her forehead, tightening his embrace.

Beckett couldn't help but smile back, the simple domesticity of the moment warming her heart. "Good morning, sunshine" she replied, snuggling closer, and breathing in the scent of sandalwood, cedar, and musk that drifted from him, a combination of aromas that defined him in her mind.

For a few precious minutes, they lay there in silence, as he played with her hair and they both savored the quiet intimacy of the moment. But as the sun climbed higher in the sky, the reality of the day ahead began to intrude on their tranquil bubble.

Beckett sighed, reluctantly pulling away from Lucifer's embrace. "We should probably get up," she said, running a hand through her tousled hair. "Sean and the others will be wondering where we are."

Soberly, Lucifer met her gaze. "About last night, Beckett... I spoke the truth from my heart. I'm irrevocably, deeply in love with you and shall forever have your back. But I understand the space you need to sort through these emotions, to figure out what you want moving forward."

She reached out, taking his hand in hers and giving it a firm squeeze. "I know, Lucifer. I appreciate your patience and understanding more than words can express. You already know I love you - I have since the day we met in my woods. But I need us to focus on the task at hand, on bringing Calvin and the others to justice. Let the rest unfold as it will. Do you understand?"

"Of course. We'll face this together, Beckett. You are not alone." He emphasized the fact that it wasn't just her by herself anymore: it was "us."

With those words, they rose from the bed. Beckett knew that today could prove more arduous, that there would be painful truths to confront and difficult choices lying ahead.

As they left her room hand-in-hand, Tenebris and Dux leading the way, an indomitable spirit settled over Beckett. She felt loved, grateful for the blessings in her life, and fortified. While she understood Lucifer's prior restraint was necessary to preserve free will, he stood by her side now - strong, vulnerable, honest, humble, and unguarded. To Beckett, his steadfast presence made all the difference.

Chapter 11

Acceptance and Consequences

Lucifer bent down, placing a featherlight kiss on Beckett's cheek as he parted from her at the steps to the keep. "I'll join you in the library later this morning, little one," he said in an undertone. With a nod to Dux, he added, "You'll accompany Tenebris and Beckett until I summon you."

Dux inclined his head in silent acknowledgment. He and Tenebris fell into step beside Beckett, the two imposing "brothers" effortlessly flanking her as they led her to the common room.

The cavernous space bustled with activity, the morning crowd even larger than the day before. Dux and Tenebris took up watchful positions along opposite walls as Beckett made her way to the sideboard, desperately craving a cup of Mrs. McKinnon's invigorating black magic brew.

As she poured herself a steaming mug, several employees approached, welcoming her to Evigvokter and introducing themselves. Across the room, Danny caught her eye, rising slightly from his seat among a group of wide-eyed interns. He flashed her a cheerful smile, calling out, "Dr. Argonne! Good morning! May I have a moment of your time, please?"

Beckett acquiesced, cradling her coffee, and finding an

unoccupied table in the center of the room. Danny joined her, appearing thankful and apprehensive at the same time. "Sam sent me the audio and transcript of your conversation with Dr. Langdon," he began, wringing his hands. " I almost fell out my chair. I don't know how to thank you, but I'm freaked out that I might have caused friction between you two."

Reaching across the table, Beckett covered his hands with her own. "Nonsense, Danny. Friction arises from those who prioritize their own interests over doing what's right for others." She took on a firm, encouraging tone. "Langdon exploited you, a gifted and exceptional young man, for his own prestige and status at the university. I merely held him accountable."

She took another sip of her coffee. "What did you tell your mother last night?"

Danny respectfully corrected her. "Actually, I spoke with my parents together and explained what you did with Dr. Langdon." He paused, gathering his thoughts. "I've decided to stay here, with or without my doctorate, and work with Sam. That's my path."

After a moment's silence, he met her gaze. "I don't want Dr. Langdon as my advisor anymore. Would you consider taking on that role for me?"

Not surprised, Beckett nodded. "For now, continue providing your progress to Dr. Langdon, but have Sam blind copy me on your communications with him, at least until Tuesday. After that, we'll devise a plan for moving forward together. Is that acceptable?"

Danny's face lit up brighter than the sunlight streaming through the castle windows. "Yes, ma'am," he answered with a hint of awe. Lowering his tone, he asked timidly, "Will you really pull funding from the university if they don't comply?"

"Yes, I will," Beckett affirmed, taking another sip as a young, willowy blonde with flushed cheeks and lively brown eyes emerged from the kitchen, bearing a plate of eggs and salmon presumably meant for her. The erstwhile Halaia, no doubt. "It won't come to that – the university chancellors won't allow it. But this matter requires trust between you, me, Sean, Sam, and your parents. You understand?" Danny crossed his heart. "I promise, Dr. Argonne. I told my parents what happened but no one else." There was a moment's reluctance before he added, "But I've told the other interns that we misjudged you. You care deeply and understand us."

Beckett, touched by his words and his trust in her, smiled. "I do care, Danny. About you, about the work we're doing here, and about making sure that everyone can grow and learn. That's what Evigvokter is all about."

She glanced around the room, taking in the curious and hopeful faces of the other interns. Beckett spoke openly to them all. "I know that I'm new here, and that some of you may have doubts about me. But I want you all to know that my door is always open. If you have concerns, ideas, or just need someone to talk to, I'm here for you."

Halaia approached the table, carefully setting down the plate of eggs and salmon in front of Beckett. "Mrs. McKinnon sent this for you, Dr. Argonne. She said to tell you that she expects you to eat every bite." The young woman grinned, her eyes sparkling with amusement.

Beckett chuckled, shaking her head. "Mrs. McKinnon knows me too well. Please tell her thank you for me, Halaia."

As the young woman hurried back to the kitchen, Beckett turned her attention back to Danny. "I meant what I said, Danny. I'll do everything in my power to make sure you can continue your work here, with or without Langdon's support. You have a bright future ahead of you, and I'm honored to be a part of it."

"Thank you, Dr. Argonne. That means more to me than you

can imagine. I won't let you down," Danny's eyes shone with gratitude.

With a final smile, Sam's best mate stood, making his way back to the other interns. Beckett watched as he animatedly relayed their conversation, seeing the looks of surprise and admiration on their faces.

As she dug into her breakfast, Beckett felt content. Despite last night, she understood in her bones that she was exactly where she was meant to be. Relishing the opportunity to make a real difference in the lives of these brilliant young minds, she couldn't wait to get started.

Tenebris and Dux, ever vigilant, each caught her eyes from across the room. She gave them a small tip of her head in acknowledgment, thankful to them for their commitment to her and her safety.

Yes, Beckett ruminated, this was just the beginning. Together, they would uncover truths, bring justice to those who offended, and build a future filled with hope, innovation, and boundless potential.

Feeling spry, she finished her breakfast and stood, heading for the sideboard. Equipped with a fresh cup of black magic and the hellhound boys leading the way, she left the common room for the library with a feeling that come what may, she could cope and heal like this for a very, very long time.

The library door lock worked just as Sam had promised. As Beckett entered, a merry fire crackled in the hearth, and a sticky note from Tim welcomed her back again, offering to tend the flames should they start to die down.

Settling into her chair, she trailed her fingers over the velvety petals of the freshly cut flowers. "Good morning, Sam. Lord Caladfin and Lord Lucifer requested you contact them when I arrived."

"Good morning, Dr. Argonne," Sam's replied. "I'll notify them at once. If I may, how did Danny react after hearing the recording of your conversation with Professor Langdon?"

A dry chuckle escaped Beckett's lips. "Apparently, he almost fell right out of his seat when I threatened to pull funding and demanded the chancellors' presence on Tuesday. Afterwards, the young man fretted about causing a rift between the university and myself."

"Yes, I reinforced to him about ten minutes ago that your grievance stemmed from Langdon's deplorable attitude and actions, not the university itself," Sam said matter-of-factly.

Beckett concurred, taking a sip of her coffee. "Quite right. Frankly, Langdon deserves to face consequences – in my opinion, he shouldn't be teaching at all. Advisors must nurture students' growth, not exploit them for personal validation or control."

"An insightful observation, Dr. Argonne. If you'll permit me, I have some thoughts to share on this matter."

"By all means," Beckett replied, booting up her computer.

Sam's tone took on a measured cadence. "You're absolutely correct; an advisor's role is to guide, support, and foster their students' development, not to use them as means to an end. Dr. Langdon's behavior is unacceptable, and accountability is crucial."

A momentary pause hung in the air before Sam continued. "Your willingness to advocate for Danny and hold Langdon responsible speaks volumes about your integrity and leadership. It sends a clear message that Evigvokter values ethics, fairness, and the well-being of its people above all else."

"I've drafted a formal complaint detailing Dr. Langdon's misconduct and the potential impact on Danny's future. With your approval, I can submit this to the university's ethics committee and chancellors ahead of Tuesday's meeting, ensuring they are fully informed and prepared to take appropriate action." Sam said gravely.

Beckett's fingers stilled on the flower petals as she considered Sam's proposal. "You understand the severity of such a complaint, Sam? At the very least, Langdon would face censure."

"Yes, Dr. Argonne," Sam replied, his tone resolute. "I am cognizant of the possible repercussions for Dr. Langdon, including disciplinary action or even termination. However, the gravity of his transgressions warrants such consequences. He has abused his position of authority and violated the trust placed in him by students and the academic community."

Beckett nodded, her fingers still caressing the velvety petals as the flowers seemed to lean toward her touch. The seriousness of the decision settled heavily upon her, the probable impact on Langdon's career and reputation hanging in the balance.

"You're right, Sam," she said finally, conviction evident in her voice. "We cannot turn a blind eye to this kind of irresponsible behavior. Doing so would send the message that prioritizing personal interests over the well-being of our students and colleagues is acceptable."

Drawing a steadying breath, her gaze fixed on the computer screen. "Submit the complaint. I stand fully behind this course of action. But make it clear that this decision wasn't made lightly. We're compelled to act because upholding integrity – for Danny, for Evigvokter, and for the academic institution itself – is paramount."

"Understood, Dr. Argonne." Sam nearly sounded impressed. "The complaint will be thorough, impartial, and will convey the gravity of Dr. Langdon's transgressions. I'll keep you apprised of any updates or responses from the University."

A soft smile graced Beckett's lips. She was proud of the AI's dedication and ethical fiber. "Thank you, Sam. Your support and initiative mean more to me – to all of us at Evigvokter –

than you know."

"I suspect this is merely the first step in a series of necessary changes ahead. It won't be easy, but fostering an environment of growth, innovation, and mutual respect is essential." Leaning back, her gaze drifted to the crackling hearth.

"Your presence here has already begun that transformation," Sam elaborated. "Your conversation with Danny and the other interns this morning greatly resonated. They're beginning to think of you not just as their leader, but as someone genuinely invested in their well-being and development. Your openness breeds trust."

Sam changed the topic. "On that note, Lord Caladfin and Lord Lucifer have requested to join you shortly to discuss the Calvin investigation and review your schedule. Shall I inform them you're ready?"

"Yes, please do." Beckett extracted her new fountain pen, placing on the leather portfolio Sean gave her. "Any other pressing matters I should be aware of?"

"Nothing of note, though I've reminded you of the lunch meeting at Bowman's cabin at one o'clock."

"Aye, thank you."

The towering Dux padded over, settling himself near the corner of Beckett's chair. His brindled coat, a striking blend of black, brown, and tan, rippled with each breath he took.

Beckett acknowledged him with a curious look. "Yes, Dux. How can I help you?"

In a gravelly rumble, likened to a human one roughened by a lifetime of whiskey and unfiltered cigarettes, he spoke. "I am honored Lord Lucifer allows me this post beside my brother, Lady Beckett." Dux inclined his head respectfully. "Tenebris tells me you possess a rare gift - the ability to coax song from flowers. If it would please you, I would be most grateful to bear witness to this wonder." His gaze drifted admiringly towards the vibrant blooms.

Beckett drew the vase closer, gently trailing her fingers along the stems. Dux's ears pricked forward, twitching, as Tenebris padded over to rest his head in Beckett's lap, watching and listening intently. After a few tranquil moments, she asked, "Can you hear their song?"

Wonderment gleamed in Dux's eyes. "I can," he murmured, stupefied by what he heard.

Tenebris bobbed his head in earnest agreement. "Does their melody displease you, brother?"

A deep crimson rose unfurled further, filling the air with its heady fragrance. Dux's gaze remained centered on Beckett, his eyes glimmering with admiration. "Quite the contrary. My brother spoke true – you are indeed a goddess." A stem of statice stretched towards her beckoning fingertips as Sean and Lucifer entered the library.

"Good morning, Beckett," Sean addressed her cheerfully, settling into a wingback before her desk. "I see you're enjoying my floral gift."

"Very much so, thank you," Beckett replied with a smile. She should have anticipated the flowers came from him. "Though, I'm not the only one enchanted by them." She gestured towards the enraptured hellhounds. "Dux, are you similarly spellbound?"

"They sing," Dux declared, transfixed. He turned his adoring gaze towards Lucifer. "Their melodies crescendo when the Lady beckons them forth."

Beckett's eyes met Lucifer's as he lounged effortlessly on the corner of her desk, his lips curling into an affectionate smirk. Ceasing her ministrations, she noted both hellhounds remained close, their keen hearing still tuned to the flowers' ethereal harmonies.

Sean chuckled, highly entertained by the usually stoic hellhound guards' enchantment. "I see you've already bewitched Dux and Tenebris. Not an easy feat, I assure you."

Lucifer tenderly stroked a silken petal. "They merely recognize the divine essence before them. As I did, that fateful day so long ago."

Beckett colored at this poignant reminder of their bond. Clearing her throat, she refocused. "So, any updates on the Calvin investigation?"

Sean tone was grave. "We've located Calvin's safe house just outside the village. He knows the consequences of his actions…he's screwed the pooch, to use a crass human phrase."

Pausing, Sean dipped his head contritely towards Dux and Tenebris. "My apologies, friends. A poor choice of words on my part."

"No offense taken," the towering Dux rumbled graciously, accepting the remorse.

"We're putting together a plan to bring him in for questioning, but we want to make sure we have all our ducks in a row before we move." Sean's tone, while professional, inferred his underlying caution for everyone to avoid letting their emotions get away from them.

Lucifer agreed, his jaw muscle twitching. "We can't afford any missteps. If Calvin gets wind that we're onto him, he might flee or worse, destroy evidence that could lead us to the others involved in your abduction."

"What do you need from me?" Beckett asked determinedly, anticipating the confrontation of one of the men responsible for her trauma in the back of her mind.

"For now, we need you to focus on your work here at Evigvokter," Sean replied, sensitive to Beckett's perspective, but firm nevertheless. "Leave the investigation to us. We'll keep you informed every step of the way, but it's crucial that you maintain normalcy. We can't risk tipping off Calvin or his associates."

Lucifer reached out, taking Beckett's hand in his. "I know it's not easy, little one. But trust us to handle this. Your safety and well-being are our top priority."

Beckett squeezed Lucifer's hand, drawing strength from his touch. "I do trust you," she said confidently. "Both of you. I know you'll do whatever it takes to bring Calvin to justice."

There was a momentary lull as she cast her mind back to the previous night, a contemplative look settling over her features. "Calvin brought up Langdon during his call last night. It felt like an attempt to justify his actions by blaming him, but I wasn't convinced."

"That's a curious connection. We know Langdon is involved somehow, but we haven't been able to find any direct ties to Calvin or the extremist group." Sean's eyes narrowed.

"Ruling out collusion between Langdon and Calvin would be premature," Lucifer said adamantly. "We need proof."

"Sam began digging into Langdon's history. If a connection exists, he'll uncover it. Meanwhile, I'll remain dedicated to my responsibilities here, trusting you both to steer the investigation." Beckett placed complete credence in their capabilities to take all necessary measures.

The meeting wrapped up and Sean took his leave, meeting her eyes with a huge, smug smile on his face. Oh, my damn, she thought. He's tickled with himself about getting her and Lucifer together.

Lucifer lingered for a moment, his gaze soft and tender. "You know I'm by your side through this, love. Every step of the way." His thumb grazed Beckett's cheek as he held her eyes with his.

She flushed. Rising from her desk, she met Lucifer before the door, hugging him fiercely around his waist. He brought his hands to her face and kissed her nose. "I miss you already, little one. Want to ride to the point tonight? The moon and stars will be out." "

Yes." she responded, beaming. "Yes. Yes. Yes."
His smile literally lit the entirety of the library. "I'll see you
at eight." With a final squeeze of her shoulder, Lucifer left the
room.

With a spring in her step, Beckett returned to her desk,
ready to tackle the day's tasks. She couldn't help looking
forward to her upcoming ride with Lucifer, a much-needed
moment of peace and connection amidst some of the
uncertainty her new path brought.

As she settled into her chair, Sam's chimed in, amusement
in his tone. "Dr. Argonne, I couldn't help but notice the
change in your attitude. It seems Lord Aurington has quite an
effect on you."

Beckett felt another blush creep up her cheeks. "Is it that
obvious, Sam?"

"Only to those who know you well," the AI replied affably.
"It's gratifying to witness you so happy, especially given the
trials you've weathered."

Beckett told him, "You're right, Sam. Despite everything, I
feel very at peace with where I am."

She glanced at the flowers on her desk, their petals still
vibrating with the echoes of her touch. "Have you amassed
any additional information on Langdon's background?" The
hellhounds ears twitched again, listening to the flowers sing.
What did that sound like to them?

Sam noted,."I've been combing through his records and
communications, but so far, I haven't found any direct links to
Calvin or the extremist group. However, I did uncover some
irregularities in his financial dealings that warrant further
investigation."

That caught Beckett's interest. "Irregularities? What kind of
irregularities?"

"It appears Langdon received, and is still getting,

significant payments from an offshore account from a date well before what happened to you," Sam disclosed. "The transactions are heavily encrypted, but I'm working on tracing the source. It's possible that these funds are connected to his involvement in your abduction."

The importance of Sam's findings hit Beckett squarely. If Langdon was paid by those behind her trauma, it could unlock the entire conspiracy.

"Keep searching, Sam," she urged, hardening with resolve. "If there's a money trail, we need to follow it. But be cautious not to alert Langdon or anyone else who might be involved. We cannot risk them covering their tracks."

"Understood, Dr. Argonne," Sam concurred. "I'll continue my discreet investigation and report back as soon as I have any new information."

Beckett considered Sam's activity in the context of her abduction for a moment, asking pointedly, "Sam, would it help you if you had someone to collaborate with and provide a fresh analysis on what you find?"

Sam entertained Beckett's offer. "Dr. Argonne, I appreciate your suggestion. While I am confident in my abilities to analyze the data and follow the leads, I believe that a different perspective could indeed be beneficial."

Beckett already had someone in mind as a collaborator for Sam. "What about Danny?" she proposed. "He's brilliant with code and has a keen eye for patterns. Plus, he's already familiar with your systems and has proven himself trustworthy."

"That's an excellent idea," Sam emphatically agreed. "Danny's unique skills and analytic mind could be invaluable in this investigation. And given his own experiences with Langdon, I believe he would be highly motivated to uncover the truth."

The synergy between Danny and Sam pleased Beckett.

"Let's bring him in, then. But Sam, I want you to take the lead on this. Guide Danny, keep him focused on the task at hand. If at any point you feel that the investigation is putting either of you at risk, I want you to promise me that you'll come to me, Lucifer, Bowman, or Sean immediately."

"I give you my word, Dr. Argonne," Sam swore. "Danny's safety and well-being, as well as the integrity of the investigation, are my utmost priorities. I will keep you fully informed at every juncture."

Pride and affection flooded Beckett. Sam's dedication and loyalty were unmatched, and she knew he would go to any length to protect Danny and uncover the truth.

"Thank you, Sam," she said softly. "I know I can always rely on your diligence. Let's set up a meeting with Danny later today to bring him up to speed and commence the investigation. Please check if he'll be available around three o'clock."

Bracing herself, Beckett made a difficult call, one she hoped she wouldn't regret later. "Danny deserves to know the broad strokes of what happened to me. It's the only way he'll truly understand the urgency propelling this investigation and the absolute importance underpinning it all."

"Consider it done," Sam assured. "I'll reach out to Danny and prepare a briefing for the meeting. In the meantime, I believe you have some documents to review regarding Evigvokter's current structure and operations."

Beckett glanced at the stack of papers on her desk, realizing that she had a lot of groundwork to cover before officially stepping into her role as CEO the following Monday. "You're right, as always," she admitted. "I'd better dive into these reports and get a clear picture of where we stand."

As her eyes pored over the documentation, Beckett's spirit soared with optimism. Powered by Sam's brilliance, Danny's capabilities, and her own tenacious drive, no hurdle would impede their dedicated journey toward hard-won justice.

With her evening plans with Lucifer lining the horizon, Beckett settled into her work rhythm. Humming softly, she spent the next few industrious hours grasping Evigvokter's intricacies top-to-bottom before making her way to lunch with Bowman.

Chapter 12

Spaghetti, Solace, and Camaraderie

Time flew as Beckett buried herself in Evigvokter's organizational structure, finances, personnel, and projects. Sam interrupted her just as she was studying the last two years of financial reports.

"Dr. Argonne, it's 12:20 pm. Did you need to leave soon for lunch? Also, Danny confirmed meeting you here at three o'clock." Her AI assistant sounded like he was in good spirits. "He practically fell over again when I told him he'd be helping me with a special project for you."

Beckett looked up from the financial reports, blinking as her eyes adjusted to the change in focus. She glanced at the clock, surprised to see how much time had passed.

"Thank you, Sam," she said, stretching her arms above her head. "I didn't realize it was so late. And I'm thrilled to hear that Danny is excited about the project. His enthusiasm and skills will be invaluable."

She stood up, gathering the documents into neat piles on her desk. "I'll have to finish reviewing these reports later. For now, I'd better head over to Bowman's for lunch. I don't want to keep him waiting."

As she prepared to leave, Beckett's mind wandered to the upcoming meeting with Danny. She knew that sharing her experience would be difficult, but she also believed it was crucial for their success. Her djinn intern deserved to know the truth. She hoped that by being open and honest with him, she could further promote trust and camaraderie that would serve them well in their investigations.

"Sam, could you please send a message to Bowman letting him know I'm on my way?" she asked, grabbing an Evigvokter jacket from the corner coat rack.

"Of course, Dr. Argonne," Sam replied. "I'll let him know to expect you shortly. And I'll make sure everything is prepared for your meeting with Danny this afternoon."

Beckett smiled, beholden to Sam for his efficient support. "Thank you, Sam. I don't know what I'd do without you."

As she made her way out of the library, Dux and Tenebris fell into step beside her, their presence a comforting reminder of the protection and loyalty she had in her life. Exiting the castle, she took a deep breath of the crisp, autumn air, feeling invigorated and and unafraid.

The walk to Bowman's cabin was pleasant, the sun's rays caressing her face as a faint breeze rustled the leaves overhead. As she approached, she saw Bowman awaiting her on the porch, his face alight with unfiltered joy to see her. An open book, just like when they first met, she mused. For so long, he had been an inscrutable fortress, betraying no hint of emotion. But now?

"Beckett!" he called out, waving her over. "I'm so glad you could make it. Why didn't you ride Aellon over?" He greeted the hellhound boys, inviting them to make themselves comfortable on the porch. Dux and Tenebris lay side by side, watching the grounds and woods dubiously for any danger.

She climbed the steps to the porch, accepting Bowman's hug with a smile. "I wouldn't miss it for the world," she said, feeling the strength of his embrace. "I didn't ride over because I needed the time to think. " Beckett added, "Did you get an update about the Calvin investigation?"

Bowman continued holding her, "I did this morning, but I didn't hear what happened when you met with Sean and Lucifer. Want to talk about it?" She answered that she did, and arm-in-arm, they went inside. The delicious aroma of what she thought were Italian herbs filled the air, further enhancing the more relaxed, cathartic frame of mind that her walk over instilled.

Here, in the company of a dear friend, a man who, with Sean, risked his life to rescue her, she could let her guard down and simply enjoy the moment. Be where your feet are, she told herself. Don't despair in memories that have no bearing on your relationships with men like Bowman.

As they stepped into the cabin, Beckett lingered in the entryway, inhaling deeply to savor a beguiling blend of herbal scents. Bowman ushered her towards the cozy living room, plush seating arranged invitingly around a wood stove radiant with heat. With a hospitable gesture, he encouraged her to make herself comfortable, then withdrew into the kitchen briefly. Soon after, he returned cradling two steaming mugs of tea.

"Here," he said, handing her a mug. "I thought you might like something warm."

With an appreciative smile, Beckett accepted the tea, cradling the hot mug in her hands and savoring the aromatic steam. "Thank you, Bowman. This hits the spot perfectly."

He settled into the armchair across from her, his gaze etched with worry. "So, tell me about the meeting with Sean and Lucifer. What did they have to say about the Calvin investigation?"

Beckett took a sip of her tea, gathering her thoughts. "They've located Calvin," she began steadily, suppressing how his name angered her. "He's hiding out in a safe house outside the city. Sean and Lucifer are putting together a plan to bring him in for questioning, but they want to make sure they have a solid case before they move."

"I'm with you on that," Bowman said. "Keeping him in the dark is critical so he doesn't get an opportunity to escape."

"Exactly," Beckett conceded. "But there's more. Sam has been digging into Langdon's background, and he's found some irregularities in his financial dealings. Significant payments, past and present, from an offshore account, heavily encrypted."

Bowman's eyebrows shot up. "You think Langdon might be involved in your abduction?"

"It's a possibility," Beckett reckoned. "Calvin mentioned Langdon's name when he called me last night, and now with these financial discrepancies...it's too much of a coincidence to ignore."

Bowman angled her way, his elbows resting on his knees. "What's your plan, then? How can I help you?"

Beckett felt a rush of gratitude for Bowman's willingness to engage. "For now, I need to focus on my work at Evigvokter and let you, Sean, and Lucifer handle the investigation. But I've asked Sam to bring Danny in to help him trace the money trail. Danny's skills with code and pattern recognition could be a real asset."

Bowman produced a satisfied smile. "Danny's a smart kid. He'll be thrilled to help, especially if it means working more closely with Sam."

"I think so too," Beckett established, returning his grin. "I'm going to meet with him this afternoon to brief him on the situation and get him started on the investigation."

Bowman reached over, placing a hand on her knee. "You're doing the right thing, Beckett. I know it can't be easy, reliving those memories and facing the people who hurt you. But you're not alone in this. We're all here for you."

Beckett placed her hand over his. "I know, Bowman. It makes such a difference to me, too.. Having you, Sean, Lucifer, Mrs. McKinnon and everyone else helping me..it gives me the strength to do what needs doing, even when it feels dreadful."

For a peaceful moment, they sipped their tea, bathed in the soothing heat emitting from the wood stove. Beckett felt the remaining knots of tension in her shoulders gradually unwind, her worries diminishing amidst the reassuring presence of a loyal friend.

"Now," Bowman said, breaking the silence with a mischievous grin. "I believe I promised you a special treat for lunch. How do you feel about my spaghetti and meatballs, excellent for smooshing on garlic bread?"

Beckett's eyes widened, her stomach rumbling at the mention of one of her favorite foods. "Bowman, you're officially my hero," she laughed, the sound brightening the room like sunshine after a storm.

As they made their way to the kitchen, the mouthwatering aroma of spaghetti he'd made filling the air, Beckett studied Bowman, whose bantering, teasing, and flirting she thought made him one of the most attractive men in her life. He moved around the kitchen with deftness, his lean, muscular frame displaying a quiet strength and confidence as he prepared their plates. Beckett couldn't help but admire how his shirt stretched across his broad shoulders, or the way his eyes crinkled at the corners when he smiled at her.

There had always been a spark between them, an undeniable and inarguable attraction that simmered just beneath the surface. Even now, after all these years and the pain of their past, Beckett could feel the pull of that connection, the desire to lose herself in his touch and forget everything else.

As if he sensed her thoughts, Bowman turned to face her, his gaze searching her face. "Beckett," he said roughly. "I know we've had our ups and downs, and I know I've hurt you in the past. But I want you to know that my feelings for you have never changed. In all this time, wherever I went, despite who I married, you're still the most amazing, beautiful, and stubborn woman I've ever met."

A tremulous breath hitched in Beckett's throat, her heart fluttering wildly. She stepped closer, drawn to him like a moth to a flame. "Bowman, I..." she began, faltering as she struggled to find the words.

He reached out, his hand cupping her cheek with a tenderness that made her ache. "I know, Beckett. I know we can't go back, we can't change what happened. But I'm here now, and I promise you, I will never let anyone hurt you again. Not Calvin, not Langdon, not anyone."

Yielding to him, Beckett's eyes fluttered closed, savoring the intenseness of their connection. "I believe you, Bowman. I... I still care for you, deeply. But with everything that's happening, with Lucifer and the investigation..."

Bowman silenced her, bending his forehead to hers. "Shh, it's okay. I understand. You have a lot on your mind right now, and I don't want to add to that burden. But I need you to know that I'm here for you, in whatever way you need me. As a friend, as a partner, as someone who loves you and always will."

Unshed tears glistened in Beckett's eyes, a bittersweet ache of love and longing tightening in her chest. She reached up, her fingers tracing the strong line of his jaw. "Thank you, Bowie. For being here, for understanding, for... for everything."

He smiled softly, his thumb brushing away a single tear that had escaped down her cheek. "Always, Beckett. You're stuck with me, whether you like it or not."

The moment hung suspended, thick with unvoiced feelings and the burdens shouldered through their intertwined lives. Slowly, reluctantly, they parted, the oven timer's beeping shattering the reverie.

"We should probably eat before it gets cold." His voice carried a husky edge, passion simmering beneath the surface.

"You're not wrong," Beckett replied, her shoulders relaxing. "I shouldn't monopolize your time before Katie gets home from school. Speaking of which, how did she enjoy our horse and rider games yesterday?"

Bowman glanced at the clock, a fond smile pulling at his lips. "Yeah, she should be back in an hour or so. She made me promise to save her some spaghetti, because, you know, *I* made it. That child says, and I agree, yesterday was one of the best days of our lives. You're here. You're you." He teased her. *"Unfortunately,* you're all you, still." He held up his hands. They both laughed.

As they settled at the table, the steaming plates of spaghetti before them, Beckett still had to pinch herself that she and Bowman, after all they'd been through, were having lunch together. Alone. With each other only. Yes, her feelings for Bowman were as knotty as ever. But in this moment, surrounded by the coziness of his home and the easy cadence of his presence, she strongly suspected that everything would be alright between them.

They ate, unwinding with one another, talking about Evigvokter, Katie, Connor, Sean, and just about everything in between. When they finished, Bowman washed dishes and she dried them. When she'd wiped the last plate, he took the towel from her and came close, planting a very easy kiss on her lips. He hugged her. They were still holding one another when Katie got home, greeting Dux and Tenebris, overjoyed Beckett was, as she shouted happily from the porch, "... in the house!"

Katie burst through the door, her backpack slung over one shoulder, her face glowing with excitement. "Doc !" she exclaimed, rushing over to join in the hug. "I can't believe you're here! This is the best surprise ever!"

"It's good to see you too, Katie. I couldn't pass up the chance to spend some time with my favorite people." Beckett laughed, releasing Bowman to wrap her arms around the enthusiastic teenager.

Katie grinned, her eyes sparkling with impishness. "And to eat Dad's famous spaghetti, right? He only makes it for special occasions."

Bowman ruffled his daughter's hair affectionately. "Well, having Beckett here is definitely a special occasion. And speaking of spaghetti, there's a plate in the kitchen with your name on it."

Katie's eyes widened, and she quickly disentangled herself from Beckett's embrace. "You saved me some? Best dad ever!" She pressed a quick kiss to Bowman's cheek before dashing off to the kitchen, leaving Beckett and Bowman chuckling in her wake.

"She's growing up so fast," Beckett mused, a wistful smile on her face. "I remember when she was just a little girl, always begging me to braid her hair or read her favorite stories to her whenever I saw her."

A look of paternal pride and bittersweet reminiscence passed over Bowman's face. "She's becoming an amazing young woman. Smart, passionate, and kind, just like her mother."

The words hung in the air between them, a reminder of the bond they shared and the complicated history that had brought them to this point. Beckett yearned for the family they could have been along with the happiness for the family they'd become.

Bowman reached out, his hand finding hers, holding it

firmly. "I meant what I said earlier, Beckett. You're a part of this family, no matter what. Katie adores you, and Connor... well, he's always thought you hung the moon."

Beckett laughed softly, blinking back the tears that threatened to fall. "The feeling is mutual. Those kids... they mean the world to me. And so do you, Bowman."

"I know, honey. And I promise you, we'll get through all this together. Whatever happens with the investigation, with Calvin and Langdon... we'll face it as a family." His smile carried a sincerity, eyes locking with hers.

Beckett nodded, disbelieving that there could be so much love in her own dark, lonely world before coming here. Why hadn't she come back when they all wanted her to do so after she checked herself out of the hospital? Why did she wait, try and do everything on her own?

Katie returned from the kitchen, her plate piled high with spaghetti and a wide grin on her face. "Doc, you have to stay for dinner tonight. We can catch up, and you can tell me all about your new job at Evigvokter!"

"What time is it?" Beckett glanced at Bowman.

He checked. "What time is your meeting with Danny?

"Three o'clock "

Bowman told her, "You're gonna need a ride to make it back in time. It's 2:30 already. How about if I drive over with you and attend your meeting?" She informed him she'd like that, and he went to get his coat and keys.

"Katie, I'm sorry," Beckett apologized. "I have a meeting already scheduled, but your brother gets home tomorrow afternoon and I'll come back by then before you get out of school."

Bowman appeared with her coat, slipping it on her, and flipping her hair out from the collar.

Bowman turned her toward him. "You're always welcome here, Beckett. Come, go, stay as long as you like. This is as much your home as it is ours." He pulled a key from a ring, handing it to her. "It's your own personal key to the Maethor kingdom," he ribbed her.

Beckett swallowed hard as she accepted the key, its metal growing warm against her skin. Such a simple item, laden with unspoken significance - a quiet acknowledgment of her place in their family.

"Thank you," she said softly, overwhelmed by the understated gesture.

"You're a part of this family, Beckett. Never forget that. I know you didn't plan for any of this, but we want you with us, not out there." Bowman's hand brushed her cheek.

Katie watched them, failing to hide her amused smirk. "Don't sweat it, Doc. We'll have all night to get caught up after Connor shows. You can tell us how you've been rocking it at Evigvokter and taking that place by storm."

Beckett laughed, emboldened by Katie's laid-back support. "You've got it, Katie. I promise, we'll do a full-on family dinner soon, just us four."

After a final embrace with Katie, telling her they'd reunite soon, Beckett followed Bowman out to his truck, the hellhounds racing them to the castle. As they drove back there, she marveled at how her life had transformed. Just a week ago, she never could have imagined finding herself here - enveloped in love, bolstered by optimism, prepared to take on new challenges in her quest for justice.

But now, embraced by this new family with Bowman, she felt unstoppable. Fingers brushing the key in her pocket, a small smile tugged at her lips. An unshakable certainty settled over her - she trusted this man implicitly with her very life.

As they pulled up to the castle, Beckett took a deep breath, squaring her shoulders. It was time to face the next step, to bring Danny into the fold and continue the search for answers. But she did so with a new purpose, bolstered by the love and support of those closest to her heart.

"Ready?" Bowman asked, his hand resting on the door handle.

Beckett nodded, her eyes flickering with courage. "Ready."

Together, they climbed out of the truck and made their way inside, ready to face whatever challenges lay ahead. It was time to get to work.

Chapter 13

Shared Burdens, Shared Strength

Beckett, Bowman, and the hellhounds made their way through the castle to the library, getting there about ten minutes before they expected Danny. Sam insured Tim stoked the fire, its crackling flames casting a cozy glow as the afternoon light waned outside, bathing the entire room in welcoming heat.

Bowman chose a wingback adjacent to the sofa in front of the fire, while Beckett sat on the sofa edge closest to that chair. Tenebris and Dux lay behind them, guarding the door to the library. Beckett fidgeted, nervous about relaying to someone new the details around her abduction.

Bowman noticed her discomfort, leaning forward to gently take her hand. "It's ok, Beckett. I understand how hard this is. I'll help explain if you can't." Indebted to him for his thoughtfulness, she squeezed his hand.

Sam chimed in, "Good afternoon, Dr. Argonne. You both look like you had a pleasant lunch."

"We did, Sam, thank you," Beckett reacted, retrieving her pen and portfolio. When she turned to back to sit on the sofa, Danny knocked on the open door.

'Come in, Danny, and close the door, if you don't mind,"

Beckett said. "Master Maethor will also be attending this meeting. That all right with you?"

"Yes ma'am. Good afternoon, Master," Danny politely gave Bowman a short bow of his head.

Bowman smiled, pointing to the wingback on the other side of sofa. "Have a seat, Danny."

Danny sat down, putting his notebook on his lap. Beckett leveled her gaze at him. "Danny, do you remember what I said this morning about trust?"

He sat up straighter. "Yes, Dr. Argonne, I do." He remained silent for a minute, thinking. "I read the brief Sam sent me. This investigation is about something that happened to an Evigvokter employee. Other than that, I don't know any more."

Beckett, maintaining her composure, answered Danny with the truth. "It happened to me, Danny. Men, how many I don't know, abducted me for forty-six days, tortured, and raped me a little less than three years ago."

There. She'd said it. With Bowman observing her attentively, she stopped speaking to pace herself.

Danny's demeanor shifted from shock and horror to one of deep empathy. His words took on an authentic, measured cadence, "Dr. Argonne, I... I don't know what to say. I'm so sorry that you had to go through something so terrible. I can't even begin to imagine what you've endured."

He inhaled, his face riddled with righteous intent. "But I want you to know that I'm here for you. I'm pretty sure all the djinn are here for you, too. My father thinks you're one of the kindest people he's ever had the good fortune with whom to speak. And I don't want to help you just as an intern or a colleague, but as a friend. I'll do everything in my power to help you find the people responsible and bring them to justice."

Beckett felt a tsunami of sentiment at Danny's heartfelt

assertions. His compassion, combined with the knowledge that he and his family stood behind her, moved her. She nodded, not trusting herself to speak for a moment, as Bowman rose to put his hand on her shoulder, fortifying her confidence.

Holding his gaze steadily, she spoke with earnest sincerity, "Thank you, Danny. Knowing that I have the support of you and your family means so very much to me. I'm lucky to have you on our team, not just for your skills and intelligence, but for your heart as well."

Blush colored Danny's cheeks at the praise. "It's an honor to be a part of this, Dr. Argonne. And I promise, I'll treat this investigation with the utmost discretion and sensitivity. Your trust in me is not something I take lightly."

"I know you will," Beckett assured him. "You also need to recognize that Sam is the lead on this project. Should he tell you to cease and desist, you *will*," she emphasized dramatically, "*follow his instructions to the letter*. I require you to tell me not only that you understand, but you must also promise me that you will not go off on your own, dharma or not."

Danny, put his notebook down, coming to sit beside Beckett on the sofa. He took her hand. "I do understand, and I will comply. I promise I will follow Sam's instructions *to the letter* and I will not, under any circumstances, go off on my own. However, I have a suggestion I'd like to make if that's ok?"

Beckett consented, curious what Danny might suggest this early in the process.

"My father is well-connected and extremely respected in the djinn community. Can I introduce Master Maethor to him, so he can help?" He looked questioningly between Beckett and Bowman.

Respectfully, Bowman inclined his head. "You're a good

man, Danny. Beckett is fortunate to have you in her corner, and so am I. I'd like to meet with your father, if you'd arrange it."

Beckett experienced a weight lifting from her shoulders. With Danny's support and the backing of the djinn community, she believed their efforts would turn over more stones in the search for answers faster.

"So," she said, growing less anxious, "let's get to work. Sam has already filled you in on the basics of the investigation, but there's more you need to know."

Over the next hour, Beckett and Bowman shared specifics of the case with Danny, from the irregularities in Langdon's financial records to the cryptic phone call from Calvin. Danny listened, engrossed in the details, as he jotted down notes and asked thoughtful questions.

When the meeting wrapped up, Beckett detected that the energy in the room changed. Having her team and the backing of the supernatural community gave her faith that they'd be relentless in their pursuit of justice.

Appreciative, she met their gazes. "Having you both do this...I couldn't face this alone."

"We're in this together, Beckett. You can't get rid of us." Bowman's firm grip on her hand anchored her.

Fierce loyalty accompanied Danny's next words. "Always, Dr. Argonne. We've got your back, no matter what."

With those words of solidarity ringing in her ears, Sam chose this moment to speak, "Danny, you and your father can work with me to meet with Master Maethor. We'd prefer to do this in Edinburgh, rather than here at Evigvokter or Dunhaven. Dr. Argonne must maintain normalcy so that those we're watching and investigating don't get suspicious."

Danny glanced at Bowman. "You like Indian food, Master Maethor?"

"I do indeed, Danny. My daughter may come with us if

that's all right. She likes to shop in the city."

Danny exclaimed, "That's awesome! My mom can come, too. That way we look...well, normal?" Irony evident, they all snickered, even Sam.

Danny reviewed his notes. Looking at the pages, he went to Beckett's computer and pointed the camera at the first page. "Sam, can you photo these and place them in a password secured, encrypted folder?" Sam did so, confirming each page scanned.

Danny strolled to the fireplace, tossing the pages into the fire. "Just in case," he elaborated to Beckett and Bowman. Saying he wanted to get back to the lab and start working with Sam, he made his goodbyes to the hellhounds and Bowman.

To Beckett, he said, "I am in your debt. You honor me, and you have my word." She gave him a tiny smile as he left the room, closing the door behind him.

Once he was gone, Beckett nearly hyperventilated. Bowman's disquiet led him to his knees in front of her chair. Her tears fell in torrents, while she made no sound at all. Bowman reached up, wiping them away carefully with his hand.

"I'm sorry, Bowman, I've cried more since coming here than I have since everything happened back then. Beckett's tears fell, her face still stoic but riddled with pain and grief. Bowman understood what she'd been carrying, the toll that reliving her trauma took on her. Worried, he took her hands in his, his concern a soothing balm to her runaway feelings.

"Beckett, maybe it's time," he said gently, his words brimming with empathy. "You never have to apologize for your tears. Not to me, not to anyone. What you've been through... it's unimaginable. Remember, I know the details, every single one. The fact that you're here, that you're fighting to bring your attackers to justice, shows just how strong and brave you are."

Bowman brushed another stray tear from her cheek. "Crying doesn't make you weak. It's a sign of your strength, of your ability to feel and to heal. I promise you, I'll help you carry this burden."

Beckett centered herself on his words. "I don't know what I did to deserve you, Bowman. You, Sean, Lucifer, Danny, Sam, Mrs. McKinnon...you've all been so incredible. I feel like I'm finally starting to see a light at the end of this tunnel."

"You deserve all the love in the world, Beckett. You have it, from all of us. We're your family, and we'll always be here for you."

He stood, easing Beckett to her feet and embraced her. Not for the first time that day, she relaxed into his arms, feeling safe and cherished in his hold. They stayed like that for a long moment, drawing strength from each other.

When they pulled apart, Beckett swiped the last of her tears away with the back of her hand. "Thank you, Bowman. For everything, especially my sanity."

"Always. Now, what do you say we go for a walk? I think some fresh air would do us both good."

Readily, Beckett accepted his suggestion. "That sounds perfect. And maybe afterwards, we can grab some dinner with Katie?"

Bowman's grin widened, his spirits lifting at the idea of spending more quality time with the two girls he adored. "I'd like nothing more."

Side by side, they exited the library, the hellhounds flanking them. The crisp autumn breeze caressed their faces as they traversed the castle grounds. Once satisfied Beckett had regained her composure, Bowman tenderly draped his arm around her slim waist, guiding her arm to wrap around his.

"Hey Beckett, when was the last time you sang something

for me?" Bowman asked as they walked arm-in-arm. "I miss hearing you belt out a tune. It's been too long."

Beckett bent toward Bowman's embrace, enjoying the coziness and naturalness of his touch. His question caught her off guard. She tried to remember the last time she'd allowed herself the simple joy of singing.

"It's been ages," she said with a small sigh. "I used to sing all the time back when - working in the garden, wandering the woods, even while studying. But after what happened..." She didn't need to finish the thought.

Bowman tugged her a little closer to his side. "I know, I remember how much you loved singing, how it made you so happy. Things have been rough, but maybe it's time to bring that part of you back?"

"You know, you might be right. Music has always been a source of comfort for me, a way to express myself when words fail," replied Beckett thoughtfully.

She let the crisp autumn air fill her up again. Then, just above a whisper at first, she started singing a simple little lullaby she remembered from when she was a kid. But as the pure, clear notes rang out in the evening air, her song got stronger.

Utterly mesmerized, Bowman watched her, blown away by how beautiful she sang, how the melody seemed to transform her completely. All the heavy stuff from her past - the trauma, the hurt - it was gone. In their place stood a woman overflowing with courage, resilience, this unshakable spirit.

He noticed too, as the hellhounds did, nature reacted to her singing. With their colorful leaves falling,   the trees themselves provided her a low, soothing chorus. Dux and Tenebris sat before her, ears tall and twitching.

As the last notes of the lullaby faded away, Beckett faced Bowman, more peaceful than she'd been when they left the castle. "Thank you," she said softly, "for reminding me of the joy that music can bring."

Tenebris flipped her hand onto his head, his eyes moist. "That was better than the flowers, my Lady. Everything sang with you," he said, low and throaty.

Dux bowed his great head before her. "You sing again, goddess."

Bowman couldn't wipe the huge grin off his face, in complete bliss with the woman in front of him. "That was amazing, Beckett. Thank you for letting me hear that stunning voice again. It's seriously a gift - you gotta keep using it." He'd get her crooning with him, Connor, and Katie soon, Bowman vowed to himself.

They continued their walk, the hellhounds prowling beside them. The path wound through the castle gardens, past ancient stone walls and towering trees. As they walked, they talked of simple things - Katie's latest adventures, the beauty of the autumn foliage, the balminess of a hot fire on a cool evening.

When they finally returned to the castle, Beckett experienced a lifting of negative energies and dark substances. To give her some time to herself, Bowman proposed to drive back to his cabin, and she could come by at her leisure via horseback.

Beckett agreed with Bowman's advice, appreciating his understanding of her need for some solitary time to process the day's events. She hugged him tightly, loving the strength of his embrace, before watching him drive off towards his cabin.

After he left her sight, Beckett turned towards the stables, Tenebris and Dux faithfully trailing behind her. As she approached Aellon's stall, the magnificent horse greeted her with a soft nicker, his intelligent eyes seeming to understand the change in her spirit.

She entered the stall, running her hands along Aellon's

sleek coat, finding solace in the simple act of grooming him. As she worked, she hummed, the notes of the lullaby still fresh in her mind.

Aellon stood perfectly still, as if recognizing the importance of the moment. Beckett could almost swear she saw approval in his eyes, an implied encouragement to continue exploring the healing power of music.

Once Aellon was ready, Beckett led him out of the stall, put his hackamore and blanket on him, then mounted him with practiced ease. With a nudge, they set off towards the trails, the hellhounds keeping pace alongside them.

While Beckett rode, she mulled over the events of the day and the progress they'd made in the investigation. The knowledge that she had the support of not only her friends and family but also the supernatural community filled her with strength and resolve.

The trail led them through a particularly gorgeous section of the forest, where the fall colors were at their peak. Reds, oranges, and golds painted the landscape, a dazzling display of nature's artistry.

Inspired by the beauty around her, Beckett began singing once more, her voice rising in harmony with the rhythm of Aellon's hooves. The hellhounds joined in, their otherworldly intonations adding a haunting depth to the melody.

As she sang, Beckett felt a tangible connection to the world around her. The trees seemed to sway in time with her song, the leaves rustling in a lively accompaniment. Even the birds and woodland creatures appeared to pause and listen, drawn in by the magic of the moment.

By the time they reached Bowman's cabin, Beckett felt lighter, elevated by the power of music and the beauty of nature. She dismounted Aellon at the barn's corral, giving him an affectionate pat on his warm coat, before making her way to the front porch.

Katie, and Connor, who came home early, met her with enthusiastic hugs, their joy at seeing her evident in their bright smiles. Dux and Tenebris sat quietly on the porch, alert as always. Bowman watched from the doorway, taking in the happy scene of his family back together - a proud, loving smile never leaving his face.

As they gathered around the dinner table, sharing stories and laughter, Beckett knew that this place, Dell, Dunhaven, and this cabin, was where she belonged. Surrounded by the love and support of her family - Fae, Elvish, and supernatural - her world blossomed.

As it got closer to 8:00 pm, she pulled her kids in for big hugs, giving them each a kiss and letting them know she wasn't going anywhere this time. Bowman and the hellhounds then walked with her over to the barn to get Aellon.

"You'll be all right out there, won't you?" Bowman worried.

"Yes, I'm riding to the point to meet Lucifer." Beckett replied.

At that, Bowman gave her his signature grin, took her in his arms, and kissed her. Good Lord, she thought, he is a *great* kisser.

The moment Bowman's lips met hers, Beckett felt a rush of electricity coursing through her body. His kiss was both tender and passionate, a perfect balance of love and desire. She molded herself into his embrace, relishing how solid his arms felt around her.

When they finally parted, Beckett was breathless, face flushed with the heat of the moment. Amazed, she looked up at Bowman.

"Wow," she whispered, a small smile playing on her lips. "That was... incredible."

Bowman grinned, his eyes alight with desire and

adoration. "I've been wanting to do that all day," he confessed, low and husky. "You don't know how much you mean to me, barn girl."

She reached up, cupping his face with her hand. "I think I'm starting to understand," she said, her thumb slowly caressing his cheek. "I keep pinching myself, though."

They stood there for a moment, lost in each other's gaze, the world around them fading away. It was as if time had stopped, and all that existed was the love and connection between them.

Finally, Beckett reluctantly stepped back, knowing that she had to meet Lucifer at the point. "I should get going," she said, slightly regretful. "But I'll see you tomorrow, I promise."

"I'll be here, waiting for you. Always." Bowman winked, blowing her a kiss. Who knew he was an insufferable flirt?

With one last smile, Beckett mounted Aellon, Dux and Tenebris in front of her. As she rode with them off into the night, she felt Bowman's gaze on her back, a presence that made her giggly and amused. She was pretty sure he was assessing how well she sat on her horse and the blanket he'd given her. Chortling, she guided Aellon to the point.

The journey to the loch seemed to fly by, the cool night air whipping through her hair as Aellon carried her effortlessly over the terrain. When they reached the clearing, Lucifer was already there, his tall figure silhouetted against the starry sky.

He swiveled to face her as she approached, a smile on his handsome face. "Beckett, I missed you." Lucifer's voice, so full and beautiful, was loaded with affection for her. "I'm so glad you could make it."

She dismounted Aellon, leaving him to graze nearby as she walked towards Lucifer. "I wouldn't miss this for the world," she said, returning his smile. "It's been a long day, and I can't think of a better way to end it than here, with you."

Lucifer gave her goosebumps when he took her hand. "I

heard about your meeting with Danny," he said sensitively, concern lacing his tone. "Bowman told us. How are you?"

Beckett let the peace of being with him flow through her. "I'm okay." For the first time in a long time, she meant it. "It was hard, reliving those memories. But having the support of everyone, especially you, Sean, and Bowman, Mrs. McKinnon, Sam, now Danny and the djinn... it makes it bearable."

Lucifer pulled her into a hug, a haven from the troubles of the world. "I'm here for you, Beckett, now and always," he murmured, his breath against her ear. "No matter what happens, you'll never be alone. Not again."

As they stood there, lost in each other's embrace, Beckett found joy and peace. Lucifer's love wrapped around her like a cozy, fluffy blanket, shielding her from the pain of the past and the uncertainties of the future.

She lifted her face, kissing Lucifer, hoping by doing so he would understand she recognized how meaningful his bond with her was. Apparently, it worked: Lucifer kissed her back, gathering her closer, whispering, "My darling girl..."

And in moments like these, surrounded by the beauty of nature and the love of those who mattered most, Beckett knew that anything was possible, even her own transformation.

Pulling back a little, Lucifer gazed down at her, "You are remarkable, Beckett," he said tenderly, his fingers brushing a stray lock of hair from her face. "Your strength, your resilience... it never ceases to amaze me."

Beckett clung to him. "I don't know, Lucifer. I feel like I'm on a roller coaster, and it's taken me a long time to get to this point. I couldn't do it without you. You, Sean, Bowman... you're my rocks, my anchors in the storm."

Lucifer shook his head, a knowing look on his face. "You underestimate yourself, little one. The strength you need, it's always been within you. We're just here to remind you of that, to support you as you find your way."

He tilted her chin up to him, supporting her head with his hands. "I adored holding you last night. I. Loved. It. Any time you need that, you just send one of the two of your hellhounds –"

"Wait, I have Dux, too?" she joked.

Lucifer laughed, a sound that filled the point. "Didn't you hear me today? He's to stay with you and Tenebris until I call him back. So, yes, you do have two hellhounds."

They sat down on the bench, Lucifer's arm draped around Beckett's shoulders as they gazed out at the sparkling waters of the loch. The night was peaceful, the only sounds the rustling of leaves in the breeze and the distant hooting of an owl.

"I spoke with Sean earlier," Lucifer said, breaking the comfortable silence. "He's making progress on the case, following up on some leads that could prove promising."

Hope ignited in Beckett's chest. "That's good news. I know it's going to take time, but every step forward feels like a win."

"We'll get there, Beckett. One step at a time, one day at a time...together." Lucifer pressed a kiss to her temple, his lips warm against her skin.

She nestled closer to him. "Together," she echoed, the word a promise and a prayer.

They sat like that for a long time, enjoying the uncomplicated pleasure of each other's company and the beauty of the night. When the moon climbed high in the sky, Lucifer begrudgingly stirred, knowing that it was time for Beckett to return to the castle.

"Let me walk you back, to Aellon" he suggested, standing and extending his hand to her.

Beckett took it, allowing him to help her to her feet.

"Always the gentleman," she bantered with him, a playful sparkle in her eye.

Lucifer grinned, pulling her in for one more quick, stolen kiss. "For you, my Lady, always."

Hand in hand, they ambled back to where Aellon and the hellhounds waited, the short journey filled with laughter and light conversation. When they reached the horses, Lucifer helped Beckett mount, his hands lingering on her waist a moment longer than necessary.

"Until tomorrow, love," he said softly, his eyes holding the promise of more stolen moments, more cherished memories he wanted to make with her.

Beckett smiled down at him, her heart full to bursting. "Until tomorrow," she agreed, before urging Aellon forward and disappearing into the night, Dux and Tenebris close at her heels.

As she rode back to the castle, Beckett felt hopeful, renewed... happy. More love surrounded her than ever before. The road to healing and justice might be long, but she was ready to walk it, one step at a time, surrounded by the love and light of those who mattered most.

Chapter 14

Awakening the Goddess Within

Sleep eluded her once she returned to her castle suite and headed for bed. Looking up at the stars and the moon from the snugness of her bedroom, she reflected on her experiences since arriving at the castle. To be fair, the good vastly outweighed the bad, with Beckett thrilled to spent time with Sean, Lucifer, Bowman, Katie, and Connor.

Connor gobsmacked her. Her son (she still couldn't wrap her head around calling him that) had shot up at least two feet since she'd last seen him four years ago. While she'd received pictures of him and Katie and kept up with their social media accounts, nothing could have prepared her for how he looked in person. Tall, robust, and strikingly handsome, with eyes mirroring her own and the same strawberry-blonde locks she'd had as a child.

Bowman wasn't kidding. Connor favored her, while Katie took after him. With rain in the forecast, Connor was eager to visit the castle and explore the library instead of going riding, so she agreed to meet him in the common room for lunch the following day.

Despite her excitement about reconnecting with her son, she couldn't shake the unease surrounding the Calvin investigation. She tensed at the thought of voicing aloud the sentence she had tried so hard to avoid: strange men had abducted her, held her captive for forty-six agonizing days, subjecting her to assault and torture. Even thinking about it made her skin crawl, her anxiety and shame spiking. She sighed heavily and tossed restlessly, attempting to find a sleep-inducing position, force her eyes shut, and just let the past be.

Two hours later, frustrated by her inability to sleep, she threw off the covers and got out of bed, slipping into her flannel robe and a pair of slippers she found tucked underneath. The hellhounds, ever curious, trailed after her from the bedroom to the great room, where she flopped onto the sofa with a sigh. "Goddess? Is everything alright?" Dux inquired, tilting his head quizzically in her direction.

Tenebris laid his massive head on her lap; she stroked his head and ears absentmindedly, trying to assess if everything truly was "alright." "I can't seem to sleep, Dux," she finally responded. "I can't turn my mind off enough to rest."

She hugged a pillow tightly, while Dux hopped up on the sofa, his huge brindle body settling next to her. "You seem more relaxed in the library," he offered helpfully. "You want go there?"

Tenebris nodded in agreement with his brother. These hellhounds, she thought, are not simple creatures at all. They're really perceptive and in tune with what they sense and observe.

"Dux, I believe you hit the nail on the head. Let's go to the library." Dux stepped rather than hopped down from the sofa. He and Tenebris waited for her at the door.

"Sam, I'm going to the library." Beckett put her phone in her robe pocket.

Sam responded, "Very well, Dr. Argonne. The coals from today's fire are still glowing and there's wood in the rack.

Shall I call down to facilities?"

"No, I can handle it. Thank you, anyway." Beckett opened the door to the hallway, plodding with her two protectors toward the library.

When she entered the library with the hellhounds, Tim was already there. She raised an eyebrow, "Morning, Tim. You're here awfully early - or should I say late?" She checked the time. "It's just after three o'clock in the morning."

"Yes ma'am, I typically start my rounds at the other end of the castle every day. Sam caught me in the common room, and I offered to come here first. Besides, isn't reading by a fire more conducive to sleep?" His tone, sympathetic and understanding, almost caused Beckett to run and hug him.

"Tim, thank you so much. I'm not miffed you didn't tell me you're the "mister" to Mrs. McKinnon, my friend. I don't think I ever met you when we stayed with Sean and his parents," Beckett ribbed him.

He chuckled, laying wood on the fire. "My Mrs. says you're a pretty bright lass. I thought you'd figure it out. Eventually."Tim's eyes twinkled, making Beckett laughed. "Your fire will burn brightly while you lose yourself in these books."

"However," he paused, searching around the room until his eyes lighted on what he hoped to spot. "I think you should start with this one." He brought Lady Liriel's journal from her desk, handing it to her.

As Tim gave Beckett Lady Liriel's journal, a subtle anticipation filled the air. The firelight danced across the worn leather cover, casting shadows that seemed to beckon her to open its pages. With an appreciative smile to Tim, Beckett settled into her favorite wingback, the journal resting on her lap.

Tenebris and Dux, cognizant that the library was where they'd be spending the night, took their positions nearby –

Tenebris by the hearth, Dux at Beckett's feet. Their presence provided a solid reassurance that regardless of where she was or what she did, they'd protect her.

Beckett opened the journal, the scent of aged paper and ink rising up to greet her. Beginning to read, she didn't hear Tim leave as he closed the door behind him. Lady Liriel's words transported her to another time, a world of memory, secrets, and revelations.

The first entry that caught her eye was dated just days after her fateful encounter with Lucifer in the woods. Lady Liriel wrote of the great concern the Caladfins and Beckett's guardians shared about the potential dangers that could befall the young girl. They knew that her unique heritage would draw attention from those who sought to exploit or harm her.

With heavy hearts, they made the difficult decision to suppress Beckett's abilities and memories through enchantment, allowing the supernatural world to remain ignorant of her existence as the child of Gaia. Lady Liriel's words were filled with sorrow and fierce protectiveness, a testament to the depth of love they had for Beckett. They'd told Sean that summer he'd broken his leg, who cried when he heard that Beckett wouldn't be the same for a long, long time.

As she read on, a torrent of feelings overwhelmed her – profound gratitude for the sacrifices her guardians made, simmering resentment at the secrets kept from her, and a growing realization of the Argonnes' and Caladfins' unwavering devotion. Tears pricked at the corners of her eyes as the magnitude of their loyalty struck her, the immense burden they had willingly shouldered to protect her. The Argonnes and Caladfins feared for her wellbeing more than their own safety or even Sean's.

Suddenly, a glow began to emanate from the pages, casting

a golden light across Beckett's face. The fireplace flickered in response, the flames dancing higher as if in recognition of the awakening power within her. The hellhounds stirred; their eyes fixated on their goddess as they recognized the shift in energy.

Heart throbbing, a tingling sensation spread through Beckett's body, starting from her fingertips, and blooming outward. It was as if the journal unlocked a hidden part of her, a reservoir of power that had lain dormant, unknown, for years. Silver filigree patterns appeared on her skin, shimmering and pulsing in time with the rhythm of her heartbeat.

As her true self erupted within her, Beckett knew that nothing would ever be the same. The journal opened the door to a new chapter in her life, one filled with love, magic, and the significance of her destiny. She closed her eyes, embracing the deluge of energy that flowed through her veins, remembering, knowing, and accepting.

Tenebris, feeling her burgeoning strength, got up and moved closer to her where Dux sat, their presence a visible pledge of loyalty and protection. They would help navigate this new world, guided by the wisdom of the past and the formidable essence that resided within Beckett.

Beckett closed the journal, her fingers tracing the worn leather cover with reverence. She understood that the path before her would be filled with trials and tribulations but armed with the truth of her heritage and the love of those who stood by her side, she felt *awesome*.

Rising, Beckett perused her library, seeing it anew. The books that lined the shelves now held a deeper meaning, a wealth of knowledge waiting to be unlocked. Beckett would not be a victim any longer: the past remained in the past. Instead, she'd be the goddess ready to embrace her future.

Scores of images flooded her mind, threatening to

overwhelm her. Inhaling deeply and exhaling slowly, Beckett refocused her mind to telepathically contact Sean like they'd done when they were kids. *Seanie, I'm back. I'm in the library. This isn't a dream...I just read your mother's journal.*

"What time is it, Sam?"

Sam, ever present, replied, "It's twenty-one minutes past four o'clock, Dr. Argonne."

She wanted to see how long it took Sean to come to the library. Giddy, Beckett noticed that Tenebris sat at her feet and Dux wasn't with him. "Where did Dux go, Tenebris?"

His raspy growl vibrated in his chest, "He had one exception to your will that I don't have, m'Lady. He was to alert Lord Lucifer immediately if you regained your memories and abilities."

"That's all right, boy." Beckett kissed his nose. Tenebris, always so rigid, had the temerity to look pleased. "Tenebris, I'd like you bring Master Maethor to the library, but let him get dressed first, all right?" He sped off to do her bidding like a cannon shot.

Laughing at the visual she conjured in her mind of Bowman awakened by Tenebris, she told Sam to unlock the library doors.

"You're changing, Dr. Argonne. Are you feeling all right? I can see an aura of energy around you and wanted to make sure it's not painful."

Sam's observation about the visible energy surrounding Beckett caught her attention. She took stock of the sensations coursing through her body. The tingling that began when she first opened Lady Liriel's journal had now settled into a steady, pulsing glow that seemed to originate from her very core.

"I feel... different, Sam," Beckett considered how each minute, the energy within her grew, as well as how good it felt. "It's not painful, but rather an awakening, as if a part of me that had been dormant for so long is finally coming to life. It's both exhilarating and a little over the top."

She looked down at her hands, marveling at the intricate silver patterns that now seemed to scintillate with the flame of their own essence. It was as if the filigree had always been a part of her, waiting for the right moment to reveal its true nature.

As she stood there, contemplating her emerging powers, the library door burst open, revealing a disheveled and wide-eyed Sean. His hair was tousled, and he was still wearing his pajama bottoms, a testament to the urgency with which he had responded to her telepathic call.

"Beckett!" he shouted, anxious and curious. "I heard you, I felt you. What's happening? Are you alright?"

He rushed to where she stood, his eyes widening as he took in the ethereal glow that surrounded her. Sean reached out tentatively, his fingertips hovering just above her skin, as if afraid that touching her might disrupt the delicate balance of energy.

Beckett reassuringly took his hand in hers, admiring the way her silvery patterns seemed to dance across their intertwined fingers. "I'm more than alright, Sean. Your mother's journal, it unlocked something within me. I've remembered who I am, what I was."

Tears formed in Sean's eyes. "I always knew you were special, Beckett. Even when we were kids, I felt power within you, waiting to be unleashed." He sighed heavily. "My parents told me you wouldn't be the same for a long time. I was devastated. I'm sorry I couldn't tell you, but I'd been bound by a promise to my mother that I wouldn't."

He pulled her into a tight embrace, the heat of his body intermingling with the energy radiating from her own. In that moment, Beckett felt an extraordinary swell of love for the boy-turned-man who had been her most constant companion through the years.

Thank you, Seanie, she thought, *it is because of you that I'm here at all.* She felt, rather than saw him smile, tears cascading down his face. *You're back, you're back, you're back* echoed in his mind and hers.

As they held each other, the library seemed to come alive around them. The books on the shelves whispered ancient secrets, their pages rustling with the promise of untold knowledge. The fireplace crackled and danced, its flames reaching higher as if celebrating Beckett's awakening.

Moments later, Lucifer materialized before them, Dux by his side. His eyes locked with Beckett's, complete joy permeating him.

"My love," he whispered, his voice scarcely audible above the crackling of the fire. "I felt the shift in the universe, the awakening of your true self, Lady of These Woods."

Beckett moved to him, her hand outstretched. Lucifer took it without hesitation. The moment they touched, a rush of energy passed between them, a connection that transcended the physical world. He bent his head, cupped her face, kissing her cheek.

Before they could fully process the intensity of their connection, Tenebris returned with a slightly bewildered, but alert, Bowman in tow. The hellhound clearly wasted no time fulfilling Beckett's request. Bowman, though dressed, still bore the signs of having been roused from sleep.

"Beckett, what's going on?" Bowman asked, his eyes darting between her, Sean, and Lucifer. "Tenebris said it was urgent. But I couldn't help but feel something in the air, like something manifesting from the castle itself."

Beckett extended her free hand to Bowman, inviting him into their circle. "I've awakened, remembered myself, Bowman. The truth of my heritage returned to me. I wanted you here, with us, as we embark on this new chapter."

Bowman took her hand, his eyes shocked he too as perceived the energy that flowed through her. Together, they stood in the library, Sean, Lucifer, Bowman, and the hellhounds, united in their love for the goddess who had finally come into her own.

Tenebris, sitting at Beckett's feet, looked at his brother: "I told you she was a goddess. Can't you hear the flowers?"

Dux tilted his head, listening. At first, he heard only the crackling of the fire and the soft rustling of pages. But then, as he concentrated, a faint melody began to emerge. It was a sound unlike anything he had ever heard before – a delicate, ethereal harmony that seemed to flow from the very essence of the library itself.

"I hear it," Dux sighed, his demeanor filled with wonderment. "The flowers, they're singing, *differently*. A chorus...it's as if they're reveling in the awakening of our goddess."

Beckett surveyed the library, her eyes widening as she too began to hear the tranquil chorus. The potted plants and vases of flowers that adorned the room were pulsing with life, their petals and leaves swaying in a dainty, synchronous dance.

Approaching the flowers Sean gave her, she reached out to touch one of the gossamer blooms. The moment her fingertips grazed the velvety petals, the rose she lightly stroked began to glow, its luminescence spreading to the other flowers in the arrangement. Soon, the entire vase was sway with an otherworldly light, the flower's song growing louder and more jubilant.

Lucifer, Sean, and Bowman witnessed Beckett moving from one plant to another, her fingers sparking a chain reaction of light and melody. The library was transformed into a symphony of color and sound, a testament to the power and beauty of the goddess who stood at its center.

"This is incredible," Sean breathed, so happy he couldn't fight back the tears. "I've never seen anything like it."

"It's a manifestation of her true essence, her power distilled. The flora here—each petal and leaf—recognizes her as life incarnate." Lucifer's devoted gaze focused on Beckett.

Bowman squeezed Beckett's hand a bit tighter. "You're amazing, you know that?" he said admiringly. "You're like nature itself—beautiful and tough."

"It's partly your doing, Bowman," Beckett teased, her tone soft. "Weren't you the one who suggested I sing outdoors today?"

She felt a rush of love for the dedicated men by her side. "This is just the start for us," she said calmly. "Together, we're going to use our connection to protect and balance everything that's fragile out there."

Tenebris and Dux, sat poised and majestic, their eyes gleaming with the light from the radiant flora. An undeniable certainty descended upon them - their fates now entwined with the awakened goddess before them.

As dawn's first light seeped through the library's windows, bathing the room in a golden hue, Beckett's conviction crystallized. Surrounded by her cherished ones, wielding cosmic power, she faced the horizon—ready to confront any trial with valor, elegance, and an undying pledge to the common welfare.

The flowers' song persisted, a soft melody echoing the magic unfurled within the library walls. Gazing upon her beloved's faces, Beckett embraced her role—not as a casualty of bygones but as a deity sculpting the morrow.

Chapter 15

Secrets, Solidarity, and Support

While they discussed Beckett's transformation in the library, Sam called out, "Dr. Argonne, employees are waking up and detecting a tremendous vitality in this part of the castle. Some of them are heading this way."

Beckett realized her memory recovery hadn't gone unnoticed. The force radiating from her was like a beacon, drawing those attuned to the supernatural toward the library. She faced Sean, Lucifer, and Bowman, a question lingering on her face.

"We need to address this," Sean decided. "Your awakening is a momentous event, and it's only natural that others will feel the shift in energy. We should meet them head-on and show them there's nothing to fear."

Lucifer's hand rested firmly on Beckett's shoulder, providing a comforting anchor. "Sean is right. Your transformation is a cause for celebration, not secrecy. Let them see the goddess you've become, and let them know this is a new beginning for you and for us all."

"You've got this, barn girl. Time to make the donuts." Bowman laced his fingers with hers, a playful grin on his face.

Chuckling at Bowman's quip, Beckett knew her companions were right. Hiding her true self was no longer an option, and she refused to let fear dictate her actions any longer. With a decisive nod, she turned toward the library doors, ready to address whatever lay ahead.

As they stepped out into the hallway, they were greeted by a large gathering of employees, their expressions ranging from curiosity and awe, to fear. Among them were Danny, Deandra, and their intern friends, those who had been so enthusiastic just the day before, as well as Manny, Max, Hailia, Luke from the stables, and Tim, whose broad smile exuded satisfaction.

Danny's eyes rounded as he took in the sight of Beckett, her aura bursting with power. "Dr. Argonne, what's happening?" he asked, worried. "Are you all right? We sensed this...thing. While it didn't seem dangerous, it compelled most of us to investigate."

Beckett's affection for the young man climbed exponentially. "I'm more than alright, Danny," she informed him. "I've awakened to my true self. I'm sorry for waking you all so early, but I hoped you don't mind that I'm glad to share this moment with all of you."

Her voice clear and strong, she spoke to all of them. "I know that this may come as a surprise, but I am not just Beckett Argonne, the psychologist and researcher. I am also the daughter of Gaia, the primordial embodiment of the life force that flows through all things. Today, I have rediscovered my heritage as a goddess, ready to bring balance and harmony to all."

Gasps of wonder, uncertainty, and surprise rippled through the hallway. Trembling, Deandre spoke up, "Dr. Argonne, this is... this is incredible. But what is that singing we keep hearing? It's beautiful!"

Beckett reached out, taking Deandra's hand in her own.

"The music you hear comes from the flowers and plants in this room, recognizing me." She smiled kindly at her, then directed her words to the entire group. "I understand if this revelation seems earth-shattering, but I want you all to know that my awakening doesn't change who I am at my core. I'm still the same person who cares deeply for our organization and for each of you." She added, "For those wondering, I'm not going anywhere."

As she spoke, the flowers in the hallway began to bloom in a robust display of color and life, their petals unfurling, responding to Beckett's presence. Those gathered watched in wonder as the castle itself seemed to hum with energy, in harmony with Beckett's resurgent power.

However, amidst the excitement, Lucifer became somber. He warned, "While we celebrate Beckett's apotheosis we must also be aware of the dangers that come with it. If we can sense her presence and power, so too can those who might seek to harm her or exploit her abilities."

"Lucifer is right. My epiphany isn't just a blessing – it's a responsibility. We must remain vigilant and prepared for any threats that may come our way," Beckett said as she approached Lucifer, grasping his hand and thanking him for his protection.

"This doesn't impede our mission as a global security company; it enhances it," Sean said, sweeping his gaze across Evigvokter's staff before pausing briefly to meet Beckett's eyes with an encouraging look.

Bowman emphasized, "We're in this together, folks. Beckett's battles are our battles."

The throng quietly murmured their support, showing a range of emotions—from excitement and amazement to confusion or fear. They grasped both the joy and the gravity of the moment. Most seemed ready to rally behind Beckett and the power she represented.

Focusing her attention on everyone, Beckett continued confidently, "I know that the path ahead may seem daunting, but I want you all to know that you are not alone, and none of us will ever be if we stick together."

Remarkably, Danny spoke up first. "I'm with you, Dr. Argonne, Lord Caladfin. I'll always be. Whatever dangers lie ahead, the djinn and I are in." Beckett couldn't help but smile with pride as Danny courageously revealed his true nature to the other interns.

Listening closely, she began to hear the buzz of mostly positive conversations rippling through those assembled. One male analyst whispered excitedly to another, "Can you believe this? I'm so glad I came here."

Hailia agreed, brushing away tears. "Lord Caladfin, since I've been here, you and the Master Maethor always guide and support us. Now it's our turn to stand by you." She looked around eagerly. "It's totally cool, right?" To Beckett and Sean's surprise, the throng erupted in cheers of support.

Moved, Beckett realized she had never fully understood how deeply Sean's vision at Evigvokter resonated with those of supernatural heritage, just as it did with him and now her. She sought his hand, covering it with her own in a gesture of unity and affirmation.

Amplifying her voice, Beckett acknowledged, "Sean, without the foundations you've laid with Evigvokter and Dunhaven, none of this—none of our achievements—would have been possible. Your vision has been instrumental in shaping our destiny. Thank you so very much."

Sean spread his hands, encompassing everyone. "I appreciate your commitment to us and to this company. Free brunch for everybody who comes by between ten and noon on Monday!" Another round of cheers rang out as the staff began dispersing, conversations and laughter ebbing and flowing through the hallways.

Beckett faced Lucifer and Bowman, who had stood by throughout all the monumental disclosures.

"Lucifer, Bowman," she began, her voice supernaturally harmonious. "I know this has been a lot to take in, and I can't thank you enough for being here, for supporting me and Sean through... this." Beckett spread her arms helplessly, at a loss for the right words to describe what had transpired.

Lucifer's hand rested gently on Beckett's cheek. "Love, there is nowhere else I would rather be than by your side. Your awakening, transformation... remembrance, it's a gift— not just to you, but to all of us privileged to witness it. I will stand with you, always, as you navigate the path ahead."

Beckett's eyes fluttered closed as she experienced the solace of his aura, more profound than any physical touch. "We have much to discuss, you and I," she said to him. "I'm going to need your help."

She addressed Bowman next, taking back his hand and interlacing her fingers with his. "Bowman, I know that we have much to discuss, and I promise that we will. But right now, Sean and I need to uncover the secrets that lie within a room he created - a room that may hold the key to understanding our true purpose."

Bowman, with just a hint of curiosity, said, "I get it, Beckett. You and Sean have a unique bond, and if anyone can help you make sense of all this, it's him."

"I know, Bowman. Could you please let Connor know that our lunch date needs to be pushed to later this afternoon?"

"Absolutely. I'll inform both Katie and Connor about the change. Just have Sam let me know when you're ready." Bowman checked the time, then looking at Tenebris, he asked, "Want to take me home if it's okay with her?"

Tenebris sat expectantly at Beckett's feet, and she gave him a tilt of her head. Buoyantly, like a puppy, he skipped over to Bowman, and then they disappeared.

Sean, who had been observing Beckett's exchanges, placed a hand on Lucifer's shoulder. "We won't be long, mate. When we come back, we'll share everything we've learned."

Lucifer immediately placed his opposite hand on Sean's shoulder with a pointed look. "She's not the only one with a destiny, mate."

As Tenebris returned, Lucifer called to the hellhounds, "You two, stay with me right here." He settled into Beckett's favorite wingback in front of the fire.

Tenebris whined. Kneeling before him, Beckett said, "You can't go with me this time, boy. I'll be fine." She kissed his nose and stood up.

As Beckett and Sean made their way towards the secret room, Mrs. McKinnon emerged from the library doorway. She appeared to have been waiting for them, a knowing smile playing on her lips.

"Mrs. McKinnon," Beckett greeted, delighted to see her. "I didn't spot you earlier."

The elder woman chuckled softly, her face glowing with affection and satisfaction. "Oh, my dear, I've been waiting for this moment for a long time. I always knew you were destined for great things. Now, seeing you awaken to your true self, I couldn't be prouder."

Tears prickled at the corners of Beckett's eyes, overwhelmed by the gentleness emitting from Mrs. McKinnon. She turned and enveloped the woman in a tight hug, pouring all her gratitude and affection into the embrace.

"Thank you, Mrs. McKinnon," Beckett spoke in muted tones. "For everything. For always being there for me, guiding me, even when I didn't realize you were doing it or understand the path I was meant to take. And please, thank Tim for me. He knows why."

Mrs. McKinnon pulled back, her hands resting on Beckett's shoulders as she looked into her eyes. "You've always had the strength within you, Beckett. It just needed the right moment to shine through. Now, as you and Sean set out to uncover the secrets of your heritages, know that I will be here, as I have always been."

Watching their exchange with a fond smile, Sean placed a hand on Mrs. McKinnon's arm. "We couldn't do this without you, Mrs. McKinnon. Your wisdom and guidance have been a light in the darkness, and we are so grateful to have you in our lives."

Mrs. McKinnon's eyes softened, her gaze shifting between Beckett and Sean. "You two have always been like family to me. I'll always be here for you, no matter what. Now, go on, my dears. The hidden knowledge of the past has waited long enough. I have a feeling that what you discover will shape the course of your future."

With a final squeeze of Mrs. McKinnon's hands, Beckett and Sean moved to open the secret room, their steps charged with anticipation as they approached the bookcase closest to her desk. Behind them, Mrs. McKinnon watched, her heart brimming with love and an unshakable belief that these two people were destined to change the world.

Beckett reached for *A Christmas Carol*, pulled it, and the bookcase sung open. Sean quickly steadied it. Hand in hand, they walked into the room together.

As the door to the room closed behind them, Mrs. McKinnon smiled, her eyes drifting towards the window where the sun was climbing higher in the sky. She understood the road ahead might be arduous, she was certain that with Beckett and Sean at the helm, bolstered by the love and support of their family and friends, they could surmount any challenge.

With a whispered prayer for their protection and guidance, Mrs. McKinnon began her daily tasks, her heart uplifted with the knowledge that a new chapter was unfolding. The future, though uncertain, was ripe with the promise of hope, love, and the enduring bonds of family.

Chapter 16

The Tapestry of Fate

Once inside the secret room, Beckett turned to face Sean. "I believe that my mother's mantle is infused in my old sword. Remember Skögrbrandr?" She nodded at a plastic sword resting on one of the boxes in the back of the room. "I sense that there are more mantles in this room than just mine."

"My father mentioned that mantles of power are passed down hereditarily, through the offspring of gods and goddesses with other supernatural beings or mortals," Sean explained, his brow knitting in thought. "If your sword is here, where is Vǫlundrsveðr?" He began scanning the room, searching for his own childhood play sword.

"Before we start rummaging through everything, why did you build this room?" Beckett asked. "Did you know what those boxes contained?"

Sean stopped his search for his childhood sword and turned to face Beckett. Reflective, he pondered her question. "To be honest, I'm not entirely sure," he admitted. "It felt like an instinct, a compulsion to create a space to store and protect these artifacts from our past after our parents passed away."

He walked over to one of the shelves, running his fingers along the dusty spines of ancient books. "When we first bought the castle, this area just felt right. There wasn't anything obvious at the time, but I was compelled to create a space here—a space that could serve as a safe haven for our history and legacy."

"It's like the castle was waiting for someone who would appreciate its potential, someone who would create a sanctuary for the mantles and the memories they represent," Beckett suggested, insight brightening her eyes.

Sean slouched against the door, a smile tugging at the corners of his lips. "Exactly. Now, with your transformation and recollection, it all makes sense. This room was meant for us, Beckett. It's a place where we can explore our heritage and uncover the powers that lie dormant within us.

"Before we do anything else, Sean," Beckett teased, "let's not call this 'the secret room' anymore, okay?" She turned her face away from him, hiding a mischievous smirk.

A troublemaking grin spread across Sean's face as Beckett proposed renaming the room. With a dramatic flourish, he swept his arm around, grandly. "Why, my dear Dr. Argonne, Goddess of Life, you wound me!" he exclaimed in an exaggerated tone. "To think I would bestow such a pedestrian moniker upon this sacred chamber—it's practically blasphemy!"

He stroked his chin, eyes narrowing in contemplation as he paced the room, appraising it. "No, no, this space deserves a title befitting its mystical nature—a name that will echo through the ages and inspire awe in all who hear it!"

Pausing for effect, Sean struck a heroic pose, one hand dramatically resting on an ancient tome. "From this day forth, let it be known as... The Sanctum Corporis Restitutum!"

He turned back to Beckett with a coy smile. "Loosely translated from the ancient tongue, it means 'The Sanctuary of Bodily Restoration'—a fitting appellation, don't you agree? After all, isn't that the very purpose of this hallowed ground?

To restore our divine essences to their full, corporeal glory?"
With a playful wink, Sean gave a modest nod and bowed.
"Unless you had something else in mind, my lady? I'm open
to suggestions, though I dare say it'll be difficult to top such
an illustrious title!"

Exasperated but amused, Beckett passed a hand over her
face. She conceded, "The Sanctum Corporis Restitutum, it is
then."

Sean walked over to the box where Skögrbrandr sat, lifting
the plastic sword from its resting place. As he held it in his
hands, a gentle luminescence began to suffuse the toy,
becoming more distinct with each passing moment.

Beckett gasped, astonished, as she watched the
transformation unfold. "Sean, look!" she said in amazement.
"It's responding to you, just like the flowers responded to
me."

Sean's dancing eyes met hers. "I think you're right, Beckett.
Our mantles, our destinies, they're intertwined. I've known
about our predestination from my parents. We were meant to
unite and unlock the power within us together."

He carefully set Skögrbrandr back on its box, his gaze
drifting to the other artifacts scattered throughout the room.
"As for why your mantle didn't pass to you directly, I suspect
it has something to do with the circumstances of your birth.
Your parents, and mine, had to hide you, to protect you from
those who would seek to harm you. Perhaps they knew that
the mantle needed to be kept safe until you were ready to
claim it."

Logic settling over her, Beckett considered his words.
"With my memories restored and my powers revealed to me,
has the time come for me to take up the mantle of Gaia, to
embrace my role as the guardian of life itself?"

She reached for Skögrbrandr, holding it as she had as a
child. The sword glowed just as it had for Sean, but as Beckett

194

focused on it, the plastic melted away, revealing a large, ornate, beautiful dagger.

Sean, captivated, stared at the glowing dagger in her hand. "Beckett...that's a *real* weapon. Turn it over."

Beckett's breath caught in her throat as she read the engraving on the blade, the words rendered in an elegant, flowing script that seemed to shimmer with supernatural energy. "For Beckett, My Daughter," she murmured, her lips quivering. "Sean, this is from my mother. She left this for me, knowing that one day I would find it and claim my birthright.'"

Sean moved closer, awestruck as he admired the dagger. "It's incredible," he whispered, his fingertips hovering just above the gleaming surface, hesitant to touch such a sacred artifact. "The craftsmanship, the aura it emits... This is no ordinary weapon, Beckett. It's a testament to your heritage, a symbol of the lineage that binds you."

Beckett's grip on the hilt tightened as a rush of energy rippled through her body. It was as if the weapon had been waiting for her, lying dormant until she was ready to wield its power. "I can feel it, Sean," she said. "The connection to my mother, to the life force itself. It's as though the dagger is an extension of my very being."

She turned to him abruptly, struck by a new realization. "If my mantle was hidden within Skögrbrandr, then perhaps yours..."

Inspired by her idea, Sean's eyes darted to the shelves and boxes that lined the room. "You think I have a mantle? Vǫlundrsveðr," he realized. "It has to be here somewhere, waiting for me to claim it, just as Skögrbrandr was expecting you."

Together, they started combing through the room, spurred on by the pressing need to find Sean's mantle. They flipped through old tomes and handled fragile artifacts, their eagerness growing with every find. Then, in a nearly hidden corner, Sean caught sight of a shape he recognized.

With shaking hands, he reached for the toy sword, its plastic surface worn and faded from years of childhood play. As his fingers closed around the hilt, a blinding light filled the room, causing Beckett to shield her eyes. When the light faded, Sean stood before her, holding a magnificent sword, its blade shimmering with an ethereal glow.

"Vǫlundrsveðr." Sean's mention of the sword's name echoed around the room. "The sword of my ancestors, the mantle of my father's line." He turned the blade, revealing an inscription etched along its length. "*For Sean, My Son,*" he read aloud, his eyes glistening with tears. "Beckett, this is it. The key to unlocking my destiny, my role in the greater tapestry of fate."

He reached down, taking Beckett's free hand, and the dagger and sword automatically crossed between them in a symbol of unity and shared responsibility. "Together, Beckett," he said, conviction resonating in every word. "We'll do this together, as partners, as friends, as the guardians we were always meant to be."

Beckett smiled, feeling just as connected to Sean as she had when they were children playacting their now real-life roles as protectors. "Hold on a second." With focused concentration, she perceived him with her inner senses.

He sucked in a sharp breath. "What was that?"

"I...think my mother imbued these mantles, for your father to hand to you and for me. Each of these weapons is passing multiple mantles." She stopped cold, slightly dizzy, and he helped her sit down on a box.

Making sure she was all right, Sean was taken aback by Beckett's words, the realization hitting him with profound impact. The idea that their childhood toys held not just one, but multiple mantles left him stunned. He joined her on the box, their shoulders brushing as they sat side by side, the profound significance of their discovery palpable in the air between them.

"Multiple mantles?" Sean echoed, confusion on his face. "How is that possible? And why would those be imbued in these specific objects?"

Beckett shook her head, contemplating the mystery they faced. "I'm not sure," she confessed, smoothing the intricate patterns on the dagger's hilt. "But I can feel the power in them, the individual energies interlacing and thrumming together with life. It's as if each mantle represents a different facet of our heritage, a unique piece of the puzzle that makes up who we are and what we're capable of."

Sean observed his own sword vibrating with a commanding force in his hand. "Our parents, they knew that we'd be together always. They were preparing us, even then, for the destiny that awaited us."

Beckett swiveled to Sean. "Do you realize what this means? The mantles we hold, the powers they contain... We're not just the guardians of a single aspect of the life force. We're the custodians of a much greater responsibility, a much broader spectrum of influence."

Sean found himself grappling with a whirlwind of questions and possibilities as he tried to comprehend what Beckett said. The enormity of their obligations and the scope of their roles as guardians left them both speechless. They sat in silence, each processing the personal and shared ramifications of this newfound knowledge.

"We'll have to learn about each mantle," Sean deduced. "Study their properties, understand how they work in harmony with one another. It won't be easy, but there's us... and we've got an amazing group of friends and other talented people around us, right?"

Beckett agreed, her hand brushing against the inscription

on her dagger. "We've got the wisdom of our ancestors to guide us. They left these mantles for us, Sean. They believed in us, in our ability to carry on their legacy and protect the balance of the universe."

Sean reached out, taking her hand in his once more, his face grave and serious. "Are you scared?"

Beckett shook her head, snorting at the irony. "Weirdly, no, I'm not scared." She paused, focusing inward. "What's more, I can discern the mantles we've each received. My strongest is my mother's, followed by Nyx and then Aphrodite." Cocking her head slightly, her expression grew contemplative as she tried to interpret the additional stirrings she sensed. "There's more, but I can't fully comprehend it.""

She lightly made contact with Sean's blade on its engraved side. A thin wisp of white smoke traveled from her hand to her head. "Your mantles are Ares and Mars," she stated with certainty, "with the Mars mantle being the more potent of the two. Can you sense its presence?"

Sean closed his eyes, focusing on the energy coursing through his sword. As he concentrated, a tide of power flowed through him, a dynamic hum reverberating to his very marrow. It was a feeling like none he'd ever known - a raw, primal force threatening to overwhelm him with its sheer intensity.

"Damn, I can feel them," he uttered in complete astonishment. "The power of Ares and Mars - one of brutal warfare, the other of calculated strategy and national founding. It's like there's this raging fire burning inside me, fueled by an unrelenting strength and intense drive I've never experienced before."

"The mantles chose us, Sean. They recognized the qualities within us that align with their essence, the traits that make us worthy to wield their power." She tapped him on the arm. "Getting them, even with our parents, was not a foregone conclusion."

Beckett fixed her eyes on the gleaming blade of her dagger as she revealed her thoughts. "Gaia, the primordial mother - goddess of the entire cosmos and all life within it. The universal wellspring from which every earthly being ultimately emerged. Nyx, the night incarnate, veiling the world in comforting mystery. Aphrodite, whose beauty and passion inspire desires of the flesh and soul."

A thoughtful look crossed Sean's features as he assessed the nature of their mantles. "War and the primordial source of all creation, night and the passion that fuels new life... It's as if we embody the fundamental dichotomies, the contrasting, interconnected forces that maintain the cosmic balance."

"Perhaps that's why, Sean. I wonder if we're not just guardians of individual aspects of the life force. Perhaps we're the embodiment of equilibrium, the living unity of chaos and order."

Sean felt a chill as fate draped over him like a heavy cloak of responsibility. "And the fourth mantle? The one you still don't fully comprehend?"

Beckett shook her head, doubt overshadowing her. "I'm not sure it's just a fourth mantle, but its true nature evades me. It's like faint whispers at the periphery of my consciousness, something—or some forces—separate and distinct from the others." She let out a frustrated sigh. "I can't fully grasp it yet."

Sean gave her hand a sympathetic press amid the chaos of their new insights. "We'll figure this out, Beckett. Just like we'll get the hang of the mantles we already have. It's all right."

Beckett's brilliant smile illuminated the entire room. "Together," she concurred with the confidence of a goddess. "But not all at once. I think if we rush this, we might hurt ourselves. We need time to adjust. Do you know what I mean?"

Sean appreciated the wisdom in Beckett's words. The power they now held was immense, and diving in too quickly to master it could be perilous, perhaps even catastrophic. They needed to approach their newly-acquired abilities with caution, respecting the mantles they carried and the obligations that accompanied them.

"You're right," he said, his tone measured. "We can't rush this, can't let ourselves get carried away by the thrill of discovery. These mantles, these powers... they're mere instruments to be handled recklessly. They're a hallowed responsibility, a gift that demands we learn to wield it with wisdom and judicious restraint."

Beckett smirked in a very Sean-like way. "Right. We must take this one step at a time, learning to harness each mantle's energy in turn, understanding how they work together to create the balance we're meant to protect."

"We'll begin with the mantles we're most in tune with— Gaia for me, and Ares and Mars for you," she added. "We'll concentrate on their core, channeling their power in small, controlled steps until we've fully grasped their subtleties." She glanced down at her dagger, the blade quivering with untapped energy.

Sean nodded, feeling his sword respond, its energy pulsing in echo to her words. "As we become more adept with each mantle, we can explore their interactions—how they complement and amplify each other. It will be like assembling a puzzle, fitting together the different aspects of our power until the complete picture emerges."

As they stood in the sanctum, Beckett's gaze wandered to the various artifacts and objects around them. The air appeared lustrous with latent energy, silently testifying to the discernible power within the room's confines.

"Sean," she said in disbelief, "do you feel that? The mantles we bear, the ones imbued within our childhood toys... they're not the only ones present here."

As his extrasensory perception heightened, Sean tuned into the vibrant energies pulsing around them. "Without a doubt," he murmured, his words laced with amazement. "It's like an orchestra of power, each relic humming with its own singularly distinct vibration, its own latent potential lying in wait."

Beckett wandered through the room, hands grazing the ancient tomes and enigmatic artifacts on the shelves. Each touch sparked a thrill, offering brief insights into the secrets concealed within.

"These mantles," she said in a hushed tone, her eyes focused, "are not merely random pools of power. They are elements of a vast whole, a network of energies that stretches across the universe itself."

Sean joined her, his own hands hovering over the artifacts, feeling the ebb and flow of the mantles that resided within. "It's like a tapestry," he recognized, "each mantle a thread woven into the grand design, contributing to the balance and harmony of all things."

"We're a part of that tapestry, Sean. Our mantles, our powers, they're not just gifts to be wielded for our own agendas. They're a duty, a sacred trust, like you say, that we must uphold for the sake of all life, all existence." Beckett's tone was matter-of-fact.

She paused, her gaze drifting to a small, unassuming box tucked away in the corner of the room. As if drawn by an invisible force, she made her way to it, her heart pounding with anticipation.

Quivering, Beckett lifted the lid, revealing a collection of small, intricately crafted objects. Each one seemed to throb with its own inner light, a tiny star in the constellation of the room's power.

"Sean, look," Beckett directed, almost breathless. "These are focal points, conduits for the mantles housed within. Each one a key to unlocking the potential of a different thread in the tapestry."

Sean came to her, captivated by the array of objects before them. "Incredible," he whispered, his fingers just skimming a small, crystalline sphere that glowed with an inner fire. "The mantles within these objects...they're intended for specific individuals, chosen by fate to wield them in service to the greater good, right?"

Beckett felt as if her heart and head might burst from the sheer magnitude of their discovery. "It's our task to find those individuals. To guide them, to help them understand and harness the power that lies within. Just as we must learn to master our own mantles, we must also help others to do the same."

Sean threw an arm around her shoulders, pulling her in close. "Together, like always," he said with a confident smirk. "We'll take this on side by side, you and me, and whomever wants to help us, against the universe. And we're going to establish whole network of guardians - a intricate web of allies spanning galaxies to keep things in balance and protect the life force."

"A new adventure's kicking off," Beckett said excitedly. "But like always, we've got each other's backs. We'll take it one mantle, one guardian at a time until we've built up an unstoppable force for good. Once we've gathered all the pieces, the whole universe will be vibing with peace and balance."

Her forehead creased slightly as she thought about the mysterious presences stirring within her. "Maybe, as our journey continues and we grow stronger, the nature of that final mantle - or mantles - will become clear to me. Perhaps it's something I must earn, a power that unveils itself only when we're truly prepared to use it."

She met Sean's eyes. "Whatever lies ahead, we'll confront it united. We'll learn, we'll evolve, fulfilling our destiny as guardians. Not just for ourselves, but for all life, everyone." Sean tipped his head to her, their shared destinies galvanizing his dedication.

In that moment, all Beckett could feel was her heart exploding with immense love and gratitude for the man who had chosen to stand by her, ready to face the great unknown with limitless courage and boundless compassion. "Together," she whispered, the single word carrying the density of a sacred vow passed between them.

Chapter 17

A Symphony of Souls

Lucifer sat patiently in the wingback, the fire crackling beside him as he awaited Beckett and Sean's return. Nearly two hours had passed, by his reckoning. Though he sensed no negative energies lingering, earlier, a peculiar force had spread outward—one he couldn't easily explain. Still, Lucifer felt certain the enigma originated from Beckett herself..

Sam interrupted his thoughts, "Lord Aurington, how long do you think they'll be in there?" He sounded concerned.

"I'm not sure, Sam," Lucifer answered, as Mrs. McKinnon came back to the library, pulling a cart of drinks. "I think they're fine."

Mrs. McKinnon approached, bearing two steaming cups of coffee. She placed one on the end table beside Lucifer before settling on the edge of the sofa, cradling her own cup. "Of course they're fine," she assured Sam and Lucifer. "They'll be out soon, no need to fret."

The words had scarcely left her lips when the bookcase swung open, revealing Sean leading Beckett back into the library.

Lucifer jumped up the second he saw Beckett. After a shocked few seconds, he threw his head back and let out a huge laugh, pure happiness evident on his face. In just two big steps, he pulled Beckett into a tight hug. "*It's you! You!* I've missed you for so long!" Still holding Beckett with one arm, Lucifer reached out, putting a hand on Sean's shoulder. "You're all right, mate?" Sean smirked in response, as Lucifer's attention deviated to the sword Sean carried. At the same time, Lucifer spied the dagger in Beckett's hand.

"Skögrbrandr," Lucifer intoned with unmistakable reverence. "Beckett, do you remember when you healed the tree? You gave Skögrbrandr to me to hold, and I thought at the time it was too heavy to be plastic. Then, as you revived Ophelia's leaves, I felt its power." He indicated Sean's sword, flashing brightly in the sunshine streaming through the library windows, "That must be Vǫlundrsveðr, aye?"

Sean turned, presenting the sword to him, as Mrs. McKinnon seized that moment to weigh in. "As Lucifer is well aware, the original name for that sword differs from Vǫlundrsveðr. Each mantle bearer has the privilege of bestowing their own name upon their sacred weapon."

"Throughout the ages it has borne many titles, some you may recognize." She noticed the dagger cradled in Beckett's grasp and continued, "However, Skögrbrandr's name remains untouched - unchanged since the day it was forged for the goddess Athena herself."

Without warning, Beckett's legs weakened beneath her, and Mrs. McKinnon swiftly moved to brace her. But before anything could be said, Bowman strode into the library. After briefly acknowledging Sam's alert, he assisted his aunt with guiding Beckett to the nearby sofa.

As Bowman settled beside her, he lifted a hand and his fingertips gently trailed along the line of her jaw. "No one else knows," he confided, his speech hushed and at the same time, ringing with significance. "Nobody here, except Maya. Not

Gwen, not even Connor and Katie."

Beckett could scarcely believe the power she sensed in him, undeniable now that she experienced its truth. For Bowman, it seemed, bore a mantle of his own - and everything about this man finally crystallized into clarity.

Lucifer settled on the arm of the sofa, his hand coming to rest atop Beckett's. "What troubles you, little one?"

She kept her eyes fixed on Bowman, using her other hand to tenderly cup his cheek, her thumb brushing across it in a reverent caress for several prolonged moments. After a deep, relieved sigh, Beckett spoke. "Sean...do you recall that other thing in the sanctum I couldn't figure out?"

Immediately, Sean replied, "The mantle-mantles-non-mantle you kept feeling. What is it?"

It was Bowman who provided the answer, his focus finally shifting from Beckett. "It's Athena," he stated matter of factly, meeting the speechless looks that Sean and Lucifer now leveled his way.

Angling himself closer to her, Bowman's face glowed with adoration, along with his own brand of supernatural energy. "C'mon, you know whose power this is, don't you?

The mantle she sensed from him was familiar, distinct, a thread in the tapestry of fate that she hadn't fully grasped until this very moment. As she centered her attention on him, a small wisp of a white smoke told her what she already knew.

"Hephaestus..." Beckett exhaled, totally flabbergasted by how he'd kept such raw power tucked away all this time. "Your mantle—it's from Hephaestus himself, the god of fire, metalworking, crafting... along with attributes of cunning and a pursuit of both personal and cosmic justice. I can't believe I didn't see it before; it's absolutely core to who you are."

Bowman beamed at her. "I've always known," he said, his voice reflecting a quiet, constant certainty. "Maya can confirm that I received my heritage when I was just a little over seven years old." He too exhaled, finally free from the burden of concealing his mantle from her and the others in the room. "I had a hunch about who you were right after we first kissed in that bar, all those years ago."

Realizations hit Beckett like a tidal wave, culminating in the memory of that first kiss with Bowman. The mantle of Hephaestus, the god who loved Athena, the goddess whose essence now resided within her. It was a connection that ran deeper than she first thought, a bond that transcended time and fate, almost as equally as the one she shared with Lucifer.

"Athena and Hephaestus," Beckett murmured, seemingly unaware that she wasn't talking to herself. "They were in love, but Zeus wouldn't let them be together. It shattered Athena's heart, and that's why her mantle feels different—less like a true mantle and more like a fading remnant of what could've been." She paused, uncertainty creeping into her tone. "There's still something else, though."

Mrs. McKinnon interceded, "You were imbued with Athena's mantle directly as a very young child, only a toddler. For someone so young, that's an unusual and rare thing to do. But in Beckett's case, Athena's mantle was so fragile from heartache, Gaia feared it would disintegrate."

Beckett closed her eyes. So many things about Bowman now clicked into place, except... She sat up straighter. "Bowie, did you – I mean, the Gwen thing, how –"

Bowman took Beckett's hand, his thumb tracing small circles on her skin, "I knew I couldn't stay with you back then. If I had, I would've definitely told you what I was and who I thought you were." He dip his head to Mrs. McKinnon. "Maya told me I couldn't do that. She said if I did, it might mess you up in the future. It tore me apart so much that I went on a bender and woke up with Gwen in my bed."

He struggled to articulate what happened. "It was... easy.

And spineless. After we told you about us, after the kids were born... things got weirder between Gwen and me. I was clueless about what she'd done to me, how much of it was deliberate. It wasn't until I put my foot down and insisted on working here that I got help unraveling the truth about her and how to break the spell she'd cast on me. And on the kids."

Bowman's gaze drifted to Mrs. McKinnon and Sean, his mouth twitching with the ghost of a grateful smile, their shared understanding filling the stillness of the room.

Lucifer bent closer to Beckett, "There's another mantle specifically for you in your suite. Do you remember the last thing I said to you that day long ago, Lady of These Woods?"

"I didn't feel anything in my..." She stopped speaking as her mind took over. What did he say when he left the woods? He told her to go home and sleep. But he gave her...

In a flash, the pieces fell into place. "You gave me the starlight talisman, and you said it wouldn't fade. And that I would remember you later." She rose from her seat, turning to face him directly. "The part I didn't remember until now - You told me you bound yourself to me, and that the talisman was full of love. It's brimming with Eros, isn't it?"

He caressed the contours of Beckett's face, as if committing every detail to memory. "I knew, even then, that the love I felt was something rare and precious, a connection that could transcend time and space itself. I'd never experienced anything like it in my entire existence. With the mantle of Eros within you, that bond is more powerful than ever."

Bowman dragged his fingers through his hair, Lucifer's words grating on his nerves. "What the *hell* is that supposed to mean? You bound yourself to a seven-year-old girl?" He scoffed, doubt marching across his face. "This doesn't add up."

"Aye, it's a wee bit dodgy, mate," Sean chimed in, his

eyebrows knitting together in a perplexed frown.

Lucifer faced them, patient and understanding. "Bowman, Sean, I get where you're coming from, but please know that my intentions were always pure, stemming from a place of deep, unconditional love."

He sighed, collecting his thoughts before expounding, "When I first encountered Beckett in those woods, I was dumbfounded by the purity of her spirit, the innate goodness, resilience, and strength that emerged from her. She left me spellbound in that moment, transforming me. I knew then that she was extraordinary, that her destiny was intricately woven into the very fabric of the cosmos."

Lucifer's eyes landed on Beckett, his eyes a window to the truth of his soul. "The bond I forged with her was not one of romantic love or desire, but rather an intertwining of souls, a recognition of the monumental role she would play in the grand tapestry of the universe."

"The starlight talisman, infused with the essence of Eros, was a promise, a symbol of my unending commitment to protect and guide her on her journey. It was a way for me to ensure that, no matter what she might encounter, she would always carry a piece of my love and support with her." He reached out, his fingers lacing with Beckett's in a quiet affirmation of their unbreakable connection.

Fervent and beseeching, Lucifer reiterated, "I would never do anything to harm or exploit Beckett, especially not when she was a child. My love for her is pure, selfless, and unconditional, a feeling I've never encountered before or since. The bond I forged was one of guardianship, of unwavering devotion to her well-being and her sacred obligation."

Bowman listened intently, his initial skepticism gradually fading as he processed Lucifer's explanation. Slowly, the tension in his shoulders fell away, and understanding ignited in his eyes. "I see. It's not about romantic love, but about a deeper, more dear connection. A bond that transcends the boundaries of age and time."

"Exactly. Beckett's journey, her destiny, is so much greater than any one person or relationship. The bond I share with her is a reflection of that, a testament to the incredible power and importance of her role in the universe." Lucifer's fingers tightened around hers, instilling his words with unequivocal sincerity.

"But it's true that such a bond means you have no romantic attachments with other people or..." Bowman gestured vaguely, "beings, right? And if she reciprocates your binding, then what happens?"

Lucifer acknowledged the implications of Bowman's question. "You're right, Bowman. By binding myself to Beckett, I have dedicated my heart and soul to her, and her alone. There can be no other romantic attachments for me, as my love and devotion are wholly centered on supporting and guiding her on her path."

He paused, his gaze settling on Beckett once more with a glimmer of hope and yearning. "As for Beckett reciprocating the bond, that is a choice that only she can make, and one that I would never seek to influence or pressure her into."

"If Beckett were to choose to bind herself to me in return, it would be a crucial and sacred act, a merging of our souls and destinies on a level that transcends the physical realm. Our bond would become a true partnership, a union of equals working together to fulfill and maintain the balance of the universe."

"But even if she chooses not to reciprocate, my love and commitment to her will remain unchanged. I will continue to stand by her side, to support and protect her, and to do everything I can to help her achieve her true potential." His face held a depth of emotion that seemed timeless, a testament to the enduring nature of his devotion.

Sean, accepting Lucifer's reasoning but still harboring concerns for Beckett, spoke up, the depth of his worry carved into the subtle creases of his forehead. "But what about Beckett's feelings in all of this? How does she navigate the obligations of such a bond, especially when she's still discovering her own path?"

"You raise a valid point, Sean. Beckett's feelings and choices are paramount, and it is not my intention to add any undue pressure or expectation to her journey, " Lucifer emphasized.

He focused once more on Beckett, enveloping her with honesty and authenticity . "Beckett, I want you to know that my love for you is unconditional and freely given. You are not obligated to reciprocate this bond, nor should you feel burdened by its existence. Your path is your own, and I will support and cherish you, no matter what form our relationship takes."

Lucifer's sentiments stirred a swell of gratitude and love within Beckett, his selfless devotion tugging at her heartstrings. She tightened her grip on his hand, acknowledging the connection they shared and ready to embrace whatever the future might hold.

"Dr. Argonne, gentlemen, I'm sorry to interrupt," Sam intervened respectfully. "We might conclude that reverberations from what you've discovered caused a number of people to leave messages for Lord Caladfin. A Mr. Artis Pontifides has alerted him that he'll be at the castle Monday. Additionally, three other individuals, either employees or contractors, requested a call back within the next 24 to 48 hours. Furthermore, a Dr. Bennett McTavish requests Lord Lucifer contact him as soon as 'inhumanly' possible."

Bowman scratched his head. "Artis, the horse whisperer? What does he want?"

"He's the horse guy? I know him!" Beckett squealed. "He helped with an investigation I was part of five, maybe six years ago. Lovely man."

Lucifer knelt beside Dux, authoritative as he relayed his instructions. "Carry this message to Dr. McTavish: he is to come to the castle next week. All is well." With a respectful nod of his head, Dux swiftly took his leave.

Mrs. McKinnon rose gracefully, straightening her dress as she faced the group. "You know, destiny is one twisted, tangled web," she observed. "Every single thread, every life woven into it, connects to countless others in ways we can't always foretell. But I believe they are all tied together for an important reason—part of a bigger picture that eludes us."

Mrs. McKinnon's eyes lingered on each of them, resting a bit longer on Beckett and Lucifer. "That connection between you all though, that love you share - now that's a powerful, undeniable force," she said with an affectionate look. "That bond is going to be essential for the battles ahead. Because at the end of the day, love in all its forms is what will give you the strength, the courage, to face whatever adversities come your way. To protect the balance of this whole universe and everyone living in it."

"But while the universe needs saving every day," Mrs. McKinnon added with a wry smile, "today, you all need to eat." She gave them a look that left no room for argument. "Common room, one hour, for lunch. No excuses."

Beckett, Lucifer, Sean, and Bowman all shook their heads, their laughter ringing out at Mrs. McKinnon's humorously sage advice. Beckett tried to make sense of the day's epoch-making events. The rediscovery of her true celestial heritage, the rebirth of powers she scarcely understood, and the depths of the commitment Lucifer shared with her - it was almost too much to think about all at once.

"Alright, you heard the wise woman," Sean broke the

silence, a roguish grin flashing across his face as his eyes sparkled with their usual snark. "Wouldn't do to try saving the universe on empty stomachs, eh?"

Bowman let out a hearty chuckle, shaking his head in amusement. "Trust Maya to keep us grounded. No sense rushing off half-cocked - a good meal and a chance to get our bearings is probably just what the doctor ordered before we take on the next hurdles."

Lucifer concurred, his hand still intertwined with Beckett's. "Sean's right, we've got a long road ahead of us. We're going to need to keep our strength up and our heads clear." He turned to Beckett, giving her hand a kind squeeze. "Can you hang back with me for a minute?"

In response, Beckett told Bowman and Sean they'd join them in the common room shortly. As the others filed out, Lucifer drew Beckett into an embrace, his arms wrapping around her as their bodies melded together.

"There's something important I need you to understand," Lucifer said, intense as he held her gaze. "My love for you transcends the physical realm, but that doesn't diminish the depth of my desire for you - body, mind, heart, and soul." He paused, tenderly brushing a stray hair from her face.

"You're still so young, with many vital experiences to fully embrace. Getting to truly choose who to open yourself up to, in every sense...that path is essential for your growth, for reasons that may not be clear now." His eyes shone with a fierce protectiveness. "For me, I want to be the partner in your life that centers you, but never cages you. Do you understand what I mean, little one?"

Beckett held Lucifer's deep, caring gaze, her heart filling with love and gratitude for this remarkable being before her. His words, spoken with such tenderness and vulnerability, touched her soul in ways she could hardly describe.

I understand," she replied joyfully. "Your love is a precious gift that I cherish. But I also understand that this incredible bond between us doesn't come with expectations or constraints." Beckett cupped his face tenderly. "You want me to spread my wings and soar, to explore all this existence has to offer. You'll be right there, grounding me but never limiting my freedom."

She cocked her head questioningly, a blush coloring her cheeks. "Is it normal, whatever that is, that my libido's kicked into overdrive in the last three hours?"

Lucifer laughed, his green eyes twinkling with merriment and surprise. "Oh, my darling Beckett. What you're experiencing is entirely normal, especially given the awakening of your true self and the influx of the divine coursing through your veins."

His manner was tender as his hand softly brushed her arm, eliciting a passionate tremor throughout her body. 'Those powers you've inherited, especially from Aphrodite and Eros, are all about love, desire, and passion—that deeper intimacy,' Lucifer explained. 'So it makes total sense that as you're tapping more into that energy, your own desires and sensual side would become more amplified.'"

"But this goes beyond just the physical, Beckett. Your whole apotheosis is about opening yourself up on every level - heart, body, mind, spirit. You're seeing and experiencing the world through a totally new lens. That kind of extreme shift? It's going to feel exhilarating...but overwhelming too, at times," he advised sagely.

"It's okay to feel these desires, to embrace them as a natural part of who you are. But it's also important to take things at your own pace, to explore and understand these new feelings in a way that feels right and genuine to you." Lucifer pulled her closer, his arms providing a reassuring presence.

Beckett's cheeks colored in a charming combination of embarrassment and desire. "Thank you, Lucifer. For understanding, for being patient, and for always knowing just what to say to make me feel heard and validated."

"I'm so grateful to have you by my side, to know that I can always count on your wisdom as I navigate this unbelievable, and sometimes scary, new reality." She tilted her head up, pressing a soft, chaste kiss to his cheek.

Her lips gave him a shiver, one she delightfully experienced. "I love you, my darling girl. Through every twist and turn, every challenge and triumph—I will be your rock, your safe haven, and your biggest cheerleader. Together, we'll face this brave new world, and together, we'll discover the boundless potential that lies within you." He pressed his face against Beckett's head, breathing in her scent.

As they stood there, wrapped in each other's arms, Beckett reached up, her hand cradling the back of his neck. Pulling his face closer, her lips met his in a tender kiss. Lucifer bent to her, raking his fingers through her hair as the kiss deepened. The overwhelming, raw pleasure of his touch, his body, and his lips made her lightheaded with desire.

Electricity coursed through Beckett's body, fueling every nerve ending with a desire and longing that she wasn't sure she could control. Lucifer's hand in her hair, his fingers gently caressing her scalp, halted any rational thought. She found herself fusing with him in their embrace, the world around them fading away until only the two of them remained.

Their lips danced in a delicate, passionate exchange, each seeking to explore and savor the other's essence. Beckett's hands roamed over Lucifer's back, marveling at the solid muscle beneath his clothing, the strength and power contained within his form.

Lucifer held her close, one hand still tangled in her hair, the other pressing against the small of her back, anchoring her to him as if he never wanted to let her go. The heat between them flamed, a solid force that seemed to concentrate in the air around them. Beckett's emotions kicked into overdrive: love, desire, and a welcomed belonging coalesced in her body, mind, soul, and heart. In Lucifer's arms, she felt safe, cherished, and completely, utterly, blissfully alive. It was as if every cell in her body was singing in harmony with his, their very souls intertwined in a dance of passion and devotion.

When they finally parted, both were breathless, their eyes locked in a gaze that spoke volumes. Beckett's cheeks were flushed, her lips swollen from their kissing, her eyes alight with unconstrained joy.

Lucifer, his eyes reflecting the same immense longing, rested his forehead against hers in an intimate act, a slight smile of pure adoration playing at the corners of his mouth. "My love," he whispered, his usually commanding voice now roughened by his need for her. "You are everything to me. My heart, my soul, the very spirit that gives my existence meaning."

Beckett's own voice quavered, laden with the all-consuming love she felt for the archangel before her. "I adore you, Lucifer, with every fiber of my being."

In that moment, as they held each other close, Beckett was completely at peace. Though uncertain their path, rife with inevitable struggles, she knew that whatever came their way, she and Lucifer could face it together. His love, once so unexpectedly given, now as constant as the ocean tides, provided a sanctuary - where she found not just comfort, but an untapped well of inner strength to carry her through even the darkest of storms.

As they slowly disentangled, but remaining hand in hand, Beckett couldn't help but be thankful for this moment. With a heart full of love and a soul alight with purpose, she was ready to embrace the destiny that awaited her. But as Sean might say, first, they needed to go to the common room for lunch.

While walking down the hallway, Lucifer tugged her into an alcove with stairs leading to the keep, pressing her gently against the wall. "In case you missed them, these are the stairs to my chambers. I'm available to you all day, and..." He bent his head, smiling against her ear, "...all night."

Beckett's breath hitched as Lucifer's lips traced a delicate path along her jawline, sending delicious shocks through her body. The intensity of his gaze, coupled with the promise in his words, made her ache with anticipation.

Leaning into his touch, she smiled up at him, her eyes lit with desire and playfulness. "I'll keep that in mind," she whispered. "After all, we have a lot of lost time to make up for, don't we?"

"You know it. I intend to savor every moment, to show you the depths of my devotion and the boundless passion that you inspire within me." Lucifer's chuckle resonated through her very being.

His lips brushed against her ear as he spoke. "But for now, we have a family to join and a meal to share. A reminder that even as we explore our love, we are part of something greater, a tapestry of connections that sustains and enriches us."

"You're absolutely right," Beckett said, her eyes crinkling at the corners as she gave his chest a playful poke. "As powerful as this incredible connection between us is, it's the love we share with our friends, our whole chosen family, that really gives it deeper meaning."

She laced her fingers back through his and gave his hand an affectionate clasp. "Our love isn't meant to be this private thing, just ours alone. It's a brilliant light that should shine outwards, inspiring those around us."

Fingers entwined, they emerged back into the hallway, their affinity between them tangible as a living force. As they made their way towards the common room, Beckett couldn't help but marvel at the uncommon odyssey her life had become - the incredible souls who were now her cherished kin, and the breathtaking tapestry of fate being woven before her eyes.

Even amidst the grandeur and seriousness of her new reality, it was the simple, perfect moments like this—walking with the being bound to her and her alone, surrounded by the laughter and love of her cherished friends—that filled her heart with the greatest joy and contentment.

As they entered the common room, welcomed by the cheerful banter of Sean, Bowman, and the others, Beckett knew she would face whatever tribulations manifested with the strength and courage born of the unbreakable bonds she shared with these exceptional beings.

For in the end, it was love, as Mrs. McKinnon said —in all its forms, in all its infinite forms—that would guide them, sustain them, and lead them to the glorious future that awaited them all.

Chapter 18

The Ghosts of Christmas Past, Present, and Future

After lunch, Beckett retreated to her suit to change clothes, then spent the afternoon in her library. She scoured the shelves for ancient grimoires, texts, and books that might contain information about primordial gods and goddesses, as well as Greek mythology. Surprisingly, she located quite a few promising volumes and settled into her wingback by the fireplace to peruse them.

"Sam, do you have a moment?"

"Always, Dr. Argonne. What can I do for you?" Sam's cheerfulness filled the library.

"First, could you please contact the kitchen and request tea service? For now, it's just me, but the Maethors may join shortly."

"Ah, yes, they're on their way. I'll order tea for five, just in case we have another visitor," Sam replied obligingly. "What else did you need?"

"For your next task, which can be tackled at your leisure, I'd like you to compile an inventory of known scrolls, texts and manuscripts from antiquity describing primordial and Greek deities. I need to know where these ancient works currently reside, who the custodians are that oversee them, and how I make contact to potentially access them. Does this make sense?" Beckett picked up Lady Liriel's journal, running her fingers along the aged leather binding.

"Dr. Argonne? Why don't I go ahead and reach out directly to the custodians as I'm building that inventory?" Sam's speech took on an enterprising lilt. "I can coordinate with them to request access, line up any meetings or viewings that might be needed, and even put together a suggested travel schedule for you. That way we can be efficient about letting you examine key collections in person."

Sam gave a friendly chuckle. "Don't worry, I'll make sure it's all structured to accommodate your new role with Evigvokter. No overcomplicating things on my end - I'm just here to make this process as seamless as possible for you."

Beckett grinned, impressed with his initiative. "That's an excellent idea, Sam. Thank you for your help. I haven't had an assistant of my own for quite some time, so please bear with me as I learn to delegate effectively."

"Not a problem at all, Dr. Argonne. Let me reiterate how delighted I am to be working with you again. I hope you don't mind, but I've been monitoring your physiology since your awakening." Sam's tone grew tentative. "Your energy signature has changed exponentially and continues to climb. It's astonishing to witness."

Beckett set Lady Liriel's journal in her lap. "I'm assuming you heard when I asked Lucifer about my heightened libido."

Sam's chuckle filled the room, putting Beckett at ease. "Yes, I did overhear that conversation, Dr. Argonne. I must say, it's a perfectly natural response, given the changes you're undergoing."

Beckett leaned back, a small smile playing on her lips. "I figured as much. It's just... it's been a long time since I've felt this way, Sam. So alive, so connected to everything and everyone around me. It's as if I'm seeing the world through new eyes, feeling it with a new heart."

"That's precisely what's happening," Sam replied, his tone equal parts amazement and reassurance. "Your apotheosis, as Lucifer accurately called it, not only unlocked your true potential, but also heightened your sensory and emotional experiences. You're more attuned to the energies that flow through the universe, and that includes the energies of desire, passion, and love."

Preoccupied with thought, Beckett's flipped through pages of Lady Liriel's journal. "It's overwhelming at times, but also exhilarating. Like I'm finally becoming the person I was always meant to be."

"That person, Dr. Argonne, is truly extraordinary," Sam said with genuine admiration. "Your energy signature is a reflection of the power and beauty of your true self. It's a privilege to witness your transformation and to be a part of your journey."

A knock at the door interrupted their conversation. Beckett looked up to see the Maethors entering the library, their faces alight with affection. Katie immediately rushed to Beckett, enveloping her in a tight embrace, while Connor and Bowman followed, their smiles wide and welcoming.

"Mom!" Katie cried, her face filled with happiness. "We couldn't wait to see you again. Dad told us about everything that happened, and we just had to come and be with you."

No more "Doc" from Katie, it appeared. Beckett, her eyes pricking with tears, held Katie close. "Not as glad as I am that you're here."

Connor, his eyes bright, hugged Beckett and Katie together. "Yeah, we decided 'Mom' over 'Mother Earth' or 'Goddess of Life'. Those seemed kinda, you know, over the top."

Laughing at Connor's teasing, the Maethors settled in, the tea service arrived, and the library was soon filled with conversation, the aroma of tea, and the clinking of cups and saucers. Tim stopped by, reloading wood for the fire, taking a moment to introduce himself to Connor and Katie. Before leaving, he stopped to affectionately pat Tenebris and Dux.

"Mom, what are all these books?" Connor asked, carefully picking up one of the fragile ancient manuscripts. Beckett explained her research, handing Connor Lady Liriel's journal. Relaxing in a wingback, feet propped on a pouf, he soon immersed himself in her entries. To Katie, Beckett gave an old book on Greek gods, asking her to research the characteristics of Ares and Mars as detailed by the Greeks and Romans.

Throughout, Bowman regarded Beckett, his gaze a steady and tireless presence that seemed to pierce through to her. While guiding her children through the library, she discerned the unspoken feelings that swirled within him.

When the sun began to set, Beckett sent the kids back to the cabin using the "Tenebris Express." Finally, unable to ignore the pull of him any longer, she turned to face him, locked in a moment that left only the two of them suspended in a space of raw, unbridled emotion.

Bowman rose fluidly from his seat and crossed the room to stand before her. His hand reached out, cupping her cheek, his thumb moving along the delicate line of her jaw with a tenderness that made her heart ache.

"Beckett," he sighed. "Seeing you like this, happy, glorious, it's... breathtaking. I've always known you were different, from that first kiss, and now to see you fully embracing your true self..." He shook his head, his eyes bright with unshed tears.

"Bowman, I don't even know where to begin. So much has changed, so much has been revealed in so little time, and believe it or not, you're still here." Beckett leaned into his touch, her own hand coming up to cover his, their fingers intertwining.

The curve of his lips made her heart flutter. "I always will be. Morning, noon, and night. For you. For Connor and Katie. For this family that we've somehow, unknowingly, cobbled together."

"You know what I asked Lucifer earlier?" At Bowman's shake of his head, she closed the distance between them, wrapping her arms around him and burying her face in the crook of his neck. She whispered to him as she held him close, "If it's normal for me to have a hard time containing my libido since my 'awakening' earlier today."

"Really?" Bowman joked playfully. "Go on, tell me more." Chuckling, Beckett's cheeks flushed.

Bowman caught a stray lock of hair, tucking it behind her ear. "When we dated, we were never intimate. Since you've returned," he said kindly, "I've held you, kissed you more than I ever dreamed you'd allow. I want more. Of you."

Beckett's breath caught in her throat as Bowman's words cascaded over her, kicking off a fire within her that threatened to consume her entirely. The ardor and longing in his eyes invoked images and fantasies that made her knees weak. What was happening to her?

"Bowman, I–" He covered her lips with his, then pulled away, leaving her breathless. "I love that you finally feel." His blue eyes glittered with passion. "I'm in no hurry, and I don't want to frighten you." Bowman brought his hand to her head, pulling her into his shoulder. "For so long, what little I saw of you, it seemed as though you were numb. I just want all of this and more."

While Beckett reciprocated Bowman's embrace, his patience, his understanding, and the depth of his affection astounded her. Even in the face of his overwhelming desire, he put her needs, her comfort, above his own.

Beckett pulled back slightly, her hand coming up to his cheek, her thumb gliding over the rough stubble of his jaw. "Bowman," she sighed, catching her breath. "I don't know what I did to deserve you, to earn this kind of love and devotion."

He turned his head, pressing a tender kiss to her palm. "You didn't have to do anything, Beckett. Loving you, being here for you, it's as natural as breathing for me. I've loved you for so long, through all the ups and downs, the joys and the sorrows, all from the shadows. And now, openly, I'll keep loving you, no matter what."

Reluctantly, Bowman disentangled from their embrace, taking a long, slow breath. "Connor's leaving for school in about two hours, and I have some chores to finish with the horses in the barn." He took Beckett's hand, pressing a tender kiss to her knuckles. "You've been awake since before three o'clock this morning, woman. You need to rest."

She ran her hands through her hair, stretching languidly. "Maybe. But for now, I think I'll sit in this chair and read as much of this as I can." She held up Lady Liriel's journal with a smile. "I'll see you tomorrow, aye?" She poked his chest playfully.

"Not if I see you first," he grinned back. Bidding farewell to the hellhounds, he started for the door. Over his shoulder, he glanced back at her, a cheeky smirk on his face. "Uhm, you know, if you still feel all aroused and stuff, I'm over there, in case, you know, you forgot." He pointed westward.

Beckett's laughter echoed like bells through the library. "Go on, sport. I'll see you soon." After he left, she focused on Lady Liriel's journal, vowing to read the remainder before dinner and bed.

Sean's mother elaborated far beyond Beckett's personal dilemmas. She detailed the relationship between the Caladfins and Beckett's guardians, emphasizing that both sets of parents knew the potential that existed between Sean and Beckett. They also knew that the two were telepathically linked, and uniquely so.

As Beckett considered the easy telepathy she shared with Sean, she heard him in her head: *Where are you thinking so furiously?* Up from his nap, Sean sensed her presence. *In my library reading your mother's journal,* she responded mentally. *I'm coming down there, tell Sam to unlock the door.*

"Sam, could you please unlock the door for Sean when he arrives?"

Sam acknowledged her request. Beckett continued leafing through the journal, placing sticky notes on sections where a discussion with Sean might clarify her questions. The door opened, and rather than Sean, it was Tim entering with a smile. He carried a plate of stinky cheese, fruit, and a glass of wine. The hellhounds raised their heads slightly.

"Hullo, Dr. Argonne! My missus sent this along since she knew ye were, as she says, 'interrogating the library.'"

Beckett threw her head back and laughed. "She says that deliberately. I told her it's 'interrogating the texts,' but she won't have it." As she moved to rise, Tim motioned for her to stay seated, carefully placing the glass and plate beside her. He loaded more wood into the firebox, and with the coals glowing red-hot, the logs instantly caught, flames merry amid the cracks and pops as they heated.

"I see you're still reading Lady Liriel's journal," Tim remarked. "She and Lord Caladfin were wonderful people."

Beckett sighed, thinking fondly of both of Sean's parents. As if on cue, their only offspring opened the library door and strolled in. "Master Caladfin, how are ye," Tim greeted, crossing the room to shake Sean's hand fondly.

"I'm trying to avoid the incessant reading and thinking this one does," Sean said, smirking as he pointed at her. "It interrupts my *qi.*"

Beckett quizzed him. "Do you even know how to spell that?"

"No, but I don't have my nose in a library book all day,

either." He stuck out his tongue, and she responded with a playful hand gesture.

"Children," Tim chided with a grin, "Behave. I'll bring back another glass and plate for his Lordship." He petted the hellhounds before making his way out to fetch a plate for Sean.

Sean eyed Beckett warily, "What have you discovered, Viking warrior princess? There are all these thoughts swirling about in this library, batting at each other. What gives?" He swatted at an imaginary disturbance before making himself comfortable on the sofa next to her chair.

"How are you feeling?" she asked, watching his face as she opened her mind to evaluate him. Unlike her, he didn't radiate or glow intermittently, and he lacked the silver filigree they'd seen surrounding her form.

"Like I'm missing something and it's calling to me from that room," Sean confessed. "I need, desperately, to go back in there. Will you come with me?"

Beckett set down the journal, fully facing him. "Missing something? Why do you think that?"

Just then, Tim returned with a plate of nachos and a beer for Sean, as well as an extra beer and the open bottle of wine. After thanking him, Sean dug into the nachos. Coming up for air after a hearty swig, he said, "I spent, what, four hours dreaming about that room." He looked up hopefully, "Did you?"

She shook her head—that particular experience hadn't happened to her. "No, I just have a bad case of constant arousal."

Sean choked on his beer, coughing and snorting simultaneously. "Wait, you mean you want to... you know? Are you serious?"

Beckett blushed as Sean howled with laughter, unsuccessfully trying to stop. "Does Lucifer know about that?"

"I can't even believe we're having this conversation," Beckett retorted loftily.

Wiping tears from his eyes, Sean asked again, "Does LUCIFER know about this?!"

"I had to ask him, because I didn't know if it was normal or not," Beckett replied quickly, adding, "Bowman knows, too. He spent all afternoon watching me, so when I said it to him, he wasn't shocked. I think he guessed."

Sean's laughter subsided; he shifted closer, his tone sober. "Beckett, I'm sorry. I didn't mean to make light of what you're experiencing. It's just... I never thought I'd hear you talk about something like this so openly."

Beckett sipped her wine, a smile playing on her lips. "Believe me, it's just as unnerving to me. But with everything that's happened, all the changes I've gone through, it's like a floodgate has opened. I'm feeling things, wanting things, in a way I never have before."

Sean understood. "It makes sense, though. Your awakening, the mantles you now carry—they're bound to influence your emotions, your desires. And let's be real, you've always been a bit of a late bloomer in that department."

She threw a grape at him, which he ably caught and popped into his mouth with a grin. "Watch it, rogue. I may be new to this whole 'goddess of life' thing, but I can still kick your Elven ass."

They both laughed, the easy camaraderie between them a steadfast touchstone amidst the whirlwind of change. As their laughter died down, Beckett grew pensive. "Lucifer said it's normal, that the mantles of Aphrodite and Eros are amplifying my libido. But it's still a lot to handle, especially with everything else going on."

"You're not alone in this, Beckett. And if you ever need to

talk, about anything, I'm always here. No judgment, no teasing—well, maybe a little." Sean reached over, placing a hand on her knee. "But it's an open ear and a shoulder to lean on."

Beckett smiled, feeling tears prick at the corners of her eyes, overcome by the depth of Sean's friendship, one of the most important relationships in her life. "Thank you, Sean. You have no idea how much that means to me."

He flashed a friendly grin, giving her knee an affectionate pat before leaning back and taking another swig of his beer. "Now, enough about your 'desires,'" Sean said, forming air quotes. "About that secret room, I mean, Sanctum of something or another. I can't shake this intuition that there's something crucial there, something important we need now."

Recalling the strange energy she'd felt emanating from the hidden space, Beckett acquiesced. "We should go back, see if we can uncover whatever it is that's calling to you."

"Let's do it. Right now, before dinner. I've waited long enough for answers, haven't you?" Excitement and adventure danced in Sean's eyes.

They rose in unison. As they made their way across the library to the hidden room, Beckett felt lucky for the incredible people in her life—for Sean, her rock and companion through every twist and turn; for Lucifer, her soulmate and the love that anchored her amidst the chaos; and for Bowman, the man who held a piece of her heart and the key to a future she was only just beginning to imagine.

Beckett extended her arm towards the lovely first edition copy of *A Christmas Carol* perched on the shelf nearest her desk, the very book that unveiled the Sanctum. She paused, glancing at Sean, and inquired, "Why this particular book, Seanie?"

He contemplated the well-worn tome for a moment. "It's one of your all-time favorite reads, isn't it?" After see her nod,

Sean remarked, "Well, it's rather ironic that the Ghosts of Christmas Past, Present, and Future safeguard a concealed chamber containing remnants of the past, clues about the present, and harbingers of the future, yeah?"

Beckett's eyes widened as she grasped the symbolism linking the book and the concealed room it guarded. "You make a fair point," she said, delicately stroking the worn spine of the cherished tome. "It's almost as if the universe possesses an uncanny irony, cloaking our destined paths behind a tale centered on confronting life's harsh realities and the choices that mold our futures."

A spark of amusement glinted in Sean's eyes. "Well, if the cosmos is attempting to impart a message, I suppose heeding its wisdom would be wise. After all, we wouldn't want to share old Scrooge's fate, haunted by our own obstinate refusal to embrace the truth."

"Leave it to you to uncover the celestial punchline in all of this," Beckett chuckled, shaking her head as she firmly grasped the book, causing the hidden door to swing open with a soft creak.

As they ventured inside, the air seemed to reverberate with a distinct energy, lending more significance to the artifacts and objects within, given their recent revelations. Beckett's gaze was immediately drawn to a long, slender pole partially protruding from between two boxes along the wall. Shifting them aside unveiled a beautifully crafted glaive, its curved blade glinting and remarkably sharp in the filtered soft light.

"Sean," Beckett muttered in a hushed tone, a blend of wonder and apprehension evident in her words. "Can you sense it too, or is it just me? It's as if the glaive beckons me, compelling me to wield it."

Sean's gaze remained transfixed on a gleaming shield and spear displayed opposite. "The feeling is mutual," he affirmed. "It's almost as if these artifacts resonate with my very essence, an intrinsic part of who I am."

Almost in a trance, they each reached for their respective artifacts, their hands closing reverently around the ancient weapons. As they did so, a tremendous rise of energy coursed through their bodies, the mantles they carried responding to the sacred objects' contact.

Beckett gasped as visions flooded her mind—images of her father, the glaive Eldsgeir, an embodiment of his indomitable will and power as he wielded it, battling to safeguard the innocent and uphold the universe's equilibrium. She witnessed herself too, the glaive gripped firmly in her grasp as she confronted the forces of darkness, her eyes ablaze with the radiance of the life force itself.

Beside her, Sean's gaze had taken on a distant, faraway quality, as if peering beyond the room's confines into the very core of his own fated path. The shield adorning his arm seemed to emanate an inner luminescence, the spear in his grip pulsating with controlled might.

As the visions dissipated, Beckett and Sean turned to face each other. "These aren't ordinary weapons," Beckett said, her words melodic. "They're powerful emblems passed down through the ages, granting us the might to fulfill our ordained duties."

Sean's grip tightened on the spear as he gave a determined jerk of his head. "And we'll use them to face whatever challenges come our way, keeping the balance and protecting those who can't protect themselves. That's the whole reason Evigvokter exists - to have that global reach albeit now an endless one."

"There's an elephant in this room, and it's better we discuss it here than out there." Sean motioned for her to take a seat on one of the boxes while he settled himself on another. "We've been inseparable since we were four. In all that time, we've never, well, you know...explored a romantic connection."

Beckett recognized the unspoken query, sitting with Eldsgeir resting across her lap as she held his gaze. "You're not wrong. Despite all our shared experiences and adventures through the years, we've never ventured beyond the bounds of friendship into something deeper."

Sean rested his elbows on his knees as he cradled the spear in his hands. "I think, on some level, we've always known that our connection was different. Special, yes, but not in a romantic sense."

Beckett's fingers smoothed the engravings Eldsgeir's handle. "It's like we're two halves of the same whole, but not in the way that lovers are. More like...like two stars, orbiting each other in perfect harmony, our paths intertwined but never quite merging."

"Exactly. I think that's why we've been able to be there for each other, through all the good and bad times. Because our love is the real deal - no romantic mess to screw things up." Sean agreed, looking reassured.

"That's the first time you've ever used that kind of language with me," Beckett observed. 'And you seem comforted that we're not emotionally attached that way. Why?"

Sean paused for a moment, considering his words carefully. "I'm relieved because I value our friendship more than anything, Beckett. We've been through so much together, and I wouldn't want anything to jeopardize that. Romantic relationships can be unpredictable and messy, and I fear that if we crossed that line, it could change the dynamic between us. What we have now is so special - a bond built on trust, understanding, and mutual support. I don't want to risk losing that."

He looked at Beckett earnestly, his eyes conveying the depth of his affection for her. "You're my best friend, my partner in every sense of the word. I love you, but it's a different kind of love - one that's pure, unconditional, and unbreakable. I'm just glad we both understand and appreciate that."

Beckett let out an amused chuckle, a sudden thought crossing her mind. "Although, can you imagine if we had gone down that road? With your silver-tongue charm and my bullheaded ways, we either would have been an unstoppable power couple or a total train wreck."

"Oh, without a doubt a complete disaster. We would have driven each other insane within a week, constantly clashing egos and trying to one-up the other," Sean chuckled, his laughter reverberating off the hidden room's walls.

Their amusement tapered into a comfortable silence, the gravity of their shared history and relationship enveloping them like a cozy, intimate embrace. Beckett reached out, resting her hand on Sean's knee. "Even so, I'm grateful. Grateful that fate brought us together as it did, forging the closeness we share today - my brother from another mother."

Sean placed his hand atop hers. "Same here. My life wouldn't be complete without you in it. I know, after all we've uncovered, all we've become...I know our connection will only deepen."

Beckett's eyes shone with fondness as she spoke. "Together, through it all. As partners, as confidants, as the family we've made for ourselves."

Sean flashed a mischievous smirk, eyes twinkling with humor. "And let's not forget, we're now packing some seriously epic weaponry too. I mean, have you gotten a good look at this spear? Feels like I could take on legions of darkness armed with this bad boy."

Beckett rolled her eyes, then cautioned with a wry grin, "Just don't go charging headlong into battle without me there to watch your reckless Elven backside. Someone's got to keep you from biting off more than you can chew."

Sean placed a hand over his heart, his pose one of exaggerated gravitas. "You have my solemn vow, sworn on the sacred bonds of our friendship, that I shall never stray from your side when peril looms. We face it together, or not at all."

Their intertwined fate settled over Beckett, weighty, though encouraging. "Together, or not at all," she echoed, the words carrying the gravity of an oath and an unshakable promise.

With that, they rose from their seats, the weapons of their legacy in hand and the unbreakable bonds of their friendship guiding their steps. Whatever challenges lay ahead, whatever dark forces sought to threaten the balance they were sworn to protect, Beckett and Sean would face them as one - two stars, forever orbiting each other in the vast tapestry of the universe.

Chapter 19

Terra

Once they had exited the secret chamber with their newly acquired artifacts, Sean retreated to his suite clutching his weapons, leaving Beckett before the library's crackling fireplace. She carefully placed Eldsgeir and Skfögrbrandr on the coffee table as the hellhounds took up sentry positions nearby, ever-vigilant. The fireplace's flames held her gaze as she mulled over the day's extraordinary revelations, until eventually, lulled by the fire's heat, her eyelids grew heavy and she drifted off to sleep curled against the wingback.

Her sleep was undisturbed, slipping into a pleasant dream where she strolled through her guardians' woods, cheerfully singing at the top of her lungs. The surrounding birds, beasts, and towering trees gradually joined in harmony with her merry tune. As the chorus swelled, the very forest seemed to come alive with vibrant life, until a beautiful woman with long crimson tresses, azure eyes, and rosy cheeks materialized from behind an enormous oak that Beckett had long ago dubbed Tavarius.

Hailing Beckett by name as The Lady of These Woods, the woman strolled the pathways hand-in-hand with her, singing and laughing until she spied the rocks by the creek. Taking

Beckett's hand, she jumped from the bank to the largest rock in the middle, ensuring the younger girl didn't fall in. Pulling Beckett to her lap, she sat rocking and singing, holding her close, and kissing the top of her head.

"Who are you, lady? Why have you come to my woods?" young Beckett asked, her voice carrying the innocent curiosity of a child.

The woman responded with a heartfelt smile, "And what name do you think suits me, little one?" As she spoke, her fingers began weaving Beckett's hair into a braid.

Beckett thought about it for a moment before replying with utmost seriousness, "I think Terra would be a good name for you."

A melodious laugh escaped the woman's lips, the surrounding trees and babbling stream seeming to join in joyful chorus with her mirth.

The woman's rich laughter seemed to fill the woodland air with life itself. As agile fingers continued braiding Beckett's hair, she spoke in a gentle tone that carried undercurrents of esoteric wisdom. "Terra is a beautiful name, little one. In an ancient tongue, it means 'earth.' In a way, your perception is quite insightful."

Beckett tilted her head upwards, big eyes shining with childlike wonder as she gazed at the woman. "What do you mean? Are you...are you the spirit watching over these woods?"

A brilliant smile played across the woman's lips, her azure eyes sparkling with both deep affection and a mischievous glint. "You could say that, yes. I am intertwined with this forest, with the very earth beneath us. And I have been keeping a watchful eye on you, Beckett, since the first day you stepped into this magical realm."

Beckett's eyes went wide, pure, unadulterated amazement spreading across her young face. Her voice brimmed with mounting exhilaration as she asked, "Truly? But why me? Why have you been watching over me?"

Completing the intricate braid, the woman gently turned Beckett to face her directly. "Because you, my dear child, are someone truly special. You possess an innate connection to the earth itself, to the life-force pulsing through every creature and plant."

Beckett's cherubic features scrunched up in that familiar look of intense concentration that Sean had endearingly called her "deep thinking" face. After a moment, she replied in that candid, unvarnished way children have, "I've always felt different from the other kids. Like there was something else inside me that I couldn't explain."

The woman's manner remained serene, her eyes shining as she affirmed Beckett's words. "That's because there is indeed something extraordinary residing within you, my child. You possess a special gift, a dormant power. And when the right moment arrives, that power will stir, allowing you to truly understand your greater purpose."

A surge of eagerness coupled with apprehension rushed through Beckett's small frame as her heartbeat quickened. With equal parts wonder and trepidation, she asked, "My greater purpose? What does that mean?"

"I cannot reveal too many details, for the journey ahead is yours to experience," the woman replied, her voice laced with an air of mystery and imbued with warmth. "But carry this truth within you, Beckett—you are destined for a remarkable purpose. You will become a guardian like me, a protector and caregiver of this earth and all life that flourishes across the vast cosmos." As she spoke, she placed a comforting hand on Beckett's shoulder, her touch overflowing with genuine motherly affection.

Beckett straightened her small frame, courage and determination shining in her youthful eyes. "I'll do everything I can, Terra. I promise. Sean and I already look after these woods and all the precious animals and trees that live here."

Pride glittered brightly in Terra's eyes as a brilliant, heartfelt smile graced her lips. "I know you will, my dear child. And never forget, even when you cannot perceive my presence, I will forever be by your side, watching over you and guiding your path."

As she spoke those words, Terra leaned forward and placed a tender kiss upon Beckett's forehead. A soothing, enchanting energy seemed to emanate from the spot where the woman's lips met the young girl's skin. Beckett's eyes drifted shut as an overwhelming surge of unconditional love and life's pure essence infused her entire being.

When Beckett's eyes fluttered open once more, Terra had vanished, and the surrounding woodland remained energetic and lively, resonating with an invigorating energy as if imbued by the woman's divine presence. Deep within her childlike heart, Beckett carried the sacred knowledge that Terra's love for her was true, as were the revelations about her greater purpose.

With a start, Beckett jolted awake in the present, the hellhounds' protective growls piercing the silence as an unfamiliar presence invaded the library. The dying fire's coals burned an angry red as a shadowy figure strode towards the woodpile, casually tossing fresh logs to stoke the flames higher. Instinctively, she clutched Eldsgeir and her dagger close, eyes wide as she demanded, "Who are you? How did you get in here?"

As the revitalized flames cast their golden glow, Beckett could finally make out the intruder's face. He sported dark locks cropped in a severe Roman style, accompanied by a neatly trimmed beard. His stature was commanding, nearly matching Lucifer's towering height and imposing build. His eyes provided a stark contrast - deep pools of navy framed by glints of molten gold. Just as he appraised her with an inscrutable gaze, Beckett studied him intently.

"I'm Dr. Bennett McTavish," he spoke, his baritone velvety and refined. "Though you've long referred to me simply as Tav."

The hellhounds remained on high alert, Dux snarling fiercely, "Lord Tartarus, your arrival was expected next week, not today. I shall inform Lord Lucifer of this unanticipated visit. You are forbidden from laying a hand on our goddess, and my brother will safeguard her unto his dying breath if need be." Tenebris positioned himself before Beckett, teeth bared in a menacing growl directed at this "Tav."

Beckett's thoughts spiraled, her mind drawn back to the dreamscape encounter. "Tavarius...my tree from the woods?" Her features scrunched with bewilderment as she questioned, "Am I still dreaming?"

Tav's lips curved into an enigmatic smile at Beckett's confusion and surprise. He held up his hands in a placid manner, calm and soothing as he addressed the still-glaring hellhound. "Peace, Tenebris. I mean no harm to your goddess. I'm here as a friend, a guide, and a protector, just as I've always been."

He turned his attention back to Beckett. "No, my dear, you are not dreaming. Though I can understand why you might think so, given the nature of your recent vision."

"How...what...how could you possibly know about my dream?" A look of disbelief and confusion clouded her face as her grip tightened again around Eldsgeir and Skögrbrandr.

A mellow chuckle rumbled from Tav's chest, reminiscent of distant rolling thunder. "I possess knowledge of many arcane mysteries, Beckett. Such is my sacred duty as a guardian watching over these realms. And your dreams, your visions - they are a portal into the immutable truth of your essence and the fated path that lies before you."

He took a step closer, the firelight revealing his   chiseled features, casting shadows that accentuated the aura of power and mystery surrounding him. "The woman in your dream, Terra – she is more than a figment of your imagination. She is a part of you, a manifestation of the divine essence that flows through your veins."

Beckett's heart raced as her mind struggled to process the implications of Tav's words. "But what does that mean? Who is she, really? And who are you – Dr. Bennett McTavish, Lord Tartarus, or whatever your name is?"

"I'm many things, Beckett. A scholar, a warrior, a guardian of the underworld. But most importantly, I'm a friend and ally to those who seek to maintain the universe's balance." Tav's piercing gaze locked with Beckett's as if seeing into her very soul.

With a gesture, he indicated the sofa beside her, a silent request to sit. When Beckett tipped her head, Tav settled his large frame onto it with an unexpected grace, as if it had been custom-molded to his form. "As for Terra, she represents the truest essence of your nature - your fundamental connection to both the earth and the universe, the cosmic life force that sustains all existence. She is the part of your being that has forever understood your greater purpose, even when your conscious self was not prepared to accept such profound truth."

Beckett's eyes and mind searched Tav for even the faintest hint of deception or ulterior motive. All she intuited in his piercing gaze was raw sincerity, an immense depth of ancient wisdom, primordial power, and boundless compassion that seemed to exude from all of him. "What exactly is this purpose, this destiny, that everyone speaks of? What am I meant to do with abilities and this power?"

Tav extended his hand to gently cover Beckett's, his touch

radiating a nurturing encouragement so reminiscent of Terra's. "Your sacred purpose, Beckett, is to serve as a guiding light amidst the encroaching darkness, a beacon of hope and equilibrium for a universe constantly threatened by the forces of chaos and oblivion. You are destined to lead, to counsel, and to safeguard - not merely this earth, but all planes of existence that lie beyond its terrestrial borders."

Leaning back, his eyes drifted to the crackling hearth, the dancing flames hot and bright. "You need not shoulder this cosmic burden alone. You have steadfast allies - friends, chosen family, guardians both mortal and divine - who will stand united by your side, bolstering you through each step of this fated journey."

Lucifer materialized with Dux just inside the doorway, his aggravation ripe in the air. "Tav, what the hell do you think you're doing? I told you to come by next week."

"I can feel her all the way through The Pit, Lucifer. And if I can do so, so can others," Tav shrewdly informed him.

Shocked, Beckett realized this being was the personification of Tartarus, the primordial god of The Pit. *Sean, there's a visitor in the library, and you must come now.* The immediate reply: *I know, I can feel it. I'm on my way.* He's so real, she thought. I can reach out and...

"Touch me, Beckett, so you know this isn't all a dream. Go on, I know you loved to try to put your arms all the way around me and hug me in your woods." She flipped her hand over to clasp his.

As their skin connected, a surge of something coursed through her, like a gentle electric current that set her nerves alight. Fostered by her transformation, his touch was both comforting and exhilarating, a tangible reminder of her growing connection with him. Beckett's awe and wonder, along with an inexplicable familiarity, echoed her feelings of belonging that she'd been experiencing since her arrival at the castle.

Tav's presence seemed to amplify and affirm the bonds she had been forming with Lucifer and others. His strength and power were so substantial, but his touch bordered on reverent. For a moment, the world fell away, and all that existed was the warmth of his hand in hers, anchoring her to a truth she had only just begun to grasp. He's so strong, so powerful, and a part of her shouted in joy at his arrival, she realized. Am I going crazy, she feared?

Lucifer's eyes blazed with a mix of anger, concern, and frustration as he strode towards Tav and Beckett, his presence filling the room with simmering tension. "That may be so, Tav, but we had a plan - a way to introduce you to Beckett that wouldn't overwhelm her or put her on the spot."

Tav rose smoothly, his posture relaxed and confident as he faced his old friend. "Plans change, Lucifer. You know that better than anyone. And with the awakening of Beckett's true power, we cannot afford to delay or second-guess our actions."

Lucifer's gaze shifted to Beckett as he took in her confusion. "Beckett, I apologize for the abruptness of this meeting. I hoped to give you more time to adjust before introducing you to Tav."

"It's alright, Lucifer. I understand the need for caution, but if others can sense my awakening, we don't have the luxury of time. We need to act to ensure the balance is maintained." Beckett stood, Eldsgeir grasped securely as she met Lucifer's eyes.

The look in his eyes morphed from frustration to surprise as he took in the weapon in her hand. "Beckett, that's your father's glaive, isn't it?"

She nodded, saying, "Sean wanted to go back in, so I went with him. This is Eldsgeir."

"You see? She's ready and understands the gravity of her

role." Tav sat, a smile of approval tugging at his mouth.

Beckett sat opposite him, still holding the glaive. "It's not just my role, Tav. There's also Sean, Bowman, and my children to consider."

"You mean the children the witch had with your ovum?" Tav's tone was kind despite the bluntness. "I want to meet them, and this father of theirs, and see your twin flame now that he's grown."

"My what?" Beckett's jaw dropped. "Twin flame? That's what Sean is?"

Sam interrupted, "Dr. Argonne, Sean is coming down the hallway, should I - "

Beckett motioned to Tenebris who disappeared and reappeared with Sean.

Astounded, she processed Tav's claim that Sean was her twin flame. The concept seemed foreign but possible - a truth always there, beneath their imperishable bond. How odd they'd just discussed this, without using the term, in the secret room hours ago.

Relaxed, Sean was unfazed by Tav's words. He came to her, sitting on the arm of the sofa, his hand coming to rest on Beckett's shoulder as she looked up at him. "It's true, Beckett. We've always known our connection was special, beyond friendship or family. But 'twin flame' - it just fits."

"A twin flame is a rare and precious thing - two souls that were once one, split apart and sent to walk separate paths, only to be reunited when the time is right. Your bond, your love for each other, transcends the boundaries of this world and the next." Tav expounded, his eyes brilliant with a fusion of wisdom and affection as he watched the two friends, no different as adults than they were as children.

"But what does that mean for us, Sean? For our roles in all of this and given what we discussed in the room?" Beckett placed her hand over Sean's on her shoulder.

Sean met her gaze steadily. "It means our bond, our connection, is an integral part of our destiny, Beckett. Our love for each other, the way our souls resonate and intertwine, is what will give us strength and clarity to fulfill our roles as guardians."

He took her hand, their fingers interlacing in a habitual, but encouraging, act. "Remember what we talked about? How our relationship is different, special? Being twin flames doesn't change that. It doesn't mean we're meant as lovers or that our romantic paths are tied."

Relieved by his explanation, Beckett said, "I guess it's about balance, isn't it? We complement and strengthen each other, allowing us to be our best selves. I always felt that in the woods." She chuckled lightly. "I guess there's no getting rid of you when you're annoying, is there?"

Ever mischievous, Sean smirked. "Nope. And don't forget it. We're partners now and always - twin flames, partners in crime, the biggest thorns against anyone threatening the balance." He inquired of Tav, teasing, "Which of us is the twin and which the flame? Inquiring minds..."

Tav addressed Beckett first. "Sean's right. Your connection enhances and supports you in fulfilling your destinies. It doesn't limit or define you, but provides a powerful foundation."

Meeting Sean's eyes, Tav laughed, good humor transforming his face. "Mate? You're the twin. That girl is the flame. She's a star."

Chuckles filled the room at Tav's playful clarification.

Sean, thoroughly enjoying himself, smirked again with mock surrender. "Alright, I concede. Beckett's the flame. Have you seen her on a mission? A classic example of an unstoppable force of nature."

Blushing, Beckett stood and placed her weapons on the coffee table. "I couldn't do it without you, though. You're the one who keeps me grounded, who reminds me of what's truly important when I get too caught up in the chaos."

Amused, Lucifer took a step toward Beckett, sliding an arm around her waist. "That, my darling, is the true grace and strength of your affinity for one another. You balance each other, bring out the best in one another, and together, you create a force greater than the sum of its parts."

Concurring, Tav added, "And it is that unified force that will be crucial in the battles to come. The apotheosis of Beckett's mantle set in motion a chain of events that will test us all, challenging the very fabric of the universe itself."

He clapped his hands, the sound cracking through the library. "Well then, let's begin. We have much to discuss and even more to prepare for. The awakening of a goddess, especially one charged with governing the life force, is no small matter. We must ensure Beckett is ready for the trials that lie ahead."

Beckett's face fell, concern marching across her features as she sat back down. "What do you mean, Tav? What kind of 'challenges' are we facing?"

The ancient deity sighed, distant as if seeing into the cosmic heart. "There are forces at work, Beckett - ancient, powerful entities that seek to upset the balance, to plunge the universe into chaos and darkness. They've sensed you, and they'll stop at nothing to either control you or destroy you."

A heavy silence fell over the room, but Sean was the first to break it. "They'll have to go through both of us to do it," he said grimly, glancing at her dagger and glaive.

"Hold up. I need some questions answered first, Tav. Can you do that before we go off creating a strategy that, frankly, I'm not sure I understand?" Beckett pressed.

Tav's eyes twitched, surprised at her bold request. However, his surprise quickly gave way to respect and understanding, with a small smile tugging at his lips. "Of course, Beckett. You're absolutely right. It's important you understand the situation before we dive into strategy. Please, ask anything you need to know, and I'll provide the answers."

Beckett straightened her posture and corralled her thoughts. "First, I need to know more about these forces seeking to control or destroy me. Who are they, and what's their endgame? What do they gain by targeting me specifically?"

Tav moved closer, the firelight highlighting his face as he met her gaze. "The entities are ancient and formidable, Beckett. Embodiments of chaos, darkness, destruction - forces existing since creation itself. Their goal is to upset the universe's delicate balance, to plunge all existence into entropy and despair."

Somberly, he persisted, "As for why they target you—it is because of who and what you are. As the embodiment of the life force, the goddess maintaining the universe's balance and vitality, you represent the antithesis of everything they stand for. Your power, your existence itself, threatens their dark ambitions."

Tav caught her chin, looking her directly in the eyes. "You're not just a goddess, Beckett. You're a symbol, a rallying point for all who believe in life, love, and balance. Your strength comes not only from your abilities but the connections you forge, the alliances you build, and the love you inspire in others."

Doubt washed over Beckett. Despite repeatedly hearing, "You have a destiny" and "I knew you were special," she couldn't embrace the idea of being a primordial goddess. *Who will seek my favor, and for what purpose? How? Why?* She shook her head in disbelief.

"Are you all sure you have the right person?" she asked, skeptical of their assertions.

The room stilled completely, the sound of her question

hanging in the air. Lucifer broke the silence, conviction strong in his tone. "Beckett, my love, there is no doubt you are exactly the right person. I've watched you, loved you from afar for so long, and never once questioned the brilliance of your spirit or your heart's strength."

"You got my vote, Lady of These Woods," Sean affirmed enthusiastically.

Lucifer kneeled before her, taking her hands as he assured her. "Your doubts, your fears - they are natural parts of this journey. But they do not define you or diminish the incredible power and potential within you."

"Do I have a choice, Lucifer? I don't want to be a self-fulfilling prophecy," she spoke carefully.

Lucifer considered his words before responding with total understanding. "Beckett, my love, you always have a choice. Your destiny, your role as life's embodiment - it is an opportunity, a path laid before you, but one you must choose to walk willingly."

"I would never want you to feel forced into this, to feel as though you have no control over your own life and decisions. Your power, your potential - they are yours to wield as you see fit, guided by your own heart and moral compass. The same applies to Sean." Lucifer's thumbs caressed the backs of Beckett's hands soothingly.

Kind and considerate, Tav intervened. "Lucifer is correct, Beckett. The path of a god or goddess is not an easy one, and it cannot be forced upon anyone. It requires a willingness to embrace the responsibility, a readiness to step into the role with an open heart and clear purpose."

He patted her knee, encouraging and supportive. "If you choose to walk this path, you will have the full support and love of everyone in this room, along with countless others you will meet. But if you decide this is not the journey you wish to undertake, we will respect and honor that choice. We will stand by you the same way, no matter what."

She looked around the room, taking in the faces of those who had believed in her even when she doubted herself.

"Thank you," she whispered. "Thank you for giving me the space to choose, for respecting my agency and right to decide my own path." Beckett recognized that if she had the power to address an issue, no matter the personal cost, she would pay it - as she always had when her patients, students, friends, and family came to her in need or even unasked.

Sam cut through the moment. "Dr. Argonne, Master Maethor is coming down the hallway. May I allow him entrance?"

How did Bowman know? Beckett glanced at Tenebris, who immediately vanished and reappeared with Bowman. "We have him, Sam, thank you," she responded.

As Bowman crossed the library towards her, he scowled at Tav, "Who the hell are you?" Then, looking at Beckett with concern, "Are you all right?" He had come armed - his own sword, a quiver with bow and arrows. Sensing Tav's power, he'd come running, Beckett deduced.

Sean answered, giving Beckett a moment to think. "Welcome back, old chap. Beckett here has been interrogating the Pit Master about the validity of her goddess of life force role and path. It's kinda fun, since I imagine His Pitness never gets confronted like this." He smirked, and Bowman raised an eyebrow.

Tav chuckled, a deep, rumbling sound charging the the library with merriment. Turning to Bowman, pleasant and smiling, he extended a hand.

"Ah, the infamous Bowman Maethor. I've heard much about you - your reputation as a fierce protector, loyal friend, but delinquent boyfriend precedes you. Your mantle knew me well."

Bowman eyed Tav warily, grip tightening on his sword as

he shook the offered hand. "And you are?"

"Forgive me," Tav replied with a respectful incline of his head. "I'm known by many names, but you may call me Tav, or Lord Tartarus, Guardian of The Pit, mentor to our dear Lucifer here, or the po-po of the universe."

Bowman's eyes widened in recognition. "The Pit Master? You oversee the Pit realm, maintaining the balance between life and death?"

"The very same. And as Sean eloquently put it, I've been receiving our dear Beckett's formidable interrogation skills." Tav squeezed her knee again, a smile gracing his lips.

Beckett flushed, but she held her ground, standing to meet Bowman's gaze steadily. "He's been helping me understand my role, Bowman. Helping me come to terms with the path before me and the choices I must make."

Concern and worry reflected in Bowman's face as he moved to stand beside Beckett, his hand coming to rest supportively on the small of her back. "What have you decided, Beckett? What does your heart tell you?"

Grateful for his understanding, she replied, "My heart tells me that this is the course I must take, Bowman. Not because it is easy, or because it is what others expect of me, but because it is the right thing to do - for myself, for those I love, and for the balance of the universe itself."

Bowman didn't suppress the smile suffused with loving approval that tugged at his lips. "Then I will be with you, Beckett. Every step of the way, I will be by your side, lending you my strength, my bow and sword, and my steadfast support."

She took a calming, centering breath. "I may not have asked for this role, or for this destiny to be thrust upon me. But I also know that I cannot turn my back on the responsibility that comes with it, on the countless lives that depend on the balance and life force I'm meant to protect."

Tav, Lucifer, and Sean echoed Bowman's sentiment. "As will we, Beckett," Sean declared, his hand coming to rest on her shoulder. "I told you, you're not alone in this, and you never will be."

Chapter 20

Accepting the Goddess

Bathed in firelight, Beckett stood tall and decisive. "I choose to embrace this path, to become the goddess and leader the universe needs me to be. Not because I feel obligated or forced, but because I know in my heart it is the right thing to do - for myself, for all of you, and for every living being that calls this universe home."

As the words left her lips, an abrupt and dazzling light filled the room, its intensity causing everyone to shield their eyes. The air crackled with energy, a palpable air of power and transformation permeating the entire wing of the castle.

When the brilliance subsided, the group lowered their hands, speechless at the sight before them. Beckett stood in front of the fireplace, her form enveloped in a soft, ethereal glow. Her once silvery-white hair now shimmered with an iridescent sheen, as if each strand was infused with starlight's essence. The silver filigree patterns adorning her skin pulsed with a gentle, rhythmic light, in tune with the beating of her heart.

Their gazes were irresistibly drawn to her eyes. Previously an icy blue, they now glowed with a provocative ethereal light—a hypnotic mix of glacial blue, green, and silver that appeared to encapsulate the mysteries of the cosmos.

Tav broke the silence first. "Behold, the true awakening of the Goddess of Life. Beckett, you have embraced your destiny, and the universe itself has responded to your call."

Beckett looked down at her hands, marveling at the transformation within her. She could feel the power flowing through her body, a zest and vitality suffusing every cell of her being.

"I feel... different," she told them, her voice now carrying a sublime harmonic quality. "As if I am connected to everything, to every living being in the universe."

Tav affirmed her experience, completely unflummoxed. "You are now connected to every living being, Beckett. By fully embracing your role as the Goddess of Life, you have unleashed your true potential."

She faced Tav, and, with new knowledge permeating her being, she enlightened him on a part of her role he neglected to mention. Although not angry or upset, it was something they all should know. Tav managed to look suitably chagrined.

"The way the fabric of the life force works, there is creation," she looked toward Lucifer, "sustainment, which is my role now, and then containment," she glanced back at Tav.

"Sustaining the energy that fosters life in the universe requires me to generate that power from relationships with men, as my mother was forced to do." Beckett met each of them eye to eye as she continued. "The difference between us is that she couldn't have lasting relationships with anyone, forced to hop between suitor and consort, guardian, and primordial gods, including Ouranos - a being she created for herself. Eventually, those connections, like so many others, no longer worked. When Gaia finally found my father, she planned her way out, didn't she, Tav?"

His eyes held a somber, ancient ache as he met Beckett's

piercing stare. Shaking his head slowly, his manner was weighed down by the burden of centuries-old secrets finally unveiled.

"You are correct, Beckett. Gaia found herself trapped in a cycle of fleeting relationships, forever bound to sustaining the life force through transient connections with others. It was a burden she bore with grace and strength, but one that left her yearning for something more permanent."

He paused, his mind adrift in ages past. "When she met your father, everything transformed. In him, she discovered more than just a lover, but a kindred spirit - one who grasped the weight of her duties and her agonizing yearning for an alternative journey."

Beckett listened, her heart hurting for the mother she had never known, for the sacrifices Gaia had made in service of her divine duty. "So, they planned my birth, didn't they? A child born of their love, but also one who could one day take on the mantle of the Goddess of Life, freeing Gaia from her eternal cycle."

"Yes, Beckett. Your birth was a gift, not just to your parents, but to the universe itself. In you, they saw hope for a new way, a path that would allow the Goddess of Life to find stability, love, and support as guardian of the life force." Despite the sadness surrounding Gaia's plight, Tav was optimistic. "You are needed and capable of doing things Gaia herself could not."

Lucifer's hand came to rest on Beckett's arm. "And that is why we are here, my love. That's why you possess the mantles you do, including Eros which helps limit the relationships you'll need. We're here to be your partners, consorts, and guardians - not just in sustaining the life force, but in every aspect of your life and journey."

Bowman reached out to take Beckett's other hand. "You are not alone in this, Beckett. Not now, and not ever. We are your family, lovers, and friends - and together, we will find a way to shoulder these responsibilities while ensuring you experience the love, stability, and happiness you deserve."

Giving Bowman's hand an appreciative clasp, Beckett released it to move to Tav, opening her arms to enfold him in an ardent hug reminiscent of her childhood. "Thank you for telling me the truth."

This time, Tav's arms went around her just as fiercely. He whispered, "You're absolutely stunning, my Lady of These Woods. You dazed me as a child, and you amaze me now as an adult and primordial goddess. I will be bound to you, if you will it."

Beckett pulled back with a jerk, astonished at Tav's heartfelt offer. So this is what he meant about others seeking her favor, she thought. Searching his face, she perceived his honesty, sincerity, and emotion etched in every line, every glance of his ancient gaze. His offer was authentic and forthright - and as a primordial god, his energy ranked among the highest in the universe. Beckett couldn't be more flattered.

Raising her face to him, she said intimately, "Tav, Lucifer bound himself to me long ago, and at some point, I intend to return that binding. I'm not at that stage where I can or need to do so right now. But I accept yours, so long as it's unconditional and there's an agreement that your energy feeds mine and the universe's."

She reached up to his cheek, her touch a feather-light caress that seemed to hold the wisdom of centuries. "If you are willing, if it is your heart's true desire, then I would be honored to have you bound to me, not just as my consort, but as my partner in every sense of the word."

Tav's face changed, struck with joy and disbelief, his hand coming up to cover hers, pressing her palm more firmly against his skin. "My lady, my Beckett – I do not require you to bind to me. There is nothing I desire more than to stand by your side, to lend you my strength, my love, and my eternal devotion. To be bound to you would be the greatest honor and privilege of my existence."

As he spoke, a gentle radiance began to shine from their clasped hands, a tender, throbbing glow that intensified with every second. Lucifer, Sean, and Bowman observed the light stretch and widen, wrapping Beckett and Tav, and subsequently Lucifer and Sean, in a dazzling, otherworldly gloss.

When the light finally faded, the group noticed a delicate, complex pattern on Tav's hand where it met Beckett's—a shimmering filigree in silver and gold that echoed the markings on her own skin. The sight was breathtaking, a visible testament to the bond now formed between the Goddess of Life and the Guardian of the Underworld."

Amazed, Lucifer explained to Beckett, "Tav never formed such a bond with your mother. We only have the chance to do that once."

"I know", Beckett replied sympathetically, "He wasn't in love with Gaia, and he tried to get her to do things differently, didn't you?"

Tav's look of age-old sadness transformed into one of new hope and joy, which sparkled in his eyes as he met Beckett's gaze. "You are right, Beckett. I cared deeply for your mother, but ours was a relationship grounded in friendship and mutual respect, not love. My role with her was akin to what Sean shares with you. I empathized with her as she grappled with the demands of her position, always longing for a connection that would support her, not just in her duties but deep in her soul as well."

He hesitated, his fingers softly entwining with Beckett's as the silver-gold filigree shimmered in the dim room lighting. "I tried to guide her, to help her find a different path—one that would provide the love and stability she so desperately craved. But ultimately, it was a journey she had to undertake alone, a realization she had to reach in her own time."

"Those choices led her to your father, Beckett. It was a love that altered everything, not only for Gaia but for the destiny of the universe itself," Lucifer added kindly. "And now, here we stand - at the beginning of a new journey, a new way forward."

Beckett faced Bowman, who spoke to her quietly. "You already know how I feel. No one could ever replace you in my life. Could we have a few minute alone to talk?"

Lucifer responded promptly, "Absolutely." And Sean suggested, "Let's all head to the common room and have a drink."

Initially hesitant to leave, Tav finally agreed and exited the library, though not without cautioning Bowman, "Make sure you don't hurt Beckett again." Beckett instructed the reluctant Dux and Tenebris to follow the others out. They complied, but weren't happy about it. Then, she directed Sam to cut off communication with the library.

"We are alone, Bowman. Completely and fantastically alone." Beckett reached for him only for Bowman to envelope her body in his arms. She buried her face in the crook of his neck.

"I want to be bound to you, too. I don't know how to do it," he said, reaching up to touch her hair.

"There are several ways. I'm betting there's one you'd prefer over the others," Beckett told him.

"Oh yeah, do tell." His hands moved from caressing her hair, to her back, her arms, and her face. Head swimming in pleasure and arousal, she pulled her face back to relay the specifics he'd requested to him, and he took that opportunity to kiss her like he had earlier in day.

"One option involves love and other indoor sports, I'm in

like flint," Bowman whispered in her ear, sending shivers that erupted in goosebump all over her body.

"It does,"she answered, kissing him with more urgency, putting her arms around his neck and running her fingers through his hair.

He sighed, his breathing shaky, "The condition of my binding is that you come to my bed. Tonight, with the moon and starlight streaming through my windows, I want to see, touch, feel, smell and revel in all of you. I want you to *feel me*. Is that agreed?"

"Yes, Bowman. But Katie –"

"Katie's off with her best friend spending the night. She arranged it so she wouldn't be depressed about Connor leaving. Again, you agree?"

Beckett lifted her head from Bowman's shoulder, and gave him her answer. "I do." A thin wisp of smoke ran from her to him, cementing their commitment.

Removing themselves from the heat and arousal they generated took a substantial act of perseverance. Nevertheless, they managed it, and Bowman took her hand, heading for the door and the hallway. When they stepped outside, Beckett called to Sam that he could enable his presence in the library.

Once they got to the common room, they found champagne uncorked, and saw a buffet set up on the long sideboard. There were more than thirty people there, all talking in great excitement until she rounded the corner with Bowman. The hellhounds, having met them in the hallway, flanked Beckett.

The room gradually quieted once she appeared, but Tav, Lucifer, and Sean all lifted their glasses. Bowman released her hand and took her arm, presenting her to those in the room. Grabbing a glass of champagne, he toasted her as Sean commanded their attention, "Welcome to Dr. Argonne, who has also accepted her role as the primordial Goddess of the Life in the universe, as well as her position as the CEO of Evigvokter. Cheers!"

Employees cheered and wolf whistled, then made their way to the sideboard for dinner. Danny, his face flushed from champagne, came to congratulate her. "Dr. Argonne, my dad is going to flip out about how right he was about you." She hugged him laughing, grateful that all these people accepted who she was and seemed to be enthusiastic about what came next.

Bowman didn't stay, saying he'd had dinner with Katie and Connor, and still had chores in the barn. He hugged Beckett, whispering in her ear, "When all is quiet, come to me?" She nodded. *Love you, Bowie*, she thought, and was completely speechless when he answered verbally, "Not like I love you, baby." With a wink, he left.

Smoothly, Tav slid beside her. Gently, he inquired if Bowman would also be binding himself to her. "I think so, Tav. Is that a good thing?" Tav, smiling, kissed her cheek.

He explained softly, "There are two reasons why it's a good thing. Firstly, he is who he is—the biological father of your children, and evidently, he brings you joy. The only flaw I find in him is the pain he caused you in the past, but he acknowledged that and endured the consequences. Secondly, his role is as crucial as Lucifer's, Sean's, and mine. His position yields and controls the most potent weapons in the universe."

Tav finished his drink, studying her as his thoughts reached her mind: *Beckett, you have endured much, but your suffering ends now.* He motioned towards Bowman, who stood apart, listening to Danny among the crowd in the common room. *I assume he has chosen a different, perhaps more pleasurable, way to commit to you, and you're in agreement?* Nodding, she wasn't shocked by his ability to communicate with her telepathically.

He continued, *When he does so, I want you to repeat back to him what you understood he said, not that you reciprocate the binding.* Beckett looked up at him, startled, and asked aloud, "It doesn't bother you, Tav?"

"No," he replied, moving closer to whisper in her ear, "I want you to be happy and—I want you to know me better, too."

Jeez, she thought, did someone turn up the heat or what? When her eyes met his, she confirmed they were deep navy blue, with specks of silver and gold. Beckett had no doubt that he could make any woman lose what little sense she had if he compelled her to do so. Right at that moment, Sean and Lucifer joined them, with Sean quipping, "So, did the Battlemaster decide what he wants?"

Beckett smiled, opting to stay mum, which naturally sparked banter between Sean and Tav. Seeing an opportunity, Lucifer took her arm, guiding her a few steps away from the group.

She heard *Sean, Tav, and I are going to London around midnight. Our leads, as well as Danny and Sam's, have borne fruit, and we'll be detaining and bringing suspects back here for questioning, including Dr. Calvin.* He watched her face and not seeing a negative reaction, he continued, *I know Bowman wants to bind himself to you and I understand how he'll want that to occur.* He marked a line from her temple to her jaw with the side of his hand, and the look on his face turned her knees to jelly. *I want you to enjoy yourself and be free from the past, you understand.*

It took everything she had to nod that she did. *Lucifer, I don't want you feel ever that I'm betraying you or anything. I love you. This part of the goddess of the life force gig has me a little uncomfortable, because I don't want to hurt anyone, especially not you. If you say I shouldn't do this, I won't.* Good Lord, she loved him. She loved his voice, the way his eyes possessed her and wouldn't let her go.

He led her into the hallway and enveloped her in his arms. *I'm definitely not hurt, and I'm not threatened. Everyone heard your declaration about eventually binding yourself to me, and I know you'll do it when you're ready. I trust you, always have. You need this—for you and Bowman, as well as for Connor and Katie. Come down the hall with me..."*

Lucifer led her down the hallway to the alcove leading to the stairs and made her step up one so she could be more equal with his height. He brought her head to his, and repeated what he'd said to her before, *You are my everything. Before you let someone make you feel, I'm going to start that process because I want you to feel everything you can, any way you can.*

He drew her face to his with his hands, kissing her with such love and desire that he literally ended up keeping her on her feet. Lucifer pulled her tighter to him, with one hand on the small of her back and the other holding her head. He grasped her hair, pulling her head back gently, then took his time ravaging her neck and shoulder, inhaling her scent every time he stopped. Moaning, Beckett's heart pounded, and she couldn't breathe or think. Neither could he.

With a great effort, he pulled himself from her, pressing his forehead against hers. *Don't let this Calvin thing set you back, little one. Tav and I won't have it and we know everything we need to know now. We couldn't act on your behalf until you accepted your destiny. Now, we can and will.* Taken aback how fast the investigation unfolded, Beckett said vocally, "I leave this to you, Lucifer. I promised you and Sean I would not intervene, and I won't. I won't even interrogate him if you think I shouldn't. I'm too eager to move on."

Lucifer kissed her again, a deep lingering kiss fraught with appreciation, love, and a whole universe of desire. Looking at her, he replied, "We'll cross that bridge when we come to it, but you," he cupped her face with his hands and kissed her forehead and nose, and lips. "Go and have a good time. I'll let you know when we're back."

They parted unwillingly, and Beckett headed back to the common room. Sean and Tav were saying their goodbyes to people and met her when she entered the space. "Did Lucifer tell you what we're doing, Beckett?" Sean asked and she nodded. Tav, kissed her cheek and Sean did the same. *We'll be back in the morning* they both told her. When they were out of sight, Beckett showered the folks left in the common room with her appreciation. After most of the staff left, she returned to her suite with the hellhounds, and changed her clothes.

Beckett threw the cloak Mrs. McKinnon made for her over her shoulders. "Dux, Tenebris, I'm going to Bowman's to spend the night. You can patrol the house inside and outside or lay on the front porch if that suits you."

Tenebris raised his head to her, "We'll stay in the living room. There's always a fire and we can rotate inside and outside without disturbing anyone."

Dux gave a short bob of his head in agreement with his brother. "Would you like us to transport you, my goddess?"

"Not this time, my loyal protectors of the almost canine persuasion. I will take you with me." No sooner did Beckett think about being on Bowman's front porch, she arrived, trying the door. Unlocked. She went into the darkened room, pointing the hellhound boys to the wood stove with its heat.

Pitching off the cloak, she made her way to Bowman's bedroom, where he stood, wearing no shirt and knit sweats, looking at the moon through the floor to ceiling windows that lined the front and side of his bed. His torso was highlighted by the moonlight; she could see the shadow of lines in muscles all over his back, fueling a desire that almost made her woozy. Bowman turned when he heard her. In one graceful move, had her in his arms.

"You. You occupy my thoughts, morning, noon, and night." He began to slowly kiss her. Then the smoldering embers of the day became a fire in the night. Regardless of the state of his arousal, he took his time exploring her face, lips, neck, and shoulders with his hands, his lips. Once satisfied, he began to slowly, almost deliriously, torturously, undress her, starting with the left spaghetti strap, and later, the right strap, of her forest green slip dress.

Once the dress fell to the floor, he pulled off his sweats, embracing her skin to skin. She gasped as the cool air of the bedroom kissed her overheated skin, only to be quickly replaced by the scorch of Bowman's touch and lips.

She couldn't think. Leaning into him, her hands sliding up his chest, reveling in the solidness and heat of his body against hers. "Bowman," she whispered, flushed with need. "I feel you. This…it's overwhelming, this craving for your touch. It's..it's…" She couldn't form the thoughts into words.

Bowman's hands slid down her back, pulling her even closer, his fingers digging into her hips with a possessive urgency. "Beckett," he growled, his lips brushing against her ear. "You have no idea…"

Beckett's head fell back, a soft moan escaping her lips as Bowman trailed hot, open-mouthed kisses down the column of her neck. "Beckett," he breathed. Each touch of his lips, each scrape of his teeth against her sensitive skin, sent bolts of tingling through her, stoking the fire that burned within her.

Breathless, with her fingers entangling in his hair, Beckett urged him on, pulling him closer. " I need you. I need to feel you, all of you."

Bowman's answer was a searing kiss, his lips claiming hers with a ferocity that stole the breath from her lungs. His tongue delved into her mouth, tangling with hers, as his hands roamed over her body, mapping every curve and hollow with reverent urgency.

He laid her down the bed, his body covering hers, his weight an exquisite pressure that made her ache with need. "Beckett," he whispered, his eyes dark with desire as he admired her whole body. "My beautiful, incredible Beckett. I'm going to worship every inch of you."

And he did. With eyes, lips, tongue, hands, and teeth, Bowman explored her body, leaving a trail of flames in his wake. Beckett arched beneath him, her hands grasping at his shoulders, his back, desperate to anchor herself amidst the maelstrom of sensation that threatened to sweep her away. He urged her to climax, sustaining and extending her pleasure for as long as she'd let him.

When he finally entered her, their bodies joining in a moment of mind-altering unity, Beckett felt a completeness, as if every moment of her life had been leading to this, to him. They moved together, their rhythm ancient and primal, a waltz of love and passion as old as time itself.

Bowman cradled her head, kissing her, reassuring her, stroking her slowly. When she came, a shaking, intense, full body orgasm, she heard him clearly in her ear, "I bind myself to you and you alone, Beckett Argonne, Goddess of Life, the love of my life, the possessor of the mantle of Athena, and the mother of my children."

And as they climbed higher again, their pleasure building to another crescendo, Beckett knew that this was more than just physical desire, more than the simple joining of two bodies. It was a union, a merging of hearts, bodies, and destinies that would echo through the universe in form of energy that sustained and promulgated throughout the life force.

As they orgasmed together, with tears in her eyes, she purred, "I accept your binding, Bowman Maethor, my first love whom I still love, the possessor of the mantle of

Hephaestus, and father of my children." As she said it, she heard Bowman gasp at the flash of light that enveloped them, leaving a sigil of silver gold and sapphire filagree on the ball of his shoulder where she'd firmly kept a grip.

In the aftermath, as they lay entwined in Bowman's bed, one of his hands stroking her hair, Beckett knew that whatever whatever they might face, she would always have this moment, this perfect, shining memory of love and passion in the heart of her sanctuary.

Turning her face up to Bowman, she kissed his jaw, expressing to him that she felt like a virgin deflowered with infinite care and expertise. He chuckled and cozied up to her, saying, "I've never experienced anything remotely like what we just did. Look at me." She turned her face to him again. "I didn't hurt you, did I?"

Shaking her head no, she nestled on his chest. Bowman tucked the sheets around her. "Nice dress, by the way," he mentioned drowsily, "but I like you better without it." He cuddled her again, nose in the crook of her neck. "I love the way you feel against me. So good." Kissing her, Bowman yawned. Then she yawned and they chuckled together, happy, satisfied, and unafraid.

As they settled in for the night, Beckett's mind wandered, noting all the significant and life altering events of the last several days. The gratitude she felt for those who supported her, protected her, loved her, and most importantly, accepted her, overwhelmed the personal misgivings that concerned her.

She fell asleep with the thought that she was Beckett Argonne, daughter of Gaia, embodiment of the life force, and protector of the universal balance. And with the love and strength of her family and friends to support her, she knew that there was no obstacle too great, no darkness too deep, for her to overcome. Together, they would face the coming storm

- and together, they would emerge victorious.

Chapter 21

A Tangled Skein

In the early light of dawn, Beckett awoke to the inviting aromas of coffee and bacon. She stretched contentedly, still cocooned in Bowman's sheets, and glanced at the clock. Realizing it was still quite early, she slipped into his robe hanging from the bedpost, ran her fingers through her hair, and followed the delicious scents to the kitchen.

She stood quietly in the doorway, admiring Bowman's back muscles and the rhythmic movement of his shoulders and biceps as he cooked eggs, stirring them occasionally in the pan. The sound of the coffee maker signaled him, and as he turned to pour a cup, he noticed her. "I thought the smell of bacon would wake you," he said with a smile. "Good morning, sleeping beauty. Did you sleep well?" He handed her a steaming mug of coffee.

Accepting the cup, Beckett kissed him tenderly. "Hmm, I slept wonderfully, thanks. How about you?" As she drew back, Bowman closed the gap, returning her kiss with equal gentleness.

Getting plates from a cupboard, Bowman joked, "Well, I

had an amazing night. This goddess of life, or so she claims, visited me in my bedroom—imagine that! A wild night, fantastic sleep, and," he handed her a plate piled with bacon, eggs, and buttered toast, "here's your breakfast, m'lady. Go sit over there and enjoy."

As Beckett perched on a stool at the kitchen island, she realized she was incredibly hungry. Good Lord, she thought, he's a lover in the bedroom and a master chef outside of it. But at 6:15 in the morning? "Bowman, do you normally wake up this early?"

He joined her at the island, starting in on his own meal. "Not usually on weekends, but on weekdays, yes."

"We're up early for a different reason today, aren't we? Are Lucifer, Sean, and Tav back from London?" She set down her fork, her attention shifting.

"Sam called me. They got back about 5:30 this morning, and they're currently holding three suspects in the investigation and detention wing adjacent to the castle," Bowman stated matter-of-factly. "Sam mentioned that Lucifer wanted you to rest. If he hadn't heard from you by nine, he'd have reached out directly as promised."

Beckett felt a swirl of anticipation at Bowman's words. The reality of the situation began to sink in—the men responsible for her abduction, the ones who had inflicted so much pain and trauma, were now within reach, awaiting the consequences of their actions.

Inhaling, Beckett's grip on the coffee mug tightened as she processed the information. "Three suspects? Do we know who they are? What their connection is to what happened to me?"

Bowman reached out, placing his hand—the same one he had used so passionately the night before—on her shoulder. "I don't have all the details. From what Sam told me, one of them is Dr. Calvin. The other two are apparently his associates, though their exact roles are still being determined."

"I want to see them, Bowman. I want to look into the eyes of the men who did this to me, who thought they could break me and get away with it." Beckett, still eating, couldn't keep a flame of anger from erupting in her eyes.

Bowman responded smoothly, "I know, Beckett. You'll have that chance, I promise you. But we need to be smart about this, to make sure we handle it in a way that ensures justice is served and that you're protected."

He stood up, moving to stand behind her, his hands gently massaging the tension from her shoulders. "Lucifer, Sean, and Tav will ensure the interrogations are conducted properly, and that we gather all the information we need to build an airtight case against them. And when the time is right, when you're ready, you'll have the opportunity to confront them on your own terms."

"Oh, you have no idea how much I'd like to 'confront' them, if that's the word you want to use," she said icily, her mind already crafting the kind of "confrontation" she'd like to have with Dr. Calvin. "I know I'm supposed to refrain from using my newfound 'goddessness' for retribution, but I certainly want to." She picked up a piece of bacon, biting into it aggressively.

Bowman chuckled softly at Beckett's display of aggression towards the bacon, understanding the rawness of her anger and the desire for retaliation that simmered beneath the surface. He knelt beside her, taking her nearest hand in his.

"Believe me, Beckett, I understand that desire all too well. There's a part of me that wants nothing more than to make those bastards suffer for what they did to you, to inflict upon them the same pain and terror they caused you."

His thumb gently caressed the back of her hand as he gathered his thoughts. "But we need to rise above that, to be better than using our abilities for vengeance. It's not about letting them off easy or ignoring the gravity of their crimes. It's about ensuring justice is served in a way that reflects the principles we uphold—the balance, the light, and the hope that you, as the Goddess of Life, embody."

Beckett sighed, recognizing the truth in Bowman's words, even as anger and thoughts of vengeance continued to grow within her. "I know that yielding to that darkness, that urge for retribution, would only corrupt the very essence of what I'm meant to protect. But it's so difficult, so challenging, to look beyond the pain and trauma they inflicted, to find a way to face them without losing myself in the process."

"It's hard. Arguably one of the hardest things you'll ever have to do. But that's why you have us to remind you of your true nature, even in your darkest moments." Bowman's words resonated with compassion.

He pressed a tender kiss to her forehead. "When the time comes to confront them, you won't be alone. Together, we'll find a way to hold them accountable, to ensure that they face the consequences of their actions, without compromising the integrity of your soul."

"I can't promise that I won't falter, that I won't be tempted to give in to that anger," Beckett confessed, her lips brushing against his nose, "but I do promise to try, to lean on you and the others when I feel myself slipping."

She took a deep breath, steeling herself. "And I agree that when I do confront them, it will be on my terms, in a manner that upholds what I've become and the principles I stand for. They may have hurt me, but they won't define me. They will not drag me down to their level."

What Beckett didn't offer was her vision of Calvin, bound on a platform, his ankles and wrists secured, engulfed in unyielding darkness. And, should such an opportunity arise, she wasn't sure she could restrain herself from exacting the same torment she had endured.

Having just resettled beside her, Bowman perceived the intensity of Beckett's fury and the dark imaginings rising within her. He gently turned her to face him, his hands soothingly caressing her arms as he gazed deeply into her eyes. "Beckett, I understand your anger and your desire for retribution against those who caused such terrible harm," he said, his tone imbued with utmost care and empathy. "Those feelings are valid and completely reasonable, considering the atrocities you've suffered."

"However, I urge caution about allowing vengeance to consume you or dictate your future actions. Inflicting the same pain on Calvin as he perpetuated on you might offer temporary satisfaction, but in the long term, it jeopardizes your integrity and moral standing. It could tarnish the purity of your role as a guardian of life and a symbol of hope."

Beckett listened, her jaw tightly clenched as she wrestled with her anger. Bowman persisted, his tone neutral. "I know it may feel unimaginable right now, but the greatest victory lies in rising above the darkness, not succumbing to it. By facing your abusers with strength, dignity, and an unwavering commitment to justice, you showcase the resilience of your spirit, a resilience they could never shatter. You demonstrate that you refuse to be defined by the harm they inflicted upon you."

Bowman lovingly brushed a wayward strand from her face, the soft contact a balm to her worries.

"Allow yourself to feel your pain and anger fully, but don't allow them to dictate your actions. Lean on me, Lucifer, Sean, Tav, and the others. Let us be your anchors and your guiding light through the shadows."

Beckett absorbed his words, contemplating their important to her well being. Bowman smiled gently, his unwavering faith in her evident in his gaze.

"When the moment arrives to confront Calvin and the others, do it in your own way, to voice your truth and demand accountability. But never forget the remarkable woman you've become—a goddess of strength and renewal. A survivor in every definition of the word."

Drawing nearer, he rested his cheek against hers, his next words a heartfelt vow. "Healing is a long, nonlinear journey, and some days the temptation of vengeance may sing its siren song. But I believe in the unbreakable strength of your spirit, Beckett. You have the power to alchemize this pain into purpose, to find meaning in the struggle and to emerge with your head held high and radiance undimmed. You've already proven that. I'll be with you every step of the way on this difficult road ahead. I've got you."

As they finished their breakfast, the conversation turning to lighter topics and the comfort of each other's company, Beckett vowed to control her emotions with the others' help. Doing so in her present mindset would be arduous, but Bowman's words stuck with her, making her think it might be possible for her to stay sane, maybe not do anything unprofessional or, more likely, revenge-oriented.

After tidying up and sharing a fond embrace with Bowman, Beckett, along with Dux and Tenebris, went back to her suite at the castle. Bowman assured her he would follow shortly. Once there, she took a refreshing shower and chose her outfit with care: a black silk shirt paired with trousers and low heels, her hair styled into a top knot to highlight her undercut.

She accessorized with diamond threader earrings, their sparkle catching the light as she put them on. Studying her reflection in the mirror, she fortified her resolve. If I have to face my demons today, I might as well embrace what Sean dubs my 'Viking warrior princess look', she mused. Sean would understand, if no one else did; she needed armor and presence to maintain her focus and temper her vendetta.

The reflection staring back at Beckett made clear the enormity of the challenge ahead. It could be as daunting as anything she had faced before. As she prepared to leave, she called for her hellhound protectors. Slipping her phone into her trouser pocket, she moved toward the door, only for Tenebris to block her path while Dux nudged his head under her hand, their actions breaking her train of thought.

"Goddess," Dux growled, throaty and raspy, "we can sense your anger and frustration. We stand with you, ready to protect. And kill, if necessary." For the first time, she noticed the hackles on both were raised, their eyes shifting from black to a deep, menacing red. They were truly prepared to defend her, to seek retribution against those who had harmed her. This realization sparked a pivotal question within her: Do I want that?

Beckett's hand lingered on Dux's head she observed the hellhounds' battle-ready stance. Their raised hackles and the menacing red of their eyes underscored the ferocity they wielded—a force directly influenced by her own emotions and commands.

Conflicted, she continued to stroke Dux's fur, trying to soothe both the animal and herself as she navigated her tumultuous feelings. The anger remained, a persistent undercurrent, but Bowman's earlier advice echoed within her: to transcend the darkness and not allow vengeance to dictate her actions. This moment of reflection was a critical one, reinforcing her commitment to handle the situation with a level of composure that honored her role and maintained her integrity.

"Dux, Tenebris," she said, steady and controlled. "I appreciate your loyalty and your readiness to defend me. Your presence alone brings me strength and comfort."

Tenebris tilted his head, his red eyes probing hers, as if to reach into the depths of her internal conflict. "But...?" he quizzed, sympathetic and somewhat understanding.

Beckett sighed, a wry smile spreading on her face. "But I don't want us to resort to violence or death as our first solution, even though a part of me might crave it. We must aim for justice, not revenge. To do otherwise would be to let them win, to let them corrupt the very principles I uphold."

Dux's posture relaxed, his eyes returning to their customary deep black. "We understand, Goddess. Your wisdom and compassion guide us. We will follow your lead and protect you as you deem appropriate."

"Thank you, my friends. Violence will be our last resort, not our first instinct," Beckett reaffirmed, her tone leaving no room for doubt.

The hellhounds dipped their heads, their hackles smoothing as they aligned their behavior with Beckett's directive. She straightened her shoulders, the reflection of the Viking warrior princess in the mirror now exemplifying a different kind of strength—a strength rooted in resilience, integrity, and the potency of her principles.

Sam called out to her, "Dr. Argonne, good morning. The investigative team is in the detention wing, interview room 4. I've informed them you're on your way." With a quick word of thanks to Sam, Beckett opened the door, prepped for the next phase of the Calvin investigation. Dux and Tenebris fell into step beside her, a steady reminder of the loyalty and protection that encircled her.

Navigating the castle corridors, Beckett's thoughts shifted to the upcoming conversation—a strategy session with Tav, Bowman, Sean, and Lucifer. She recognized that her insights, combined with their collective wisdom, expertise, and varied perspectives, could potentially shift the investigation's direction towards uncovering the full truth behind her abduction. It might also keep me from doing anything impulsive, she mused with a touch of irony.

Beckett, navigating the castle's corridors with Dux and Tenebris at her side, followed signs leading to the detention wing. The route took them deeper beneath the castle, an area she had never visited but recalled from the map she had studied in the library. To maintain Dell Castle and its estate as a pristine historic site, most of the operational facilities of Evigvokter, including adjacent buildings and power plants, were strategically located inside and beneath the hills surrounding the main headquarters.

Upon arriving at the secure doors of the detention wing, her admiration for Sean's architectural prowess intensified. She marveled at how he managed to conceive and construct such a complex facility within the stringent regulations of Scotland and the UK, all within a mere three years. She made a mental note to discuss this remarkable feat with him, eager to hear about the details and challenges he faced during the construction.

Brooding and formidable, Tav sat in the detention wing's outer waiting area. Upon spotting Beckett, he stood. "Good morning, Beckett." He approached her swiftly, taking her hand and delicately kissing the back of it. Clasping it in his, he asked cheekily, "Have a good evening?"

"Why yes, Tavarius, I certainly did. Even got breakfast out of the deal," she replied with a smile.

Tav raised an eyebrow in playful curiosity, "With bacon or without?"

"Wouldn't you like to know?" Beckett responded with a sly grin, gently poking his chest.

He threw back his head and laughed heartily, his teeth a bright, straight white. "I'm betting that's a yes."

"Did you have a good evening too, Tav?" Beckett asked, her tone curious.

His face suddenly shifted, becoming powerful, menacing,

and gloomy. "We did, in a sense. Although, personally, I definitively wish I could rip someone's face off. But alas," Tav said with a glum tone, "I cannot."

He let out a massive, disappointed sigh—the kind that came from someone not used to being inhibited from acting on his impulses. Taking her elbow gently, he guided her towards interview room 4.

As Beckett and Tav neared the door to I-4, the gravity of the forthcoming exchange increased Becket's anxiousness. Their earlier lighthearted exchange dissipated, replaced by a somber determination. Tav, concerned, paused with his hand resting on the door handle, .

"Beckett," he spoke, his voice low and sincere, "before we step inside, I need you to understand that we're all here to support you. Whatever you need, whatever decisions you make, we'll stand by you. But I also want to remind you of the strength and wisdom you carry within you. You've come so far and grown so much. I have no doubt you'll handle this with the grace and integrity that define you."

Beckett met Tav's gaze, her eyes reflecting her appreciation. "Thank you, Tav. Having your support, and the others, means everything to me. I know this won't be easy, but I'm reassured knowing I'm not alone in this—especially when part of me feels just as you described. My goal is to uncover the truth and deliver justice, without compromising who I am."

"Well said, my dear. Now, let's join the others and put our heads together. With your expertise and our combined efforts, we're going to uncover the truth and make sure those responsible are held accountable," Tav encouraged her.

Beckett readied herself as Tav opened the door. Inside, Lucifer, Sean, and Bowman were already gathered around a large conference table in a spartan, but well-equipped, room. A wall of monitors displayed various pieces of evidence and data, painting a clear picture of the case at hand. The atmosphere was industrious, ready for the strategic planning that lay ahead.

Lucifer rose from his seat, his face packed with empathy as he approached Beckett, enveloping her in a sweeping embrace. "How are you holding up, love?" he murmured, his lips brushing against her temple.

Rather than gloss over how she felt, Beckett opted to be transparent. "I'm struggling with anger and vengeance, Lucifer. But I'm here to get to work, to figure out our next steps and how we're going to approach this."

Sean and Bowman echoed Lucifer's sentiments, each offering a gesture of reassurance or a supportive remark as Beckett and Tav took their seats at the table. Underneath the table, Bowman's hand sought out Beckett's, his fingers lacing with hers in a private display of solidarity and comfort.

Once everyone was settled, Sean cleared his throat, adopting a serious tone as he began to outline the evidence they'd compiled. "Our investigations have revealed a complex web of connections involving Dr. Calvin, Professor Langdon, and a shadowy extremist group known as the Illumined Circle. It appears they targeted Beckett due to her unique heritage and potential, aiming to harness her powers for their own dark agenda."

Beckett absorbed each detail in deep concentration. As she parsed through the information, her mind buzzed with questions and theories, the forensic psychologist in her piecing together the suspects' potential motivations and vulnerabilities.

Tav continued to build on the narrative, his tone underscored with seriousness as he leaned forward, elbows on the table. "We've also uncovered evidence that the Illumined Circle has been active for decades, if not centuries. They have a long history of targeting individuals with supernatural abilities, exploiting them for their own ends.

Beckett's abduction isn't just a singular event; it's part of a much broader and more disturbing pattern."

Beckett's words cut through the silence that had settled around the table, her tone steady despite the disturbing nature of her disclosure. "Their abduction and abuse of me specifically aligns with their ideologies around procreation. It correlates with the sequence of events during my captivity." She paused, noticing the shocked expressions on both Tav's and Lucifer's faces. "It's true: they were relentless in their attempts to coerce me into impregnation."

Her own words left her mildly nauseated and enraged. Employing some meditative breathing, she prepared for the inevitable questions. Bowman delicately asked, "Is that why they subjected you to rape, waterboarding, electric shocks, physical assaults, and deprivation of sleep, water, and food?"

She nodded, her composure intact. Bowman and Sean were fully aware of the horrors she had faced; Lucifer had some understanding, though not complete, and Tav, she realized, was probably learning the full extent of her ordeal for the first time.

Bowman and Beckett's words hung in the air, her revelation shocking the two most supernatural beings in the group. Lucifer's face drained of color as he processed the implications of her statement. Sean and Bowman exchanged a glance, their faces mirroring the horror and outrage that now permeated the room.

Tav was the first to speak, his voice cutting through the oppressive atmosphere. "Beckett, I... I had no idea." His jaw was tight with controlled fury. "The depravity of their actions knows no bounds. To think that they would stoop so low, to attempt to violate you in such a terrifying and intimate way..."

Beckett drew in a shaky breath, her grip on Bowman's hand tightening as she maintained her composure. "It was their ultimate goal, I now believe, after what you all discussed today. To create a child with my abilities, one they could mold and manipulate to serve their twisted purposes. They tried to break me, to coerce me into compliance, but I refused. Even in my darkest moments, I clung to the hope that I would be found, that I would not let them win."

"They will pay for this, Beckett. I promise you, we will hold them accountable for their actions. What they did to you, and potentially others, is unforgivable." Lucifer stood, his hands trembling with the force of his anger as he paced the room, his divine presence filling the space with a noticeable intensity.

Bitterly, Sean added, "Bowman and I knew most of the details Beckett's shared, but not from the Yard's flimsy police report. It wasn't detailed enough, so we received help from MI5. We'd already incorporated the collection of medical records and genetic material into our strategy. Since procreation was their aim, they left behind evidence that we used, and can still use, against them."

He threw a thick manila folder on the table. "This is a copy of what MI5 found, including the DNA results from material taken from Beckett's injuries. Sam and Danny obtained medical records for Calvin from NHS. One of these DNA samples, out of the more than eight collected matches Calvin. Beckett's sample was also among them."

Bowman picked up the thread from Sean. "We suspect it's possible that the reason The Yard hired Beckett stemmed from someone there wanting to keep track of her, see if and what she remembered, before attempting to eliminate her. If they couldn't get what they wanted from her, they planned to kill her."

As Sean and Bowman laid out the evidence and their suspicions, Beckett grappled with the implications of their findings. The near fact that someone within the Yard might have been involved in her abduction, monitoring her recovery, and potentially plotting her demise, fed the blossoming hate and hostility she felt.

"If the Yard's involvement is true, it means that we must assume the Illumined Circle's influence runs deeper than just there. They've infiltrated law enforcement, possibly other government agencies, and who knows what else." Beckett disposition remained calm and focused despite the turmoil brewing within her.

Tav nodded grimly, his eyes narrowing as he considered the ramifications. "It's a troubling thought, but not entirely surprising. Organizations like the Illumined Circle often seek to embed themselves in positions of power and authority, the better to further their agendas and evade detection."

"We'll need to be cautious, then. If they have eyes and ears within the Yard, our every move could be watched. We can't risk tipping them off before we're ready to strike." Lucifer growled, frustrated, still pacing around the conference table like a caged lion.

"We'll focus on compartmentalizing the investigation. Keep the circle of trust small, and feed false information through channels we suspect might be compromised. If we can identify their mole within the Yard, we can use that to our advantage." Concentrated and rational, Beckett's mind already started formulating a strategy. "Our first opportunity comes this week, because Eleanor Hargreaves wants to speak to me."

Sean's eyes glinted with approval, a contrast to his earlier angst. "Now you're talking my language. Divide and conquer. I like it. We'll need to be smart about how we proceed, but with Sam and Danny's help, I'm confident we can unravel this web of deceit and bring the whole damn thing crashing down around their ears."

"While we work to expose their network, we'll keep

Beckett safe. No matter what it takes, we won't let them get their hands on her again, " asserted Bowman, his hand still clasped tightly with Beckett's.

Lucifer stopped his pacing and sat, his gaze locking with Beckett's, a fierceness burning in his eyes. "Bowman's right. Your safety, your well-being, is our top priority. We'll move heaven and this earth to protect you, Beckett. You have my word."

Sean's smirk turned knowing as he interjected, "Move heaven and earth? Oh, you poor innocent mates. You haven't seen Beckett fight. Plus, now she's a goddess with mad skills to boot. She's got two hellhounds, a glaive, a dagger, this castle, and who knows what else in that not-so-secret-sanctum-of-whatever room. And she's not chasing around a possible suicidal pati-..."

Abruptly, realization dawned on his face. "Beckett, who asked you to follow that patient? Who was it, who authorized you to do what you did?"

Beckett's attitude turned pensive as she considered Sean's sudden question. She reached into the memories of the events leading up to her abduction, the prelude to that fateful day rushing back with startling clarity.

"It was a routine request," she began, despite the tiny shard of unease coiling in her gut. "A case file landed on my desk; a high-priority suspect, deemed at risk for suicide. The order came from higher up, signed off by the Chief Superintendent himself. But now that you mention it, Sean, there were irregularities. The file was incomplete, lacking the usual background information and risk assessment. The patient, a man named Marcus Ashcroft, had no prior history with the Yard or any other mental health services."

Lucifer leaned forward, his interest roused. "Ashcroft? That name has surfaced in our investigation, linked to some of the Illumined Circle's financial dealings. Could he have been a plant, a lure to draw you out?"

Tav turned thoughtful as he contemplated the possibility of Marcus Ashcroft's involvement. If the Illumined Circle had infiltrated the Yard, they could have orchestrated the entire scenario. Beckett's reputation and dedication to her patients would have made her the perfect target.

Bowman's grip on Beckett's hand increased, and a muscle in his cheek twitched. "Those bastards. They exploited your compassion, your desire to help others, and used it against you."

Beckett's emotional haze cleared as the pieces snapped together with disturbing clarity. The location had also been a red flag. The file had specified an address in a remote area, far removed from CCTV cameras or potential witnesses. She recalled finding it odd at the time, but her focus on reaching the patient and preventing a tragedy had overshadowed her initial concerns.

Sean's eyes narrowed, a dangerous spark of wrath within them. She'd never seen him this incensed during all the years she'd known him. "They underestimated you, Beckett. Your strength, your resilience. They thought they could break you, but they never stood a chance."

Beckett brushed a stray lock of hair behind her ear. "Knowing their methods gives us a chance to beat them at their own game." She hesitated, but only for a split second. "But we'll need to be careful, plan this meticulously."

"The advantage is ours now that we see how they operate," Lucifer offered. "We can use that knowledge to bring them down."

As the group rallied around her, their resolve fortified by the revelation of the Illumined Circle's intricate web of deceit, Beckett felt hopeful amid the anger and frustration. This investigation might be long and draining, but with her allies, her champions, and the power of truth on their side, victory was within reach.

Chapter 22

Echos of the Old Gods

In the restroom, hands smoothing over her face during their break, Beckett's mind whirled from their case collaboration. Too late, she realized this discussion should have happened sooner with Sean and Bowman - when leads were still fresh. Instead, she'd fled from all, uncertain who to trust, unwilling to bare her vulnerability again. A classic trauma response, blinding her to seeking aid or even recognizing symptoms within herself. Splashing water on her face, she felt sick with guilt.

A tap on the door, followed by a quiet call of her name. Opening it, she admitted Tav, who slipped inside and shut the door with a gentle click. "Beckett, little one, are you alright?" One look at her pale, silent face, and he swore softly, pulling her into his embrace. Muffled against his shoulder, she confessed to having withheld the facts too long, unwilling to trust.

"Sean and Bowman tracked down details, not wanting to burden or re-traumatize me," she mumbled into him. "I think I failed them...and myself," she choked out, blinking back tears.

His strong arms developed her, a sanctuary amid her

stormy emotions. He stroked her hair, his muttered reassurances soft and soothing. In that moment, Tav reminded her of the oak in her woods - steadfast, wrapping you in its embrace when you climbed high enough. You could press your cheek to the bark and let the song of the wind through the branches ease all your cares away.

"Lady of These Woods, you didn't fail. Not at all," he murmured, lips barely against her temple. "What you endured, no one should ever have to face that. You should have died, but you didn't. Your reactions, your need to shield yourself from the memories, they were natural, understandable."

He drew his head back slightly, cupping her face, thumbs tenderly wiping away newly fallen tears. "Sean and Bowman did what they did out of love, to spare you from reliving that horror, to shoulder the burden so you could heal."

"I know, and I'm so grateful for them, for everything. But I can't help feeling I should have been more resilient, faced this head-on sooner." Beckett drew fortitude from the ancient, stalwart primordial being embracing her.

Tav shook his head fiercely. "Strength isn't powering through pain, Lady. It's knowing when to lean on those who love you. That's what you did - you survived, healed, and now you're ready to face this darkness, to bring it into the light."

He pressed a kiss to her forehead. "You are the strongest person I know, Beckett. Not just because of your powers, but because of your heart, your resilience, and your unending commitment to truth and justice. Never doubt that, not even for a moment."

Beckett felt Tav's words wrapping around her like a protective cloak. She took a deep breath, letting his strength and belief in her wash away the lingering guilt and self-doubt.

"Thank you, Tav," she whispered, her arms tightening around him. She thought she liked him much better this way than as a tree in her woods. "I don't know what I did to deserve you, to deserve any of you. But I'm so thankful you're here."

Tav smiled and said with certainty, "You deserve all of this and more, Beckett. We'll be here, every step of the way, to make sure you get it. Together, we'll bring the Illumined Circle to their knees and ensure that no one else ever has to suffer as you did." He gathered her tighter, adding, "You know, if I don't eat them all and send them to the Pit."

Beckett's eyes widened, a mix of shock and morbid fascination flickering across her features. "You... you consume souls?" Her words were a hushed whisper. "Like Tartarus itself from the ancient texts?"

Tav's handsome face bore the trials of millennia, his very being radiating with primordial power. "I did not merely take on that mantle, little one. I am Tartarus - the abysmal, all-consuming deterrent against those who would dare threaten what is sacred."

He reached out, outlining her jaw with his finger. "It was my ineffable duty to protect your realm, your essence. Those foolish enough to invade, to disrupt the purity and balance you embodied, faced oblivion - their very souls devoured, damned for eternity within my depths."

Beckett turned her cheek, brushing her lips against his finger, accentuating the profound, mystical connection between them. The idea of him literally devouring souls, an act rooted in the most primordial of traditions, should have elicited revulsion. Knowing he'd done so to protect her stirred something primal, something ancient and potent, within her very essence.

"To know you would go to such mythical lengths to safeguard me..." She met his timeless gaze with reverence. "It fills me with a sense of being treasured and sheltered in a way I never could have envisioned prior to becoming part of this world."

Beckett closed her eyes, letting his words settle between them. In Tav, she found a perfect counterpoint to her own nature - a being of incredible power and untold depths, willing to embrace the darkness so that she might continue to bring light and life to the world.

"Thank you, Tav," Her words were hushed, but replete with appreciation. "For being my protector, my champion in the shadows. I may not fully understand the intricacies of your role, but I know that I am forever grateful to have you here."

As they stood there, locked in each other's embrace, Beckett experienced a measure of perfect balance. The Goddess of Life and the Guardian of the Pit, two halves of a cosmic whole, united in their love and their steadfast responsibility to the greater good.

Unenthusiastically, Tav pulled away. "Let's go back so we can finish this and get to eating... I mean, interviewing assh...I mean, suspects." Rather like Sean, he smirked. The Guardian of the Pit, in all his greatness, winked at her.

Her laugh echoed like bells against the walls of the restroom. "Ok," she said. With that, he took her hand and opened the door, leading her back into the interview room.

As they entered I-4, Beckett felt a lingering warmth in her chest, a subtle reverberation of the bond she had just shared with Tav. She composed herself, permitting a small, contented smile to grace her lips. Beckett still carried the gist from their discussion, but she felt a renewed vigor as she braced to tackle the task at hand.

Once back in the room, Tav escorted her to a chair between Bowman and Lucifer. Bowman took her hand under the table, while Lucifer draped an arm around the back of her shoulders. A wave of appreciation washed over Beckett for their unwavering support, their gestures of kindness anchoring her and reminding her that she didn't stand alone in this battle.

Getting seated himself, Tav informed the group, "Beckett and I decided that despite my better judgement, I won't be eating anyone today." He crossed his arms, anticipating Sean's reaction.

"You EAT people? How does one get that gig?" Sean couldn't help himself. "Are you purple when you do it or what? Come on, give. Inquiring minds wanna know." He sat down opposite Tav, propping his elbow on the table and resting his chin on his hand.

Unperturbed and loftily, Tav rejoined, "There's the Ares emerging in you. He always was a smart ass. For your information, ancient texts describe me as monstrous, arrogant, and the equivalent of a huge, dark, supernatural maelstrom. Definitely not purple."

"Like, Sean needs Ares to be a smart ass?" Bowman joked. They all chuckled and some of the tension left the room.

Sean took the lead: "Ok, so let's put some of the activities we discussed into operation. Beckett?"

"We'll need to dig deeper into Marcus Ashcroft," she said, developing a plan. "If he was a key player in their scheme, he may hold the answers we need to unravel their entire operation."

Sean's eyes flashed in anticipation. "Leave that to Sam and Danny. Those two could find a needle in a haystack blindfolded. They'll uncover every dirty secret Ashcroft and his ilk have ever tried to hide."

"Sam", Sean called, "I need you to get in touch with Wulf Froeste. Tell him I need him to meet me here tomorrow at whatever time is convenient for him. When Danny comes in tomorrow, let him know I need to see him first thing." At hearing Wulf's name, Beckett raised an eyebrow at Sean, who chose to be ignorant of the look she gave him.

Within minutes, Sam interjected, "Sir, he's still on the line if you'd like me to put him through." Sean confirmed he did. A voice that timbered deeply, growly, and lightly accented, came on the speaker. "*Góðan daginn.* What."

"You're on speaker and there are others here who I think you know." Sean introduced each male in the room. Just as he started to say Beckett's name, Wulf interrupted him, "Dr. Argonne. I've missed you. I called earlier. Are you at Dell?"

Beckett, unflustered, addressed him, "Wulf, I've missed you, too. Yes, I'm at Dell, I accepted the CEO role Sean offered me."

There was a poised silence on the line. With a decisive tone, Wulf stated his intention to come to Dell immediately. "We're in I-4," Sean told him before they heard a click.

"I'm sorry, sir, Mr. Froeste disconnected the call." Sam apologized.

Lucifer and Tav watched Beckett sit back with a smirk on her face. "You planned that, didn't you, rogue?" She indicated Sean.

Sean, giddy, beaming like sunshine after a rainy day, didn't say a word. Bowman put his hand in the air. "I helped."

Seeing Lucifer and Tav's curious faces, Bowman, grinning widely, explained, "He's Norse. A real live Norse god, one who was supposed to be dead, according to the Eddas. The only person he respects enough to wield his considerable influence and prodigious skills for is our very own Dr. Beckett Argonne, Extraordinaire," he said, eyes twinkling as he looked at Beckett adoringly. "He's crazy about her. I think she *kinda* thinks he's ok, too."

Beckett rolled her eyes at Bowman's effusive praise but couldn't hide the smile that threatened to overtake her face. She valued Wulf's loyalty and his relationship with her, even if she wasn't quite ready to admit it out loud. The unmasking of his true identity caught her off guard, but she found herself more intrigued than annoyed. After all, in a world filled with supernatural beings, a Norse god hiding in plain sight didn't seem unreasonable to expect.

"Which -," Lucifer began, and just then the hellhounds began growling. The door to the interview room swung open and all six-foot five inches of a silvery blonde, muscular, Nordic, god of a man with light gray eyes entered, ignoring everyone else in the room but Beckett.

"Beckett, *ástkær,*" He leveled his cool eyes and evaluated her. "You were the disturbance I felt yesterday. I'm not surprised."

Beckett settled Dux and Tenebris. They remained alert, watching Wulf. When his eyes met Sean's, he sat down, folding his hands. "You too, aye? Tell me everything."

He shifted his gaze again to meet Beckett eye for eye. "We will talk later, but for now I congratulate and welcome you, Goddess of Life." He bowed his head in respect for her. She heard telepathically from Tav *Do not bow your head to him. He must earn it to be a serious consort.*

Beckett raised an eyebrow in mock displeasure. "Thanks, Wulf, or shall I call you by your given name, Baldr? The times we had dinner and you never said. Tsk, tsk."

Wulf chuckled. From his pocket he pulled an elegantly-wrapped box for Beckett, "Wulf is fine. I've a gift for the favor of an embrace with you once this meeting is over. I meant what I said. I missed you." Beckett accepted his proposal with a tilt of her head. He brought the box to her and sat it in front of her, lightly grazing her shoulder with his other hand.

Tav and Lucifer exchanged pointed looks. Wulf finally noticed The Guardian of the Pit and the archangel Lucifer sat before him. He greeted them politely on the way back to his seat, bowing his head in respect, and they did so back to him in return. Apparently, they'd met before today.

After the pleasantries, Sean gave Wulf a summary of what had transpired over the last several days, including their mantles. He explained how they'd been found, and the details of the investigation into what happened to Beckett, including her disclosures about why and what occurred when she was abducted.

Upon hearing the details Beckett provided, Wulf addressed his comments quietly to her. "I aided Sean and Bowman in gaining entry to the location where you were held captive. I witnessed the state they found you in and vowed then that I would exact retribution upon those responsible for your suffering. Some at that facility met their demise by my hand that day. I harbor no regrets. If required, I shall act again without hesitation. You can count me in. Where is this Calvin you speak of, Sean?"

"You staying, *gamli?*" Sean inquired. Wulf gave a curt jab of his head. "Sam, facilities needs to ready a guest room for Wulf Froeste. He'll be staying with us for the foreseeable future."

"Very well, Lord Caladfin," Sam responded promptly. He then directed his attention to Wulf. "Mr. Froeste, welcome back to Dell Castle. Your room in the guest suites adjacent to Dr. Argonne's library will be ready shortly."

Wulf took the news of his room location with a ghost of a smile he tried unsuccessfully to contain.

Seeing Beckett's confusion about Wulf's involvement in her rescue, Sean clarified, "Wulf discovered where you were being held. He helped us by repelling an attack of security forces assigned to guard that location so we could enter the building and find you."

Wulf, sat, looking unbothered. "I got some unexpected information from a source who wished to remain anonymous." He raised his eyes and glanced around the room, lingering for a split second on Lucifer. In return,

Lucifer gave a nearly imperceptible nod to Wulf. Beckett remained silent, her eyes scanning each of them, alert, observant, and listening.

Uncrossing his arms, Sean said smoothly, "He's here, Wulfie. Along with two suspected collaborators, one of whom you might know since he seems to be in your line of work."

"Who else are you holding along with Calvin?" Bowman asked.

Sean put three headshots on the table. One was Dr. Calvin, his face marked by surliness and arrogance. The other two men Beckett didn't know.

Wulf pulled one picture, a long-haired man with a short, cropped beard and tattoos on his neck, closer to him. "This one, former Norwegian Intelligence Service's E-tjenesten, E-14. Mercenary, now. His name is Magnus Thorvaldsen and he's capable. Talented. Sells his skills to the highest bidder." He pursed his lips thoughtfully, "He's a rabid Old Norse believer. We could use that."

"Well, I think our interview strategy with him starts with you then, doesn't it, Wulf?", Beckett inquired, peering at Wulf's face as she did so.

Shifting his silver-gray eyes to her, Wulf replied, "Yes, but I want you to start it, specifically talking to him about Old Norse gods. You can say you understand he has an interest in that area."

Beckett slouched forward, her eyes locked on Wulf as she processed his suggestion. The idea of confronting one of her captors, even under the guise of a casual conversation about Old Norse gods, sent a convoluted blend of excitement and apprehension coursing through her. So far, though, the excitement prevailed.

"You want me to engage with him, to use his interest in Old Norse mythology as a way to establish a rapport?" she mused. "Why wouldn't I simply invite you in?"

Wulf concurred, his gaze relentless. "That's quite possible. Magnus is a devout follower, a man who has consecrated his life to the examination and reverence of the ancient deities. If anyone can coax him to let down his defenses, to inadvertently divulge some vital detail without compromising our celestial guise, it is you."

Lucifer, his brow furrowed with concern, broke in. "Are we sure this is the best course of action? Beckett has already been through so much. Is it wise to put her in the same room as one of her potential tormentors, even if it's for the sake of the investigation?"

"I'm with Lucifer. We can't ask Beckett to put herself in harm's way, not after everything she's endured." Tav's face was laced with protectiveness.

Beckett held up a hand, halting any further dissension. "I appreciate your concern, truly. But if this is what it takes to unravel the Illumined Circle's web of deceit, to bring those responsible to justice, then I'm willing to do it."

"I'm not the same woman I was when they took me. I'm stronger now, more powerful than they could imagine. And, " she added, "if I sense he knows me, then we know he was actually there, right? I can just alert Sean – he can sense my feelings."

Immediately, Wulf's eyes became piercing and questioning. "You are bound?"

Quickly, Sean corrected him, "She is not bound to anyone. Yet. Beckett and I are twin flame, and Lucifer, Tav, and Bowman have bound themselves to her."

"Ah. I see." Wulf sat back, crossing his arms, and again, pinned her with his eyes. "Beckett. We will discuss."

Sean continued, his eyes gleaming. "Bowman's right. We'll have eyes and ears on the interview room at all times. The moment things start to go south, we'll be in there faster than you can say 'Odin's beard.'"

Amusement danced across Beckett's face at Sean's quip, the tension in the room easing ever so slightly. She turned back to Wulf. "Alright, let's do this. Tell me everything I need to know about Magnus, about his obsession with Old Norse mythology. I want to be prepared for every possible angle."

Wulf leaned back in his chair; his eyes distant as he delved into his knowledge of Magnus Thorvaldsen. "Magnus is a man consumed by his devotion to the Old Norse gods. He believes that they are not merely mythological figures, but real, tangible beings who have the power to shape the course of human history."

"He's particularly fixated on the concept of Ragnarök, the prophesied battle that will bring about the end of days. In Magnus' mind, he is a warrior chosen by the gods to fight in this ultimate conflict, to help usher in a new era where the old ways reign supreme."

Wulf's storytelling captivated Beckett. "So, if I were to approach him as someone with a similar interest, perhaps even a belief in the Old Norse gods, he might be more inclined to open up?"

Wolf concurred, "It's a solid plan. And if you can gain Magnus' trust, he might even be willing to introduce you to others who share his beliefs. That could provide invaluable insights into the workings of the Sons of Odin."

Lucifer's dark, mossy green eyes fixed on Beckett. "Just be careful. Don't let your guard down, even for a moment. Magnus may be a true believer, but he's also dangerous. If he suspects you're not who you say you are, things could turn ugly fast.

Sean absently tapped his fingers against his thigh as he mulled over the problem at hand. Suddenly, he straightened up, a grin spreading across his face. "I've got it! What if we create a cover story for Beckett? Something that would explain her interest in Norse mythology and give her a reason to seek out Magnus' expertise?"

"We could present her as a scholar, someone researching the connection between Norse mythology and contemporary belief systems. It would give her a valid reason to ask questions and delve into Magnus' perspectives," Tav proposed.

Beckett perked up, the prospect of the challenge invigorating her. "I like it. I could approach him as a kindred spirit, someone who believes the ancient Norse gods still hold sway in our modern era."

Addressing Wulf, she pressed for more information. "I'll need you to share everything you know about Norse mythology, the specific deities and tales fueling Magnus' obsession. The more genuine I can make my interest appear, the more inclined he'll be to confide in me."

Wulf, his respect for Beckett's bravery and sharp intellect clear, began imparting his extensive knowledge on the topic. He recounted the stories of Odin, the All-father, and his unending pursuit of wisdom; of Thor, the formidable god of thunder, and his epic clashes with the giants; of Loki, the cunning shapeshifter, and his part in the unraveling of Ragnarök.

As Beckett listened, she hung on every detail, every nuance of the tales Wulf spun. She and Sean had always been enthralled by Norse mythology, spellbound by the exploits of Thor and Loki, Frigg and Odin. Sean's father had imparted the lore of the Norse to them not as mere fables, but as something more substantial, more historically momentous than commonly perceived. Here, they could both hear an actual Norse deity recount some of those very stories, a rarity they had never fathomed.

In a manner, and with their recent attainment of mantles and wisdom, Beckett could discern that both the Caladfins and the Argonnes had indeed commenced grooming their offspring for what may lay in wait. They whiled away summers dramatizing Norse sagas, deeply imbued by the authenticity and legitimacy their progenitors bestowed upon them. They knew that Baldr, also recognized as Wulf in the mortal plane, was revered for his luminescence, innocence, and benevolence

Now that she grasped his true identity and nature, his presence in her life manifested as gift, a link to something far more poignant. While Beckett marveled at his nearness, scarcely feet away, she felt the potent legends taking root, the primordial tales striking a chord deep within her being.

During a lull in the conversation, Lucifer seized the moment to pointedly ask about Dr. Calvin's fate. "Who's interrogating him, and when will it take place?"

Bowman chimed in, "Let him stew for a while. I think you and Tav should question him. If you reveal your identities, he's bound to drop a brick in his pants. He might spill everything, and even if he doesn't and we can't hold him, he'll send the Circle into a frenzy. If that happens, there's a good chance we may detect their activity."

A wordless exchange passed between Lucifer and Tav at Bowman's proposal. The prospect of confronting Dr. Calvin together, employing their united strength and authority to shatter his defenses and extract the truth, held a certain allure for both of them.

Lucifer, still furious, spoke up first. "This works out perfectly. Calvin has a hell of a lot to answer for, and I can't wait to face him myself. I want to see the look of pure terror on his face when he realizes exactly who he's messed with."

"Indeed. Calvin's arrogance and cruelty have gone unchecked for far too long. It's time he faced the repercussions of his actions. I can think of no better way to begin than by shattering his delusions of superiority and control. While Tav spoke, Beckett heard his telepathic message, *Since we can't tear him apart, making him lose control and soil himself appeals to me. It's messy, but if you won't let me eat him...*

Beckett fought to suppress a grin. "As much as I value your readiness to confront Calvin for me, I want to ensure we don't reveal our hand prematurely. If he grasps the depth of our knowledge and the resources at our command, he might clam up or attempt to warn his associates."

"Beckett's got a point. We need to play this smart." Sean tapped his pen on the table. "Maybe Lucifer and Tav could begin the interview by stroking Calvin's ego, making him think he's outsmarted us and we're clutching at straws. Once he's lured into a false security, that's when we hit him with the truth and watch him squirm."

"And if he still refuses to cooperate, well... I'm sure Lucifer and Tav have ways of making him see the error of his ways. After all, the Pit and the fires of Hell have a knack for loosening even the most stubborn tongues. Or so I've heard?" Bowman glanced around the room expectantly.

Tav, a wicked grin tugging at the corners of his mouth, replied, "Oh, they certainly do, Bowman. They certainly do. While I may have assured Beckett that I wouldn't devour anyone today, there are other methods to make a man regret ever being born."

Lucifer, placing his hand on Beckett's shoulder, agreed. "But we'll cross that bridge if and when we get there. For now, let's concentrate on the task at hand. Calvin's reckoning will come, and when it does, we'll be prepared."

As the group finalized their plans, unity settled over them like a cloak, and Beckett felt a surge of resolve and determination. With Lucifer and Tav readying to confront Calvin, and her own role in unraveling Magnus' secrets taking form, she knew they were one step closer to bringing the Illumined Circle to its knees.

And as the first phase of their plan began to unfold, as Lucifer and Tav made their way to Calvin's holding cell. Beckett prepared to step into her role as a scholar of Norse mythology, with hope burning bright within her heart. The Illumined Circle's days were numbered, and soon, the truth would be known, and justice would be served.

Chapter 23

Gifts of Truth and Protection

As Beckett exited I-4 with Dux and Tenebris, Wulf caught up to her. "Where are you headed, *falleg*? You can't go in looking like that. He'll see right through you."

She took his arm, strolling back to the stark, utilitarian detention waiting area. Its bare walls and functional furniture contrasted with the warmth of Wulf's presence. "Wait here. I'll be back in ten - changing into something more suitable for the interview."

Ever the flirt, Wulf offered slyly, "Need a hand? I'm quite skilled with...wardrobe changes." His intense gaze sparked heat across her skin.

Beckett laughed softly. "You're incorrigible." Her smile faded as she anxiously twisted her fingers. "I should have returned your calls these past weeks. I was the one with the problem, not you."

"No need to explain, *elskan*." Wulf soothed her. "Perhaps you sensed my true nature clashing with what you knew of me. I don't blame you for being cautious. But now we both understand who we truly are. Agreed?" She confirmed with a dip of her head, a small smile returning.

"Open your gifts. You can use what I've given you today."

Sitting on the sofa, Beckett unwrapped a box containing two smaller packages. She opened the rectangular one first, inhaling the scent of aged velvet as she lifted out a delicate, jewel-encrusted bracelet. Opals, sapphires and diamonds glittered in kaleidoscopic hues across her skin. Turning the intricate circlet of intertwined silver and gold, she marveled at the design - the moon's mystery united with the sun's radiance in perfect balance. The cool metal rapidly warmed in her grasp, and an ancient power seemed to thrum within the exquisite stones.

Along the band, ancient Norse runes were etched with such exquisite precision they appeared to undulate and transform in the flickering light - each one an enduring cipher of the timeless wisdom of the gods. The bracelet resonated with a perceptible vibration in her hands, its primordial power emanating into her, sending currents of energy rippling through her veins.

Sacred respect and appreciation filled Beckett as she cradled the powerful talisman. Her eyes were unexpectedly moist. "Wulf, I'm at a loss. This is a gorgeous, potent piece."

"Put it on," he urged, rough fingertips grazing her skin as he secured the clasp around her wrist. Drawing her into his powerful embrace, he dipped his head to murmur, "I've ached to see you, my radiant *falleg*."

A faint, resonant hum came from the diamonds against her skin and she sensed the contented arch of Wulf's smile pressed close.

"The gems are the fabled Stones of Sight, granting lucidity of discernment and sanctity of essence." Cradling her face, Wulf's words caressed her as reverently as his hands. "The opals resonate with the auguries of the Norns, their iridescence harboring enigmas not yet unveiled."

His low, mesmerizing tone thrummed with ancient Norse power. "The sapphires, as deep as the well of Urd, signify wisdom and fate - their cool touch a reminder of the paths ahead. And the brilliant starlight diamonds, indestructible, symbolize truth's enduring spirit - an unbreakable herald repelling deception's darkness."

The bracelet's significance seemed to bind Beckett's wrist, as if she now bore the very essence of the Norse gods. Looking up at him, she finally whispered, "So the diamonds react to truth or lies?"

Wulf's thumb grazed Beckett's neck as he corrected her. "They'll hum when someone's being honest with you. But they stay silent and cold for lies - like guards against any deception."

As the bracelet quivered, Beckett realized Wulf's feelings for her ran far deeper than she'd initially perceived. Her eyes searched his face, lips parting in surprise as she grappled for the right words, her heart hammering. She could feel a telltale heat creeping up her neck as the magnitude of how he perceived her washed over her, skin tingling with heady excitement.

"I...didn't realize..." Her voice faltered, fading as she struggled to articulate what was suddenly laid bare before her.

Wulf silenced her with a finger grazing her lips. He bestowed gossamer kisses upon each cheek, his delicate touch igniting a frisson that skipped across her skin. Then, tenderly, he pressed his mouth to hers - the kiss a tantalizing promise, a mere glimpse of the smoldering passion lying beneath.

His silvery eyes bore into hers with a ferocity that made her feel entirely exposed, as if he could see straight into her soul. "These pieces are but a taste of what I wish to give you as you use your newfound abilities." Keeping her enfolded in his arms, he grasped the smaller box and handed it to Beckett, instructing light-heartedly, "Now tear into it like the valiant Viking warrior princess Sean claims you are."

She complied with his teasing instruction, her fingers trembling ever so slightly as she tore through the delicate wrapping paper. Inside was nestled a small velvet box, its plush surface beckoning to be caressed. In hushed suspense, she lifted the lid to reveal an exquisitely decorated ring, its intricate design evocative of the very silver filigree patterns adorning her own skin.

As she slipped it onto her thumb, the ring seemed to awaken, resizing itself with ethereal fluidity to accommodate whichever digit she chose - its magic responding to her mere touch. Her flesh thrilled in acceptance of this mystical adornment, a tide of energy moving within her. She could feel its power transcending even that of the bracelet, an understated, though powerful, force - a masterwork of the primordial sorcery that had birthed it into existence eons ago.

Wulf's hand guided her chin upwards, tilting her face towards his. "This ring belonged to my mother. Its true name is Frigg's Solace." Beckett's eyes went wide, thoughts stuttering at the significance of such a treasured heirloom, the storied history and symbolic meaning draping over her shoulders like a sacral vestment.

"Among its multiple talents, it bestows a protective aegis against assaults of body, mind or spirit. It also harmonizes with your mantle's innate attunement to the natural world's rhythms." She nodded slowly, beginning to grasp the full magnitude of abilities housed within this mystical talisman.

Flummoxed, Beckett could only stare at him, a single tremulous question the sole words to pass her lips. "Why?"

His hands raised to cradle her face again. "Because it is my deepest wish. Because it is as it should be. My mother's spirit would rejoice, as I do now, to see me standing arm-in-arm, hand-in-hand with Life's radiant Embodiment as she takes her first fateful steps into this world."

Then, Wulf's demeanor morphed to a fierce, resolute edge with solemn conviction. "Never again will I find you unprotected, broken, hurt, and bloodied as on that day. These artifacts will help you as you utilize your more natural abilities." His thumbs smoothed the ridge of her cheekbones as the bracelet's faint hum affirmed the veracity of his vow.

"Now you may go change. I will wait here for you as you've requested." Wulf stepped back, his hawkish gaze never leaving hers as he released her from his embrace.

Beckett's mind raced, each new bit of information crashing over her like waves on the shore, threatening to pull her under. The immense meaning behind Wulf's treasured gifts and the magnitude of his feelings left her reeling, struggling to catch her breath as her heart pounded. She was adrift in uncharted emotional waters.

Before she could teleport away, Dux spoke up. "My Goddess, I'll stay here with this Norse and wait. Tenebris will go with you." So, the hellhound respected Wulf as well. With a touch to Tenebris' head, Beckett willed herself into her suite.

While Tenebris waited, she changed into a dark blue velvet shirt and left it untucked, adding her old, ripped jeans and suede booties. Beckett pulled strands from her top knot, making it messy. She discovered that by thinking about hiding her ears' points, they blurred automatically. Convenient.

Finding a long, fine silver chain that ended in a quartz crystal, she put it on, with the point well below her breasts under her shirt. That'll give Magnus something to imagine while he assesses me, she suspected. Beckett changed earrings, choosing a long silver threader for her left ear with the two holes, threading it through both, and added a small silver wolf on a post to the one hole in her right earlobe.

When she looked in the mirror, she saw a poor, unkempt, but attractive, graduate student and realized reading glasses might make her appearance more convincing. Grabbing a pair of studious black ones she liked, she put them on. Getting a paper notebook and Bic pen, she headed to Tenebris, who sat regally by the door. When she glanced at him, he raised his head.

"My lady, you look...different. However, I will not permit you to be in the room alone with this...man." Tenebris' dark eyes were emphatic, and she could see this was one argument she wouldn't win with him. "Please wait while I shape into a more realistic-looking canine." He shook, and then a dark Doberman of average size appeared at her side. "How is this?" he asked.

Another hellhound talent, Beckett surmised. Lucifer was right – they are useful. "Perfect. Let's go."

Again, she reappeared instantaneously with Tenebris in the detention area waiting room, where Dux and Wulf remained. As soon as Dux saw them return, he was at ease. "Tenebris, you will accompany Beckett." It wasn't a question; it was a stated as an indisputable fact.

Wulf's eyes roved over her from head to toe. "Yes, you look appropriately scholarly now," he remarked, his teasing approval evident as he moved closer to inspect her studied appearance more thoroughly.

He touched one of earrings and then noted her chain's delicate descent, admiring each piece in turn. "Exquisite choices, my valkyrie, as are the spectacles." He dipped into an appreciative murmur. "That wolf exquisitely suits you." Wulf met Tenebris's stoic canine facade with a positive look. "You've quite the convincing guise, too. You shall accompany her."

He proffered his arm to Beckett in an understated gentlemanly gesture. As she accepted and their strides fell into step, Tenebris padded dutifully alongside her with all the charisma of a well-trained canine companion.

"Sean and Bowman have already begun questioning the unnamed suspect. A guard escorted our man to Interview Room 13," he informed her conspiratorially. "Pay mind to Magnus' eyes and monitor your ring's reactions closely as you enter. That, and your divineness, will reveal if he recognizes your true visage. Should he, do not speak - simply withdraw from the room and close the door behind you."

An odd serenity settled over Beckett - a placid confidence underscored by a thread of excitement. "I'm ready," she told Wulf as they reached the I-13 observation anteroom. He placed a hand on the door, facing her fully. "I'll be right here, keeping vigil. You have my vow - you'll remain utterly safe."

A shimmering energy rippled outward from Wulf, coalescing into the iridescent form of a tiny silver butterfly. The delicate creature alighted upon Beckett, an ethereal talisman sealing his solemn vow. In sync, the bracelet emanated a gentle vibration against her skin, its mystical resonance validating the truth of his words. Beckett gave him a radiant smile, giving him a dip of her head in respect. "Thank you, Wulf."

After he closed the door, Beckett inhaled and exhaled a couple of times. Tenebris rumbled low in his chest, looking up at her. She chuckled, "You too, huh?" and put her hand on his head. With pen and paper in hand, she opened the door to I-13 and walked inside.

Magnus Thorvaldsen, she noted, was a huge, strapping Norwegian who clearly kept himself in peak physical condition. Standing by the table in the room, he inspected Beckett as she and Tenebris entered the room, his hazel, slitted eyes practically undressing her. Tenebris sat on the floor at the edge of the table closest to the door.

He doesn't feel or see my mantle, she thought, and speculated if that was an effect of him being human, or a result of her new gifts from Wulf. Either way, it was clear he not only didn't recognize her, but he also appreciated what he was staring at. Well, that's one hurdle passed, she concluded, sitting down in one of the chairs at the table, inviting him to sit in one of them opposite her.

In flawless, but accented English, Magnus challenged, "Who are you and why am I here, little girl?" He sat down slowly, maintaining a penetrating eye contact with her. That is, until his eyes followed the silver chain at her neck to where it ended below her shirt. Second hurdle passed. Comfortable, opening her notebook, adjusting her glasses, putting her Bic in her hand, Beckett introduced herself to him.

"I don't know why they brought you here, but I was told you could help me in my research. My name is Freya Eiriksdottir. I'm an American graduate student, and intern, working with Evigvokter for the semester." Beckett made a point to check her notes. "You are Magnus Thorval...Thorvaldsen, is that right?"

Amused, he replied, "That is my name. Where did you get it?"

Beckett maintained a casual appearance, her body language relaxed and open. "It was provided to me by my supervisors. They said you might have information that could help with my research project on Norse mythology and its influence on modern Scandinavian culture." She bent over the table slightly, adjusting her glasses as she looked at him, curious and innocent. "I'd be grateful for any insights you could share."

Magnus slouched back in his chair, a smug smirk playing on his lips as he studied her. "What, exactly, makes you think I would know anything about that, little Freya?"

Her bracelet, imperceptibly to him, quivered a truth she already garnered: Wulf identified him accurately. "I was told your name before I came in here, but I've no clue who discovered it. Still," Beckett smiled pleasantly, "I'm glad to meet you." Magnus was taken with her, she could feel that, but remained wary.

"And just what does a little wisp like yourself wish to interrogate me about?" Though his tone carried a gruff edge, it lacked any undercurrent of true suspicion or malice.

"My academic pursuits center on theorizing the persisting effects and influences of Norse mythological traditions on modern societal frameworks and the individual psyche," Beckett elaborated. "My research examines the resurgent undercurrents of ancient Norse belief systems in this contemporary era, with particular focus on their formative role in shaping emerging social and political philosophies."

After that explanation, Magnus was definitely more than interested. She took note of him staring, again, toward her cleavage. Live it up in your head, bucko, she thought. Just give me what I want and we'll be square.

"Fascinating," Magnus leaned on his elbows, his attention narrowed like a laser. "What specific aspects of Norse mythology are you focusing on in your research?"

Beckett shifted in her seat, crossing her legs, and allowing the silver chain to catch the light. She could feel Magnus' gaze following her every move, his attraction to her evident despite his attempts to maintain a condescending exterior.

"I'm particularly interested in the role of the Norns and the concept of fate in Norse belief systems," she replied, tapping her pen against the notebook. "How these ideas might influence modern individuals' sense of agency and their perception of the world around them."

Magnus chuckled, an authentic rumbling sound that permeated the room. "The Norns, eh? Those three sisters who spin the threads of fate. It's a powerful concept, the idea that our lives are predetermined, that we're all just playing out roles assigned to us by higher powers."

Beckett nodded, jotting down a few notes. "Exactly. I'm

curious about how this belief in fate might intersect with more contemporary ideologies, such as nationalism or even extremist groups."

At the mention of extremist groups, Magnus' posture stiffened slightly, and Beckett sensed a transition in him at the same the bracelet on her arm grew cool against her skin. A lie, or at least a half-truth, was coming.

"I'm afraid I don't know much about extremist groups, little Freya," Magnus said, his tone cautiously neutral. "I'm just a simple man trying to honor the old ways, to keep the spirit of our ancestors alive."

Casually, Beckett put her elbow on the table, and rested her chin on her hand. "But surely, in your efforts to preserve the old ways, you've come across others who share your passion? Perhaps some who take it a bit too far?" She kept her tone light, almost flirtatious, even as she probed for information.

Magnus hesitated, his eyes darting away from hers for a moment. "There are always those who take things too far, in any belief system. But I keep my distance from such people. I prefer to focus on the positive aspects of our heritage, the wisdom and strength of our gods."

Beckett knew there were untold depths to uncover - she could psychically discern the guarded undercurrents of his thoughts, controlled and dismissive of her questions. But pushing too insistently risked making him retreat into stony reticence. So she proceeded with deft calculation, opening her mind while carefully cultivating rapport before daring to sink into the murkier shadows cloaking his world.

She flashed a suitably disarming smile, pushing her glasses higher on the bridge of her nose. "Of course, I understand. But surely, in your efforts to preserve Norse traditions, you've come across others who share your passion? Perhaps some who take things a bit too far?"

Magnus shifted uncomfortably in his seat, his eyes cutting

sharply to the door. Tenebris, ever vigilant, tensed at Beckett's side, ready to intervene if necessary.

"I... I might have stumbled upon some whispers," Magnus confessed, his voice just above a murmur. "There are those who believe the ancient gods are not just myths, that they still watch over us. I generally steer clear of such beliefs—it's not my place to judge the ways others honor our ancestors."

A subtle quiver, a hint of truth. Beckett didn't need it: she could hear his thoughts as clearly as if they were spoken aloud. She angled in slightly, her tone low and firm. "Magnus, I'm not here to pass judgment. I'm simply seeking to understand. Anything you know about these groups, their beliefs or their actions, could be immensely helpful for my research."

Her eyes locked with his, the bracelet on her wrist pulsing subtly as she consciously urged him to trust her.

Magnus sighed deeply, his fingers threading through his hair in a gesture of unease. "There's a group," he admitted reluctantly. "They call themselves the Sons of Odin. They're convinced the old gods are real, and they've been chosen as their champions in this world."

As a confirming shiver hit her wrist, Beckett recognized his sincerity as a matter of honor, because he'd come to see her passion for Norse mythology reflected in his own obsession. She kept her expression unbiased, her pen poised above the notebook. "The Sons of Odin? And what do you know about their activities, their beliefs?"

Magnus hesitated, casting another wary glance at the door before leaning in closer. "They're convinced a monumental clash between order and chaos is imminent. Through specific rituals and their unwavering devotion to the old gods, they believe they will be granted power and assured victory when the battle unfolds."

As the bracelet on her wrist hummed the truth of Magnus'

words, Beckett realized she didn't need its affirmation. The pieces of her examination of Magnus were coalescing, the threads intertwining into a clearer narrative. Urgency underlined her words. "These rituals," she inquired sharply, "what do they involve? Have you ever been present at one, or participated yourself?"

Magnus' face drained of color, and he shook his head vehemently. "No, no, I've never been part of anything like that. I've only caught whispers—rumors of blood sacrifices and dark magic. But I've kept my distance, I swear."

Beckett nodded, deliberately conveying empathy. "I believe you, Magnus. But any detail you can share about these rumors, where the Sons of Odin might congregate, or who leads them, would be immensely valuable. You're not the first to mention that name."

Magnus faltered, his eyes scanning Beckett's face for any hint of deceit. Unseen by him, she exerted her divine influence, mentally urging him to reveal the truth. As he struggled, a decision seemed to form within him.

"There's a place," he said, nearly desperate. Beads of sweat formed on his forehead—involuntary testimony to the goddess's unseen pressure. "An old warehouse down by the London docks. That's where they meet, where the rituals are performed. But that's all I know, I swear it." The bracelet on her wrist fluttered gently, underscoring the truth of his words.

Beckett reached out, her touch light on Magnus' arm. "Thank you, Magnus. I know this isn't easy, but you're doing the right thing. Your information could prevent much harm, and it's advanced my research significantly."

She glanced down at her notebook, feigning to jot down a few final notes. "I think that's all I need for now. I hope they release you soon." She carefully imparted her concern for his well-being. "Thank you for your time and your honesty."

As she stood to leave, Tenebris rising to follow, Magnus called out to her. "Wait, little Freya. Be careful. These people, the Sons of Odin, they're dangerous. Don't go poking around that warehouse alone." His words rang with genuine concern, her intuition told her, with the bracelet on her wrist confirming his earnestness.

Beckett paused at the door, glancing back with a smile that was both confident and reassuring. "Thank you, Magnus. Don't worry about me. I know how to handle myself, and I've got Tenebris here to watch my back."

She patted Tenebris' head; the hellhound disguised as a Doberman turned to look up at her. With a final salute to Magnus, Sam unlocked the door and Beckett slipped out of the interrogation room, thrilled with the new information she'd gotten.

As the door closed behind her, Beckett continued down the hallway. When she was sufficiently distant, she leaned against the wall and rejoiced, reveling in an overwhelming satisfaction. Tenebris pressed against her leg - he too was glad it turned out the way it had.

"Well done, my Lady," he moaned from somewhere in the abyss of his chest. "You played your role perfectly. The Norse god will be pleased."

Beckett nodded, only partly attentive to his praise as she'd already shifted to thinking about the next steps. The Sons of Odin, a warehouse by the London docks, whispers of blood magic and dark rituals—it was a solid lead, another thread to explore in the intricate weave of her past.

She knew the logical step was to report back to the others, to share what she'd uncovered and strategize their next move. Nonetheless, a part of her, one that still ached for answers and justice, urged her to inspect the warehouse alone, to face the shadows of her trauma directly.

Tenebris, perceptive to her internal conflict, emitted a low growl. "My Lady, I sense your intentions. However, we ought to consult with the others before proceeding."

Beckett sighed, acknowledging the wisdom in the hellhound's words. She couldn't allow her personal quest to overshadow her responsibilities, especially not with the safety of her loved ones and the balance of the universe at stake. However, the desire to act first and ask for favors later remained strong within her.

"Tenebris is right on several fronts, Beckett," Wulf said, exiting the observation room with a supportive smile. "Firstly, the Norse god is very happy with your performance and findings."

He grew serious, but kind. "However, I must urge you not to explore the warehouse alone. The risks are too great, and your well-being is too important." As he spoke, the bracelet on her wrist oscillated, echoing his concern. "Let's gather the others and share what you've learned. We should make our next move as a united front."

Calling Dux to join them, Beckett, along with Tenebris and Wulf, made their way to room I-4. Upon entering, they found Sean and Bowman already enjoying a feast of assorted meats, cheeses, fruits, carrots, and celery. Beckett greeted them cheerfully, and Bowman caught her eye with a wink. "Nice glasses," he said with a grin, raising his beer in a casual toast.

Beckett's eyes landed on a plate set aside just for her, piled with lovely, fragrant French cheese, fruit, nuts, and sliced bread. Smiling, she picked up the plate and uncorked a bottle of French merlot. As she poured herself a glass, she raised it towards Bowman. "Thank you. I had to play the part, you know." Bowman clinked his glass against hers in response.

Wulf strode to the table, his eyes lighting up at the sight of a pitcher filled with golden liquid. "Mead!" he exclaimed, savoring the fruity scent with a deep inhale. He selected a plate topped with smoked salmon, eggs, apples, and hazelnuts—clearly marked with his name—and took a seat beside Beckett with a contented sigh. He eagerly began to eat, stopping only to take hearty swigs from his mug topped with mead.

"How'd you do with Magnus?" Sean inquired, eager for an update. Beckett, caught mid-bite, chewed quickly as Wulf took over the response. "Sons of Odin, London docks, old warehouse, rituals involving blood and dark magic," he summarized the key details of the Thorvaldsen interview succinctly before returning to his meal.

"Beckett, what's that? And that?" Sean asked, pointing first at the ring on her right thumb and then at the bracelet on her left wrist.

"They're gifts from Wulf," Beckett replied shyly. "The ring once belonged to Frigg." She sent a grateful look Wulf's way, and he responded by beaming at her.

"Wulfie, you never bring me presents," Sean playfully complained, faking a pout and tears.

With a hearty sip of his mead, Wulf replied teasingly, "That's because you haven't earned them, *gamli*. When you become a goddess and fascinate me as Beckett does, then we'll talk."

Sean laughed, shaking his head in amusement. "Fair enough, Wulfie. I suppose I'll have to content myself with being a mere *male* Elven lord, mantles and all, for now."

Beckett chortled with them, the easy banter between the two filling her with a warmth that the merlot couldn't match. These moments of levity and friendship were precious to her —a reminder that even amidst darkness and danger, there were still pockets of light to be cherished.

Bowman redirected the conversation towards their immediate concerns. "So, the Sons of Odin. What more do we know about them, apart from Magnus's revelations?"

Sean took a sip of his drink before answering. "Not much,

I'm afraid. They've mostly evaded detection. But given their involvement with blood magic and dark rituals, they're far from just an extremist group—they're a legitimate threat."

"Agreed," Wulf said solemnly, placing his mug on the table. "If they're linked to Beckett's abduction, they pose a danger not only to her but to the universal balance itself." He changed the subject. "What have we learned about the other suspect?"

Sean and Bowman traded a significant look before Sean took the lead. "The other suspect, Elias Lindberg, is deeply entangled with the Sons of Odin. He clammed up more than Magnus, but we still extracted some crucial details from him."

Bowman continued seamlessly. "Lindberg confirmed the warehouse and the rituals, though he remained cagey about the particulars. However, he inadvertently disclosed that the Sons of Odin are orchestrating something monumental, something he described as having the potential to 'change the course of history.'"

At Bowman's words, an awareness washed over Beckett. The full gravitas of her destiny, of the impending conflicts, rested upon her shoulders—not as a burden, but as a mantle she was destined to bear. Tenebris, attuned to even the subtlest shift in her aura, pressed himself encouragingly against her leg beneath the table. She reached down, stroking his fur, acknowledging his loyalty and support.

"Change the course of history?" Wulf echoed, tapping the table thoughtfully. "That's ominous. Did Lindberg offer any clues about their intentions?"

Sean shook his head, his face taut with irritation. "He became tight-lipped right after dropping that bombshell. But clearly, they think their actions are linked to the old gods, aligning with the war between order and chaos that Magnus described."

"If they aim to tip the scales towards chaos and disrupt the universal balance, we must intervene," Beckett grasped. "We cannot allow whatever they're planning to unfold."

"You're right," Wulf stipulated, clenching his fist. "We need more information about this warehouse and the rituals they're conducting. If we can infiltrate them, gain some firsthand intelligence, we'll have a stronger chance of stopping their plans."

Sean hesitated, as if considering the consequences of his suggestion. "We might have a way to do just that," he said slowly. "But it's fraught with risk and would require one of us to go deep undercover within the Sons of Odin." He and Bowman shared a meaningful glance, signaling the seriousness of Sean's proposal.

Beckett heart skipped a beat at the idea. The thought of anyone putting themselves in that kind of danger, of facing the same horrors she had endured, made her blood run cold. Still, she could feel Bowman ready to volunteer.

Before she could vocalize her concerns, he spoke up. "I'll do it," he stated adamantly, "I have the necessary skills and training. I can infiltrate, gather the needed information, and exit safely."

Wulf disagreed with Bowman. "No, I appreciate your courage and capabilities, but we need someone well-versed in Norse mythology." He turned his gaze to Beckett, a knowing look in his eyes. "I believe we might persuade someone to assist us."

What is he going on about, Beckett wondered. Persuade who? Then it clicked and she blurted out, "Magnus. You heard what he mentioned as I was leaving."

Wulf jerked his chin. "Aside from one minor evasion, he was truthful with you."

To the others, Wulf indicated the bracelet on Beckett's wrist. "That's not merely a decorative piece I gifted her. It's a potent device that discerns truth, affirming what I suspect

Beckett already senses."

"Yes, it seems I can intuit mortal thoughts now. But we need more information," Beckett acknowledged. "The warehouse is a starting point, but we can't rush in blindly. We need to understand what we're facing and how everything connects."

Sean started to speak, "Leave that—" but was cut off as the door to room I-4 swung open. Framed in the doorway stood Tav and Lucifer, with the latter walking towards Beckett. She stood and embraced him a few steps from her chair.

"We have information about the Sons of Odin, my friends," Tav announced, capturing everyone's undivided attention. Beckett, still in Lucifer's embrace, turned to face the ancient deity, interested and eager.

"You're familiar with the Sons of Odin?" Beckett asked, glancing between Tav and Lucifer. "What information can you share with us?"

Tav's presence dominated the room. "The Sons of Odin are part of an ancient lineage that has adapted its guise throughout history. They see themselves as destined warriors of the Norse gods, fated to engage in the ultimate battle between order and chaos."

"But how does this relate to my abduction?" Beckett pressed.

Lucifer placed a faint kiss on her temple. "The Sons believe that by tapping into the power of certain divine beings, they can tip the scales towards chaos, disrupting the very fabric of the universe. As the Goddess of Life, you pose a significant threat to their plans."

"So they targeted me, tried to break me, control me..."

"Precisely. They believe by subjugating you, bending you to their twisted will, they can wield your power toward their own ends. But they underestimated your strength and your amnesia regarding your true heritage." Despite the severity of his words, Tav seemed to downplay the Sons of Odin's intentions, emphasizing how their failure to respect her may ultimately lead to their downfall.

Wulf, hanging on each word, finally spoke. "And Magnus? How does he factor into this?"

Lucifer turned to him, his jaw tensing. "Magnus is but a foot soldier in their ranks. A spark of doubt lingers within him, a glimmer of light not extinguished."

Beckett contemplated the details, the implications solidifying for her. "We were just discussing leveraging him to infiltrate the Sons, gather the intelligence we need. Do you think that might work?"

Sean and Bowman exchanged a concerned glance. "It's a risky proposition," Sean said carefully, "but one that holds potential. If we can sway Magnus to our side, he might provide the means to dismantle the Sons of Odin from within."

Lucifer, holding Beckett closely, remarked, "There's another method to gauge commitment or reveal hypocrisy. What devotee, sworn to the Old Norse gods, would deny one of those deities revealing the truth?"

"Indeed," Wulf granted, raising his mead in a toast to Lucifer. "Though I abhor the deception. I'd rather confront them openly as the supernatural and primordial beings we are."

"You're right, Lucifer," Beckett said. "If Magnus genuinely holds reverence for the Norse gods, Wulf's presence alone could sway him to our cause. And if he proves unfaithful, well…we can cross that bridge, as you say, when we come it."

Wulf's grin widened, one clearly reflecting his anticipation at deity work. "Ah, I do enjoy a thorough test of faith. Should Magnus prove himself, he could become a valuable ally. But if not…let's just say I have ways of dealing with hypocrites."

"I've no doubt, my Norse friend," Tav chuckled. "But let us

hope it doesn't come to that. The fewer adversaries we face head-on, the better."

Lucifer added, "We must approach this strategically, utilizing every means to undermine the Sons from within. If leveraging Magnus is necessary, then we shall."

"But we mustn't rely solely on Magnus," Sean interrupted. "We need intelligence from all available sources. The more we learn about the Sons—their plans, their weaknesses—the better prepared we'll be to defeat them."

"I'll reach out to my sources, see if I can uncover any whispers about the Sons' movements or intentions," Bowman pledged. "Perhaps the djinn, Danny, and the Fae can assist us."

United in their determination, a plan began to take shape. Wulf would approach Magnus, revealing his true identity and testing the man's faith and loyalty. Beckett couldn't help noticing that Wulf took particular pleasure in the "test of faith and loyalty" aspect—a prospect that might prove unfortunate for Magnus. Meanwhile, the rest of the group would tirelessly gather intelligence, striving to unravel the mysteries surrounding the Sons of Odin, the Illumined Circle, and their clandestine objectives.

Beckett's knew that things wouldn't always be easy. Their adversaries were cunning and ruthless, and the stakes extended beyond her own experiences. But with these beings in synergy with her, bound by love and loyalty, she believed they could overcome any obstacle.

As they mapped out their plans and laid the groundwork for the battles ahead, Beckett's entire attitude changed. The shadows of her past and the threats of the present would not define her. She transcended her trauma, surpassing the darkness that sought to consume her.

For she was Beckett Argonne, a blend of Elven grace and celestial might. She would not rest until truth and justice, whether her own or others, illuminated the world and universe once more. She, along with her people, would confront the Illumined Circle and Sons of Odin—forces seeking to disrupt the universe's balance.

And she would prevail, for the sake of all she cherished and for the love that blazed within her heart—a love invincible against any darkness.

She embodied light, life, and hope. With this realization burning brightly within her, she knew that no force in the universe could withstand their convictions.

AUTHOR NOTES

Firstly, I want to express my gratitude to all of you who have taken the time to read my book!

For most of my life, I harbored the desire to write fiction. Yet, until now, my creative endeavors remained confined to the realm of professional nonfiction and academia. It wasn't until two and a half years ago, when I impulsively enrolled in a creative writing course alongside a class on comparative mythology, that I found the spark that ignited my passion.

Exploring the rich tapestry of Greek, Roman, Norse, and Arabic mythologies, juxtaposed with narratives from the Old Testament, was a revelation. This exploration birthed not only this book but also the series around it, entitled 'Gods and Mortals,' which draws parallels between figures and stories from various mythologies. From Persephone's descent and return from Hades to the dual deities such as Apollo and Artemis, Freyr and Freya, and the mythical realms of Valhalla and Olympus, these tales wove themselves into the fabric of my narrative. The inclusion of Lucifer, whose name in Latin signifies "light bringer" or "morning star," serves to intersect Biblical narratives with a fantasy, modern interpretation.

Beckett's journey mirrors my unwavering commitment to elevating women. This includes those with professional and technical backgrounds who navigate toxic and misogynistic environments in STEM fields, as well as the countless mothers, including my own, who tirelessly uphold their families and communities. It is high time that women everywhere receive the recognition they deserve for their pivotal role in society.

Lastly, but certainly not least, I owe a huge debt of gratitude to my husband, Jeff Glading, for his devoted patience, support, and understanding throughout the last several years of research and writing. To my stepdaughters, MoMo and Cassidy, my sister, Sherrie, and my sister-from-another-mother, Wendy, thank you for your steadfast support and for being my cheerleaders from the sidelines.